HIDDEN RICHES

Nora Roberts

HOT ICE	TRUE BETRAYALS
SACRED SINS	MONTANA SKY
BRAZEN VIRTUE	SANCTUARY
SWEET REVENGE	HOMEPORT
PUBLIC SECRETS	THE REEF
GENUINE LIES	RIVER'S END
CARNAL INNOCENCE	CAROLINA MOON
DIVINE EVIL	THE VILLA
HONEST ILLUSIONS	MIDNIGHT BAYOU
PRIVATE SCANDALS	THREE FATES
HIDDEN RICHES	BIRTHRIGHT

Anthologies

FROM THE HEART
A LITTLE MAGIC
A LITTLE FATE

The Once Upon Series
(with Jill Gregory, Ruth Ryan Langan, and Marianne Willman)

ONCE UPON A CASTLE
ONCE UPON A STAR
ONCE UPON A DREAM
ONCE UPON A ROSE
ONCE UPON A KISS
ONCE UPON A MIDNIGHT

Series

The Key Trilogy	*Three Sisters Island Trilogy*
KEY OF LIGHT	DANCE UPON THE AIR
KEY OF KNOWLEDGE	HEAVEN AND EARTH
KEY OF VALOR	FACE THE FIRE

The Gallaghers of Ardmore Trilogy	*The Born In Trilogy*
JEWELS OF THE SUN	BORN IN FIRE
TEARS OF THE MOON	BORN IN ICE
HEART OF THE SEA	BORN IN SHAME

The Chesapeake Bay Saga	*The Dream Trilogy*
SEA SWEPT	DARING TO DREAM
RISING TIDES	HOLDING THE DREAM
INNER HARBOR	FINDING THE DREAM
CHESAPEAKE BLUE	

NORA ROBERTS

HIDDEN RICHES

BERKLEY BOOKS, NEW YORK

A Berkley Book
Published by The Berkley Publishing Group
A division of Penguin Group (USA) Inc.
375 Hudson Street
New York, New York 10014

PRINTING HISTORY
G. P. Putnam's Sons edition / July 1994
Jove mass-market edition / May 1995
Berkley trade paperback edition / July 2004

Berkley trade paperback ISBN: 0-425-19722-0

The Library of Congress has cataloged the G.P. Putnam's Sons edition of this book as follows:

Roberts, Nora
Hidden riches / Nora Roberts.
p. cm.
ISBN 0-399-13948-6
1. Antique dealers—Fiction.   2. Philadelphia (Pa.)—Fiction.   I. Title.
PS3568.O243 H5 1994   93037425
813'.54—dc20

PRINTED IN THE UNITED STATES OF AMERICA

10 9 8 7 6 5 4 3 2 1

To Mom,
because she loves trinkets,
and a good bargain

PROLOGUE

HE didn't want to be there. No, he hated being trapped in the elegant old house, prodded and pinched by restless ghosts. It was no longer enough to shroud the furniture in dustcovers, lock the doors and walk away. He had to empty it and, by emptying it, purge himself of some of the nightmares.

"Captain Skimmerhorn?"

Jed tensed at the title. As of last week he was no longer captain. He'd resigned from the force, turned in his shield, but he was already weary of explaining it. He shifted aside as two of the movers carried a rosewood armoire down the staircase, through the grand foyer and out into the chilly morning.

"Yes?"

"You might want to check upstairs, make sure we got everything you wanted put in storage. Otherwise, looks like we're all done here."

"Fine."

But he didn't want to go up those stairs, walk through those rooms. Even empty they would hold too much. Responsibility, he mused as he reluctantly started up. His life had been too crowded with responsibility to ignore one now.

Something nudged him along the hallway toward his old room. The room where he had grown up, the room he had continued to inhabit long after he'd lived here alone. But he stopped in the doorway just short of crossing the threshold. Hands jammed into tight fists in his pockets, he waited for memories to assault him like sniper fire.

He'd cried in that room—in secret and in shame, of course. No Skimmerhorn male ever revealed a weakness in public. Then, when tears had dried, he'd plotted in that room. Small, useless childish revenges that had always boomeranged back on him.

He'd learned to hate in that room.

Yet it was only a room. It was only a house. He'd convinced himself of that years before when he had come back to live there as a man. And hadn't he been content? he asked himself now. Hadn't it been simple?

Until Elaine.

"Jedidiah."

He flinched. He'd nearly brought his right hand out of his pocket to touch a weapon that was no longer there before he caught himself. The gesture, and the fact that he'd been so lost in his own morbid thoughts that someone could have come up behind him, reminded him why the weapon no longer hung at his side.

He relaxed and glanced back at his grandmother. Honoria Skimmerhorn Rodgers was neatly wrapped in mink, discreet daytime diamonds winking at her ears, her snowy hair beautifully coiffed. She looked like a successful matron on her way out for lunch at her favorite club. But her eyes, as vivid a blue as his own, were filled with concern.

"I'd hoped I'd convinced you to wait," she said quietly, and reached out to lay a hand on his arm.

He flinched automatically. The Skimmerhorns simply weren't touchers. "There was no reason to wait."

"But there's a reason for this?" She gestured toward the empty room. "There's a reason to empty out your home, to put aside all of your belongings?"

"Nothing in this house belongs to me."

"That's absurd." The faint whisper of her native Boston crept into her tone.

"By default?" He turned his back on the room to face her. "Because I happen to still be alive? No, thanks."

If she hadn't been so worried about him, the curt answer would have earned him a ringing reprimand. "My dear, there's no question of default. Or any kind of fault." She watched him close in, shut off, and would have shaken him if it would have helped. Instead, she touched his cheek. "You only need some time."

The gesture left his muscles taut. It took all of his willpower not to jerk away from the gentle fingers. "And this is my way of taking it."

"By moving out of the family home?"

"Family?" He laughed at that, and the sound of it echoed nastily down the hall. "We were never a family here, or anywhere."

Her eyes, previously soft with sympathy, hardened. "Pretending the past doesn't exist is as bad as living in it. What are you doing here? Tossing away everything you've earned, everything you've made of yourself? Perhaps I was less than enthusiastic about your choice of profession, but it was your choice and you succeeded. It appears to me that you made more of the Skimmerhorn name when you were promoted to captain than all your ancestors did with their money and social power."

"I didn't become a cop to promote my damn name."

"No," she said quietly. "You did it for yourself against tremendous family pressure—including my own." She moved away from him to walk down the hall. She had lived here once, years before as a bride. An unhappy one. "I saw you turn your life around, and it awed me. Because I knew you did it for no one but yourself. I often wondered how you were strong enough to do that."

Turning back, she studied him, this son of her son. He had inherited the bold good looks of the Skimmerhorns. Bronzed hair, tousled by the wind, swept around a lean, rawboned face that was taut with stress. She worried, woman-like, because he had lost weight, though the fining down of his features only heightened their power. There was strength in the tall, broad-shouldered build that both accented and defied the romantic masculine beauty of pale gold skin and sensitive mouth. The eyes, a deep striking blue, had come from her. They were as haunted and defiant now as they had been in the young, troubled boy she remembered so well.

But he was no longer a boy, and she was afraid there was little she could do to help the man.

"I don't want to see you turn your life around again, for the wrong reasons." She shook her head, walking back toward him before he could speak. "And I might have had reservations when you moved back in here alone after your parents died, but that, too, was your choice. And for some time, it seemed you'd made the right one again. But this time your solution to a tragedy is to sell your home, throw away your career?"

He waited a beat. "Yes."

"You disappoint me, Jedidiah."

That stung. It was a phrase she rarely used, and had more bite than a dozen of his father's raging insults. "I'd rather disappoint you than be responsible for the life of a single cop. I'm in no shape to command." He looked down at his hands, flexed them. "I may never be. And as for the house, it should have been sold years ago. After the accident. It would have been sold if Elaine had agreed to it." Something backed up in his throat. Guilt was as bitter as bile. "Now she's gone too, and it's my decision."

"Yes, it's yours," she agreed. "But it's the wrong one."

Rage sizzled in his blood. He wanted to hit something, someone, pound his fists into flesh. It was a feeling that came over him all too often. And because of it, he was no longer Captain J. T. Skimmerhorn of the Philadelphia Police Department, but a civilian.

"Can't you understand? I can't live here. I can't sleep here. I need to get the hell out. I'm smothering here."

"Then come home with me. For the holidays. At least until after the first of the year. Give yourself a little more time before you do something irreversible." Her voice was gentle again as she took his rigid hands in hers. "Jedidiah, it's been months since Elaine—since Elaine was killed."

"I know how long it's been." Yes, he knew the exact moment of his sister's death. After all, he'd killed her. "I appreciate the invitation, but I've got plans. I'm looking at an apartment later today. Over on South Street."

"An apartment." Honoria's sigh was ripe with annoyance. "Really, Jedidiah, there's no need for that kind of nonsense. Buy yourself another house if you must, take a long vacation, but don't bury yourself in some miserable room."

He was surprised he could smile. "The ad said it was quiet, attractive and well located. That doesn't sound miserable. Grandmother"—he squeezed her hands before she could argue—"let it be."

She sighed again, tasting defeat. "I only want what's best for you."

"You always did." He suppressed a shudder, feeling the walls closing in on him. "Let's get out of here."

1

A theater without an audience has its own peculiar magic. The magic of possibilities. The echoing voices of actors running lines, the light cues, the costumes, the nervous energy and vaulting egos that bound from center stage to the empty back row.

Isadora Conroy absorbed the theater's magic as she stood in the wings of the Liberty Theater, watching a dress rehearsal for *A Christmas Carol.* As always, she enjoyed the drama, not only Dickens, but also the drama of edgy nerves, of creative lighting, of the well-delivered line. After all, the theater was in her blood.

There was a vibrancy that pulsed from her even in repose. Her large brown eyes glinted with excitement and seemed to dominate the face framed by a swing of golden-brown hair. That excitement brought a flush to ivory skin, a smile to her wide mouth. It was a face of subtle angles and smooth curves, caught between wholesome and lovely. The energy inside her small, compact body shimmered out.

She was a woman interested in everything around her, who believed in illusions. Watching her father rattling Marley's chains and intoning dire predictions to the fear-struck Scrooge, she believed in ghosts. And because she believed, he was no longer her father, but the doomed miser wrapped for eternity in the heavy chains of his own greed.

Then Marley became Quentin Conroy again, veteran actor, director and theater buff, calling for a minute change in the blocking.

"Dora." Hurrying up from behind, Dora's sister, Ophelia, said, "We're already twenty minutes behind schedule."

"We don't have a schedule," Dora murmured, nodding because the blocking change was perfect. "I never have a schedule on a buying trip. Isn't he wonderful, Lea?"

Though her sense of organization was hampered, Lea glanced out on-stage and studied their father. "Yes. Though God knows how he can stand to put on this same production year after year."

"Tradition." Dora beamed. "The theater's rooted in it." Leaving the stage hadn't diminished her love of it, or her admiration for the man who had taught her how to milk a line. She'd watched him become hundreds of men onstage. Macbeth, Willie Loman, Nathan Detroit. She'd seen him triumph and seen him bomb. But he always entertained.

"Remember Mom and Dad as Titania and Oberon?"

Lea rolled her eyes, but she was smiling. "Who could forget? Mom stayed in character for weeks. It wasn't easy living with the queen of the fairies. And if we don't get out of here soon, the queen's going to come out and run through her list of what might happen to two women traveling alone to Virginia."

Sensing her sister's nerves and impatience, Dora swung an arm around Lea's shoulders. "Relax, honey, I've got her covered, and he's going to take five in a minute."

Which he did, on cue. When the actors scattered, Dora stepped out to center stage. "Dad." She took a long look, skimming down from the top of his head to his feet. "You were great."

"Thank you, my sweet." He lifted an arm so that his tattered shroud floated. "I think the makeup is an improvement over last year."

"Absolutely." In fact, the greasepaint and charcoal were alarmingly realistic; his handsome face appeared just short of decay. "Absolutely gruesome." She kissed him lightly on the lips, careful not to smudge. "Sorry we'll miss opening night."

"Can't be helped." Though he did pout just a little. Although he had a son to carry on the Conroy tradition, he'd lost his two daughters, one to marriage, one to free enterprise. Then again, he did occasionally shanghai them into a minor role. "So, my two little girls are off on their adventure."

"It's a buying trip, Dad, not a trip to the Amazon."

"Just the same." He winked and kissed Lea in turn. "Watch out for snakes."

"Oh, Lea!" Trixie Conroy, resplendent in her costume complete with bustle and feathered hat, rushed out onstage. The Liberty's excellent acoustics carried her throaty voice to the rear balcony. "John's on the phone, dear. He couldn't remember if Missy had a scout meeting tonight at five, or a piano lesson at six."

"I left a list," Lea muttered. "How's he going to manage the kids for three days if he can't read a list?"

"Such a sweet man," Trixie commented when Lea dashed off. "The perfect son-in-law. Now, Dora, you will drive carefully?"

"Yes, Mom."

"Of course you will. You're always careful. You won't pick up any hitchhikers?"

"Not even if they beg."

"And you'll stop every two hours to rest your eyes?"

"Like clockwork."

An inveterate worrier, Trixie gnawed on her bottom lip. "Still, it's an awfully long way to Virginia. And it might snow."

"I have snow tires." To forestall more speculation, Dora gave her mother another kiss. "There's a phone in the van, Mom. I'll check in every time we cross a state line."

"Won't that be fun?" The idea cheered Trixie enormously. "Oh, and Quentin, darling, I've just come from the box office." She gave her husband a deep curtsy. "We're sold out for the week."

"Naturally." Quentin lifted his wife to her feet and twirled her in a graceful spin that ended in a deep dip. "A Conroy expects nothing less than standing room only."

"Break a leg." Dora kissed her mother one last time. "You too," she said to Quentin. "And Dad, don't forget you're showing the apartment later today."

"I never forget an engagement. Places!" he called out, then winked at his daughter. "Bon voyage, my sweet."

Dora could hear his chains clanging when she hit the wings. She couldn't imagine a better send-off.

*   *   *

To Dora's way of thinking, an auction house was very like a theater. You had the stage, the props, the characters. As she had explained to her baffled parents years before, she wasn't really retiring from the stage. She was merely exploring another medium. She certainly put her actor's blood to good use whenever it was time to buy or sell.

She'd already taken the time to study the arena for today's performance. The building where Sherman Porter held his auctions and ran a daily flea market had originally been a slaughterhouse and was still as drafty as a barn. Merchandise was displayed on an icy concrete floor where cows and pigs had once mooed and squealed on their way to becoming pot roasts and pork chops. Now humans, huddled in coats and mufflers, wandered through, poking at glassware, grunting over paintings and debating over china cabinets and carved headboards.

The ambience was a bit thin, but she'd played in less auspicious surroundings. And, of course, there was the bottom line.

Isadora Conroy loved a bargain. The words "On Sale" sent a silvery tingle through her blood. She'd always loved to buy, finding the basic transaction of money for objects deeply satisfying. So satisfying that she had all too often exchanged money for objects she had no use for. But it was that love of a bargain that had guided Dora into opening her own shop, and the subsequent discovery that selling was as pleasurable as buying.

"Lea, look at this." Dora turned to her sister, offering a gilded cream dispenser shaped like a woman's evening shoe. "Isn't it fabulous?"

Ophelia Conroy Bradshaw took one look, lifted a single honey-brown eyebrow. Despite the dreamy name, this was a woman rooted in reality. "I think you mean frivolous, right?"

"Come on, look beyond the obvious aesthetics." Beaming, Dora ran a fingertip over the arch of the shoe. "There's a place for ridiculous in the world."

"I know. Your shop."

Dora chuckled, unoffended. Though she replaced the creamer, she'd already decided to bid on that lot. She took out a notebook and a pen that boasted a guitar-wielding Elvis to note down the number. "I'm really glad you came along with me on this trip, Lea. You keep me centered."

"Somebody has to." Lea's attention was caught by a colorful display of Depression glass. There were two or three pieces in amber that would add nicely to her own collection. "Still, I feel guilty being away from home this close to Christmas. Leaving John with the kids that way."

"You were dying to get away from the kids," Dora reminded her as she inspected a lady's cherrywood vanity.

"I know. That's why I'm guilty."

"Guilt's a good thing." Tossing one end of her red muffler over her shoulder, Dora crouched down to check the work on the vanity's brass handles. "Honey, it's only been three days. We're practically on our way back. You'll get home tonight and smother the kids with attention, seduce John, and everybody'll be happy."

Lea rolled her eyes and smiled weakly at the couple standing beside her. "Trust you to take everything down to the lowest common denominator."

With a satisfied grunt, Dora straightened, shook her chin-length sweep of hair away from her face and nodded. "I think I've seen enough for now."

When she checked her watch, she realized it was curtain time for the matinee performance back home. Well, she mused, there was show business, and there was show business. She all but rubbed her hands together in anticipation of the auction opening.

"We'd better get some seats before they—oh wait!" Her brown eyes brightened. "Look at that."

Even as Lea turned, Dora was scurrying across the concrete floor.

It was the painting that had caught her attention. It wasn't large, perhaps eighteen by twenty-four inches with a simple, streamlined ebony frame. The canvas itself was a wash of color, streaks and streams of crimson and sapphire, a dollop of citrine, a bold dash of emerald. What Dora saw was energy and verve, as irresistible to her as a red-tag special.

Dora smiled at the boy who was propping the painting against the wall. "You've got it upside down."

"Huh?" The stock boy turned and flushed. He was seventeen, and the sight of Dora smiling at him reduced him to a puddle of hormones. "Ah, no, ma'am." His Adam's apple bobbed frantically as he turned the canvas around to show Dora the hook at the back.

"Mmm." When she owned it—and she certainly would by the end of the afternoon—she would fix that.

"This, ah, shipment just came in."

"I see." She stepped closer. "Some interesting pieces," she said, and picked up a statue of a sad-eyed basset hound curled up in a resting pose. It was heavier than she'd expected, and pursing her lips, she turned it over and over for a closer inspection. No craftsman's mark or date, she mused. But still, the workmanship was excellent.

"Frivolous enough for you?" Lea asked.

"Just. Make a terrific doorstop." After setting it down she reached for a tall figurine of a man and woman in antebellum dress caught in the swirl of a waltz. Dora's hand closed over thick, gnarled fingers. "Sorry." She glanced up at an elderly, bespeckled man who gave her a creaky bow.

"Pretty, isn't it?" he asked her. "My wife had one just like it. Got busted when the kids were wrestling in the parlor." He grinned, showing teeth too white and straight to be God-given. He wore a red bow tie and smelled like a peppermint stick. Dora smiled back.

"Do you collect?"

"In a manner of speaking." He set the figurine down and his old, shrewd eyes swept the display, pricing, cataloguing, dismissing. "I'm Tom Ashworth. Got a shop here in Front Royal." He took a business card from his breast pocket and offered it to Dora. "Accumulated so much stuff over the years, it was open a shop or buy a bigger house."

"I know what you mean. I'm Dora Conroy." She held out a hand and had it enveloped in a brief arthritic grip. "I have a shop in Philadelphia."

"Thought you were a pro." Pleased, he winked. "Noticed you right off. Don't believe I've seen you at one of Porter's auctions before."

"No, I've never been able to make it. Actually, this trip was an impulse. I dragged my sister along. Lea, Tom Ashworth."

"Nice to meet you."

"My pleasure." Ashworth patted Lea's chilled hand. "Never does warm up in here this time of year. Guess Porter figures the bidding'll heat things up some."

"I hope he's right." Lea's toes felt frozen inside her suede boots. "Have you been in business long, Mr. Ashworth?"

"Nigh onto forty years. The wife got us started, crocheting doilies and scarves and what-all and selling them. Added some trinkets and worked out of the garage." He took a corncob pipe from his pocket and clamped it between his teeth. "Nineteen sixty-three we had more stock than we could handle and rented us a shop in town. Worked side by side till she passed on in the spring of eighty-six. Now I got me a grandson working with me. Got a lot of fancy ideas, but he's a good boy."

"Family businesses are the best," Dora said. "Lea's just started working part-time at the shop."

"Lord knows why." Lea dipped her chilly hands into her coat pockets. "I don't know anything about antiques or collectibles."

"You just have to figure out what people want," Ashworth told her, and flicked a thumbnail over a wooden match to light it. "And how much they'll pay for it," he added before he puffed the pipe into life.

"Exactly." Delighted with him, Dora hooked a hand through his arm. "It looks like we're getting started. Why don't we go find some seats?"

Ashworth offered Lea his other arm and, feeling like the cock of the walk, escorted the women to chairs near the front row.

Dora pulled out her notebook and prepared to play her favorite role.

The bidding was low, but certainly energetic. Voices bounced off the high ceiling as the lots were announced. But it was the murmuring crowd that fired Dora's blood. There were bargains to be had here, and she was determined to grab her share.

She outbid a thin, waiflike woman with a pinched mouth for the cherrywood vanity, snapped up the lot that included the creamer/slipper for a song and competed briskly with Ashworth for a set of crystal saltcellars.

"Got me," he said when Dora topped his bid yet again. "You're liable to get a bit more for them up north."

"I've got a customer who collects," Dora told him. And who would pay double the purchase price, she thought.

"That so?" Ashworth leaned closer as the bidding began on the next lot. "I've got a set of six at the shop. Cobalt and silver."

"Really?"

"You got time, you drop on by after this and take a look."

"I might just do that. Lea, you bid on the Depression glass."

"Me?" Horror in her eyes, Lea gaped at her sister.

"Sure. Get your feet wet." Grinning, Dora tilted her head toward Ashworth's. "Watch this."

As Dora expected, Lea started out with hesitant bids that barely carried to the auctioneer. Then she began to inch forward in her seat. Her eyes glazed over. By the time the lot was sold, she was snapping out her bid like a drill sergeant commanding recruits.

"Isn't she great?" All pride, Dora swung an arm over Lea's shoulders to squeeze. "She was always a quick study. It's the Conroy blood."

"I bought all of it." Lea pressed a hand to her speeding heart. "Oh God, I bought all of it. Why didn't you stop me?"

"When you were having such a good time?"

"But—but—" As the adrenaline drained, Lea slumped in her chair. "That was hundreds of dollars. Hundreds."

"Well spent, too. Now, here we go." Spotting the abstract painting, Dora rubbed her hands together. "Mine," she said softly.

By three o'clock Dora was adding half a dozen cobalt saltcellars to the treasures in her van. The wind had kicked up, stinging color into her cheeks and sneaking down the collar of her coat.

"Smells like snow," Ashworth commented. He stood on the curb in front of his shop and, with his pipe clenched in his hand, sniffed the air. "Could be you'll run into some before you get home."

"I hope so." Pushing back her flying hair, she smiled at him. "What's Christmas without it? It was great meeting you, Mr. Ashworth." She offered her hand again. "If you get up to Philadelphia, I'll expect you to drop by."

"You can count on it." He patted his pocket where he'd slipped her business card. "You two ladies take care of yourselves. Drive safely."

"We will. Merry Christmas."

"Same to you," Ashworth added as Dora climbed in the van.

With a last wave she started the van and pulled away from the curb. Her eyes flicked up to the rearview mirror and she smiled as she saw Ashworth standing on the sidewalk with his pipe in his teeth and his hand lifted in a farewell salute. "What a sweetheart. I'm glad he got that figurine."

Lea shivered and waited impatiently for the van to heat. "I hope he didn't overcharge you for those saltcellars."

"Mmm. He made a profit, I'll make a profit and Mrs. O'Malley will add to her collection. Everybody gets what they want."

"I guess. I still can't believe you bought that hideous painting. You'll never be able to sell it."

"Oh, eventually."

"At least you only paid fifty dollars for it."

"Fifty-two seventy-five," Dora corrected.

"Right." Twisting in her seat, Lea looked at the boxes packed into the rear of the van. "You know, of course, that you don't have room for all this junk."

"I'll make room. Don't you think Missy would like that carousel?"

Lea imagined the outsize mechanical toy in her daughter's pink-and-white bedroom and shuddered. "Please, no."

"Okay." Dora shrugged. Once she'd cleaned up the carousel, she might let it spin in her own living room for a while. "But I think she'd go for it. You want to call John and tell him we're on our way back?"

"In a little while." With a sigh, Lea settled back. "This time tomorrow, I'll be baking cookies and rolling out pie dough."

"You asked for it," Dora reminded her. "You had to get married, have kids, buy a house. Where else is the family going to have Christmas dinner?"

"I wouldn't mind if Mom didn't insist on helping me cook it. I mean, the woman never cooked a real meal in her life, right?"

"Not that I remember."

"And there she is, every Christmas, underfoot in my kitchen and waving around some recipe for alfalfa and chestnut dressing."

"That one was bad," Dora recalled. "But it was better than her curried potatoes and succotash casserole."

"Don't remind me. And Dad's no help, wearing his Santa hat and hitting the eggnog before noon."

"Maybe Will can distract him. Is he coming alone or with one of his sweeties?" Dora asked, referring to their brother's list of glamorous dates.

"Alone, last I heard. Dora, watch that truck, will you?"

"I am." In the spirit of competition, Dora gunned the engine and passed the sixteen-wheeler with inches to spare. "So when's Will getting in?"

"He's taking a late train out of New York on Christmas Eve."

"Late enough to make a grand entrance," Dora predicted. "Look, if he gets in your hair, I can always—oh, hell."

"What?" Lea's eyes sprang open.

"I just remembered, that new tenant Dad signed up is moving in across the hall today."

"So?"

"I hope Dad remembers to be there with the keys. He was great about showing the apartment the last couple of weeks while I was tied up in the shop, but you know how absentminded he is when he's in the middle of a production."

"I know exactly how he is, which is why I can't understand how you could let him interview a tenant for your building."

"I didn't have time," Dora muttered, trying to calculate if she'd have an opportunity to call her father between performances. "Besides, Dad wanted to."

"Just don't be surprised if you end up across the hall from a psychopath, or a woman with three kids and a string of tattooed boyfriends."

Dora's lips curved. "I specifically told Dad no psychopaths or tattoos. I'm hoping it's someone who cooks, and hopes to suck up to the landlord by bringing me baked goods on a regular basis. Speaking of which, do you want to eat?"

"Yeah. I might as well get in one last meal where I don't have to cut up anyone's food but my own."

Dora swung toward the exit ramp, cutting off a Chevy. She ignored the angry blast of horns. There was a smile on her face as she imagined unpacking her new possessions. The very first thing she would do, she promised herself, was find the perfect spot for the painting.

HIGH in the glittery tower of a silver building overlooking the cramped streets of LA, Edmund Finley enjoyed his weekly manicure. The wall directly across from his massive rosewood desk flickered with a dozen television screens. CNN, *Headline News* and one of the home-shopping networks all flashed silently across the wall. Other screens were tuned in to various offices in his organization so that he could observe his employees.

But unless he chose to listen in, the only sounds in the vast sweep of his office were the strains of a Mozart opera and the steady scrape of the manicurist's nail file.

Finley liked to watch.

He'd chosen the top floor of this building so that his office would over-look the panorama of Los Angeles. It gave him the feeling of power, of om-nipotence, and he would often stand for an hour at the wide window behind his desk and simply study the comings and goings of strangers far below.

In his home far up in the hills above the city, there were television screens and monitors in every room. And windows, again windows where he could look down on the lights of the LA basin. Every evening he would stand on the balcony outside his bedroom and imagine owning every-thing, everyone, for as far as his eye could see.

He was a man with an appetite for possessions. His office reflected his taste for the fine and the exclusive. Both walls and carpet were white, pure white to serve as a virgin backdrop for his treasures. A Ming vase graced a marble pedestal. Sculptures by Rodin and Denaecheau filled niches carved into the walls. A Renoir hung in a gold frame above a Louis Quatorze com-mode. A velvet settee reputed to have been Marie Antoinette's was flanked by gleaming mahogany tables from Victorian England.

Two high glass cabinets held a stunning and esoteric display of objets d'art: carved snuff bottles of lapis and aquamarine, ivory netsukes, Dres-den figurines, Limoges ring boxes, a fifteenth-century dagger with a jew-eled handle, African masks.

Edmund Finley acquired. And once he acquired, he hoarded.

His import-export business was enormously successful. His smuggling sideline more so. After all, smuggling was more of a challenge. It required a certain finesse, a ruthless ingenuity and impeccable taste.

Finley, a tall, spare, distinguished-looking man in his early fifties, had begun to "acquire" merchandise as a youth working the docks in San Francisco. It had been a simple matter to misplace a crate, to open a trunk and to sell what he took. By his thirtieth year he had amassed enough capital to start his own company, enough savvy to play heavily on the dark side and win and enough contacts to ensure a steady flow of merchandise.

Now he was a wealthy man who preferred Italian suits, French women and Swiss francs. He could, after decades of transactions, afford to keep what appealed most to him. What appealed most was the old, the priceless.

"You're all done, Mr. Finley." The manicurist placed Finley's hand gently on the spotless blotter on his desk. She knew he would check her work carefully while she packed up her tools and lotions. Once he had raged at her for ten minutes for missing a minute speck of cuticle on his thumb. But this time, when she dared to glance up, he was smiling down at his buffed nails.

"Excellent work." Pleased, he rubbed his thumbs and fingertips together. Taking a gold money clip from his pocket, Finley peeled off a fifty. Then with one of his rare and disarming smiles, he added another hundred. "Merry Christmas, dear."

"Oh—thank you. Thank you very much, Mr. Finley. Merry Christmas to you, too."

Still smiling, he dismissed her with a wave of his buffed fingertips. His sporadic generosity came as naturally as his constant greed. He relished both. Before the door had closed behind her, he had swiveled in his chair, folded his hands over his silk vest. Through the stream of sunlight he studied his view of Los Angeles.

Christmas, he thought. What a lovely time of year. One of goodwill toward men, ringing bells and colored lights. Of course, it was also the time of desperate loneliness, despair and suicide. But those small human tragedies didn't touch or concern him. Money had catapulted him above those fragile needs for companionship and family. He could buy companionship. He had chosen one of the richest cities in the world, where anything could be bought, sold, possessed. Here youth, wealth and power were admired above all else. During this brightest of holiday seasons, he had wealth, and he had power. As for youth, money could buy the illusion.

Finley scanned the buildings and sun-glinted windows with his bright green eyes. He realized with a vague sense of surprise that he was happy.

The knock on his office door made him turn as he called out, "Enter."

"Sir." Abel Winesap, a small, stoop-shouldered man with the heavy title of "Executive Assistant to the President," cleared his throat. "Mr. Finley."

"Do you know the true meaning of Christmas, Abel?" Finley's voice was warm, like mulled brandy poured over cream.

"Ah . . ." Winesap fiddled with the knot of his tie. "Sir?"

"Acquisition. A lovely word, Abel. And the truest meaning of this delightful holiday, don't you agree?"

"Yes, sir." Winesap felt a shiver whisper down his spine. What he had come to report was difficult enough. Finley's happy mood made the difficult more dangerous. "I'm afraid we have a problem, Mr. Finley."

"Oh?" Finley's smile remained, but his eyes frosted. "And what might that be?"

Winesap gulped in fear. He knew that Finley's frigid anger was more lethal than another man's rage. It had been Winesap who had been chosen to witness Finley's termination of an employee who had been embezzling. And he remembered how calmly Finley had slit the man's throat with a sixteenth-century jeweled dagger.

Betrayal, Finley believed, deserved quick punishment, and some ceremony.

Winesap also remembered, to his dismay, that it had been he who had been delegated to dispose of the body.

Nervously, he continued with his story. "The shipment from New York. The merchandise you were expecting."

"Has there been a delay?"

"No—that is, in a manner of speaking. The shipment arrived today as expected, but the merchandise . . ." He moistened his thin, nervous lips. "It isn't what you ordered, sir."

Finley placed his pampered hands on the edge of the desk and the knuckles turned bone white. "I beg your pardon?"

"The merchandise, sir. It isn't what was ordered. Apparently there was a mix-up somewhere." Winesap's voice petered out to a whimper. "I thought it best to report it to you at once."

"Where is it?" Finley's voice had lost its jovial warmth. It was a chilly hiss.

"In Receiving, sir. I thought—"

"Bring it up. Immediately."

"Yes, sir. Right away." Winesap escaped, grateful for the reprieve.

Finley had paid a great deal of money for the merchandise, and a great deal more to have that merchandise concealed and smuggled. Having each piece stolen, then disguised, transported from various locations to his factory in New York. Why, the bribes alone had run close to six figures.

To calm himself, he paused by a decanter of guava juice and poured generously.

And if there had been a mistake, he thought, steadier, it would be rectified. Whoever had erred would be punished.

Carefully, he set the Baccarat low-ball glass aside and studied himself in the oval George III mirror above the bar. He brushed a fussy hand over his thick mane of dark hair, admiring the glint and gleam of silver that threaded through it. His last face-lift had smoothed away the sags under his eyes, firmed his chin and erased the lines that had dug deeply around his mouth.

He looked no more than forty, Finley decided, turning his face from side to side to study and approve his profile.

What fool had said that money couldn't buy happiness?

The knock on his door shattered his mood. "Come," he snapped out, and waited as one of his receiving clerks wheeled in a crate. "Leave it there." He jabbed a finger toward the center of the room. "And go. Abel, remain. The door," he said, and Winesap scurried to shut it behind the departing clerk.

When Finley said nothing more, Winesap blanched and walked back to the crate. "I opened it as you instructed, Mr. Finley. As I began to inspect the merchandise, I realized there had been an error." Gingerly he reached into the crate, dipping his hand into a sea of shredded paper. His fingers trembled as he pulled out a china teapot decorated with tiny violets.

Finley took the teapot, turning it over in his hands. It was English, a lovely piece, worth perhaps $200 on the open market. But it was mass-produced. Thousands of teapots exactly like this one were on sale across the world. So to him it was completely worthless. He smashed it against the edge of the crate and sent shards flying.

"What else?"

Quaking, Winesap plunged his hand deep into the crate and drew out a swirling glass vase.

Italian, Finley deduced as he inspected it. Handmade. A value of $100, perhaps $150. He hurled it, barely missing Winesap's head, and sent it crashing against the wall.

"There's—there's teacups." Winesap's eyes darted to the crate and back to his employer's stony face. "And some silver—two platters, a candy dish. A p-pair of crystal goblets etched with wedding bells."

"Where is my merchandise?" Finley demanded, biting off each word.

"Sir, I can't—that is, I believe there's been . . ." His voice drained out to a whisper. "An error."

"An error." Finley's eyes were like jade as he clenched his fists at his sides. DiCarlo, he thought, conjuring up an image of his man in New York. Young, bright, ambitious. But not stupid, Finley reminded himself. Not stupid enough to attempt a double cross. Still, he would have to pay, and pay dearly for this error.

"Get DiCarlo on the phone."

"Yes, sir." Relieved that Finley's wrath was about to find a new target, Winesap darted to the desk to place the call.

As Winesap dialed, Finley crunched shards of china into the carpet. Reaching into the crate, he systematically destroyed the rest of the contents.

2

JED Skimmerhorn wanted a drink. He wasn't particular about the type. Whiskey that would burn a line down his throat, the seductive warmth of brandy, the familiar tang of a beer. But he wasn't going to get one until he'd finished carting boxes up these damn rickety back steps and into his new apartment.

Not that he had a hell of a lot of possessions. His old partner, Brent, had given him a hand with the sofa, the mattress and the heavier pieces of furniture. All that remained were a few cardboard boxes filled with books and cooking utensils and other assorted junk. He wasn't sure why he'd kept even that much when it would have been easier to put it all in storage.

Then again, he wasn't sure of a lot of things these days. He couldn't explain to Brent, or to himself, why he'd found it so necessary to move across town, out of the huge old Colonial and into an apartment. It was something about fresh starts. But you couldn't start fresh until you'd ended.

Jed had been doing a lot of ending lately.

Turning in his resignation had been the first step—perhaps the hardest. The police commissioner had argued, refusing to accept the resignation and putting Jed on extended leave. It didn't matter what it was called, Jed mused. He wasn't a cop anymore. Couldn't be a cop anymore. Whatever part of him had wanted to serve and protect was hollowed out.

He wasn't depressed, as he'd explained to the department shrink. He was finished. He didn't need to find himself. He just needed to be left alone. He'd given fourteen years of his life to the force. It had to be enough.

Jed elbowed open the door to the apartment and braced it with one of the boxes he carried. He slid the second box across the wooden floor before heading back down the narrow hallway toward the outside steps that served as his entrance.

He hadn't heard a peep from his neighbor across the hall. The eccentric old man who had rented him the place had said that the second apartment was occupied but the tenant was as quiet as a mouse.

It certainly seemed that way.

Jed started down the steps, noting with annoyance that the banister wouldn't hold the weight of a malnourished three-year-old. The steps themselves were slick with the sleet that continued to spit out of the color-less sky. It was almost quiet in the back of the building. Though it fronted on busy South Street, Jed didn't think he'd mind the noise and Bohemian atmosphere, the tourists or the shops. He was close enough to the river that he could take solitary walks when he chose.

In any case, it would be a dramatic change from the manicured lawns of Chestnut Hill, where the Skimmerhorn family home had stood for two centuries.

Through the gloom he could see the glow of colored lights strung on the windows of neighboring buildings. Someone had wired a large plastic Santa and his eight tiny reindeer to a roof, where they were caught in the pretense of flying day and night.

It reminded him that Brent had invited him to Christmas dinner. A big, noisy family event that Jed might have enjoyed in the past. There had never been big, noisy family events in his life—or none that could have been called fun.

And now there was no family. No family at all.

He pressed his fingertips to the ache at his temple and willed himself not to think of Elaine. But old memories, like the ghost of past sins, snuck through and knotted his stomach.

He hauled the last of the boxes out of the trunk and slammed it with a force that rattled the reconditioned Thunderbird down to its tires. He

wasn't going to think of Elaine, or Donny Speck or responsibilities or regrets. He was going to go inside, pour a drink and try to think of nothing
at all.

With his eyes narrowed against the stinging sleet, he climbed the steep
steps one last time. The temperature inside was dramatically higher than
the wind-punched air outside. The landlord was generous with the heat.
Overly generous. But then, it wasn't Jed's problem how the old guy spent
his money.

Funny old guy, Jed thought now, with his rich voice, operatic gestures
and silver flask. He'd been more interested in Jed's opinion on twentieth-
century playwrights than in his references and rent check.

Still, you couldn't be a cop for nearly half your life and not understand
that the world was made up of a lot of odd characters.

Once inside, Jed dumped the last box onto the oak table in the dining
area. He dug through crumpled newspaper in search of that drink. Unlike
the crates in storage, these boxes weren't marked, nor had they been
packed with any sort of system. If there had been any practical genes in
the Skimmerhorn blood, he figured Elaine had gotten his share as well as
her own.

The fresh thought of his sister made him swear again, softly through
his teeth. He knew better than to let the thought dig roots, for if it did it
would bloom with guilt. Over the past month he'd become all too aware
that guilt could give you night sweats and a dull, skittering sense of panic.

Sweaty hands and panic weren't desirable qualities in a cop. Nor was
the tendency to uncontrollable rage. But he wasn't a cop anymore, Jed reminded himself. His time and his choices, as he'd told his grandmother,
were his own.

The apartment was echoingly empty, which only served to satisfy him
that he was alone. One of the reasons he'd chosen it was because he'd have
only one neighbor to ignore. The other reason was just as simple, and just
as basic: It was fabulous.

He supposed he'd lived with the finer things for too long not to be
drawn to them. However much he claimed that his surroundings didn't
matter, he would have been quietly miserable in some glossy condo or
soulless apartment complex.

He imagined the old building had been converted into shop and apartments sometime in the thirties. It had retained its lofty ceilings and spacious rooms, the working fireplace and slim, tall windows. The floors, a random-width oak, had been highly polished for the new tenant.

The trim was walnut and uncarved, the walls a creamy ivory. The old man had assured Jed they could be painted to suit his tastes, but home decorating was the last thing on Jed's mind. He would take the rooms precisely as they were.

He unearthed a bottle of Jameson, three-quarters full. He studied it a moment, then set it on the table. He was shoving packing paper aside in search of a glass when he heard noises. His hands froze, his body braced.

Tilting his head, he turned, trying to locate the source of the sound. He'd thought he'd heard bells, a tingling echo. And now laughter, a smoky drift of it, seductive and female.

His eyes turned to the brass, open-work floor vent near the fireplace. The sounds floated up through it, some vague, some clear enough that he could hear individual words if he chose to listen.

There was some sort of antique or curio shop beneath the apartment. It had been closed for the last couple of days, but it was apparently open for business now.

Jed went back to his search for a glass and tuned out the sounds from below.

"I really do appreciate your meeting us here, John." Dora set a newly acquired globe lamp beside the antique cash register.

"No problem." He huffed a bit as he carted another crate into the overflowing storeroom. He was a tall man with a skinny frame that refused to fill out, an honest face that might have been homely but for the pale, shy eyes that peered at the world from behind thick lenses.

He sold Oldsmobiles in Landsdowne and had been named Salesman of the Year two years running using a low-key, almost apologetic approach that came naturally to him and charmed the customers.

Now he smiled at Dora and shoved his dark-framed glasses back up his nose. "How did you manage to buy so much in such a short time?"

"Experience." She had to rise on her toes to kiss John's cheek, then she bent and scooped up her younger nephew, Michael. "Hey, frog face, did you miss me?"

"Nuh-uh." But he grinned and wrapped his pudgy arms around her neck.

Lea turned to keep an eagle eye on her two other children. "Richie, hands in your pockets. Missy, no pirouetting in the shop."

"But, Mom . . ."

"Ah." Lea sighed, smiled. "I'm home." She held out her arms for Michael. "Dora, do you need any more help?"

"No, I can handle it from here. Thanks again."

"If you're sure." Dubiously, Lea glanced around the shop. It was a mystery to her how her sister could function in the clutter she constantly surrounded herself with. They had grown up in chaos, with every day dawning with a new drama or comedy. For Lea, the only way to remain sane as an adult was structure. "I really could come in tomorrow."

"No. It's your day off, and I'm counting on scarfing down my share of those cookies you'll be baking." As she herded her family toward the door, Dora slipped a pound bag of M&M's to her niece. "Share," she ordered under her breath. "And don't tell your mom where you got them." She ruffled Richie's hair. "Scram, creep."

He grinned, showing the wide gap of his missing two front teeth. "Burglars might come tonight and rob you blind." Reaching out, he toyed with the long dangle of citrine and amethyst that swung at her ear. "If I spent the night, I'd shoot them for you."

"Why, thank you, Richie," Dora said in serious tones. "I can't tell you how much I appreciate that. But I'll just have to shoot my own burglars tonight." She nudged her family outside, then began to lock up immediately, knowing that Lea would wait until she had turned every lock and engaged the security alarm.

Alone, she turned and took a deep breath. There was the scent of apple and pine from the potpourri set all around the shop. It was good to be home, she thought, and lifted the box that contained the new acquisitions she'd decided to take to her apartment upstairs.

She moved through the storeroom to unlock the door that led to the inside stairway. She had to juggle the box, her purse and her overnight bag, as well as the coat she'd stripped off on entering the shop. Muttering to her-self, she managed to hit the light switch in the stairway with her shoulder.

She was halfway down the hall when she saw the light spilling out of the neighboring apartment. The new tenant. Shifting her grip, she walked to the door that was braced open with a box and peered in.

She saw him standing by an old table, a bottle in one hand, a glass in the other. The room itself was sparsely furnished with a sofa and an over-stuffed chair.

But she was more interested in the man who stood in profile to her and downed a long swallow of whiskey.

He was tall with a tough, athletic build that made her think of a boxer. He wore a navy sweatshirt with sleeves pushed up to the elbows—no visi-ble tattoos—and Levis worn white at the stress points. His hair was a bit unkempt, falling carelessly over his collar in a rich shade of ripening wheat.

In contrast, the watch at his wrist was either an amazingly good knock-off, or a genuine Rolex.

Though her appraisal took only seconds, Dora sensed her neighbor was not celebrating his new home. His face, shadowed by the high slash of cheekbones and the stubble of a beard, seemed grim.

Before she had made a sound, she saw his body tense. His head whipped around. Dora found herself fighting the instinct to step back in defense as he pinned her with eyes that were hard, expressionless and shockingly blue.

"Your door was open," she said apologetically, and was immediately annoyed that she'd excused herself from standing in her own hallway.

"Yeah." He set the bottle down, carrying the glass with him as he crossed to her. Jed took his own survey. Most of her body was obscured by the large cardboard box she carried. A pretty oval face, slightly pointed at the chin, with an old-fashioned roses-and-cream complexion, a wide, un-painted mouth that was just curving up in a smile, big brown eyes that were filled with friendly curiosity, a swing of sable-colored hair.

"I'm Dora," she explained when he only continued to stare. "From across the hall? Need any help getting organized?"

"No." Jed booted the box away with his foot and closed the door in her face.

Her mouth fell open before she deliberately snapped it shut. "Well, welcome to the neighborhood," she muttered as she turned away to her own door. After an initial fumble for her keys, she unlocked her door and slammed it behind her. "Thanks a lot, Dad," she said to the empty room. "Looks like you found me a real prize."

Dora dumped her things on a settee blooming with cabbage roses, brushed her hair back with impatient fingers. The guy might have been a pleasure to look at, she mused, but she preferred a neighbor with a modicum of personality. Marching to her candlestick phone, she decided to call her father and give him an earful.

Before she'd dialed the second number, she spotted the sheet of paper with its big heart-shaped happy face drawn at the bottom. Quentin Conroy always added some little drawing—a barometer of his mood—on his notes and letters. Dora hung up the phone and began to read.

Izzy, my darling daughter.

Dora winced. Her father was the only living soul who called her by that derivative of her name.

The deed is done. Well done, if I say so myself. Your new tenant is a strapping young man who should be able to help you with any menial work. His name, as you see on the copies of the lease awaiting your signature, is Jed Skimmerhorn. A full-bodied name that brings lusty sea captains or hearty pioneers to my mind. I found him fascinatingly taciturn, and sensed a whirlpool bubbling under those still waters. I couldn't think of anything nicer to give my adored daughter than an intriguing neighbor.

Welcome home, my firstborn babe.
Your devoted father.

Dora didn't want to be amused, but she couldn't help smiling. The move was so obvious. Put her within elbow-rubbing space of an attractive man, and maybe, just maybe, she would fall in love, get married and give her greedy father more grandchildren to spoil.

"Sorry, Dad," she murmured. "You're in for another disappointment."

Setting the note aside, she skimmed a finger down the lease until she came to Jed's signature. It was a bold scrawl, and she dashed her own name on the line next to it on both copies. Lifting one, she strode to her door and across the hall and knocked.

When the door opened, Dora thrust the lease out, crushing the corner against Jed's chest. "You'll need this for your records."

He took it. His gaze lowered, scanned, then lifted again. Her eyes weren't friendly now, but cool. Which suited him. "Why'd the old man leave this with you?"

Her chin tilted up. "The old man," she said in mild tones, "is my father. I own the building, which makes me, Mr. Skimmerhorn, your landlord." She turned on her heel and was across the hall in two strides. With her hand on the knob, she paused, turned. Her hair swung out, curved, settled. "The rent's due on the twenty-first of each month. You can slip the check under my door and save yourself a stamp, as well as any contact with other humans."

She slipped inside and closed the door with a satisfied snick of the lock.

3

WHEN Jed jogged to the base of the steps leading up to his apartment, he'd sweated out most of the physical consequences of a half bottle of whiskey. One of the reasons he'd chosen this location was the gym around the corner. He'd spent a very satisfying ninety minutes that morning lifting weights, punching the hell out of the heavy bag and burning away most of his morning-after headache in the steam room.

Now, feeling almost human, he craved a pot of black coffee and one of the microwave breakfasts he'd loaded into his freezer. He pulled his key out of the pocket of his sweats and let himself into the hallway. He heard the music immediately. Not Christmas carols, thankfully, but the rich-throated wail of gospel according to Aretha Franklin.

At least his landlord's taste in music wouldn't irritate him, he mused, and would have turned directly into his own rooms except he'd noted her open door.

An even trade, Jed figured, and, dipping his hands into his pockets, wandered over. He knew he'd been deliberately rude the night before. And because it had been deliberate, he saw no reason to apologize. Still, he thought it wise to make some sort of cautious peace with the woman who owned his building.

He nudged the door open a bit wider, and stared.

Like his, her apartment was spacious, high ceilinged and full of light from a trio of front windows. That was where the similarity ended.

Even after growing up in a house adorned with possessions, he was amazed. He'd never seen so much stuff crammed into one single space before. Glass shelves covered one wall and were loaded with old bottles, tins, figurines, painted boxes and various knickknacks that were beyond his power to recognize. There were a number of tables, and each of them was topped by more glassware and china. A brightly floral couch was loaded with colored pillows that picked up the faded tones of a large area rug. A Multan, he recognized. There'd been a similar rug in his family's front parlor for as long as he could remember.

To complement the season, there was a tree by the window, every branch laden with colored balls and lights. A wooden sleigh overflowed with pinecones. A ceramic snowman with a top hat grinned back at him.

It should have been crowded, Jed thought. It certainly should have been messy. But somehow it was neither. Instead he had the impression of having opened some magic treasure chest.

In the midst of it all was his landlord. She wore a scarlet suit with a short straight skirt and a snugly fitted jacket. While her back was to him, he pursed his lips and wondered what sort of mood he'd been in the evening before not to have noticed that nifty little body.

Under Aretha's rich tones, he heard Dora muttering to herself. Jed leaned against the doorjamb as she propped the painting she'd been holding on the sofa and turned. To her credit, she managed to muffle most of the squeal when she spotted him.

"Your door was open," he told her.

"Yeah." Then, because it wasn't in her nature to be monosyllabic like her tenant, she shrugged. "I've been recirculating some inventory this morning—from up here to downstairs." She brushed at her bangs. "Is there a problem, Mr. Skimmerhorn? Leaky plumbing? Mice?"

"Not so I've noticed."

"Fine." She crossed the room and moved out of his view until he shifted inside the door. She stood beside a pedestal dining room table pouring what smelled gloriously like strong coffee from a china pot into a delicate matching cup. Dora set the pot back down and lifted a brow. Her unsmiling lips were as boldly red as her suit. "Is there something you need?"

"Some of that wouldn't hurt." He nodded toward the pot.

So now he wanted to be neighborly, Dora thought. Saying nothing, she went to a curved glass cabinet and took out another cup and saucer. "Cream? Sugar?"

"No."

When he didn't come any farther into the room, she took the coffee to him. He smelled like soap, she realized. Appealingly so. But her father had been right about the eyes. They were hard and inscrutable.

"Thanks." He downed the contents of the fragile cup in two swallows and handed it back. His mother had had the same china, he recalled. And had broken several pieces heaving them at servants. "The old—your father," he corrected, "said it was okay for me to set up my equipment next door. But since he's not in charge I figured I should check with you."

"Equipment?" Dora set his empty cup back on the table and picked up her own. "What sort?"

"A bench press, some weights."

"Oh." Instinctively, she took her gaze over his arms, his chest. "I don't think that's a problem—unless you do a lot of thudding when the shop's open."

"I'll watch the thudding." He looked back at the painting, studied it for a moment. Again, bold, he thought, like her color scheme, like the punch-in-the-gut scent she wore. "You know, that's upside down."

Her smile came quickly, brilliantly. She had indeed set it on the sofa the way it had been displayed at auction. "I think so, too. I'm going to hang it the other way."

To demonstrate, she went over and flipped it. Jed narrowed his eyes. "That's right side up," he agreed. "It's still ugly, but it's right side up."

"The appreciation of art is as individual as art itself."

"If you say so. Thanks for the coffee."

"You're welcome. Oh, Skimmerhorn?"

He stopped, glanced back over his shoulder. The faint glint of impatience in his eyes intrigued her more than any friendly smile would have.

"If you're thinking of redecorating or sprucing up your new place, come on down to the shop. Dora's Parlor has something for everybody."

"I don't need anything. Thanks for the coffee."

Dora was still smiling when she heard his door close. "Wrong, Skimmerhorn," she murmured. "Everybody needs something."

COOLING his heels in a dusty office and listening to the Beach Boys harmonize on "Little St. Nick" wasn't how Anthony DiCarlo had pictured spending this morning. He wanted answers, and he wanted them now.

More to the point, Finley wanted answers, and wanted them yesterday. DiCarlo tugged on his silk tie. He didn't have answers yet, but he would. The phone call from Los Angeles the day before had been crystal clear. Find the merchandise, within twenty-four hours, or pay the consequences.

DiCarlo had no intention of discovering what those consequences were.

He looked up at the big white-faced clock overhead and watched the minute hand click from 9:04 to 9:05. He had less than fifteen hours left. His palms were sweaty.

Through the wide glass panel stenciled with an overweight Santa and his industrious elves, he could see more than a dozen shipping clerks busily stamping and hauling.

DiCarlo sneered as the enormously fat shipping supervisor with the incredibly bad toupee approached the door.

"Mr. DiCarlo, so sorry to keep you waiting." Bill Tarkington had a weary smile on his doughy face. "As you can imagine, we're pretty frantic around here these days. Can't complain, though, no sir, can't complain. Business is booming."

"I've been waiting fifteen minutes, Mr. Tarkington," DiCarlo said, his fury clear. "I don't have time to waste."

"Who does, this time of year?" Unflaggingly pleasant, Tarkington waddled around his desk to his Mr. Coffee machine. "Have a seat. Can I get you some of this coffee? Put hair on your chest."

"No. There's been an error, Mr. Tarkington. An error that must be corrected immediately."

"Well, we'll just see what we can do about that. Can you give me the specifics?"

"The merchandise I directed to Abel Winesap in Los Angeles was not the merchandise which arrived in Los Angeles. Is that specific enough for you?"

Tarkington pulled on his pudgy bottom lip. "That's a real puzzler. You got your copy of the shipping invoice with you?"

"Of course." DiCarlo took the folded paper from the inside breast pocket of his jacket.

"Let's have a look-see." His fat, sausage fingers moved with a quick, uncanny grace as he booted up his computer. "Let's see now." He rattled a few more keys. "That was to ship out on December seventeenth. . . . Yep, yep, there she is. She went out just fine. Should have arrived yesterday, today at the latest."

DiCarlo ran a hand through his wavy black hair. Idiots, he thought. He was surrounded by idiots. "The shipment did arrive. It was incorrect."

"You're saying the package that plopped down in LA was addressed to another location?"

"No. I'm saying what was *in* the package was incorrect."

"That's an odd one." Tarkington sipped some coffee. "Was the package packed here? Oh, wait, wait, I remember." He waved DiCarlo's answer away. "We provided the crate and the packing, and you supervised. So how in the wide, wide world did the merchandise get switched?"

"That is my question," DiCarlo hissed, his hand slamming the desk.

"Now, now, let's stay calm." Determinedly affable, Tarkington hit a few more keys. "That shipment went out of section three. Let's see who was on the belt that day. Ah, here we go. Looks like Opal." He swiveled around to beam at DiCarlo. "Good worker, Opal. Nice lady, too. Had a rough time of it lately."

"I'm not interested in her personal life. I want to speak to her."

Tarkington leaned forward and flicked a switch on his desk. "Opal Johnson, please report to Mr. Tarkington's office." He flicked the switch off, then patted his toupee to make sure it was still in place. "Sure I can't get you some coffee? A doughnut, maybe?" He tossed open the lid on a cardboard box. "Got us some nice raspberry-jelly-filled today. Some tractor wheels, too."

DiCarlo let out a sound like steam escaping a kettle and turned away. With a shrug, Tarkington helped himself to a doughnut.

DiCarlo clenched his fists as a tall, striking black woman strode across the warehouse. She was wearing snug jeans and a bright green sweater with a Nike hip pouch. Her hair was pulled back in a curly ponytail. The yellowing smudges of old bruises puffed around her left eye.

She opened the door and poked her head in. The room was immediately filled with the noise of conveyor belts and the scent of nerves. "You call for me, Mr. Tarkington?"

"Yeah, Opal. Come on in a minute. Have some coffee?"

"Sure, okay." As she closed the door, Opal took a quick scan of DiCarlo as possibilities raced through her mind.

They were laying her off. They were firing her outright because she'd fallen behind her quota last week after Curtis had knocked her around. The stranger was one of the owners come to tell her. She took a cigarette out of her pouch and lit it with shaky hands.

"We got ourselves a little problem here, Opal."

Her throat seemed to fill with sand. "Yes, sir?"

"This is Mr. DiCarlo. He had a shipment go out last week, on your line."

The quick surge of fear had Opal choking on smoke. "We had a lot of shipments going out last week, Mr. Tarkington."

"Yes, but when the shipment arrived, the merchandise was incorrect." Tarkington sighed.

With her heart hammering in her throat, Opal stared at the floor. "It got sent to the wrong place?"

"No, it got to the right place, but what was inside it was wrong, and since Mr. DiCarlo oversaw the packing himself, we're baffled. I thought you might remember something."

There was a burning in her gut, around her heart, behind her eyes. The nightmare that had plagued her for nearly a week was coming true. "I'm sorry, Mr. Tarkington," she forced herself to say. "It's hard to recall any one shipment. All I remember about last week is working three double shifts and going home to soak my feet every night."

She was lying, DiCarlo decided. He could see it in her eyes, in her body stance—and bided his time.

"Well, it was worth a shot." Tarkington gestured expansively. "Anything pops into your mind, you let me know. Okee-doke?"

"Yes, sir, I will." She crushed the cigarette out in the dented metal ashtray on Tarkington's desk and hurried back to her belt.

"We'll start a trace on this, Mr. DiCarlo. With a red flag. Premium prides itself on customer satisfaction. From our hands to your hands, with a smile," he said, quoting the company motto.

"Right." He was no longer interested in Tarkington, though he would have found some satisfaction in plowing his fists into the man's bulging belly. "And if you want to continue to enjoy the patronage of E. F., Incorporated, you'll find the answers."

DiCarlo circled the noisy shipping room and headed for Opal's station. She watched his progress with nervous eyes. Her heart was thudding painfully against her ribs by the time he stopped beside her.

"What time's your lunch break?"

Surprised, she nearly bobbled a box of cookware. "Eleven-thirty."

"Meet me outside, front entrance."

"I eat in the cafeteria."

"Not today," DiCarlo said softly. "Not if you want to keep this job. Eleven-thirty," he added, and walked away.

SHE was afraid to ignore him, afraid to oblige him. At 11:30, Opal donned her olive-green parka and headed for the employees' entrance. She could only hope that by the time she'd circled the building, she'd have herself under control.

She would have liked to skip lunch altogether. The Egg McMuffin she'd eaten that morning kept threatening to come back for a return visit.

Don't admit anything, she coached herself as she walked. They can't prove you made a mistake if you don't admit it. If she lost the job, she'd have to go back on welfare again. Even if her pride could stand it, she wasn't sure her kids could.

Opal spotted DiCarlo leaning against the hood of a red Porsche. The car was dazzling enough, but the man—tall, dark, glossily handsome and wrapped in a cashmere coat of pale gray—made her think of movie stars. Terrified, awed, intimidated, she walked toward him, head lowered.

DiCarlo said nothing, simply opened the passenger door. His mouth twitched when he caught her instinctive sigh on sliding over the leather seat. He climbed behind the wheel, turned the key.

"Mr. DiCarlo, I really wish I could help you about that shipment. I—"

"You're going to help me." He shoved the gearshift into first, and the car shot away from Premium like a slick red bullet. He'd already decided how to play her, and gave Opal two full minutes of silence to stretch her nerves. He fought back a satisfied smile when she spoke first.

"Where are we going?"

"No place in particular."

Despite the thrill of riding in a first-class car, she moistened dry lips. "I got to be back in a half hour."

He said nothing to that, only continued to drive fast.

"What's this all about?"

"Well, I'll tell you, Opal. I figured we could deal better together away from the work atmosphere. Things have been pretty harried for you the last few weeks, I imagine."

"I guess so. The Christmas rush."

"And I figure you know just what happened to my shipment."

Her stomach did a quick jig. "Look, mister, I already told you I didn't know what happened. I'm just doing my job the best I can."

He swung the car into a hard right turn that had her eyes popping wide. "We both know it wasn't my screwup, honey. We can do this hard, or we can do this easy."

"I—I don't know what you mean."

"Oh yeah." His voice held the same dangerous purr as the Porsche's engine. "You know just what I mean. What happened, Opal? Did you take a liking to what was in the crate and decide to help yourself? An early Christmas bonus?"

She stiffened, and some of her fear drained away in fury. "I ain't no thief. I ain't never stolen so much as a pencil in my whole life. Now you turn this car around, Mr. Big Shot."

It was just that kind of sass—as Curtis was fond of telling her—that earned her bruises and broken bones. Remembering that, she cringed against the door as the final word faded away.

"Maybe you didn't steal anything," he agreed after she'd started to tremble again. "That's going to make me really sorry to bring charges against you."

Her throat snapped shut. "Charges? What do you mean, charges?"

"Merchandise, which my employer considers valuable, has vanished. The police will be interested to learn what happened to that shipment once it got into your hands. And even if you're innocent, it's going to leave a big question mark on your work record."

Panic was pounding like an anvil at the base of her skull. "I don't even know what was in the crate. All I did was ship it. That's all I did."

"We both know that's a lie." DiCarlo pulled into the parking lot of a convenience store. He could see that her eyes were filled with tears, her hands twisting and twisting the strap of her shoulder bag. Almost there, he thought, and shifted in his seat to offer her a cold merciless stare.

"You want to protect your job, don't you, Opal? You don't want to get fired, and arrested, do you?"

"I got kids," she sobbed as the first tears spilled over. "I got kids."

"Then you'd better think about them, about what could happen to them if you got into this kind of trouble. My employer is a hard man." His eyes flicked over her fading facial bruises. "You know about hard men, don't you?"

Defensively, she lifted a hand to her cheek. "I—I fell down."

"Sure you did. Tripped on somebody's fist, right?" When she didn't answer he continued to press, lightly now. "If my boss doesn't get back what belongs to him, he's not just going to take it out on me. He'll work his way through Premium until he gets down to you."

They'd find out, she thought, panicking. They always found out. "I didn't take his stuff, I didn't. I just—"

"Just what?" DiCarlo leaped on the word and had to force himself not to wrap a hand around her throat and squeeze out the rest.

"I got three years in with Premium." Sniffing, she dug in her bag for a Kleenex. "I could make floor supervisor in another year."

DiCarlo bit back a stream of abuse and forced himself to stay cool. "Listen, I know what it's like to climb up that ladder. You help me out here, and I'll do the same for you. I don't see any reason that what you tell me has to go beyond you and me. That's why I didn't do this in Tarkington's office."

Opal fumbled for a cigarette. Automatically, DiCarlo let the windows down a crack. "You won't go back to Mr. Tarkington?"

"Not if you play straight with me. Otherwise . . ." To add impact, he slid his fingers under her chin, pinching as he turned her face to his.

"I'm sorry. I'm really sorry it happened. I thought I got it right afterward, but I wasn't sure. And I was afraid. I had to miss a couple of days last month 'cause my youngest was sick, and last week I was late one day when I fell and . . . and I was so rushed I mixed up the invoices." She turned away, braced for a blow. "I dropped them. I was dizzy and I dropped them. I thought I had everything put back right, but I wasn't real sure. But I checked on a bunch of deliveries yesterday, and they were okay. So I thought I was clear, and nobody'd have to know."

"You mixed up the invoices," he repeated. "Some idiot clerk gets a dizzy spell and screws up the paperwork and puts my butt in a sling."

"I'm sorry." She sobbed. Maybe he wasn't going to beat her, but he was going to make her pay. Opal knew someone always made her pay. "I'm really sorry."

"You're going to be a lot sorrier if you don't find out where the shipment went."

"I went through all the paperwork yesterday. There was only one other oversized crate that came through that lot in the morning." Still weeping, she reached in her bag again. "I wrote down the address, Mr. DiCarlo." She fished it from her purse and he snatched it.

"Sherman Porter, Front Royal, Virginia."

"Please, Mr. DiCarlo, I got kids." She wiped at her eyes. "I know I made a mistake, but I've done real good work at Premium. I can't afford to get fired."

He slipped the paper into his pocket. "I'll check this out, then we'll see."

Her jaw dropped with the weight of hope. "Then you won't tell Mr. Tarkington?"

"I said we'll see." DiCarlo started the engine as he plotted out his next steps. If things didn't go his way, he'd come back for Opal and it wouldn't just be her face that he'd leave black and blue.

At the main counter in her shop, Dora put the finishing touch of a big red bow on a gift-wrapped purchase. "She's going to love them, Mr. O'Malley." Pleased with the transaction, Dora patted the brightly wrapped box containing the cobalt saltcellars. "And it'll be an even bigger surprise, since she hasn't seen them in the shop."

"Well, I appreciate your calling me, Miss Conroy. Can't say I know what my Hester sees in these things, but she sure does set store by them."

"You're going to be her hero," Dora assured him as he tucked the purchase under his arm. "And I'll be happy to hold the other set for you until your anniversary in February."

"That's nice of you. You sure you don't want a deposit on them?"

"Not necessary. Happy Christmas, Mr. O'Malley."

"Same to you and yours." He walked out, a satisfied customer, with a spring in his step.

There were another half a dozen customers in the shop, two being helped by Dora's assistant, Terri. The prospect of another big day before the after-holiday lull made Dora's heart swell. Skirting the counter, she wandered the main room of the shop, knowing the trick was to be helpful but not intrusive.

"Please let me know if you have any questions."

"Oh, miss?"

Dora turned, smiling. There was something vaguely familiar about the stout matron with lacquered black hair.

"Yes, ma'am. May I help you?"

"Oh, I hope so." She gestured a bit helplessly toward one of the display tables. "These are doorstops, aren't they?"

"Yes, they are. Of course, they can be used for whatever you like, but that's the primary function." Automatically, Dora glanced over as the bells jingled on her door. She merely lifted a brow when Jed walked in. "Several of these are from the Victorian period," she went on. "The most common material was cast iron." She lifted a sturdy one in the shape of a basket of fruit. "This one was probably used for a drawing room. We do have one rather nice example of nailsea glass."

It was currently in her bedroom upstairs, but could be whisked down in a moment.

The woman studied a highly polished brass snail. "My niece and her husband just moved into their first house. I've got them both individual gifts for Christmas, but I'd like to get them something for the house as well. Sharon, my niece, shops here quite a lot."

"Oh. Does she collect anything in particular?"

"No, she likes the old and the unusual."

"So do I. Was there a reason you had a doorstop in mind?"

"Yes, actually. My niece does a lot of sewing. She's put together this really charming room. It's an old house, you see, that they've been refurbishing. The door to her sewing room won't stay open. Since they have a baby on the way, I know she'd want to be able to keep an ear out, and that this would be an amusing way to do it." Still, she hesitated. "I bought Sharon a chamber pot here a few months ago, for her birthday. She loved it."

That clicked. "The Sunderland, with the frog painted on the inside bottom."

The woman's eyes brightened. "Why, yes. How clever of you to have remembered."

"I was very fond of that piece, Mrs. . . . ."

"Lyle. Alice Lyle."

"Mrs. Lyle, yes. I'm glad it found a good home." Pausing, Dora tapped a finger to her lips. "If she liked that, maybe she'd appreciate something along these lines." She chose a brass figure of an elephant. "It's Jumbo," she explained. "P. T. Barnum's?"

"Yes." The woman held out her hands and chuckled as Dora passed Jumbo to her. "My, hefty, isn't he?"

"He's one of my favorites."

"I think he's perfect." She took a quick, discreet glance at the tag dangling from Jumbo's front foot. "Yes, definitely."

"Would you like him gift-boxed?"

"Yes, thank you. And . . ." She picked up the sleeping hound Dora had purchased at auction only the day before. "Do you think this would be suitable for the nursery?"

"I think he's charming. A nice, cozy watchdog."

"I believe I'll take him along, too—an early welcoming gift for my newest grandniece or -nephew. You do take Visa?"

"Of course. This will just take a few minutes. Why don't you help yourself to some coffee while you wait?" Dora gestured to the table that was always set with tea and coffeepots and trays of pretty cookies before she carried both doorstops back to the counter. "Christmas shopping, Skimmerhorn?" she asked as she passed him.

"I need a—what do you call it? Hostess thing."

"Browse around. I'll be right with you."

Jed wasn't completely sure what he was browsing around in. The packed apartment was only a small taste of the amazing array of merchandise offered in Dora's Parlor.

There were delicate figurines that made him feel big and awkward, the way he'd once felt in his mother's sitting room. Still, there was no sense of the formal or untouchable here. Bottles of varying sizes and colors caught the glitter of sunlight and begged to be handled. There were signs advertising everything from stomach pills to boot polish. Tin soldiers arranged in battle lines fought beside old war posters.

He wandered through a doorway and found the next room equally packed. Teddy bears and teapots. Cuckoo clocks and corkscrews. A junk shop, he mused. People might stick a fancy name on it, like "curio shop," but what it was was junk.

Idly, he picked up a small enameled box decorated with painted roses. Mary Pat would probably like this, he decided.

"Well, Skimmerhorn, you surprise me." Framed by the doorway, Dora smiled. She gestured toward the box he held as she walked to him. "You show excellent taste. That's a lovely piece."

"You could probably put bobby pins or rings into it, right?"

"You probably could. Originally it was used to hold patches. The well-to-do wore them in the eighteenth century, at first to cover smallpox scars, and then just for fashion. That particular one is a Staffordshire, circa 1770." She looked up from the box, and there was a laugh in her eyes. "It goes for twenty-five hundred."

"This?" It didn't fill the cup of his palm.

"Well, it is a George the Third."

"Yeah, right." He put it back on the table with the same care he would have used on an explosive device. The fact that he could afford it didn't make it any less intimidating. "Not quite what I had in mind."

"That's no problem. We have something for everyone's mind. A hostess gift, you said?"

He grunted and scanned the room. Now he was afraid to touch anything. He was back again, painfully back in childhood, in the front parlor of the Skimmerhorn house.

Don't touch, Jedidiah. You're so clumsy. You don't appreciate anything.

He blocked off the memory with its accompanying sensory illusion of the mingled scents of Chanel and sherry.

He didn't quite block off the scowl. "Maybe I should just pick up some flowers."

"That's nice, too. Of course, they don't last." Dora was enjoying his look of pure masculine discomfort. "A bottle of wine's acceptable as well. Not very innovative, but acceptable. Why don't you tell me a little about our hostess?"

"Why?"

Dora's smile widened at the suspicion in his voice. "So that I can get a picture of her and help you select something. Is she the athletic, outdoors type, or a quiet homebody who bakes her own bread?"

Maybe she wasn't trying to make him feel stupid, Jed thought, but she was succeeding just the same. "Look, she's my partner—ex-partner's wife. She's a trauma nurse. She's got a couple of kids and likes to read books."

"What sort of books?"

"I don't know." Why the hell hadn't he just gone by the florist?

"All right, then." Taking pity on him, she patted his arm. "It sounds to me as though we have a busy, dedicated woman. A compassionate and a romantic one. A hostess gift," she mused, tapping her finger to her lip. "It shouldn't be too personal. Something for the house." With a nod, she turned away and walked to a corner that was fashioned to resemble an old-fashioned pantry. "I think this would do nicely." Dora took down a footed wooden jar trimmed in brass.

Jed frowned over it. His parents hadn't gone for novelty antiques. "What's it—like for cookies?"

"How clever of you." Dora beamed at him. "It's a biscuit jar. Victorian. This one's oak from about 1870. A practical and ornamental gift, and at forty dollars, it won't cost you more than a dozen long-stem roses or a good French wine."

"Okay. I guess she'd get a kick out of it."

"See? That wasn't so painful. Can I help you with anything else? A last-minute Christmas gift?"

"No, that's it." He followed her back into the main room. The place smelled—cozy, he decided. Like apples. There was music playing softly. He recognized a movement from *The Nutcracker* and was surprised that he suddenly felt relaxed. "Where do you get all this stuff?"

"Oh, here and there," she said over her shoulder. "Auctions, flea markets, estate sales."

"And you actually make a living out of this."

Amused, she took a box from behind the counter and unfolded it. "People collect, Skimmerhorn. Often they don't even realize it. Didn't you ever have marbles as a boy, or comic books, baseball cards?"

"Sure." He'd had to hide them, but he'd had them.

She lined the box with tissue, working quickly, competently. "And didn't you ever trade your cards?" She glanced up to find him staring down at her hands.

"Sure I did," he murmured. His gaze lifted, locked on hers. He'd felt something watching her work that had gone straight to the gut like a hot arrow. "Just like you played with dolls."

"Actually, I didn't." She couldn't quite manage a smile. For a moment there, he'd looked as though he could've taken her in one quick bite. "I never liked them much. I preferred imaginary playmates, because you could change them into any character you wanted at the time." With more care than necessary she fit the lid with its gold-embossed DORA'S PARLOR onto the box. "What I was getting at is that most children collect and trade. Some people never grow out of it. Shall I gift-wrap this for you? There's no extra charge."

"Yeah, go ahead."

He shifted, then moved down the counter. Not that he was interested in what was displayed there, but to give himself some breathing room. The sexual tug he'd felt wasn't new, but it was the first time he'd experienced it because a woman had pretty hands. And huge brown eyes, he added. Then there was that smile, he thought. She always looked as though she was laughing at some secret joke.

Obviously he'd been celibate too long if he was attracted to a woman who laughed at him.

To pass the time he picked up a baseball-shaped item with a hole in the top. The words "Mountain Dew" were painted on the side. Curious, Jed turned it over in his hand. He didn't think it could be some sort of odd drinking cup for the soft drink.

"Interesting, isn't it?" Dora set the gaily wrapped package in front of him.

"I was wondering what it was."

"A match striker." She put her hands over his on the bowl and guided his thumb to the rough edge. "You put the matches in the top, then light them on the side. Mountain Dew was a whiskey. This is from the late nineteenth century." She caught the glimmer of a smile on his face. "Do you like it?"

"It's different."

"I'm very fond of the different." She kept her hands warm over his for another moment. "Take it. Consider it a housewarming gift."

The inexplicable charm the object had for him dimmed considerably. "Hey, I don't think—"

"It's not valuable, monetarily. A neighborly gesture, Skimmerhorn. Don't be snotty."

"Well, when you're so sweet about it."

She laughed then and gave his hand a quick squeeze. "I hope your friend likes her gift." She walked away then to help another customer, but she watched out of the corner of her eye as Jed left the shop.

An unusual man, she mused. And, of course, the unusual was her stock-in-trade.

DiCarlo raced along the Van Wyck toward the airport, dialing his car phone with one hand and steering with the other. "DiCarlo," he stated, flipping the phone to speaker. "Get me Mr. Finley." With his nerves bubbling, he checked his watch. He'd make it, he assured himself. He had to make it.

"Mr. DiCarlo." Finley's voice filled the car. "You have good news, I assume."

"I tracked it all down, Mr. Finley." DiCarlo forced his words into a calm, businesslike tone. "I found out just what happened. Some idiot clerk at Premium switched the shipments. Sent ours to Virginia. I'll have it straightened out in no time."

"I see." There was a long pause. DiCarlo's bowels turned to ice water. "And what is your definition of 'no time'?"

"Mr. Finley, I'm on my way to the airport right now. I've got a flight booked into Dulles and a rental car waiting. I'll be in Front Royal before five east coast time. I have the name and address where the shipment was misdirected." His voice weakened. "I'm handling all of this at my own expense, Mr. Finley."

"That's wise of you, Mr. DiCarlo, as I don't wish for your mistake to cost me more than it already has."

"No, sir. And you have my word that this mistake will be corrected expediently."

"Very well. I'll expect you to contact me when you reach your destination. Naturally, I'll want the clerk fired."

"Naturally."

"And, Mr. DiCarlo? You do know how important that merchandise is to me, don't you? You will use any means necessary to recover it. Any means at all."

"Understood." When the connection broke, DiCarlo smiled grimly. The way this mess was screwing up his holiday, he was more than ready to use any means. Any means at all.

4

"THIS is quite a mix-up, isn't it?" While he asked this rhetorical—and to DiCarlo, unamusing—question, Sherman Porter rummaged through his dented file cabinet.

"Guess we'd have caught it here, but we had ourselves an auction going on," Porter continued as he carelessly destroyed the filing system. "Hell of a turnout, too. Moved a lot of inventory. Shitfire, where does that woman put things?"

Porter opened another file drawer. "Don't know how I'm supposed to find anything with Helen off for a week visiting her daughter in D.C. You just did catch me. We'll be closing till New Year's."

DiCarlo looked at his watch. Six-fifteen. His time was running out. As for patience, even the dregs of that had vanished. "Maybe I didn't make myself clear, Mr. Porter. The return of this merchandise is vitally important to my employer."

"Oh, you made that clear. A man wants what's his, after all. Here now, this looks promising." Porter unearthed a short stack of neatly typed sheets. "See, Helen's listed all the merchandise we auctioned, the lot numbers, selling price. Woman's a jewel."

"May I see that?"

"Sure, sure." After handing over the papers, Porter pulled open the bottom drawer of his desk. He took out a bottle of Four Roses and a couple of dusty jelly glasses. He offered DiCarlo a sheepish grin. "Join me in a drink? It's after hours now, and it keeps the cold away."

DiCarlo eyed the bottle with distaste. "No."

"Well, I'll just help myself then."

DiCarlo took out his own list and compared. It was all there, he noted, torn between relief and despair. All sold. The china hound, the porcelain figurine, the abstract painting, the bronze eagle and the stuffed parrot. The enormous and ugly plaster replica of the Statue of Liberty was gone, as well as a pair of mermaid bookends.

Inside his pocket, DiCarlo had another list. On it were descriptions of what had been carefully and expensively hidden in each piece of merchandise. An engraved Gallae vase valued at nearly $100,000, a pair of netsukes stolen from a private collection in Austria and easily worth six figures. An antique sapphire brooch, reputed to have been worn by Mary, Queen of Scots.

And the list went on. Despite the chill of the room, DiCarlo's skin grew clammy. Not one single item remained in Porter's possession. Sold, DiCarlo thought, all sold.

"There's nothing left," he said weakly.

"Said we had a good turnout." Pleased with the memory, Porter poured another drink.

"I need this merchandise."

"So you said, but that shipment came in just minutes before we started the auction, and there wasn't time to do an inventory. Way I figure it, your boss and I could sue the pants right off Premium." Because the idea held appeal, Porter smiled and drank again. "Bet they'd settle on a nice tidy sum, too."

"Mr. Finley wants his property, not a lawsuit."

"Up to him, I guess." With a shrug, Porter finished off his liquor. "Helen keeps a mailing list of our customers. Pays to send out notices when we're having an auction. Best I can say is you go through it, match up the names and addresses with the names she's got there next to the stuff we sold. You can get in touch, explain things. Of course, you'll return *my* merchandise. I paid for it, right?"

It would take days to round up Finley's stock, DiCarlo thought, sickened. Weeks. "Naturally," he lied.

Porter grinned. The way he figured it, he'd already sold one lot. Now he'd sell another—all for the price of one.

"The mailing list?"

"Oh, sure, sure." Comfortably buzzed on Four Roses, Porter shuffled through a drawer and came up with a metal box full of index cards. "Go ahead, take your time. I'm not in any hurry."

TWENTY minutes later, DiCarlo left Porter comfortably drunk. He had one bright pinpoint of hope. The porcelain figurine was still in Front Royal, the property of a Thomas Ashworth, antique dealer. DiCarlo grasped hold of the possibility that regaining possession of one piece quickly would placate Finley and buy time.

As he drove through light traffic to Ashworth's shop, DiCarlo worked out his strategy. He would go in, explain the mishap, keeping it light, friendly. Since Ashworth had paid only $45 for the figure, DiCarlo was prepared to buy it back and include a reasonable profit for the dealer.

It could all be handled quickly, painlessly. Once he had the figurine, he would phone Finley and tell him that everything was under control. With any luck, Finley would be satisfied to have Winesap contact the rest of the list, and DiCarlo would be back in New York to enjoy Christmas.

The scenario brightened his mood to the extent that DiCarlo was humming as he parked his car by the curb in front of Ashworth's shop. It wasn't until he was out of the car and across the sidewalk that his easy smile faded.

CLOSED

The large cardboard sign on the glass-fronted door glared back at him.

DiCarlo was at the door in two strides, rattling the knob, pounding on the glass. It couldn't be closed. With his breath coming quickly, he raced to the wide display window, cupping his hands beside his face as he pressed it to the glass. He could see nothing but shadows and his own misery.

Finley would accept no excuses, he knew. Would tolerate nothing so vague as simple bad luck.

Then, as his lips peeled back in a snarl, DiCarlo saw the porcelain figure of a man and woman in ball dress, embracing lightly.

DiCarlo clenched his gloved hands into fists. He wasn't about to let a lock and a sheet of glass stop him.

The first step was to move his car. DiCarlo circled the block slowly, instincts humming as he kept an eye out for cruising patrol cars. He parked two blocks away. From his glove compartment he took what he thought he'd need. A flashlight, a screwdriver, his revolver. He slipped them all into the pockets of his cashmere coat.

This time he didn't approach the shop from the front, but headed up a side street with the firm, unhurried steps of a man who knew where he was headed. But as he walked, his eyes darted from side to side, watchful, wary.

It was a small town, and on a cold, blustery night most of its citizens were home enjoying the evening meal. DiCarlo passed no one as he walked toward the rear entrance of Ashworth's shop.

Nor did he spot any evidence of a security system. Moving quickly, he used the screwdriver to jimmy the door. The sound of splintering wood made him smile. He'd nearly forgotten the simple pleasure of breaking and entering during his years of corporate thievery. DiCarlo slipped inside, shut the door behind him. He flicked on his flashlight, shielding the beam with his hand as he swung it right and left. He'd entered through what appeared to be a small, cramped office. Because he would need to cover his tracks, DiCarlo had decided to make the break-in appear to be a random burglary. Impatient with the time he needed to waste, he pulled open drawers, upended contents.

He chuckled to himself as he spotted a plastic bank envelope. It looked as though his luck had changed. A quick flip through the small bills inside and he estimated the take to be about $500. Satisfied, he stuffed the money into his pocket and used the light to guide him into the main shop.

It seemed to DiCarlo that a little vandalism was just the touch he needed. He smashed a milk-glass lamp and a Capo di Monte vase at random. Then, because it felt so good, he kicked over a table that held a collection of demitasses. On impulse, and because it had been years since he'd had the thrill of stealing, he dropped a few cloisonné boxes into his pockets.

He was grinning when he snatched up the figurine. "Gotcha, baby," he murmured, then froze as light flooded into the shop from a stairway to his right. Swearing under his breath, DiCarlo squeezed himself between a rosewood armoire and a brass pole lamp.

"I've called the police." An elderly man wearing a gray flannel robe and carrying a nine-iron inched down the steps. "They're on their way, so you'd best stay right where you are."

DiCarlo could hear the age in the voice, and the fear. For a moment he was baffled as he smelled roasted chicken. The old man had an apartment upstairs, DiCarlo realized, and cursed himself for crashing through the shop like an amateur.

But there wasn't time for regrets. Tucking the figurine under his arm like a football, he hurtled toward Ashworth, as he had once hurtled down midtown Fifth Avenue with elderly matrons' Gucci bags stuffed in his jacket.

The old man grunted on impact, teetered on the steps, his worn bathrobe flapping over fish-white legs as thin and sharp as pencils. Breath wheezing, Ashworth swung awkwardly with the golf club as he fought to save his balance. More in reaction than intent, DiCarlo grabbed at the club as it whooshed by his ear. Ashworth pitched forward. His head hit a cast-iron coal shuttle with an ominous crack.

"Ah, Christ." Disgusted, DiCarlo shoved Ashworth over with the toe of his shoe. In the spill of the upstairs light, he could see the flow of blood, the open staring eyes. Fury had him kicking the body twice before he pulled himself back.

He was out the rear door and half a block away when he heard the sound of sirens.

FINLEY was switching channels on several of his television screens when the call came through.

"DiCarlo on line two, Mr. Finley."

"Put him through." After he'd switched the phone to speaker, Finley said, "You have news for me?"

"Yes. Yes, sir. I have the porcelain figurine with me, Mr. Finley, as well as a list locating all the other merchandise." DiCarlo spoke from his car phone, and kept his speed to a law-abiding fifty-five on his way back to Dulles International.

Finley waited a beat. "Explain."

DiCarlo began with Porter, pausing every few sentences to be certain Finley wanted him to continue. "I'd be happy to fax the list to you as soon as I reach the airport, Mr. Finley."

"Yes, do that. You sound a bit . . . uneasy, Mr. DiCarlo."

"Well, actually, sir, there was a bit of a problem in recovering the figurine. An antique dealer in Front Royal had purchased it. His shop was closed when I arrived, and knowing that you wanted results quickly, I broke in to retrieve it. The dealer was upstairs. There was an accident, Mr. Finley. He's dead."

"I see." Finley examined his nails. "So I assume you took care of this Porter."

"Took care of?"

"He can link you to the . . . accident, correct? And a link to you, Mr. Di-Carlo, is a link to me. I suggest you snap the link quickly, finally."

"I'm—I'm on my way to the airport."

"Then you'll have to turn around and go back, won't you? Don't bother with that fax. After you've finished tidying up in Virginia, I'll expect you here, with the figurine. We'll discuss the next steps."

"You want me in California? Mr. Finley—"

"By noon, Mr. DiCarlo. We'll be closing early tomorrow. The holidays, you know. Contact Winesap with your flight information. You'll be met."

"Yes, sir." DiCarlo broke the connection and headed for the first exit ramp. He hoped to God Porter was still in his office and well drunk so that he could put a bullet in the man's brain with little fuss.

If he didn't get this whole mess straightened out soon, he'd never make it home for Christmas dinner.

"REALLY, Andrew, *really*, there's no need for you to walk me up." With the self-defense only a woman who'd been bored beyond redemption could possibly understand, Dora body-blocked the stairway. *Just let me get inside*, she thought, behind a locked door. Then she could beat her head against the wall in private.

Andrew Dawd, a CPA who considered bundling funds into tax shelters the height of intrigue, gave one of his hearty laughs and pinched her cheek. "Now, Dora, my mother taught me to always see the girl to her door."

"Well, Mama's not here," Dora pointed out, and inched up the steps. "And it's late."

"Late? It's not even eleven. You're not going to send me off without a cup of coffee, are you?" He flashed the white teeth that his doting mama had spent thousands to have straightened. "You know you make the best coffee in Philadelphia."

"It's a gift." She was searching for some polite way to refuse when the outside door slammed open, slammed shut.

Jed strode down the hall, his hands balled into the pockets of his scarred leather bomber jacket. It was left unsnapped to the wind over a sweatshirt and torn jeans. His hair was windblown, his face unshaven—which suited the surly look in his eye.

Dora had to wonder why, at that moment, she preferred Jed's dangerous look to the three-piece-suited, buffed and polished accountant beside her. The lack, she decided, was most certainly in her.

"Skimmerhorn."

Jed summed up Dora's date with one brief glance as he fit his key into his lock. "Conroy," he said. With that as greeting and farewell, he slipped inside and closed the door.

"Your new tenant?" Andrew's dark, well-groomed eyebrows rose into the high forehead his mother assured him was a sign of intelligence, and not male-pattern baldness.

"Yes." Dora sighed and caught a whiff of Andrew's Halston for Men, and the clashing, wild-animal scent Jed had left stirring in the air. Since she'd missed her chance to make excuses, she unlocked her own door and let Andrew in.

"He seems remarkably . . . physical." Frowning, Andrew shed his London Fog overcoat, folding it neatly over the back of a chair. "Does he live alone?"

"Yep." Too frustrated for tidiness, Dora tossed her mink, circa 1925, toward the couch on her way to the kitchen.

"Of course, I know how important it is to keep an apartment tenanted, Dora, but don't you think it would have been wiser—certainly safer—to rent to another female?"

"A female what?" Dora muttered, then paused as she poured beans into her old, hand-cranked coffee grinder. "No." While she ground beans, she glanced over her shoulder where Andrew was standing behind her, lips pursed in disapproval. "Do you?"

"Certainly. I mean the two of you do live here, alone."

"No, I live here, alone. He lives there." Because it annoyed her to have him breathing down her neck while she worked, Dora said, "Why don't you go put on some music, Andrew?"

"Music?" His blandly handsome face cleared. "Of course. Mood."

Moments later she heard the quiet strains of an old Johnny Mathis recording. She thought, Uh-oh, then shrugged. If she couldn't handle an accountant who wore Brooks Brothers suits and Halston cologne, she deserved to pay the price. "The coffee'll be a few minutes," she said as she walked back into the living room. Andrew was standing, hands on his narrow hips, studying her new painting. "That's something, isn't it?"

He tilted his head right, then left. "It's certainly bold." Then he turned to her to take a moment to admire how she looked in the short black dress covered with fiery bugle beads. "And it suits you."

"I picked it up at an auction in Virginia just a couple of days ago." She sat on the arm of a chair, automatically crossing her legs without giving a thought to the way the movement urged her skirt higher on her thighs.

Andrew gave it considerable thought.

"I thought I'd enjoy living with it awhile before I put it in the shop." She smiled, then catching the predatory look in his eye, popped off the chair like a spring. "I'll go check the coffee."

But he caught her hand and swung her, in what she imagined he considered a stylish move, into his arms. She barely avoided colliding her head with his chin. "We should take advantage of the music," he told her as he glided over the rug. His mother had paid good money for dance lessons and he didn't want to waste it.

Dora forced herself to relax. He did dance well, she mused as she matched her steps to his. She smiled and let her eyes close. She let the music and the movement take her, laughing softly when he lowered her into a stylish dip.

He wasn't such a bad guy, she mused. He looked good, he moved well. He took care of his mother and had a solid portfolio. Just because he'd bored her silly on a couple of dates didn't mean . . .

Suddenly he clamped her hard against him, shattering her mellow mood. That she could understand and certainly overlook. But, as she pressed a hand against his chest, she felt the unmistakable outline of a toothbrush he'd slipped into the inside pocket of his jacket.

As conscientious as she knew Andrew to be, she sincerely doubted he carried it with him to brush after every meal.

Before she could comment, his hands had streaked under the hem of her dress to grab her silk-covered bottom.

"Hey!" Furious, she reared back, but even as she managed to free her mouth, he was slobbering kisses over her neck and shoulder.

"Oh, Dora, Dora, I want you."

"I get the picture, Andrew." While she squirmed, one of his hands snuck up to tug her zipper. "But you're not going to have me. Now pull yourself together."

"You're so beautiful, so irresistible."

He had her pressed against the side of a chair. Dora felt her balance going and swore. "Well, resist, or I'll have to hurt you."

He only continued to mumble seductive phrases as he tumbled with her to the floor. It wasn't the indignity of being sprawled under a crazed accountant that bothered her so much. It was the fact that they'd rammed against the coffee table and sent several of her treasures crashing to the floor.

Enough was enough. Dora brought her knee up between Andrew's thighs. Even as he grunted, she popped him hard in the eye.

"Off!" she shouted, shoving at him. Groaning, he rolled, curling up like a boiled shrimp. Dora scrambled to her feet. "If you don't get up right now, I'll hit you again. I mean it."

Afraid, he heaved himself to his hands and knees. "You're crazy," he managed, and took out a snowy-white handkerchief to check his face for blood.

"You're right. Absolutely." She picked up his coat and held it out. "You're better off without me. Now run along home, Andrew. And put some ice on that eye."

"My eye." He probed at it, winced. "What am I supposed to tell Mother?"

"That you walked into a door." Impatience snapping around her, Dora helped him to his feet. "Go away, Andrew."

Struggling for dignity, he snatched his coat away from her. "I took you out to dinner. Twice."

"Consider it a bad investment. I'm sure you can find a way to deduct it." She yanked open her door just as Jed opened his across the hall. "Out! And if you ever try anything like that again, I'll blacken both your eyes."

"Crazy." Andrew scurried toward the door. "You're out of your mind."

"Come back and I'll show you crazy." She pulled off a spiked heel and hurled it like a discus. "And you're fired." The shoe hit the back of the door with a satisfying thump. Dora stood, one shoe off, one shoe on, catching her breath. The quiet sound of Jed clearing his throat had her spinning back. He was grinning. It was the first time she'd seen him grin, but she wasn't in the mood to be pleased with the way it made his usually surly face approachable.

"See something funny, Skimmerhorn?"

He thought about it. "Yeah." Because it had been a long time since he'd been quite so amused, he leaned against the doorjamb and continued to grin. "Interesting date, Conroy?"

"Fascinating." She hobbled down the hall to retrieve her shoe. Slapping it against her palm, she hobbled back. "You still here?"

"Looks like."

Dora let out a long breath, dragged a hand through her tumbled hair. "Want a drink?"

"Sure."

As she crossed the threshold into her apartment, she pulled off the other shoe and tossed them both aside. "Brandy?"

"Fine." He glanced at the broken china on the floor. That must have been the crash he'd heard. Between that and the shouting, he'd had a bad moment deciding whether or not to intervene. Even when he'd carried a badge, he'd worried more about answering a domestic dispute than collaring a pro.

He looked over at Dora while she poured brandy into snifters. Her face was still flushed, her eyes still narrowed. He had to be grateful his Seventh Cavalry routine hadn't been necessary.

"So, who was the jerk?"

"My former accountant." Dora handed Jed a snifter. "He spends the evening boring me into a coma talking about Schedule Cs and long-term capital gains, then figures he can come back here and rip my clothes off."

Jed skimmed his gaze down her glittery black dress. "Nice clothes," he decided. "Don't know why he'd waste his time with capital gains."

Dora drank again, tilted her head. "Give me a minute. I think there was supposed to be a compliment buried in there."

Jed shrugged. "Looks like he got the worst of it."

"I should have broken his nose." Pouting, she walked over and crouched to pick up broken bric-a-brac. "Look at this!" Temper began to simmer again. She held up a broken cup. "This was Derby. Eighteen-fifteen. And this ashtray was Manhattan."

Jed crouched beside her. "Expensive?"

"That's not the point. This used to be a Hazel Ware candy dish—Moroccan amethyst, with lid."

"It's trash now. Leave it be; you're going to cut yourself. Get a broom or something."

Muttering, she rose and went out to rummage in the kitchen. "He even had a toothbrush in his pocket." She came out, waving a whisk broom and dustpan like a shield and spear. "A damn toothbrush. I bet the son of a bitch was an Eagle Scout."

"Probably had a change of underwear in his overcoat pocket." Gently, Jed took the broom from her.

"I wouldn't be surprised." Dora stalked back to the kitchen for the trash can. She winced as Jed dumped a load of broken glass into the trash can. "And a couple of condoms."

"Any self-respecting Eagle Scout would have those in his wallet."

Resigned, she sat on the arm of the chair again. The theatrics, it seemed, were over. "Were you?"

"Was I what?"

"An Eagle Scout."

He dumped the last load of glass, then sent her a long look. "No. I was a delinquent. Better watch your feet over here. I might have missed some splinters."

"Thanks." Too wired to sit, Dora rose to replenish both snifters. "So what do you do now?"

"You ought to know." Jed took out a pack of cigarettes, lighted one. "I filled out an application."

"I didn't have a chance to read it. Can I have one of those?" She nodded to his cigarette. "I like to smoke in times of stress or great annoyance."

He passed her the one he'd already lighted and took out another. "Feeling better?"

"I guess." She took a quick drag, blew it out as quickly. She didn't like the taste, only the effect. "You didn't answer my question."

"What question?"

"What do you do?"

"Nothing." He smiled, but there was nothing humorous about it. "I'm independently wealthy."

"Oh. I guess it pays to be a delinquent." She took another pull on the cigarette. The smoke and the brandy were making her pleasantly dizzy. "So what do you do with yourself all day?"

"Nothing much."

"I could keep you busy."

His brow lifted. "Is that so?"

"Honest labor, Skimmerhorn. That is, if you're any good with your hands."

"I've been told I'm good enough." His fingers hovered at her back, over the zipper that had been pulled nearly to her waist. After a moment's hesitation, he zipped it neatly into place. Dora jolted, blinked.

"Ah . . . thanks. What I meant was, I need some new shelves in the storeroom. And this place always needs a little this or that."

"Your outside banister's a joke."

"Oh." Her lips moved into a pout, as though the insult had been personal. To Dora, it very nearly was. "Can you fix it?"

"Probably."

"We could work it off the rent, or I could pay you by the hour."

"I'll think about it." He was thinking about something else at the moment—about how badly he wanted to touch her. Just a brush of his thumb along the curve of her throat. He couldn't say why, but he wanted to do that, only that, and to see if the pulse at the base of that long, slender throat would throb in response.

Annoyed with himself, Jed set aside his empty snifter and moved past her to pick up the trash can. "I'll take this back for you."

"Thanks." She had to swallow. It wasn't as simple as it might have been, not with the obstruction in her throat. There was something about the way the man looked at her that sent all sorts of weird jangles through her system.

Stupid, she told herself. It had simply been a long and exhausting day. She started toward the kitchen.

"Really, thanks," she said again. "If you hadn't come in, I'd have spent an hour kicking things."

"That's all right. I liked watching you kick him."

She smiled. "Why?"

"I didn't like his suit." He stopped in the doorway to look down at her. "Pinstripes put me off."

"I'll keep that in mind." With the smile still curving her lips, she glanced up. Jed followed her gaze and studied the sprig of mistletoe over his head.

"Cute," he said, and because he was a man who'd decided to stop taking chances, started to move by her.

"Hey." Amused by the situation, and his reaction, Dora caught his arm. "Bad luck," she told him. Hiking up to her toes, she brushed her mouth lightly over his. "I don't like to risk bad luck."

He reacted instinctively, in much the same way he would have to a gunshot or a knife at the back. Thought came after action. He caught her chin in his hand to hold her still. "You're risking more than bad luck, Isadora."

And he brought his mouth down on hers in a kiss tasting of smoke and brandy and an underlying violence that had the blood draining out of her head.

Oh God, my God, was all she had a chance to think. Or perhaps she groaned it as her lips parted helplessly under his.

It was quick, seconds only, but when he released her, she rocked back down on her heels, eyes wide.

He stared down at her for another moment, cursing himself and fighting a vicious urge to do exactly what the idiot accountant had tried.

"I wouldn't try kicking me on the way out," he said softly. "Lock your door, Conroy."

He walked out, across the hall, and locked his own.

5

"WHAT are you so cranky about?" Lea demanded. She'd popped back into the storeroom to announce a $500 sale, and had been greeted, for the third time that morning, by a short snarl.

"I'm not cranky," Dora snapped. "I'm busy." She was currently boxing up a four-piece place setting of Fire-King Dinnerware, honeysuckle pattern. "People ought to be shot for trying to cram their shopping into the last two days before Christmas. Do you realize I have to take Terri off the floor and have her deliver this across town this afternoon?"

"You could have told the customer to come back in for it."

"And I might have lost the sale," Dora tossed back. "I've had these damn dishes for three years. I'm lucky to have palmed them off on anyone."

"Now I know something's wrong." Lea crossed her arms. "Spill it."

"Nothing's wrong." Except that she hadn't been able to sleep. And there was no way, absolutely no way she was going to admit that she'd let one quick kiss tie her up into knots. "I've just got too much to do and not enough time to do it."

"But you like that, Dora," Lea pointed out.

"I've changed." Dora wrapped the last cup in newspaper. "Where's that stupid packing tape?" She turned, then stumbled back against the desk when she spotted Jed at the base of the stairs.

"Sorry." But he didn't look it. "I came down to see if you still wanted me to fix that banister."

"Banister? Oh . . . oh, well." She hated being flustered. The only thing she hated more was being wrong. "You have to get wood or something?"

"Or something." He looked over when Lea firmly cleared her throat.

"Oh, Lea, this is Jed Skimmerhorn, the new tenant. Jed, my sister, Lea."

"Nice to meet you." Lea extended a hand. "I hope you're settling in all right."

"Not much to settle. Do you want the banister fixed or not?"

"Yes, I suppose. If you're not too busy." Dora found the packing tape and kept herself occupied by sealing the carton. When the idea dawned, she went with it. "Actually, you could help me out. You've got a car, right? The Thunderbird?"

"So?"

"I have a delivery—in fact, I have three of them. I really can't spare my assistant."

Jed hooked his thumbs in his front pockets. "You want me to make deliveries?"

"If it wouldn't be a problem. You'd keep track of your gas and mileage." She offered him a sunny smile. "You might even cop a couple of tips."

He could have told her to go to hell. He wasn't sure why he didn't. "How can I resist?" He eyed, with vague dislike, the box she was sealing. "Where to?"

"It's all written down. Those are the other two right there." She nodded toward the corner of the room. "You can carry them out through the side door to your car."

Saying nothing, Jed hefted the first box and disappeared outside.

"*That's* the new tenant?" Lea whispered. Possibilities were already racing through her mind as she hurried to the door to peek through. "Who is he? What does he do?"

"I just told you who he is. His name's Skimmerhorn."

"You know what I mean." She watched Jed muscle the box into the backseat of the T-Bird, then quickly stepped back across the room. "He's coming back."

"I hope so," Dora said dryly. "He's only got one of the boxes." She lifted the second one herself and passed it to Jed when he came to the door. "They're fragile," she told him, and got a grunt in response.

"Did you see his shoulders?" Lea hissed. "John doesn't have shoulders like that in my wildest fantasies."

"Ophelia Conroy Bradshaw, shame on you. John's a wonderful guy."

"I know that. I'm nuts about him, but he doesn't have any shoulders. I mean, he's got them, of course, but they're just kind of bone and . . . God!" After studying the way Jed's Levis stretched when he leaned over the trunk of his car, she patted her heart and grinned. "It's always reassuring to know the attraction cells still operate. So what's he do?"

"About what?"

"About . . . the invoices," she said quickly. "Don't forget to give Mr. Skimmerhorn the invoices, Dora." She picked them up herself and handed them over to Jed as he stepped in to pick up the last box.

"Thanks." He gave Lea an odd look, wary of the gleam in her eye. "You want me to pick up that lumber, or what?"

"Lumber? Oh, the banister," Dora remembered. "Sure, go ahead. You can slip the bill under my door if I'm not around."

He couldn't resist. He knew he should, but he couldn't. "Another hot date?"

She smiled sweetly and yanked open the door. "Kiss my ass, Skimmerhorn."

"I've thought of it," he murmured. "I have thought of it." With that, he sauntered out.

"Tell," Lea demanded. "Tell all. Don't leave out any detail, however small or insignificant."

"There's nothing to tell. I went out with Andrew last night, and Jed met him when I was kicking him out."

"You kicked Jed out?"

"Andrew—he made a pass," Dora said with the last of her patience. "And I kicked him out. Now, if we've finished our little gossip session—"

"Almost. What does he do? Jed, I mean. He must lift weights or something to have shoulders like that."

"I never knew you had such a shoulder fixation."

"I do when they're attached to a body like that one. Let's see, he's a longshoreman."

"Nope."

"A construction worker."

"You lose the trip for two to Maui. Would you like to try for the Samsonite luggage?"

"Just tell me."

Dora had spent part of her sleepless night digging up Jed's application. One of his references had been Commissioner James L. Riker of the Philadelphia Police Department. Which made sense, she mused, since Jed's last place of employment had been the Philadelphia PD.

"He's an ex-cop."

"Ex?" Lea's eyes went wide. "Christ, he was fired from the force for taking bribes? Dealing drugs? For killing someone?"

"Put your imagination on hold, sweetie." Dora patted her sister's shoulder. "I swear, you should have been the one to take after Mom and Dad on the stage. He resigned," she said. "A few months back. According to the copious notes Dad took when he called the commissioner of police, Jed's got a pot full of commendations, and they're keeping his service revolver warm for him in hopes that he'll come back."

"Well, then why did he quit?"

"That didn't seem to be anyone's business," she said primly, but she was just as curious, and just as annoyed as Lea that their father hadn't asked. "Game over." She held up her hand to ward off another spate of questions. "If we don't get back inside to help Terri, she'll make my life a living hell."

"All right, but I feel good knowing you've got a cop right across the hall. That should keep you out of trouble." She stopped dead, goggle-eyed. "Oh God, Dory, do you think he was carrying a gun?"

"I don't think he'll need one to deliver dinnerware." With this, Dora shoved her sister through the door.

UNDER any other circumstances, DiCarlo would have felt foolish sitting in an elegant reception area holding a cheap statue in his lap. In this particular reception area, decorated with muted Impressionist prints and Erté sculptures, he didn't feel foolish at all. He felt scared, bone scared.

He hadn't really minded the murder. Not that he enjoyed killing like his cousin Guido, but he hadn't minded it. DiCarlo looked at putting a small-caliber bullet between Porter's eyes as self-defense.

But he'd had a lot to worry about on the long flight from east to west coast. Considering his string of bad luck, he wondered whether by some twisted hook of fate he had the wrong statue warming in his lap. It certainly looked like the one he'd seen packed into the crate at Premium. In a just world, there couldn't be two such ugly porcelain creations in the same small town.

"Mr. DiCarlo?" the receptionist said. "Mr. Finley will see you now."

"Ah, right. Sure." DiCarlo rose, hooking the statue under his arm and straightening the knot of his tie with his free hand. He followed the blonde to the double mahogany doors and worked on fixing a pleasant smile on his face.

Finley didn't rise from behind his desk. He enjoyed watching DiCarlo nervously cross the ocean of white carpet. He smiled, coldly, noting the faint beading of sweat over DiCarlo's upper lip.

"Mr. DiCarlo, you have tidied up in the great state of Virginia?"

"Everything there is taken care of."

"Excellent." He gestured to his desk so that DiCarlo set the statue down. "And this is all you've brought me?"

"I also have a list of the other merchandise. And all the locations." At the wave of Finley's fingers, DiCarlo dived into his pocket for the list. "As you see, there were only four other buyers, and two of them are also dealers. I think it should be simple enough to go right into those shops and buy back that merchandise."

"You think?" Finley said softly. "If you could think, Mr. DiCarlo, my merchandise would already be in my possession. However," he continued when DiCarlo remained silent, "I'm willing to give you the opportunity to redeem yourself."

He rose then and ran a fingertip over the overly sweet female face of the statue. "An unfortunate piece of work. Quite hideous, don't you agree?"

"Yes, sir."

"And this man, this Ashworth, paid in good coin for it. Amazing, isn't it, what people will find appealing. One has only to look to see the lines are awkward, the color poor, the material inferior. Ah well. 'Beauty's but skin deep.' " He picked up an unused marble white ashtray from his desk and decapitated the woman.

DiCarlo, who had only hours before cold-bloodedly murdered two men, jolted when the ashtray smashed the second head away. He watched, his nerves jumping, as Finley systematically broke away limbs.

"An ugly cocoon," Finley murmured, "to protect sheer beauty." From inside the torso of the figurine he pulled a small object wrapped in layers of heavy bubble plastic. Delicately, he unwrapped it, and the sound he made was like that of a man undressing a lover.

What DiCarlo saw looked like a gold cigarette lighter, heavily ornate and studded with some sort of stones. To him it was hardly more attractive than the statue that had hidden it.

"Do you know what this is, Mr. DiCarlo?"

"Ah, no, sir."

"It is an etui." Finely laughed then, caressing the gold. For that moment, he was supremely happy—a child with a new toy, a man with a new lover. "Which tells you nothing, of course. This small, ornamental case was used to hold manicure sets, or sewing implements, perhaps a button-hook or a snuff spoon. A pretty little fancy that went out of fashion toward the end of the nineteenth century. This one is more intricate than most, as it's gold, and these stones, Mr. DiCarlo, are rubies. There are initials etched into the base." Smiling dreamily he turned it over. "It was a gift from Napoleon to his Josephine. And now it belongs to me."

"That's great, Mr. Finley." DiCarlo was relieved that he'd brought the right figurine, and that his employer seemed so pleased.

"You think so?" Finley's emerald eyes glittered. "This bauble is only a portion of what is mine, Mr. DiCarlo. Oh, I'm pleased to have it, but it reminds me that my shipment is incomplete. A shipment, I might add, that has taken me more than eight months to accumulate, another two months to have transported. That's nearly a year of my time, which is quite valuable to me, not to mention the expense." He hefted the ashtray again and swung it through the delicate folds of milady's gown. Thin shards of porcelain shot like tiny missiles through the air. "You can understand my distress, can you not?"

"Yes, sir." Cool sweat slipped clammily down DiCarlo's back. "Naturally."

"Then we'll have to see about getting it back. Sit down, Mr. DiCarlo."

With an unsteady hand, DiCarlo brushed porcelain splinters off the buttery leather of a chair. He sat cautiously on the edge of his seat.

"The holidays make me magnanimous, Mr. DiCarlo." Finley took his own seat and continued to caress the etui in intimate little circles. "Tomorrow is Christmas Eve. You have plans, I imagine."

"Well, actually, yes. My family, you see . . ."

"Families." Finley's face lit up with a smile. "There is nothing like family around the holidays. I have none myself, but that is unimportant. Since you've managed to bring me one small portion of my property, so quickly, I hate to take you away from your family at Christmas." Keeping the etui trapped between his palms, he folded his hands. "I'll give you until the first of the year. Generous, I know, but as I said, the holidays. They make me sentimental. I'll want everything that is mine by January one—no, no, make it the second." His smile spread and widened. "I trust you won't disappoint me."

"No, sir."

"Naturally, I'll expect progress reports, holidays or no. You can reach me here, or on my private number. Do stay in touch, Mr. DiCarlo. If I don't hear from you at regular intervals, I'd have to come looking for you myself. We wouldn't want that."

"No, sir." DiCarlo had an uncomfortable image of being hunted by a rabid wolf. "I'll get right on it."

"Excellent. Oh, and have Barbara make a copy of this list for me before you go, will you?"

JED couldn't say why he was doing it. He'd had no business going down to the shop that morning in the first place. He was perfectly content to spend his days working out in the gym, lifting weights in his own apartment, catching up on his reading. God knew what crazy impulse had had him wandering downstairs and somehow volunteering to make Dora's deliveries.

Of course, he remembered with what was almost a smile, he had gotten tipped pretty well at that. A few bucks, and in one memorable case a brightly colored tin filled with homemade Christmas cookies.

It hadn't been such a big deal, and it had been interesting to see how much more enthusiastically you were greeted when you knocked on someone's door carrying a box rather than a badge.

He could have crossed the whole experience off as a kind of experiment, but now he was standing out in the cold replacing a banister. The fact that he was enjoying it on some deep, elemental level made him feel like an idiot.

He was forced to work outside because Dora didn't have ten feet of unoccupied space anywhere in her building. Since her idea of tools had run to a single screwdriver and a ball peen hammer with a taped handle, he'd had to drop by Brent's to borrow some. Of course, Mary Pat had grilled him on everything from his eating habits to his love life while plying him with Snickerdoodles. It had taken him nearly an hour to escape with his sanity and a power saw.

The events of the day had taught Jed one important lesson: He would keep to himself from this point on, just as he had planned. When a man didn't like people to begin with, there was no rational reason to mix with them.

At least there was no one to bother him in the rear of the building, and he enjoyed working with his hands, liked the feel of wood under them. Once, he'd considered adding a small workshop onto the back of the house in Chestnut Hill. A place where he could have tinkered and built when the job gave him time. But that had been before Donny Speck. Before the investigation that had become an obsession.

And, of course, it had been before Elaine had paid the price.

Before Jed could switch off his mind, he saw it again. The silver Mercedes sedan sitting sedately under the carport. He saw the dull gleam of pearls around Elaine's neck and remembered inanely that they had been a birthday gift from the first of her three husbands. He saw her eyes, the same brilliant blue as his own—perhaps the only family trait they had shared—lift and look curiously in his direction. He saw the faint annoy-ance in those eyes and saw himself racing across the manicured lawn, be-tween the well-tended rosebushes that had smelled almost violently of summer.

The sun had glinted off the chrome, speared into his eyes. A bird high up in one of the trio of apple trees had trilled insanely.

Then the explosion had ripped through the air with a hot fist that had punched Jed back, sent him flying away toward the roses, where the petals were sheared off by the force of the blast.

The silver Mercedes was a ball of flame with a belch of black smoke stinking upward into the summer sky. He thought he heard her scream. It could have been the screech of rending metal. He hoped it had been. He hoped she'd felt nothing after her fingers had twisted the key in the igni-tion and triggered the bomb.

Swearing, Jed attacked the new banister with Brent's power sander. It was over. Elaine was dead and couldn't be brought back. Donny Speck was dead, thank Christ. And however much Jed might have wished it, he couldn't kill the man again.

And he was exactly where he wanted to be. Alone.

"Ho, ho, ho."

Distracted by the hearty voice behind him, Jed switched off the sander. He turned, his eyes narrowed behind his tinted aviator glasses as he stud-ied, with equal parts annoyance and curiosity, the pink-cheeked Santa.

"You're a couple days early, aren't you?"

"Ho, ho, ho," Santa said again, and patted his comfortable belly. "Looks like you could use a little Christmas cheer, son."

Resigned to the interruption, Jed took out a cigarette. "Mr. Conroy, right?" He watched Santa's face fall. "It's the eyes," Jed told him, and struck a match. They were Dora's eyes, Jed thought. Big and brown and full of secret jokes.

"Oh." Quentin considered, then brightened. "I suppose a policeman is trained to see past disguises, the same way an actor is trained to assume them. I have, of course, played many upholders of law and order in my career."

"Right."

"In keeping with the season, I've been entertaining the children at Tidy Tots Day Care." He stroked his silky white beard. "A small engagement, but a satisfying one, as it gives me the opportunity to play one of the world's most beloved characters to an audience of true believers. Children are actors, you see, and actors, children."

Amused despite himself, Jed nodded. "I'll take your word for it."

"I see Izzy's put you to work."

"Izzy?"

"My darling daughter." Quentin wiggled his eyebrows and winked. "Pretty thing, isn't she?"

"She's all right."

"Cooks, too. Don't know where she gets it from. Not her mother." Conspiratorily, Quentin leaned closer. "Not to complain, but boiling an egg is a culinary triumph for her. Of course, she has other talents."

"I'm sure she does. Dora's inside."

"Naturally. A dedicated businesswoman, my firstborn, not at all like the rest of us in that aspect—though, of course, she could have had a brilliant career on the stage. Truly brilliant," he said with some regret. "But she chose the world of retail. Genes are a peculiar thing, don't you think?"

"I haven't given it a lot of thought." A lie, he thought. A basic one. He'd spent a great deal of his life thinking about inherited traits. "Listen, I need to finish this before I lose the light."

"Why don't I give you a hand?" Quentin said with the unexpected streak of practicality that made him a good director as well as an actor.

Jed studied the padded belly, the red suit and flowing white cotton beard. "Don't you have elves to handle this kind of thing?"

Quentin laughed merrily, his booming baritone echoing on the windy air. "Everything's unionized these days, boy. Can't get the little buggers to do anything not in the contract."

Jed's lips quirked as he turned on the sander again. "Once I finish here, you can help me put it up."

"Delighted."

A patient man, Quentin sat on the bottom step. He'd always liked to watch manual labor. "Watch" being the key word. Fortunately, a modest inheritance had kept him from starving while pursuing his acting career.

He'd met his wife of thirty years during a production of *The Tempest*, he as Sebastian and she as Miranda. They had entered the brave new world of matrimony and had traveled from stage to stage, with considerable success, until settling in Philadelphia and founding the Liberty Players.

Now, at the comfortable age of fifty-three—forty-nine on his résumé—he had whipped the Liberty Players into a respected troupe who performed everything from Ibsen to Neil Simon at a steady profit.

Perhaps because his life had been easy, Quentin believed in happily ever after. He'd seen his younger daughter tidily wed, was watching his son staunchly carrying the family name onto the stage. That left only Dora.

Quentin had decided that this healthy young man with the unreadable eyes was the perfect solution. Smiling to himself, he pulled a flask out of Santa's pillow belly, took a quick nip. Then another.

"Well done, boy," Quentin said half an hour later as he heaved himself up to pat the banister. "Smooth as a lady's cheek. And it was a pleasure to watch you work. How does one secure it in place?"

"Take a hold," Jed suggested. "Carry your end up to the top."

"This is fascinating." The silver bells on Quentin's boots jangled as he climbed the stairs. "Not that I'm a complete novice, you see. I have assisted in the building of sets. We once constructed a rather spiffy Jolly Roger for a production of *Peter Pan*." Quentin twirled his white moustache, and a look of menace gleamed in his eye. "I played Hook, naturally."

"I'd have bet on it. Watch yourself." Making use of Brent's electric drill, Jed secured banister to post. Throughout the procedure, Quentin kept up a running conversation. Jed realized it was as easy to tune him out as it was to tune out the background music in a dentist's office.

"As easy as that." Back at the base of the steps, Quentin shook the rail and beamed. "Steady as a rock, too. I hope my Izzy appreciates you." He gave Jed a friendly slap on the back. "Why don't you join us for Christmas dinner? My Ophelia puts on an impressive production."

"I've got plans."

"Ah, of course." Quentin's easy smile didn't reveal his thoughts. He'd done his research on Jed Skimmerhorn much more thoroughly than anyone knew. He was well aware that Jed had no family other than a grandmother. "Perhaps New Year's, then. We always throw a party at the theater. The Liberty. You'd be welcome."

"Thanks. I'll think about it."

"In the meantime, I think we both deserve a little reward for our labors."

He pulled out the flask again, winking at Jed as he poured whiskey into the silver top. He handed the makeshift cup to Jed.

Since he couldn't think of any reason not to, Jed tossed back the whiskey. He managed to choke back a gasp. The stuff was atomic.

"By God!" Quentin slapped Jed's back again. "I like seeing a man drink like a man. Have another. Here's to full white breasts that give a man's head sweet rest."

Jed drank again and let the whiskey work up a nice buffer against the cold. "Are you sure Santa should be drinking?"

"Dear boy, how do you think we get through those long, cold nights at the North Pole?

"We'll be doing *South Pacific* next. Nice change, all those palm trees. We try to fit a couple of musicals into our schedule each year. Crowd pleasers. Have to have Izzy bring you by."

He tipped more into Jed's cup and began a rousing rendition of "There Is Nothin' Like a Dame."

It must be the whiskey, Jed decided. That would explain why he was sitting outside in the cold at dusk, finding nothing particularly odd about watching Santa belt out a show tune.

As he downed another capful, he heard the door open behind him and looked around lazily to see Dora standing at the top of the steps, her hands fisted on her hips.

Christ, she had great legs, he thought.

She spared Jed one withering glance. "I should have known you'd encourage him."

"I was minding my own business."

"Sitting on the back steps drinking whiskey with a man in a Santa suit? Some business."

Because his tongue had thickened considerably, Jed enunciated with care. "I fixed the banister."

"Bully for you." Dora strode down the steps and caught her father's arm just as Quentin was executing a fancy spin. "Show's over."

"Izzy!" Delighted, Quentin kissed her lustily and gave her a bear hug. "Your young man and I were seeing to carpentry repairs."

"I can see that. You both look very busy at the moment. Let's go inside, Dad." She took the flask and shoved it into Jed's hand. "I'll come back for you," she said under her breath, and dragged her father upstairs.

"I was minding my own business," Jed said again, and meticulously capped the flask before slipping it into his back pocket. By the time Dora returned, he was loading up Brent's tools with the care of a man packing fine china.

"So." He slammed the trunk, leaned heavily against it. "Where's Santa?"

"Sleeping. We have one rule around here, Skimmerhorn. No drinking on the job."

Jed straightened, then wisely braced himself against the car again. "I was finished." Blearily, he gestured toward the banister. "See?"

"Yeah." She sighed, shook her head. "I shouldn't blame you. He's irresistible. Come on, I'll take you upstairs."

"I'm not drunk."

"You're plowed, Skimmerhorn. Your body knows it, it just hasn't gotten through to your brain yet."

"I'm not drunk," he said again, but didn't object when she slipped an arm around his waist to lead him up the steps. "I made fifteen bucks and two dozen cookies on the deliveries."

"That's nice."

"Pretty good cookies." He bumped into her as they passed through the doorway. "Christ, you smell good."

"I bet you say that to all your landlords. Got your keys?"

"Yeah." He fumbled for them, gave up and leaned against the wall. Served him right, he thought, for drinking that hard with only a few Snickerdoodles in his system.

Sighing, Dora slid her hand into his front pocket. She encountered a hard thigh and loose change.

"Try the other one," he suggested.

She looked up, caught the easy and surprisingly charming smile. "Nope. If you enjoyed that, you're not as drunk as I thought. Fish them out yourself."

"I told you I wasn't drunk." He found them, then wondered how he was supposed to fit the key into the lock when the floor was weaving. Dora guided his hand. "Thanks."

"It's the least I can do. Can you get yourself to bed?"

He braced a hand on the doorjamb. "Let's get this straight, Conroy. I don't want to sleep with you."

"Well, that certainly puts me in my place."

"You got complication all over you, baby. Those big, brown eyes and that tough little body. I just want to be alone."

"I guess that kills any hope I've been harboring that I'll bear your children. But don't worry, I'll get over it." She steered him toward the couch, shoved him down, then propped up his feet.

"I don't want you," he told her as she pried off his boots. "I don't want anyone."

"Okay." She looked around for a blanket, and settled on a couple of towels he'd hung over his bench press. "Here you go, nice and cozy." She tucked them neatly around him. He looked awfully cute, she thought, all drunk and surly and heavy-eyed. Going with impulse, she leaned over and kissed the end of his nose.

"Go to sleep, Skimmerhorn. You're going to feel like hell tomorrow."

"Go away," he muttered, closed his eyes and tuned out.

6

SHE was right. He felt terrible. The last thing Jed wanted was someone pounding on his door while he was trying to drown himself in the shower. Cursing, he twisted off the taps, wrapped a towel around his waist and dripped his way to the door. He yanked it open.

"What the hell do you want?"

"Good morning, Skimmerhorn." Dora breezed in with a wicker basket over her arm. "I see you're your usual bright and cheerful self."

She was wearing some sort of short-skirted outfit in vivid blues and gold that made his eyes throb. "Get lost."

"My, we are feeling nasty this morning." Unoffended, she unpacked the basket. Inside was a red plaid thermos, a mason jar filled with some sort of vile-looking orange liquid and a snowy-white napkin folded around two flaky croissants. "Since my father instigated this little affair, I thought I should see to your welfare this morning. We'll need a glass, a cup and saucer, a plate." When he didn't move, she tilted her head. "Fine, I'll get them. Why don't you go put some clothes on? You made it clear that you're not interested in me on a physical level, and the sight of your damp, half-naked body might send me into an unbridled sexual frenzy."

A muscle in his jaw twitched as he ground his teeth. "Cute, Conroy. Real cute." But he turned and strode off into the bedroom. When he came back wearing gray sweats torn at the knee, she'd set a neat breakfast on his picnic table.

"Had any aspirin yet?"

"I was working on it."

"These first, then." She offered him three pills. "Take them with this. Just gulp it down."

He scowled at the sickly orange liquid she'd poured into a tumbler. "What the hell is it?"

"Salvation. Trust me."

Because he doubted he could feel much worse, he swallowed the pills with two big gulps of Dora's remedy. "Christ. It tastes like embalming fluid."

"Oh, I imagine it's the same principle. Still, I can guarantee the results. Dad swears by it, and believe me, he's the expert. Try the coffee—it won't do much for the hangover, but you'll be fully awake to enjoy it."

Because his eyes were threatening to fall out, he pressed the heels of his hands against them. "What was in that flask?"

"Quentin Conroy's secret weapon. He has a still in the basement where he experiments like a mad scientist. Dad likes to drink."

"Now there's news."

"I know I should disapprove, but it's hard to. He doesn't hurt anyone. I'm not even sure he hurts himself." She broke off a corner of one of the croissants and nibbled. "He doesn't get surly or arrogant or nasty with it. He'd never consider getting behind the wheel of a car—or operating heavy machinery." She shrugged. "Some men hunt or collect stamps. Dad drinks. Feeling better?"

"I'll live."

"That's fine, then. I've got to go open up. You'd be amazed at how many people shop on Christmas Eve." She started out, paused with her hand on the knob. "Oh, and the banister looks good. Thanks. Let me know when you feel up to hammering together some shelves. And don't worry." She flashed him a smile. "I don't want to sleep with you either."

Dora closed the door quietly and hummed her way down the hall.

DiCarlo was feeling fine. His luck was back; the rented Porsche was tearing up 95. Neatly boxed on the seat beside him rode a bronze eagle and a reproduction of the Statue of Liberty, both easily purchased from a novelty shop just outside of Washington, D.C.

It had gone slick as spit, DiCarlo thought now. He had walked into the shop, done some nominal browsing, then had walked out again, the proud owner of two pieces of American kitsch. After a quick detour into Philadelphia to pick up the next two items on his list, he would head into New York. All things being equal, he would make it home by nine o'clock, with plenty of time for holiday celebrations.

The day after Christmas he would take up his schedule again. At this pace, he figured he would have all of Mr. Finley's merchandise in hand well before deadline.

He might even earn a bonus out of it.

Tapping his fingers along with the dance track, he dialed Finley's private number on the car phone.

"Yes."

"Mr. Finley. DiCarlo."

"And do you have something of interest to tell me?"

"Yes, sir." He all but sang it. "I've recovered two more items from D.C."

"The transactions went smoothly?"

"Smooth as silk. I'm on my way to Philadelphia now. Two more items are in a shop there. I should arrive by three at the latest."

"Then I'll wish you Merry Christmas now, Mr. DiCarlo. I'll be difficult to reach until the twenty-sixth. Naturally, if you have something to report, you'll leave a message with Winesap."

"I'll keep in touch, Mr. Finley. Enjoy your holiday."

Finley hung up the phone but continued to stand on his balcony, watching the smog clog the air over LA. The etui hung around his neck on a fine gold chain.

DiCarlo did arrive in Philadelphia by three. His luck was holding steady as he walked into Dora's Parlor fifteen minutes before closing. The first thing he noticed was a statuesque redhead wearing a green elf's cap.

Terri Starr, Dora's assistant, and a devoted member of the Liberty Players, beamed at DiCarlo.

"Merry Christmas," she said in a voice as clear as holiday bells. "You've just caught us. We're closing early today."

DiCarlo tried out a sheepish smile. "I bet you hate us eleventh-hour shoppers."

"Are you kidding? I love them." She'd already spotted the Porsche at the curb and was calculating ending the business day with a last whopping sale. "Are you looking for anything in particular?"

"Actually, yes." He took a look around the shop, hoping he'd spot either the painting or the china hound quickly. "I'm on my way home, and I have an aunt who collects statues of animals. Dogs in particular."

"I might be able to help you out." Topping six foot in her spiked heels, Terri moved through the shop like a staff sergeant inspecting troops. She'd sized up DiCarlo's suit and overcoat as well as his car, and led him toward the jade.

"This is one of my favorite pieces." She opened a curved glass cabinet and took out an apple-green carved Foo dog, one of their most expensive objects. "Gorgeous, isn't he?"

"Yes, but I'm afraid my aunt's tastes aren't quite so sophisticated." He let amusement play around his eyes. "You know how these little ladies are."

"Are you kidding? You can't run a curio shop and not know. Let's see, then." With some regret Terri replaced the jade. "We've got a couple of nice cocker spaniels in plaster."

"I'll take a look. Would it be all right if I just browsed around? I know you'd like to get out of here, and I might see something that strikes me as being Aunt Maria."

"You go right ahead. Take your time."

DiCarlo saw the plaster cockers. He saw cloisonné poodles and blown-glass retrievers. There were plastic dalmations and brass Chihuahuas. But nowhere did he see the china hound.

He kept his eye peeled for the painting as well. There were dozens of framed prints, faded portraits, advertising posters. There was no abstract in an ebony frame.

"I think I've found the perfect—" Terri backed up two steps when Di-Carlo whirled around. She was a woman who prided herself on reading expressions. For a moment there, she'd thought she'd read murder in his. "I—sorry. Did I startle you?"

His smile came so quickly, wiping out the icy gleam in his eyes, she decided she'd imagined it. "Yes, you did. Guess my mind was wandering. And what have we here?"

"It's Staffordshire pottery, a mama English sheepdog and her puppy. It's kind of sweet, isn't it?"

"Right up Aunt Maria's alley." DiCarlo kept the pleasant smile in place even after he'd spotted the four-figure price tag. "I think she'd love it," he said, hoping to buy time by having it wrapped. "I had something a little different in my mind, but this is Aunt Maria all over."

"Cash or charge?"

"Charge." He pulled out a credit card. "She used to have this mutt, you see," he continued as he followed Terri to the counter. "A brown-and-white spotted dog who curled up on the rug and slept twenty hours out of twenty-four. Aunt Maria adored that dog. I was hoping to find something that looked like him."

"That's so sweet." Terri nestled the Staffordshire in tissue paper. "You must be a very considerate nephew."

"Well, Aunt Maria helped raise me."

"It's too bad you weren't in a few days ago. We had a piece very much like you're talking about. In china, a spotted hound, curled up asleep. It was only in the shop a day before we sold it."

"Sold it?" DiCarlo said between smiling teeth. "That's too bad."

"It wasn't nearly as fine a piece as the one you've just bought, Mr. DiCarlo," she added after a glance at his credit card. "Believe me, your aunt's going to love you come Christmas morning."

"I'm sure you're right. I notice you also carry art."

"Some. Mostly posters and old family portraits from estate sales."

"Nothing modern, then? I'm doing some redecorating."

"Afraid not. We've got some stuff piled in the storeroom in back, but I haven't noticed any paintings."

While she wrote up his bill, DiCarlo drummed his fingers on the counter and considered. He had to find out who had bought the dog. If it hadn't been broad daylight, with a wide display window at his back, he might have stuck his gun under the clerk's pretty chin and forced her to look up the information for him.

Of course, then he'd have to kill her.

He glanced at the window behind him. There wasn't much traffic, vehicular or pedestrian. But he shook his head. A young girl wrapped in a parka zoomed by on Rollerblades. It wasn't worth the risk.

"Just sign here." Terri passed him the sales slip and his card. "You're all set, Mr. DiCarlo. I hope you and your aunt have a terrific Christmas."

Because she watched him through the window, DiCarlo set the box carefully in the trunk of the car, then waved cheerfully before climbing in. He slid smoothly away from the curb.

He'd go somewhere for a late lunch. When it was dark, when the shop was empty, he'd be back.

DORA gave Jed's door her best businesslike rap. She knew he was going to growl at her—it couldn't be helped. The fact was, she'd gotten used to the way he snarled and spat. She didn't look forward to it, but she'd gotten used to it.

He didn't disappoint her.

His short-sleeved sweatshirt was damp with sweat. His forearms glistened with it. She might have taken a moment to admire the basic masculinity, but she was too busy studying the scowl on his face.

Jed gripped the ends of the towel he'd hooked around his neck. "What do you want now?"

"Sorry to disturb you." She peeked over his shoulder and spotted his weight equipment scattered over the living area. "When you're so involved with building muscles, but my phone's out of order. I need to make a call."

"There's a phone booth on the corner."

"You're such a sweet guy, Skimmerhorn. Why hasn't some lucky woman snapped you up?"

"I beat them off with a stick."

"Oh, I bet you do. Be a pal. It's a local call."

For a minute, she thought he was going to shut the door in her face.

Again. But he swung the door wider and stepped back. "Make it fast," he told her, and stalked into the kitchen.

To give her privacy? Dora wondered. Hardly. Her judgment proved correct when he came back in glugging Gatorade from the bottle. Dora juggled the phone, swore softly, then dropped the receiver back on the hook.

"Yours is out, too."

"Not so surprising, since we're in the same building." He'd left his door open, as she had. From her apartment he could hear the strains of music. Christmas music this time. But it was something that sounded like a medieval choir, and intrigued rather than annoyed.

Unfortunately, Dora had exactly the same effect on him.

"You always dress like that to talk on the phone?"

She was wearing a slithery jumpsuit in silver with strappy spiked heels. A chain of stars hung at each ear. "I have a couple of parties to drop in on. How about you? Are you spending Christmas Eve lifting weights?"

"I don't like parties."

"No?" She shrugged and the silver silk whispered invitingly at the movement. "I love them. The noise and the food and the gossip. Of course, I enjoy having conversations with other human beings, so that helps."

"Since I haven't got any wassail handy to offer you, why don't you run along?" He tossed the towel aside and picked up a barbell. "Make sure your date doesn't hit the Christmas punch."

"I'm not going with anyone, and since I don't want to have to worry about how often I dip into the Christmas punch, I was calling a cab." She sat on the arm of the couch, frowning as she watched Jed lift his weights. She shouldn't have felt sorry for him, she mused. He was the last person on earth that inspired sympathy. And yet she hated to imagine him spending the evening alone, with barbells. "Why don't you come with me?"

The long, silent look he sent her had her hurrying on.

"It's not a proposition, Skimmerhorn. Just a couple of parties where you hang out and make nice."

"I don't make nice."

"I can see you're rusty, but it is Christmas Eve. A time of fellowship. Goodwill among men. You might have heard of it."

"I heard rumors."

Dora waited a beat. "You forgot bah-humbug."

"Take off, Conroy."

"Well, that's a step up from this morning. People will say we're in love." She sighed, rose. "Enjoy your sweat, Skimmerhorn, and the coal I'm sure Santa's going to leave in your stocking." She stopped, tilted her head. "What's that noise?"

"What noise?"

"That." Her eyes narrowed in concentration. "Oh boy. Don't tell me we *do* have mice."

He lowered the barbell and listened. "Someone down in the shop."

"What?"

"In the shop," he repeated. "The sound carries up through the vent. Don't you know your own building, Conroy?"

"I'm not over here that much, and not when the shop's open." She started to dismiss it, then froze. "But the shop's not open." Her voice had lowered to a stage whisper. "There's no one down there."

"Somebody is."

"No." Her hand slid up to rub at the nerves in her throat. "We closed hours ago. Terri left by three-thirty."

"So she came back."

"On Christmas Eve? She's giving one of the parties I'm going to." Dora's heels clicked smartly on the floor as she crossed to the door.

"Where are you going?"

"Downstairs, of course. Somebody must have cut the alarm and broken in. If they think they can gather up a sack of goodies from my shop, they're in for a surprise."

He swore, ripely, then took her arm, pushed her into a chair. "Stay there." He strode into the bedroom. Dora was still working out what name to call him when he walked back in, carrying a .38.

Her eyes rounded. "What's that?"

"It's a parasol. Stay in here. Lock the door."

"But—but—"

"Stay." Jed closed the door behind him. It was probably her assistant, he thought as he moved quickly, silently down the hall. Or her sister, who'd forgotten some package she'd hidden. Or the old man, looking for a bottle.

But there was too much cop in him to take chances. And too much cop to dismiss the fact that the phones were out, and that the sounds coming through the vent had been stealthy, rather than careless.

He reached the door that led down to the storeroom, eased it open. There was no generous spill of light from below. He heard a sound—a drawer closing.

Did she keep cash down there? he wondered, and swore under his breath. Probably. In some old-time canister or cookie jar.

A movement behind him had him braced and pivoting. And swearing again. Dora was three steps back, her eyes swallowing her face, and a barbell hefted in one hand.

Jed jerked a thumb. She shook her head. He curled his hand into a fist. She lifted her chin.

"Idiot," he muttered.

"Same goes."

"Stay back, for Christ's sake."

He started down, jerking still when the third step groaned under his foot. There was a rapid series of pops, and the wall inches away from his face spat plaster.

Jed crouched, took the rest of the steps in a sprint, rolling when he hit bottom and coming up, weapon drawn in time to see the rear door slam shut. He heard Dora clattering down after him, shouted for her to stay put.

He hit the door at a run, went through low. The cold air bit into his lungs like slivers of ice. But his blood was hot. The sound of running footsteps echoed off to the right. Ignoring Dora's frantic demands to stop, he raced after them.

It was instinct and half a lifetime of training. After he'd run about two blocks, he heard the roar of an engine, the squeal of tires. He knew he'd lost his quarry.

He ran on for another half a block, on the off chance that he could catch a glimpse of the car. When he returned to Dora he found her standing in the center of the small gravel lot, shivering.

"Get inside."

Her fear had already turned to anger. "Your face is bleeding," she snapped.

"Yeah?" He brushed at his cheek experimentally, and his fingers came away wet. "The plaster must have nipped it." He looked down at the barbell she still carried. "And what were you going to do with that?"

"When he grabbed you and wrestled you to the ground, I was going to hit him with it." She felt some small relief when he tucked the gun into the back of his sweatpants. "Weren't you supposed to call for backup or something?"

"I'm not a cop anymore."

Yes, you are, she thought. She might not have had much experience with the preservers of law and order, but he'd had cop in his eyes, in his moves, even in his voice. Saying nothing, she followed him toward the rear entrance of the shop.

"Ever heard of security systems?"

"I have one. It's supposed to clang like hell if anyone tries to get in."

He only grunted and, instead of going inside, hunted up boxes and wires. "Mickey Mouse," Jed said in disgust after one quick look at the mechanism.

She pouted a little, brushing her bangs aside. "The guy who sold it to me didn't think so."

"The guy who sold it to you was probably laughing his ass off when he installed it. All you have to do is cut a couple wires." He held out the frayed ends to demonstrate. "He took out the phone for good measure. He'd have seen by the lights that there was somebody upstairs."

"Then he was stupid, wasn't he?" Her teeth were chattering. "I mean, he should have waited until we were out, or asleep, then he could have walked in and stolen me blind."

"Maybe he was in a hurry. Don't you have a coat or something. Your nose is getting red."

Insulted, she rubbed it. "Silly of me not to have thought to grab my wrap. What was that noise right before you took your heroic flight downstairs? It sounded like balloons popping."

"Silencer." Jed checked his pocket for loose change.

"Silencer?" The word came out on a squeak as she grabbed his arm. "Like in gangster movies? He was shooting at you?"

"I don't think it was personal. Got a quarter on you? We'd better call this in."

Her hands slid away from his arm. The color the cold had slapped into her cheeks drained away. Jed watched her pupils dilate.

"If you faint on me, I'm really going to get pissed off." He grabbed her chin, gave her head a little shake. "It's over now. He's gone. Okay?"

"Your face is bleeding," she said dully.

"You already told me that."

"He could have shot you."

"I could have been spending the night with an exotic dancer. Shows you how far 'could have' is from reality. How about that quarter?"

"I don't . . ." Automatically, she checked her pockets. "I have a phone in my van."

"Of course you do." He strode over to her van, shaking his head when he found it unlocked.

"There's nothing in it," she began, huffing. It pleased him to see her color was back.

"Except a phone, a stereo tape deck." He lifted a brow. "A Fuzzbuster."

"It was a gift." She folded her arms.

"Right." He punched in Brent's number and waited two rings.

"Merry Christmas!"

"Hi, Mary Pat." He could hear children yelling in the background over a forceful recording of "Jingle Bells." "I need to talk to Brent for a minute."

"Jed. You're not calling to make some lame excuse about tomorrow? I swear I'll come drag you out here myself."

"No, I'll be there."

"Two o'clock sharp."

"I'll set my watch. MP, is Brent around?"

"Right here making his world-famous sausage stuffing. Hang on."

There was a clatter. "Jingle Bells" gave way to "Rudolf." "Hey, Captain. Merry, merry."

"Sorry to bust in on your cooking, but we had a little problem over here."

"Jody, let go of that cat! What sort of problem?"

"Break-in. The shop below the apartment."

"They get anything?"

"I have to have her check." He brushed wind-tossed hair from his face and watched Dora shiver. "Took a couple of pops at me. Used a silencer."

"Shit. You hit?"

"No." He checked his cheek again. The bleeding was nearly stopped. "He had a car close. From the sound of the engine, it wasn't an economy."

"Sit tight, Kimo Sabe. I'll call it in and be on my way."

"Thanks." He hung up and looked at Dora, who was dancing from foot to foot in a fruitless effort to keep warm. "Maybe you'd better break out that brandy again. Come on." Because her hands were frozen, he took them, warming them automatically as they walked back to the shop. "You can take a look around, see if anything is missing."

"I'm not supposed to touch anything, right?"

"You keep up with the cop shows."

"Can we close the door?"

"Sure." He took a brief glance at the jimmied lock, then closed out the cold. After he'd switched on the lights, he simply stood and absorbed.

The storeroom was crammed. On one wall, boxes were stacked from floor to ceiling. Shelves held uncrated merchandise in no sort of order he could discern. There were two four-drawer file cabinets shoved into a corner. The top of each was piled with more boxes.

There was a desk, which seemed to be an island of sanity. It held a phone, a lamp, a porcelain pitcher stuffed with pencils and pens, and a bust of Beethoven, which served as a paperweight.

"Nothing's gone," she said.

"How can you tell?"

"I know my inventory. You must have scared him off." She walked over to the shelves and tapped what looked to Jed to be an old perfume or lotion bottle. "This Daum Nancy is worth well over a thousand. This Castelli plate nearly that much. And this." She took down a box with a picture of a child's toy on it.

"Nando? A kid's robot?"

"Boxed, it's worth easily two thousand to a collector." She sniffed and replaced it.

"And you just leave this stuff out?"

"I have a security system. Had one," she muttered. "I can hardly drag all my stock into a vault every night."

"What about cash?"

"We deposit everything but about a hundred in small bills and change every night." She walked over to the desk, opened the top drawer. She took out an envelope, flipped through the bills inside. "Here it is. Like I said, you must have scared him off." She stepped away and heard a paper rustle under her foot. Bending down, she scooped it up. "Charge ticket," she told Jed. "Funny, this would have been filed."

"Let's see." He snatched it out of her hand. "Timothy O'Malley. Five-fifty and tax on December twenty-first. For saltcellars?"

"His wife collects."

"Five hundred for saltshakers?"

"Cellars," Dora corrected, and snatched the receipt back. "Peasant."

"Bloodsucker."

Unamused, she turned to replace the receipt in its file. "Look at this!" she demanded. "These drawers are a mess."

He came to peer over her shoulder. "They're not supposed to be?"

"Of course not. I keep very careful records. The IRS terrifies me the same as they terrify all good Americans. And Lea spent a week purging and updating these files last month."

"So he was after something in your files. What do you keep in here?"

"Nothing of value. Receipts, invoices, mailing lists, inventory printout, delivery sheets. Business stuff." Baffled, she ran a hand through her hair. The stars dangling from her ears sparkled in the light. "There's no reason for anyone to break in here for paperwork. A crazed IRS agent? A psycho-pathic accountant?"

As soon as she'd said it, Dora bit her tongue.

"What was that jerk's name the other night?"

"Don't be ridiculous. Andrew would never do anything like this."

"Didn't you say he was an accountant?"

"Well, yes, but—"

"And you fired him?"

"That's hardly any reason to—"

"Andrew what?"

She blew out a long breath, fluttering her bangs. "I'll give you his name, his address, his phone number, then you can go do cop things like harass him for his alibi on the night in question."

"I'm not a cop."

"If it looks like a cop, sounds like a cop"—she sniffed at him—"smells like a cop . . ."

"How would you know what a cop smells like?"

She angled her chin. "Gun oil and sweat. Come to think of it, you even taste like a cop."

"How's that?"

"I don't know." Very deliberately she dropped her gaze to his mouth, then lifted it slowly. "Tough, authoritative, just a little bit mean."

"I can be meaner." He edged closer so that she was trapped between him and the file cabinet.

"I figured that. Did I tell you that I've always had this problem with authority? Goes all the way back to my elementary-school days when I bucked Miss Teesworthy over quiet time."

He pressed her back. "You didn't mention it." No gun oil and sweat here, he realized. It seemed the whole room smelled like Dora, that hot, spicy scent that made a man's mouth water.

"I do," she continued. "That's one of the reasons I started my own business. I hate taking orders."

"You're lousy at taking them. I told you to stay put."

"I had this driving need to stay close to the man with the gun." She lifted her hand, rubbed her thumb over the cut on his cheek. "You scared me."

"You didn't get scared until it was over."

"No, I was scared all along. Were you?"

"No. I love having people shoot at me."

"Then this is probably just a reaction we're having." She slid her arms around his neck, found the fit to her liking. "You know, from the shock."

"I told you to back off."

"So push me away." Her lips curved. "I dare you."

They were still curved when his mouth came down. She expected him to be rough, and she was ready for it. His body slammed hers back into the file cabinet. The handles dug into her back, but she was too busy gasping with pleasure to notice the discomfort.

He knew it was a mistake. Even as he steeped himself with her, he knew. Somehow she'd already dug a hook into his mind he'd been unable to shake loose. Now she was trembling against him, making soft little sounds of shocked arousal deep in her throat. And she tasted—God she tasted every bit as hot and sweet as she smelled.

It had been so long, so very long since he'd allowed himself to tumble into that dark, soft oblivion of woman.

He drew back, wanting to clear his head, but she fisted both of her hands in his hair and pulled him against her. "More," she murmured as her mouth ravaged his. "I always want more."

With him she could have more. She knew it. With him there would be no vague sense of the incomplete. She could feast and be filled, and still have more.

For one wild moment he considered taking her there, on the floor of the cramped, dusty storeroom with gun smoke still fading from the air. Perhaps he would have, perhaps he would have had no choice, but he was still sane enough to hear the rattle at the door upstairs, and the spit of gravel under tires outside.

"The troops are here." He took Dora by the shoulders and set her firmly aside. She saw in his eyes what he would continue to deny. He was a cop again. "Why don't you go put on some coffee, Conroy? It doesn't look like you're going to make your parties after all."

She started up the stairs, keeping her back to him when she spoke. "And that's it?"

"Yeah." He wished violently for the cigarettes he'd left upstairs. "That's it."

7

DORA had brandy. Jed drank coffee. Cop, she thought nastily. After all, they didn't drink on duty—at least on TV. Wanting to ignore him as completely as he was ignoring her, she curled herself onto the couch and studied the cheerful lights of her Christmas tree.

She liked Jed's pal, though. Lieutenant Brent Chapman, with his wrinkled slacks, stained tie and easy grin. He'd come in smelling of sausage and cinnamon, his heavy horn-rims magnifying mild brown eyes. His manner was so reassuring that Dora found herself making coffee and setting out cookies as though she were entertaining unexpected guests rather than being involved in a police investigation of shots fired.

Brent's questions were slow and thoughtful and very nearly relaxing.

No, there was nothing missing as far as she could tell.

No, there was nothing in the files of any monetary value.

Yes, the shop had been crowded the past couple of weeks, but no, she couldn't remember anyone acting suspicious or asking unusual questions.

Enemies? This brought on a quick laugh. No, not unless you counted Marjorie Bowers.

"Bowers?" Brent's ears perked up. He kept his pencil hovering over his dog-eared notepad.

"We were both up for the lead in the school play. Junior year. It was a production of *West Side Story*. I creamed her in the auditions, so she started this rumor that I was pregnant."

"I don't really think—"

"With my reputation at stake, I had no choice," Dora went on. "I ambushed her after school." She flicked a glance over to Jed, who was busy frowning at the bull's-head cheese dish on her breakfront.

"That's very interesting. But I don't think it applies here."

"Well, she really hated me." Dora picked up her snifter again, shrugged. "Then again, that was in Toledo. No, I'm wrong. Junior year must have been in Milwaukee. We moved around a lot in those days."

Brent smiled. He'd taken a liking to Jed's landlord. A great many people who'd been through a break-in and gunfire didn't retain any sense of humor. "We're looking for something a bit more recent."

"Tell him about the bean counter," Jed ordered.

"For heaven's sake. Andrew wouldn't—"

"Dawd," Jed interrupted. "Andrew Dawd. He was Dora's accountant until a couple of days ago. He put some moves on her, so she gave him a black eye and his walking papers." He smiled nastily in Dora's direction. "And kicked his ass."

"I see." Brent tucked his tongue in his cheek as he scribbled the name in his book. He would have liked to have smiled, but the gleam in Dora's eye warned him to keep a sober countenance. "Did he, ah, threaten any reprisals?"

"Certainly not. Give me a cigarette, Skimmerhorn."

He lighted one for her. "Annoyed or stressed?" he asked when he offered it.

"You be the judge." She snatched it from him, took a quick puff. "The most violent thing Andrew would have done was to go home and whine to his mother."

"It wouldn't hurt to talk with him," Brent pointed out gently. "Where can we reach him?"

Dora shot Jed a look of intense dislike. "Dawd, Dawd and Goldstein, an accounting firm on Sixth and Market."

Brent nodded and picked up one of the cookies she'd spread on a pretty fluted dish at his elbow. "Hell of a way to spend Christmas Eve, huh?"

"I did have other plans." Dora drummed up a smile. "I'm sorry you had to leave your family."

"Just part of the job. Great cookies."

"Thanks. Why don't I give you some to take home? You've got kids, don't you?"

"Three." In a knee-jerk reaction, Brent reached for his wallet to show off pictures. While Jed rolled his eyes and paced away, Dora rose to admire the children's snapshots. There were two girls and a boy, all spit and polish for school pictures.

"The oldest girl looks like you," Dora commented.

"Yeah, she does. That's Carly. She's ten."

"I have a niece who just turned ten. Fifth grade."

"Carly's in the fifth, too. Over at Bester Elementary in Landsdowne."

"Missy goes to Bester." While Jed looked on, his partner and his landlord beamed at each other. "I bet they know each other."

"That wouldn't be Missy Bradshaw, would it? She has a younger brother named Richie, who's a real . . ."

"Terror, yes, that's right."

"She's been over to the house a dozen times. They only live a block over. Missy's parents and my wife and I are in the same car pool."

"Would you two like to be alone?" Jed asked.

They both spared Jed a pitying glance. "Tell me, Brent, is he always so crabby?"

"Pretty much." He tucked his wallet away and rose. There were cookie crumbs dusting his shirt and finger smudges on his glasses. Dora found him charming. "But he was the best cop I ever worked with, so you can feel safe having him across the hall."

"Thanks. I'm going to get you those cookies." Pointedly ignoring Jed, she walked into the kitchen.

"Some landlord," Brent commented, and wiggled his eyebrows.

"Get a grip. How soon will you have anything on the slugs you dug out of the plaster?"

"Jesus, Jed, it's Christmas. Give the lab boys a few days. We'll check out the prints, too, but that's pretty much a waste of time."

"If he's pro enough to use a silencer, he's pro enough to wear gloves."

"You got it."

"What do you figure—" Jed broke off when Dora walked back, carrying a paper plate covered with aluminum foil.

"Thanks, Miss Conroy."

"Dora. You will let me know if you find out anything?"

"Count on it. You just relax. Jed'll keep an eye on things."

"Well." She sent Jed a long, cool glance. "I can sleep easy now."

"There you go. Merry Christmas."

"I'll walk you out." Jed nodded to Dora. "I'll be back."

As they walked down the hall, Brent snuck another cookie from under the foil. "You've been here what, about a week?"

"Almost."

"How'd you piss her off already?"

"It's a gift. Look, why do you figure a pro would break into a junk shop and rifle a bunch of paperwork?"

"That's the sixty-four-dollar question." Brent walked through the rear door, sucking in his breath at the slap of wind. "There's a lot of valuable stuff in there."

"But he didn't go for the valuable stuff, did he?"

"Hadn't gotten around to it. You interrupted him."

"He sees lights on upstairs, he cuts the phone wires. He whacks the security system. But he doesn't go for the Daum Nancy."

"The what?"

"Never mind," Jed snapped, annoyed with himself. "He goes right for the files."

"Because he's looking for something."

"Yeah." Jed pulled out a cigarette. "But did he get it? And what would anyone look for in the files of a junk shop?"

"Receipts?" Brent offered as he opened his car door.

"Inventory lists, names, addresses."

"You can take the boy off the force, but you can't take the force out of the boy."

"I take a personal interest when somebody shoots at me."

"Can't blame you for that. We miss you downtown, Captain."

Something flickered in Jed's eyes that might have been grief, then was quickly gone. "The city seems to be hobbling along without me."

"Listen, Jed—"

"Save it." He wasn't in the mood for a lecture, or a pep talk, or a guilt trip. "Let me know what comes through."

"You'll be the first." Brent climbed into the car, rolled down the window. "Oh, and watch your butt, pal. I believe that lady could kick it."

Jed's response was a snort. He headed back inside. He wanted to make certain Dora was locked up for the night before he went back downstairs for another look.

Just as an interested civilian, he told himself.

"They've cleared out," he told her when he breezed through her open door. "You can count on Brent. He's a good detail man."

"Terrific. Sit down."

"I've got stuff to do. Lock your door."

"Sit down," she repeated, and pointed to a chair. "I'm going to clean up that cut."

"I can do it myself."

"Don't you know anything, Skimmerhorn? When you're wounded defending a woman, she's honor bound to whip out the antiseptic. If I was wearing a petticoat, I'd have to rip it into bandages."

Jed skimmed one more look over the glitter of her jumpsuit. "What are you wearing under that?"

"Excellent muscle tone." Because she was looking forward to it, Dora dragged him over to the chair. "Now you're supposed to say, 'Shucks, ma'am, it's only a scratch.'"

"It is." He smiled thinly. "But it could have been worse."

"Undoubtedly." With a whisper of silk, she knelt beside the chair and dabbed at the cut with one of the cotton balls she'd set out. "My sister would say you could have put out your eye. With Lea, everything's a potential eye poker. She inherited our mother's worry genes." Dora soaked another cotton ball and said brightly, "This may sting a bit."

As the shallow scratch erupted with fire, Jed snagged her wrist. "Goddamn it, what is that?"

"Alcohol." She fluttered her lashes. "It'll clean out any grit."

"Right down to the bone," Jed muttered.

"Don't be a baby, Skimmerhorn. Hold still."

He grimaced as she dabbed again. "You called me by my first name when you were clattering down the steps, screaming hysterically."

"I never scream hysterically."

"You did this time." He grinned wickedly. " 'Jed! Jed! Oh, Jed!' "

Dora dropped the cotton ball into a shallow enamel bowl. "At the time I thought you were about to be murdered. Unfortunately, I was wrong." She put a thumb to his chin to push his head to the side, examining the cut. "Do you want a Band-Aid?"

"No." His eyes gleamed. "Aren't you going to kiss it?"

"No." She rose then, started to pick up the bowl, set it down again. "Listen, I've got to ask. I know what you'll say. You'll say not to worry, that it was just one of those freak things that happen. But I have to ask anyway. Do you think he'll be back?"

Jed studied her face. There was a strain in her eyes she'd done a good job of hiding up until now. There was little he could, or would, do to alleviate it.

"I don't know," he said flatly.

"Great." Dora closed her eyes, drew a deep breath. "I should have known better than to ask. If you can't figure out what he was doing here in the first place, how can you tell if he'll be back or not?"

"Something like that." He could have lied, Jed told himself, uneasy that her cheeks were pale again. It wouldn't have been so hard to offer a phony reassurance to give her a peaceful night. Her eyes, when she opened them, were very dark, very tired.

"Look." He rose, and surprised them both by reaching out to tuck her hair behind her ear before snatching his hand back and stuffing it in his pocket. "Look," he said again. "I don't think you've got anything to worry about tonight. What you need to do is go to bed, tune out. Let the cops do their job."

"Yeah." It was on the tip of her tongue to ask him to stay, and only part of the reason was fear of being alone. She shook her head, rubbed her hands up and down her arms to warm them. "I'll be out most of tomorrow—at my sister's. I'll leave you the number in case . . . just in case," she finished.

"Fine. Lock up behind me. Okay?"

"You bet." She had her hand on the knob when he stepped into the hall. "You too. Lock up, I mean."

"Sure." He waited until she'd closed the door, turned the bolts. His lips quirked when he heard the unmistakable sound of a chair scraping across the floor, the rattle of the knob as it was wedged under it. Good thinking, Conroy, he decided, then went down to take another look at the storeroom.

In a pretty Federal town house shaded by stately oaks, a well-to-do matron was enjoying a glass of sherry and a showing of Bing Crosby's *White Christmas* on her big-screen TV.

At the sound of a quiet footstep behind her, Mrs. Lyle smiled and held up a hand. "Come watch, Muriel," she invited, addressing her longtime housekeeper. "This is my favorite number."

She didn't cry out when the blow came. The delicate crystal shattered against the edge of the coffee table, splattering the Aubusson rug with bloodred sherry.

Somewhere through the haze of pain that left her paralyzed, she heard the crashing of glass and a furious male voice demanding over and over, "Where is the dog? Where is the fucking dog?"

Then she heard nothing at all.

It was midnight when DiCarlo rode the elevator up to his apartment in Manhattan. His arms were laden with boxes he'd copped from the back of a liquor store.

He'd been lucky to find the receipt for the stupid dog, he told himself, and wondered idly if the bullets he'd sprayed up the stairs of the antique shop had hit anything. Or anyone.

Not to worry, he thought. The gun was untraceable. And he was making progress.

He hefted the boxes more comfortably as he walked out of the elevator into the hallway. He had the bronze eagle, the plaster Statue of Liberty, the china dog.

And a partridge in a pear tree, he thought, and chuckled to himself.

*   *   *

"So . . ." Dora snacked on a raw carrot while Lea checked the Christmas goose. "Jed goes racing out after the guy, waving this big gun while I stand there like your typical Hollywood heroine, with my hands clutched at my breasts. You got any dip for these veggies?"

"In the fridge. Thank God you weren't hurt." Harassed by the number of pots simmering on the stove, the sound of her children wreaking havoc in the family room and the very real fear that her mother would invade the kitchen at any moment, Lea shuddered. "I've been worried for years about your shop being burglarized. I'm the one who convinced you to put in that security system, remember?"

"A lot of good it did me, too." Dora dunked a spear of broccoli into sour-cream-and-chive dip, then leaned on Lea's cheery breakfast bar as she nibbled. "Jed said it was Mickey Mouse."

"Well, really." Lea paused in her stirring to be indignant. "John's cousin Ned said it was state-of-the-art."

"John's cousin Ned is a jerk. Great dip." She tried it with cauliflower. "Anyway, the cops came and did all this cop stuff—Dad would have loved the staging—and asked all these questions." Dora had purposely left out the part about the bullets. It didn't seem like Christmas conversation. "And it turns out that Jed's ex-partner is a neighbor of yours."

"Oh?" Lea chewed her knuckle as she basted her candied yams.

"Carly Chapman's father. She goes to school with Missy."

"Carly?" While she ran through her daughter's friends, Lea lifted a lid and sniffed. "Oh, yeah. Brent and Mary Pat. We carpool."

"So I hear." Dora helped herself to a glass of the wine Lea had breathing on the counter. "Here's the good part. They're going to question Andrew."

"You're kidding! Andrew?"

"Jilted accountant seeks revenge by destroying woman's tax files." Dora shrugged and passed a glass of wine to her sister. "Makes as much sense as anything. When's dinner?"

"Twenty minutes. Why don't we take what you've left of my crudité out. If we can keep Mom busy for—" She broke off, swore lightly under her breath as Trixie Conroy made her entrance.

Trixie always made an entrance, whether it was onto a stage or into the corner market. She'd dressed for the simple family dinner in a flowing caftan of bleeding colors that trailed fringe from its sweeping hem and draping sleeves. The material billowed theatrically around her willowy form. Her hair, cropped gamine short, was a bold, fire-engine red. Her face, milk-pale and unlined, thanks to religious pampering and one discreet lift, was striking. The soft blue eyes Lea had inherited were lavishly lashed, the full, sensuous mouth lushly red.

She breezed into the kitchen, trailing silks and her signature scent— one ripe with woodsy undertones.

"Darlings!" Her voice was as dramatic as the rest of her, a husky whisper that could easily carry to the last row in any theater. "It's so lovely to see my two girls together." She took a deep sniff of the air. "Oh, and those glorious aromas. I do hope you're not overheating my meatballs, Ophelia."

"Ah . . ." Lea sent Dora a desperate look and was met by a shrug. "No, of course not." Lea hadn't heated them at all, but had stuck them under the sink with hopes of palming them off on the dog later. "Mom, did you know . . . they're green."

"Naturally." Trixie buzzed around the stove, clanging lids. "I dyed them myself in honor of the season. Perhaps we should put them out now, as an appetizer."

"No. I think we should . . ." Since she couldn't think of a good ruse, Lea sacrificed her sister. "Mom, did you know someone broke into Dora's shop?"

"Damn it, Lea."

Lea ignored the muttered curse and barreled ahead. "Last night."

"Oh, my baby. Oh, my lamb." Trixie rushed across the kitchen to clasp Dora's face between her heavily ringed hands. "Are you hurt?"

"Of course not."

"Why don't you take Mom in the other room, Dora? Sit down and tell her all about it."

"Yes, yes, you must." Trixie gripped Dora's hand and dragged her toward the doorway. "You should have called me the minute it happened. I would have been there in the blink of an eye. My poor little darling. Quentin! Quentin, our daughter was robbed."

Dora had time for one speedy glare over her shoulder before she was yanked into the fray.

The Bradshaw family room was in chaos. Toys were strewn everywhere, making the practical buff-colored carpet an obstacle course. There were shouts and yips as a remote control police cruiser, operated by a steely-eyed Michael, terrorized the family dog, Mutsy. Will, looking very New York in a dark silk shirt and paisley tie, entertained Missy with bawdy numbers on the spinet. John and Richie were glassy-eyed over a Nintendo game, and Quentin, well plied with eggnog, boisterously kibitzed.

"Quentin." Trixie's stage voice froze all action. "Our child has been threatened."

Unable to resist, Will played a melodramatic riff on the piano. Dora wrinkled her nose at him.

"I wasn't threatened, Mom." Dora gave her mother a comforting pat, eased her into a chair and handed over her glass of wine. "The shop was broken into," she explained. "It didn't amount to much, really. They didn't get anything. Jed scared them off."

"I had a feeling about him." Quentin tapped the side of his nose. "A sixth sense, if you will. Were there fisticuffs?"

"No, Jed chased him away."

"I'd've shot him dead." Richie leaped onto the couch and fired an imaginary automatic weapon. "I told you."

"So you did."

"Richie, don't stand on the furniture," John ordered automatically. "Dora, you called the police?"

"Yes. And it's all in the hands of Philadelphia's finest." She scooped up Richie herself. "And the investigating officer is the father of a really, really good friend of yours, frog face. Jody Chapman."

"Jody Chapman!" Richie made gagging noises and clutched his throat.

"She sends her love." Dora fluttered her lashes and smacked her lips. The resulting din of groans and shrieks had her convinced the crisis had passed.

"Willowby!" Trixie cut through the noise with one word and a raised hand. "You'll stay at Isadora's tonight. I won't feel safe unless I know a man's keeping watch."

"Mother." It was enough to make Dora take back her wine. "I, on behalf of all feminists, am ashamed of you."

"Social and political ideals pale when it comes to the welfare of my child." Trixie gave a regal nod. "Will, you'll stay with your sister."

"No problem."

"Well, I have a problem," Dora cut in. "He leaves shaving gunk in the sink, and he makes long, obscene phone calls to his women in New York."

"I use my calling card." Will grinned. "And you wouldn't know they were obscene if you didn't listen."

"Your mother knows best." Quentin rose to help himself to more eggnog. Tonight he looked trim and dapper in a starched collar and a derby. He detoured to kiss his wife's hand. "I'll go by the shop myself tomorrow and take stock of the situation. Don't worry your pretty head, my sweet."

"Talk about obscene," Will mumbled, then grimaced. "What is that stench?"

"Dinner," Lea announced, swinging through the kitchen door. She smiled grimly at her mother. "Sorry, darling, I seem to have burned your meatballs."

A block away, Jed was trying to ease himself out the door. He'd enjoyed Christmas dinner at the Chapmans' more than he'd anticipated. It was hard not to get a kick out of the kids, who were still wide-eyed and enthusiastic over their Christmas loot. Impossible not to relax with the scents of pine and turkey and apple pie sweetening the air. And there was the simple fact that he liked Brent and Mary Pat as people, as a couple.

And the longer he stayed in their comfortable home, the more awkward he felt. There was no way to avoid comparing the homey family scene—a fire crackling in the hearth, kids playing on the rug—with his own miserable childhood memories of the holiday.

The shouting matches. Or worse, far worse, the frigid, smothering silences. The year his mother had smashed all the china against the dining room wall. The year his father had shot out the crystal drops on the foyer chandelier with his .25.

Then there had been the Christmas Elaine hadn't come home at all, only to turn up two days later with a split lip and a black eye. Had that been the year he'd been arrested for shoplifting in Wanamakers? No, Jed remembered. That had been a year later—when he'd been fourteen.

Those were the good old days.

"At least you can take some of this food home with you," Mary Pat insisted. "I don't know what I'll do with it all."

"Be a pal," Brent put in, patting his wife's bottom as he moved past her to pop the top on a beer. "You don't take it, I'll be eating turkey surprise for a month. Want another?"

Jed shook his head at the beer. "No, I'm driving."

"You really don't have to go so soon," Mary Pat complained.

"I've been here all day," he reminded her, and because she was one of the few people he felt relaxed with, kissed her cheek. "Now I'm going home to see if I can work off some of those mashed potatoes and gravy."

"You never put on an ounce. It makes me sick." She heaped leftovers into a Tupperware container. "Why don't you tell me more about this gorgeous landlord of yours?"

"She's not gorgeous. She's okay."

"Brent said gorgeous." Mary Pat sent her husband a narrow look. He only lifted his shoulders. "Sexy, too."

"That's because she gave him cookies."

"If she's Lea Bradshaw's sister, she must be more than okay." Mary Pat filled another container with generous slices of pie. "Lea's stunning—even first thing in the morning with a bunch of squalling kids in the car. The parents are actors, you know. Theater," Mary Pat added, giving the word a dramatic punch. "I've seen the mother, too." She rolled her eyes. "I'd like to look like that when I grow up."

"You look fine, hon," Brent assured her.

"Fine." Shaking her head, Mary Pat sealed the containers. "Does he say gorgeous? Does he say sexy?"

"I'll say it."

"Thank you, Jed. Why don't you bring the landlord over sometime? For dinner, or drinks?"

"I pay her rent; I don't socialize with her."

"You chased a bad guy for her," Mary Pat pointed out.

"That was reflex. I gotta go." He gathered up the food she'd pressed on him. "Thanks for dinner."

With her arm hooked around Brent's waist, Mary Pat waved goodbye to Jed's retreating headlights. "You know, I might just drop by that shop."

"You mean snoop around, don't you?"

"Whatever it takes." She leaned her head against his shoulder. "I'd like to get a look at this gorgeous, sexy, single landlord of his."

"He won't appreciate it."

"We'll see. He needs someone in his life."

"He needs to come back to work."

"So we'll double-team him." She turned, lifting her mouth for a kiss. "He won't have a chance."

In LA Finley dined on pressed duck and quail eggs. Joining him in his mammoth dining room was a stunning blonde, green-eyed, slenderly built. She spoke three languages and had an excellent knowledge of art and literature. In addition to her beauty and intelligence, she was nearly as wealthy as Finley. His ego demanded all three attributes in a companion.

As she sipped her champagne, he opened the small, elegantly wrapped box she'd brought.

"So thoughtful of you, my dear." He set the lid aside, pausing in anticipation.

"I know how you enjoy beautiful things, Edmund."

"Indeed I do." He flattered her with a warm look before reaching into the tissue paper. He lifted out a small ivory carving of a kirin, cradling it gently, lovingly in his palm. His deep, appreciative sigh whispered on the air.

"You admire it every time you dine with me, so I thought it would be the perfect Christmas gift." Pleased with his reaction, she laid her hand over his. "It seemed more personal to give you something from my own collection."

"It's exquisite." His eyes gleamed as he studied it. "And, as you told me, one of a kind."

"Actually, it seems I was mistaken about that." She picked up her glass again and missed the sudden spasm in his fingers. "I was able to obtain its twin a few weeks ago." She laughed lightly. "Don't ask me how, as it came from a museum."

"It's not unique." His pleasure vanished like smoke, replaced by the bitter fire of disappointment. "Why would you assume I would wish for something common?"

The change in tone had her blinking in surprise. "Edmund, it's still what it is. A beautiful piece of exceptional workmanship. And extremely valuable."

"Value is relative, my dear." As he watched her, cool-eyed, his fingers curled around the delicate sculpture. Tighter, tighter, until the carving snapped with a sound like a gunshot. When she cried out in distress, he smiled again. "It seems to be damaged. What a pity." He set the broken pieces aside, picked up his wine. "Of course, if you were to give me the piece from your collection, I would truly value it. It is, after all, one of a kind."

8

WHEN Jed knocked on Dora's door a little after nine on the day after Christmas, the last thing he expected was to hear a man's voice saying wait a damn minute.

There was a thud, a curse.

Will, a flowered sheet wrapped around his thin frame like a toga, and favoring the toe he'd smashed against the Pembroke table, opened the door to an unfriendly sneer.

"If you're selling anything," he said, "I hope it's coffee."

She sure could pick them, Jed thought nastily. First a pin-striped accountant with overactive glands, now a skinny kid barely out of college.

"Isadora," Jed said, and showed his teeth.

"Sure." Mindful of the trailing sheet, Will moved back so that Jed could step inside. "Where the hell is she?" he muttered. "Dora!" His voice echoed richly off the walls and ceiling.

The kid had lungs, Jed decided, then noticed, intrigued, the tangle of pillows and blankets on the sofa.

"You're not getting in here until I dry my hair." Dora stepped out of the bathroom, dressed in a terrycloth robe and armed with a hand-held hair dryer. "You can just—oh." She stopped, spotting Jed. "Good morning."

"I need to talk to you for a minute."

"All right." She combed her fingers through her damp hair. "You met my brother?"

Brother, Jed thought, annoyed with himself for the quick, unquashable sense of relief. "No."

"The guy in the sheet is Will. Will, the guy who needs a shave is Jed, from across the hall."

"The ex-cop who chased off the burglar." Will's sleep-glazed eyes cleared. "Nice to meet you. I played a drug dealer once, in a Sly Stallone film? Got killed in the first reel, but it was a great experience."

"I bet."

"Here." Dora passed Will the hair dryer. "You can use the shower. I'll make the coffee, but you have to make breakfast."

"Deal." He headed off, trailing flowered sheets.

"My mother thought I needed a man in the house after the break-in," Dora explained. "Will was the only one available. We can talk in the kitchen."

It was the same efficient galley setup as his own, but was obviously more well used, and certainly more organized. She chose what Jed now recognized as a biscuit tin and scooped coffee beans out and into a grinder before she spoke again.

"So how was your Christmas?"

"Fine. I've got a guy coming by around noon to hook up a new security system. One that works."

Dora paused. The scent of ground coffee and her shower filled the room and made Jed's juices swim. "Excuse me?"

"He's a friend of mine. He knows what he's doing."

"A friend," she repeated, going back to her grinding. "First, I must say I'm amazed you have any. Second, I suppose you expect me to be grateful for your incredible gall."

"I live here, too. I don't like being shot at."

"You might have discussed it with me."

"You weren't around." He waited while she put a kettle on to boil. "You need a couple of real locks on the doors. I can pick them up at the hardware."

With her lips pursed in thought, Dora measured coffee into a filtered cone. "I'm debating whether to be amused, annoyed or impressed."

"I'll bill you for the locks."

That decided her. Her lips curved up, then the smile turned into a quick, throaty laugh. "Okay, Skimmerhorn. You go ahead and make our little world safe and sound. Anything else?"

"I figured I might measure for those shelves you want."

She ran her tongue around her teeth, reached around him for the wicker basket of oranges. "Getting tired of being a man of leisure?" When he said nothing, she sliced through an orange with a wicked-looking knife. "I'll show you what I have in mind after breakfast. As it happens, we're not opening until noon today." After slicing half a dozen oranges, she put the halves into a clunky-looking device that squeezed out the juice. "Why don't you set the table?"

"For what?"

"Breakfast. Will makes terrific crepes." Before he could answer, the kettle shrilled. Dora poured boiling water over the coffee. The smell was all it took.

"Where do you keep your plates?"

"First cupboard."

"One thing," he said as he opened the cabinet door. "You might want to put some clothes on." He sent her a slow smile that had her throat clicking shut. "The sight of your damp, half-naked body might send me into a sexual frenzy."

It didn't amuse her at all to have her own words tossed back in her face. Dora poured herself a cup of coffee and walked away.

"Smells good," Will decided, strolling in now wearing black jeans and a sweater. His hair, a few shades lighter than Dora's, had been blow-dried into artful disarray. He looked like an ad for Ralph Lauren. "Dora makes great coffee. Hey, would you mind switching on the tube? CNN, maybe. I haven't heard what's happening out there for a couple of days." Will poured both himself and Jed a cup before rolling up his sleeves.

"Damn you, Will!"

Dora's voice made her brother wince, grin. "I forgot to wash out the sink," he explained to Jed. "She really hates to find shaving cream glopped in it."

"I'll keep that in mind if it ever becomes an issue."

"It's all right for her to hang underwear everyplace though." He pitched his voice to carry out of the kitchen and through the bathroom door, adding just a dollop of sarcasm for flavor. "Growing up with two sisters, I never went into the bathroom without fighting my way through a jungle of panty hose."

While he spoke, Will measured ingredients and stirred with careless finesse. He caught Jed's eye and grinned again. "We're all great cooks," he said. "Lea, Dora and me. It was self-defense against years of takeout and TV dinners. So about this burglary thing." Will went on without breaking stride. "Do you think it's anything to worry about?"

"I always worry when somebody shoots at me. I'm funny that way."

"Shoot?" Will's hand hovered an inch above the edge of the bowl, the egg he'd just cracked dripping inside. "What do you mean 'shoot'?"

"A gun. Bullets." Jed sipped his coffee. "Bang."

"Jesus, Jesus. She didn't say anything about shooting." Still carrying the dripping eggshell, he dashed into the living room and down the short hall and jerked open the bathroom door.

Dora nearly poked her eye out with her eyeliner. "Damn it, Will."

"You didn't say anything about shooting. Christ, Dory, you made it sound like a joke."

She sighed, tapped the eye pencil on the lip of the pedestal sink and gave Jed a hard stare over Will's shoulder. She should have looked silly with one eye lined and the other naked. Instead she looked sulky, sexy and steamed.

"Thanks loads, Skimmerhorn."

"Anytime, Conroy."

"Don't blame him." Incensed, Will took Dora by the shoulders and shook. "I want to know exactly what happened. And I want to know now."

"Then ask the big-nosed cop." She gave Will a shove. "I'm busy," she said, and shut the bathroom door, deliberately turned the lock.

"Isadora, I want answers." Will hammered on the door. "Or I'm calling Mom."

"You do, and I'll tell her about your weekend on Long Island with the stripper."

"Performance artist," he muttered, but turned toward Jed. "You," he said, "you fill me in while I finish making breakfast."

"There's not that much to tell." There was a sick feeling in Jed's gut. It didn't come from running over the events of Christmas Eve while Will whipped up apple crepes. It came from watching the brother and sister together, in seeing the concern and anger on Will's face—emotions that came from a deeply rooted love, not simply from family loyalty.

"And that's it?" Will demanded.

"What?" Jed forced himself back to the present.

"That's it? Some joker breaks in, messes with the files, takes a couple of potshots at you and runs away."

"More or less."

"Why?"

"That's what the police are paid to find out." Jed helped himself to a second cup of coffee. "Look, there's a new security system going in this afternoon. And new locks. She'll be safe enough."

"What kind of a cop were you?" Will asked. "A beat type, a narc, what?"

"That's irrelevant, isn't it? I'm not a cop now."

"Yeah, but . . ." Will trailed off, frowning down at the crepes he scooped onto a flower-blue platter. "Skimmerhorn? That's what she called you, right? Kind of name sticks in the mind. I remember something from a few months ago. I'm a news junkie." Will rattled it around in his mind, as he might lines long ago memorized. "Captain, right? Captain Jedidiah Skimmerhorn. You're the one who blew away Donny Speck, the drug lord. 'Millionaire cop in shoot-out with drug baron,' " Will remembered. "You made a lot of headlines."

"And headlines end up lining birdcages."

Will would have pressed, but he remembered more. The assassination of Captain Skimmerhorn's sister with a car bomb. "I guess anyone who could take out a top-level creep like Speck ought to be able to look out for my big sister."

"She can look out for herself," Dora announced. With a juice pitcher in one hand, Dora answered the ringing kitchen phone. "Hello? Yes, Will's right here. Just a minute." Dora fluttered her lashes. "Marlene."

"Oh." Will scooped two crepes onto his plate and gathered up his fork. "This might take a while." After taking the phone from his sister, he leaned against the wall. "Hello, gorgeous." His voice had dropped in pitch and was as smooth as new cream. "Baby, you know I missed you. I haven't thought of anything else. When I get back tonight I'll show you just how much."

"Sick," Dora muttered.

"Why didn't you tell him the whole story?"

Dora shrugged, kept her voice low. "I didn't see any need to worry my family. They tend to be dramatic under the best of circumstances. If my mother finds out I've got a stomach virus, she immediately diagnoses malaria and starts calling specialists. Can you imagine what she'd have done if I'd told her someone shot holes in my wall?"

Jed shook his head, savoring the crepes.

"She'd have called the CIA, hired two bulky bodyguards named Bubba and Frank. As it was, she stuck me with Will."

"He's all right," Jed said just as Will made kissy noises into the phone and hung up. Before he'd taken two steps, the phone rang again.

"Hello." Will's eyes gleamed. "Heather, darling. Of course I missed you, baby. I haven't been able to think of anything else. I'll get everything straightened out by tomorrow night and show you just how much."

"Nice touch," Jed said, and grinned into his coffee.

"You would think so. Since he's busy making love through AT&T, I'm turning off the television." She rose and had nearly tapped the Off button when a bulletin stopped her.

"There are still no leads in the Christmas tragedy in Society Hill," the reporter announced. "Prominent socialite Alice Lyle remains in a coma this morning as a result of an attack during an apparent burglary in her home sometime December twenty-fourth. Mrs. Lyle was found unconscious. Muriel Doyle, Lyle's housekeeper, was pronounced dead at the scene. Both Mrs. Lyle and her housekeeper were discovered by Mrs. Lyle's niece Christmas morning. Alice Lyle, the widow of Harold T. Lyle of Lyle Enterprises, remains in critical condition. A Philadelphia police spokesperson states that a full investigation is under way."

"Oh God." Hugging her elbows, Dora turned back to Jed. "I know her. She was in the shop before Christmas, buying a gift for her niece."

"It's a wealthy neighborhood," Jed said carefully. "Lyle's a prominent name. Burglaries can turn ugly."

"She bought a couple of doorstops," Dora remembered. "And she was telling me how her niece was expecting a baby." She shuddered. "How awful."

"You can't take it inside." Jed got up to turn off the television himself.

"Is that what they teach you in cop school?" she snapped, then immediately shook her head. "Sorry. That's why I never listen to the damn news. The only thing I read in the paper are the classified section and the comics." She pushed her hair back and struggled to shake off the mood. "I think I'll go down and open early, leave Will to clean up the mess before he goes back to New York."

This time he didn't resist the urge to brush his knuckles along her jawline. The skin there was as soft as rose petals. "It's tough when they're not strangers."

"It's tough when they are." She lifted a hand, touched his wrist. "Is that why you quit?"

He dropped his hand. "No. I'll head out to the hardware. Thanks for breakfast."

Dora merely sighed when the door closed behind him. "Will, when you finish your obscene call, do the dishes. I'm going down to the shop."

"I'm finished." He popped out of the kitchen and snagged the juice. "You're full of secrets, aren't you, Dory? How come you didn't tell me that your tenant was the big bad cop who took down Donny Speck?"

"Who's Donny Speck?"

"Jeez, what world do you live in?" He nibbled on little bits of crepe while he cleared the table. "Speck ran one of the biggest drug cartels on the east coast—probably the biggest. He was crazy, too; liked to blow people up if they messed with him. Always the same MO—a pipe bomb triggered by the ignition."

"Jed arrested him?"

"Arrested, hell. He whacked him in a real, old-fashioned gunfight."

"Killed him?" Dora asked through dry lips. "Is that—is that why he had to leave the force?"

"Shit, I think he got a medal for it. It was all over the news last summer.

The fact that he's the grandson of L. T. Bester, Incorporated, got him a lot of press, too."

"Bester, Inc.? As in large quantities of money?"

"None other. Real estate, Dora. Shopping malls. Philadelphia doesn't have too many loaded cops."

"That's ridiculous. If he was loaded, why would he be renting a one-bedroom apartment over a curio shop?"

Will shook his head. "You're a Conroy and you're questioning eccentricity?"

"I lost my head a minute."

"Anyway." Will filled the sink with hot soapy water. "The way I see the script here, I figure our hero, the wealthy police captain, is taking some downtime. Last summer was pretty hairy. The Speck investigation kept him in the news for months, then when his sister was killed in the car explosion—"

"Wait." She gripped Will's arm. "His sister?"

"They figured it was Speck, but I don't think they ever proved it."

"Oh, that's horrible." Paling, she pressed a hand to her grinding stomach. "Horrible."

"Worse—he saw it happen. The headlines said: 'Police captain watches sister's fiery death.' Pretty tough."

"Poor Jed," Dora murmured.

"The tabloids got a lot of play out of it, too. Can't remember it all, but there were lots of hints of scandal in the Skimmerhorn-Bester clan. The sister'd been divorced three or four times. The parents used to have public brawls. I think there was some stuff about Jed getting in scrapes as a juvenile. You know how people like to read about wealthy families suffering."

"No wonder he wants to be left alone. But," she continued after a moment, "that's not the answer." Leaning over, she kissed Will's cheek. "Lock up when you leave. See you New Year's?"

"Wouldn't miss it. Dora?"

"Hmm?"

"Do what he tells you. I like having you around."

"I like being around." She grabbed her keys and headed downstairs.

*   *   *

CUSTOMER traffic was light through the morning, which gave Dora time to think. What she didn't know about Jed Skimmerhorn could apparently fill a football stadium. The fascinating tidbits Will had dropped only made her lack of knowledge seem more acute.

"Good morning, Izzy, my darling daughter." Quentin swept into the shop with mink earmuffs clamped over his mane of striking pewter-colored hair. He was wearing an ankle-length shearling coat, a Christmas gift from his wife.

"Dad. Just the man I want to see."

"It's rewarding to be wanted by your children. Proves a man's worth in his middle years. Ah, Terri, a vision as always." He strode over to the red-head, took her hand and bowed theatrically over it. "A credit to the Liberty Players, to your humble director as well as to Dora's Parlor. What, no clientele this morning?"

"A couple of browsers, one exchange and a brisk sale of a twenty-dollar door knocker in the shape of a roaring hippo," Dora reported. "I imagine the malls are packed. Terri, you can handle things out here, can't you?"

"Blindfolded and hog-tied."

"Dad." Dora took her father's arm and drew him out of the main shop into one of the smaller display rooms. "What do you know about Jed Skimmerhorn?"

"Know?" To stall for time, Quentin took out a roll of spearmint Certs. "Let's see. He's about six-one, I'd say. A hundred seventy-five pounds, athletically proportioned. Mid-thirties. Anglo-Saxon lineage from his coloring."

"Cut it out. I know you, Quentin D. Conroy. Lea might think you'd rent the apartment to some chain-wielding biker with 'Born to Raise Hell' tattooed on his chest, but I know better."

Quentin blinked, clearly shocked. "Lea said such a thing? A serpent's tongue, by God." He slapped his fist into his palm.

"Don't change the subject. Whatever there is to know about Skimmerhorn, you know or he wouldn't be living here. So spill it. What's this business about his being from some wealthy family?"

"The Bester-Skimmerhorn clan," Quentin confirmed. Wearily, he slipped out of his coat and folded it lovingly over a balloon-back chair. "Most of the money is from his mother's side, though the Skimmerhorn branch aren't exactly pikers. Jed is the heir, if you will, as there is only himself and a couple of distant cousins remaining on the dwindling family tree."

"So he really is independently wealthy," Dora murmured. "I'll be damned."

"Independence was apparently more important." Quentin coughed gently into his hand. His cheeks pinked. "You know I dislike repeating gossip, Izzy."

"You'll only have to say it once."

He chuckled, patted her cheek. "My girl is quick. Very quick. Well then, rumor is that young Jed joined the police force against his family's wishes. They disapproved of his choice of career and threatened to cut him off." His voice had dropped into its story-telling mode, rich and perfectly paced. "In any case, the parents were notorious socialites. I say 'notorious' literally. They were given to public displays of bickering. It was no secret that they detested each other, but neither would divorce the other due to the convoluted financial connection between Bester and Skimmerhorn."

"Heartwarming," Dora murmured.

"Oh, indeed. Jed made a name for himself on the police force. He gained a reputation for being part bloodhound, part terrier. Sniffing out clues and getting his teeth into a case." Quentin smiled, enjoying his own analogy. "A bit over a year ago he was made captain, a position many feel would have been a stepping-stone leading to chief of police. Then there was Donny Speck."

"Will told me. Speck killed Jed's sister."

"That's the general assumption. As to why Jed left his position, I can only speculate. I would suggest that you ask him yourself."

"He wouldn't tell me."

"Is your interest personal or professional?"

She thought it through, then accepted the mint her father thumbed out of the roll. "I haven't decided. Thanks for the details." She kissed his cheek. "Which I shouldn't have had to ask for in the first place."

"You're quite welcome."

"Jed's back in the storeroom. You can go bother him while he puts in the new lock."

"It would be a pleasure." He picked up his coat, draped it over his arm.

"You can leave that here."

"Here . . . ah, no, no." Avoiding Dora's eye, he stroked the coat lovingly. "I'll just take it along. I might get chilly."

Might need the flask in the inside pocket, Dora corrected, and returned to work.

BACK in the storeroom, Jed was putting Brent's drill to use again. He had a nice thick dead bolt nearly installed when Quentin toddled in.

"And happy Boxing Day to you. It seems you're our man of the hour. May I extend my deepest and most sincere gratitude."

"Mr. Conroy."

"Quentin, please. After all, according to Will you've protected my little girl at the risk of your own life and limb." Quentin settled into a ladder-back chair. "Tell me, do we have any clues?"

"Call headquarters and ask Lieutenant Brent Chapman. He's in charge."

"But, my dear boy, you were on the scene, weapon drawn. Where are the bullet holes? Will told me shots were exchanged."

"In the plaster, by the stairway." Amused, Jed watched Quentin stride over to peer at the wall. He wouldn't have been surprised if the man had pulled a magnifying glass and a deerstalker out of his pocket.

"Curious, isn't it? You know, I once played Poirot in a little theater production of *Orient Express*."

"And Will played a drug dealer with Stallone. Quite a family."

"One must play the villain as well as the hero to fully develop one's art. We have theater in our blood, you know. Although Izzy's seems to lean more toward props." He came back and settled himself again. He stretched back, crossed his legs at the ankles and folded his hands on his trim belly. "Do you have the time?"

Jed twisted his wrist to read his watch. "Couple minutes shy of noon."

"That's fine then." Satisfied, Quentin reached in his coat for his flask.

"Don't bring that near me."

Quentin smiled genially. "I'm afraid I'd filled it with what we might call my high-test the other day. We have a much lower octane today."

"I'll pass just the same."

"Well, here's to all the girls I've loved." Quentin took a slow drink, sighed, then tucked the flask away again. Dora might pop in at any time. "I had another reason for dropping by this morning. I'd like to renew the invitation to our annual New Year's Eve party, at the theater. My wife would like to thank you personally for looking out for our Izzy."

"I'm not big on parties."

"I'd consider it a personal favor if you'd at least drop in. After this incident, I'm concerned about Izzy driving there alone." Having planted the seed, Quentin snuck one more nip before making his exit.

WITH business slowed to a crawl, Dora left Terri in charge and spent most of the afternoon reorganizing her files. It was nearly dusk when Jed came downstairs and, without a word to her, began measuring the wall where she'd told him to put the shelves.

Dora ignored him, too, for nearly five minutes. "This security system you've dumped on me is complicated enough for Fort Knox."

Jed scribbled down figures on a pad. "All you do is cue in a six-digit code."

"And if I forget the code, bells and buzzers go off, lights flash—and some guy with a bullhorn shouts for me to come out with my hands up."

"So don't forget the code."

"I'm not good with numbers. That's why I have an accountant."

"Had an accountant. He's clean, by the way."

"Clean? Andrew? Of course he is. His mother checks every night to see if he's washed behind his ears."

Jed's measuring tape rewound with a snap. "Why the hell did you ever go out with him in the first place?"

"He was talking about paragraph twenty-five of the new tax law. I was terrified not to." Then she smiled because at least they were having a conversation. "Actually, I felt kind of sorry for him. His mother really is a smothering old witch."

"On the night in question, Andrew was with the smothering old witch and about two dozen other people at the Dawd, Dawd and Goldstein Christmas party. He's alibied tight until ten-thirty."

"I never thought it was him anyway." She spent another few moments separating receipts from invoices. "I called the hospital."

"What?"

"Mrs. Lyle, on the news this morning? I couldn't get it out of my mind." Dora refiled a Federal Express receipt. "She's still in a coma. I sent flowers. I guess that was stupid."

"Yeah." Christ, why was he letting her get to him this way? "But people usually appreciate stupid gestures."

"I do." Dora let out a long breath and shoved back from her desk. "Skimmerhorn, you want to get out of here?"

"I'm almost finished with the measurements. Then I'll get out of your way."

"No, I mean out." Restlessly, she pulled her hand through her hair. "Do you want to go get a pizza, see a movie? I don't want to face this pile of paperwork right now."

"It's a little early for a movie."

"It won't be after the pizza." She put on her best persuasive voice. "Be a pal, Skimmerhorn. The only thing worse than going to the movies alone is going to a drive-in movie alone."

He shouldn't, he knew. After what had nearly happened between them the night before, he should be avoiding her. "What's your security code?"

"Why?"

"Because we'll have to lock up if we're going out."

The tension cleared out of her eyes. "It's twelve twenty-four ninety-three. Christmas Eve, ninety-three?" She smiled and grabbed her coat. "I figured it was a date that would stay with me."

"Good thinking." He shrugged into his jacket. After a brief hesitation he took the hand she held out. "We'll check the locks."

9

MARY Pat believed in the direct approach. The best way to satisfy her curiosity about Jed's landlord was to do a little shopping. She entered Dora's Parlor, as pleased with the ambience as she was to see her car-pool partner.

"Lea, hi."

"Well, hello." Lea set down the blown-glass cuspidor she'd been dusting. "What brings you to this part of town?"

"My mother's birthday." It hardly mattered that it wasn't for three months. "I loved the biscuit barrel Jed bought me from here, and thought I might find something unique."

"Unique we have. How are the kids?"

"Oh, driving us crazy. I'm counting the days until school starts up again."

"Who isn't?" Lea's mind worked fast. Mary Pat would be the perfect source to pump about Jed. "So, you and Jed are friends."

"For years." Mary Pat examined a collection of Goss china and looked for an opening to casually grill Lea about her sister. "He and Brent were partners before Jed made captain, were on the same squad for six years. Your sister has a charming place here. How long has she been in business?"

"Since the first grade," Lea said dryly. "She always liked to wheel and deal. But officially, for about three years."

A hard-edged businesswoman? Mary Pat wondered. A profit hound? "She certainly has some beautiful things." She edged over a price tag on a

Deco cocktail shaker, let out a soundless whistle. "I hope she hasn't had any more trouble since the break-in."

"No, thank God." Lea walked over to the silver coffee service and poured two cups. "Cream, right? No sugar?"

"Mmmm. Thanks."

"We're awfully grateful Jed was here. It eases the mind knowing that Dora's got a policeman right across the hall."

"And one of the best, too. Brent thinks if Jed pulls out of this and comes back on the job he could be chief in another ten years."

"Really?" Guiltily thinking of diets, Lea added a miserly half teaspoon of sugar to her own cup.

Mary Pat turned back the topic of conversation.

"I was surprised when he moved in here. Your sister's quite the entrepreneur—a shop owner, a landlord."

"Oh, Dora loves to run things."

Pushy, Mary Pat decided. Arrogant. She was glad, for Jed's sake, that she'd come by to snoop. She turned when she heard voices drifting in through the doorway.

"I think I know where to find just what you're looking for, Mrs. Hendershot." Dora helped an elderly woman leaning heavily on a birchwood cane through the shop.

"You'll call me," she demanded in a voice that boomed shockingly from the frail body. "My great-granddaughter's wedding is in two months. Young people, always hurrying."

"Don't worry." Dora held the woman's arm as they came to the door and, despite the thin protection of her silk suit, walked her out to the classic DeSoto waiting at the curb. "We're going to find her the perfect gift."

"Don't disappoint me." Mrs. Hendershot propped her cane on the passenger seat as she took the wheel. "Get inside, girl, you'll catch your death."

"Yes, ma'am." Dora made it to the curb before Mrs. Hendershot roared off into traffic. Dora hurried back inside, rubbing her chilled hands. "If she had the pole position at Indy, nobody would beat her."

"A woman that age shouldn't be driving," Lea stated, and poured her sister a cup of coffee.

"Why not? She handles that old tank like a pro. Good morning," she said to Mary Pat. "Is Lea helping you?"

Mary Pat had had ample time to study her quarry. She approved, with a tinge of envy, the stylishness of Dora's floral jacket, and the straight, snug skirt the color of apricots. As a woman who stood on her feet for hours on end, she marveled at Dora's choice of high-heeled pumps, and wondered if the sapphire clusters at her ears were real or paste.

"I came in looking for a birthday gift. Lea and I are neighbors."

"This is Mary Pat Chapman," Lea told her.

All of Mary Pat's preformed opinions shattered when Dora smiled and took her hand. There was instant warmth, quick friendliness. "I'm so glad you came by. I was hoping I'd get a chance to meet you. Brent was terrific the other night, keeping me calm. By the way, did you like the biscuit barrel?"

"Yes, I did." Mary Pat relaxed. "In fact, I liked it so much I came by to look for a gift for my mother." She hesitated, then set her cup down. "That's only part of the reason I came in. Mostly I'm here to check you out."

Dora's eyes laughed over the rim of her cup. "Who could blame you? Well, while you're checking me out, why don't we find Mom a present? Did you have anything in mind?"

"Not a thing. Have you ever been married?"

Dora almost giggled at the unambiguous interrogation. "Nope. I was almost engaged once. Remember Scott, Lea?"

"Unfortunately."

"He moved to LA, and our romance faded quietly away. How about something in a perfume bottle? We have several nice pieces in crystal, porcelain, blown glass."

"Maybe. She does have a vanity table. Oh, this one's lovely." She picked up a heart-shaped bottle with cut flowers decorating both front and back. "You consider your shop successful? Ah, financially?"

Dora grinned. "I'm not interested in a man's bank account, even one as nicely padded as Jed's. I'm much more interested in his body. That bottle runs seventy-five, but if you like it, I'll give you ten percent off. An introductory special."

"Sold." Mary Pat grinned back. "He is easy on the eyes, isn't he?"

"Very. Would you like this gift-wrapped?"

"Yeah." Mary Pat followed Dora to the counter. "I'm not usually so pushy, but Jed's like family."

"I understand. If I hadn't, I'd have been pushy back."

More than pleased with the results of her visit, Mary Pat laughed. "Good. You know, Dora, all Jed needs is—" She broke off when the man in question came through from the storeroom.

"Conroy, do you want these—" He stopped, narrowed his eyes. "MP."

"Hey." Her smile was quick and a little forced. "Fancy meeting you here."

He knew her well, too well. He hooked his thumbs in his pockets with forced casualness. "What are you doing?"

"I'm buying a present." She took out her credit card to prove it. "For my mother."

"And I certainly hope she likes it." With her back to Jed, Dora sent Mary Pat a slow wink. "She has thirty days to exchange it." She turned toward Jed. "Did you want something?"

Annoyance tightened his mouth. "Do you want these damn shelves fixed or adjustable?"

"You can make them adjustable? Terrific. Jed's been such a help around here." Beaming, Dora turned to Mary Pat. "I don't know what I did without him."

"There's nothing like having a handyman around," Mary Pat agreed. "Jed helped Brent finish off the family room last year. You'll have to see it sometime."

"You're about as subtle as nuclear waste, Mary Pat." Jed scowled at both of them and slammed the storeroom door behind him.

"He's such a friendly, low-key sort of guy," Dora stated.

"That's why we love him."

Mary Pat left a few minutes later, satisfied with her morning's work.

*   *   *

THE woman was asking for trouble, Jed thought grimly as he sent the power saw ripping through a board. She figured she could handle herself. It was tempting to prove her wrong. He would have done it, too, he decided, if she hadn't been so close to the truth on one single point.

He wasn't scared of her. Damned if he was. But . . . He set the saw aside and took out a cigarette. She sure as hell made him nervous.

He liked listening to her laugh. He'd even gotten a strange sort of kick at the way she'd talked back to the movie screen the evening before in the darkened theater. She didn't have any problem with conversation, he mused. Hell, he imagined he could sit alone with her for an hour without saying a word and there wouldn't be any holes in the conversation.

He'd be stupid not to admit he liked the way she looked. Big eyes and short skirts. She wasn't any wilty pushover either. He admired the way she'd taken on the accountant, her fists raised and fire in her eye.

Jed caught himself grinning and crushed the cigarette under his boot.

He wasn't going to let her get to him. He didn't need the headache. Didn't want the complication. Didn't care for the feeling of being sucked into a situation by his hormones.

Maybe he'd spent some time—too much time—imagining peeling Isadora Conroy out of one of those trim suits she wore. That didn't mean he was going to act on it.

After all, he mused, he'd been raised to be suspicious, cynical and aloof, in the best Skimmerhorn tradition. His years on the force had only heightened the tendency. As long as he didn't trust the lady, he could keep his hands to himself.

Ten minutes of standing out in the cold cooled his blood. Jed gathered up lumber and headed back inside.

She was still there, sitting at her desk. Before he could come up with an appropriately sarcastic comment, he saw her face. Her cheeks were dead white, her eyes dark and gleaming.

"Bad news?" he said, and carefully deleted any interest from his voice. When she didn't answer, he set the lumber aside. "Dora?" He stepped in front of the desk, said her name again.

She lifted her face. One of the tears swimming in her eyes spilled over and slipped down her cheek. He'd seen hundreds of women cry, some with callous expertise, some with the abandon of wild grief. He couldn't remember any affecting him more than that single, silent tear.

She blinked, spilling another, and with a strangled sound pushed back from the desk. His intellect ordered him to let her go, but he caught up to her in two strides. Firmly, he turned her around until she faced him.

"What is it? Is it your father?"

Battling fiercely for control, she shook her head. She wanted to lay her head on Jed's shoulder. Perhaps because he offered it, she refused.

"Sit down." Though she held herself stiff, he guided her back to her seat. "Do you want me to get your sister?"

"No." Dora pressed her lips together, took a deep breath. "Go away."

He'd have been relieved to oblige her, but he already had enough guilt on his shoulders. He went into the tiny adjoining bath and poured a glass of tepid water into a Dixie cup. "Here. Drink this. Then sit back, close your eyes and take some deep breaths."

"What's that? Skimmerhorn's all-purpose cure?"

Uneasy with the urge to stroke and soothe, he jammed his hands into his pockets. "Something like that."

Since her throat felt raw, she drank the water.

With her eyes closed, Jed thought she looked fragile, not at all like the vital woman who'd tweaked his libido only moments before. He sat on the edge of her desk and waited.

"Okay," she said after a moment. "It works." She sighed, opened her eyes again. "Thanks."

"What set you off?"

"The call." She sniffled, then reached in a desk drawer for a pack of tissues. "I met this other dealer on a buying trip right before Christmas. I just called down there to see if he had this piece my last customer wanted." She had to take another long breath. "He's dead. He was killed during a burglary last week."

"I'm sorry." They were two words Jed hated because they always seemed useless.

"I only met him once. I outbid him for a couple of lots. Lea and I went by his shop after the auction and he made hot chocolate." Her voice broke and she took a moment to strengthen it. "That was his son on the phone. He was killed the next night."

"Did they catch the guy?"

"No." She looked back at Jed. Both of them were relieved that her eyes were dry again. "I don't know any of the details. I didn't want to ask. How do you handle it?" she demanded, gripping Jed's hand with an urgency that surprised them both. "How do you handle being close to the horrible day in and day out?"

"You don't look at things the same way on the job as you do as a civilian. You can't."

"Did you leave because you stopped looking at things like a cop?"

"That's part of it." He pulled his hand away, distanced himself.

"I don't think that's a good reason."

"I did."

"Interesting choice of tense, Skimmerhorn." She rose, wishing her stomach wasn't still so shaky. "You should have said 'I do'—unless you've changed your mind. We could go into that, but I'm not feeling up to a debate right now. I've got to go talk to Lea."

GREGG and Renee Demosky arrived home to their Baltimore split-level at 6 P.M. sharp. They were, as usual, bickering. They had sniped at each other all during the twenty-minute drive from Gregg's dental practice, where Renee was his dental hygienist, and continued the bout in the garage, where Gregg parked their bronze BMW beside their spiffy Toyota Supra, and as they reached the door to the house.

"We could have gone out to dinner," Renee said as she slammed open the front door. She was a statuesque blonde just beginning to thicken in the middle.

"Once in a while I'd like to see people, when they don't have their mouths wide open," she complained. "We're in a rut, Gregg."

"I like being in a rut," he muttered. "Come on, Renee, ease off. All I want is to relax in my own home. Is that too much to ask?"

"And I want to have a nice night out, maybe down at the Inner Harbor." Renee yanked open the refrigerator and took out a tuna casserole.

"But no, I come home, after standing on my feet all day flossing other people's teeth, and have to fix dinner."

Gregg headed straight for the scotch in the living room.

"Don't you walk away from me when I'm talking to you." Renee shoved the casserole into the oven and hurried out on his heels.

She stopped, as her husband already had, to stare at the destruction of their living room. What wasn't missing was broken or jumbled in the center of the room, where the Persian rug had been. The entertainment corner across from the conversation pit was depressingly empty of their twenty-five-inch stereo TV, VCR and multiple-CD player.

"Oh, Gregg!" Resentments were forgotten as Renee grabbed her husband. "We've been robbed."

"Don't cry, baby. I'll take care of everything. Go in the kitchen and call the police."

"All our things. All our pretty things."

"Just things." He gathered her close and kissed the top of her head. "We can get more things. We've still got each other."

"Oh." Renee blinked tears out of her eyes as she looked up at him. "Do you mean that?"

"Sure I do." He ran an unsteady hand over her hair. "And after the cops finish up, and we figure out what the hell happened, we're going out. Just you and me."

DiCarlo was whistling along with Tina Turner on his car stereo. He had the mermaid bookends as well as $600 in cash the Demoskys had hidden in the freezer, a fine ruby-and-diamond ring Renee had left carelessly on her dresser and the profit he'd made by fencing all the electronic equipment to an old connection of his in Columbia, Maryland.

All in all, he considered it an excellent day. Making it look like a random burglary had helped pay his traveling expenses. He was going to treat himself to a first-class hotel after he'd picked up the parrot in Virginia.

That would leave only another quick trip to Philly for the painting.

In another day or two, Finley would have to admit just how reliable and how creative Anthony DiCarlo could be. And, DiCarlo mused, he was bound to earn a substantial reward for services rendered.

10

A well-mannered fire simmered in the grate of the Adam fireplace. It threw pretty, dancing lights over the Oriental carpet and silk-papered walls. A distinguished vermouth picked up the subtle lighting and sparkled in the heavy, faceted Baccarat glass. Van Cliburn played an elegant Chopin étude. Tasteful hors d'oeuvres had been offered on Georgian silver by the aged and discreet butler.

It was exactly the sort of room Jed had skulked through during his childhood, with the carefully placed bric-a-brac whispering of old money. But there was a subtle difference here. In this room, in this house, he had known some transient happiness. In this room he hadn't been threatened or berated or ignored.

Yet it still reminded him, painfully, of the boy he had been.

Jed rose from the miserably uncomfortable Louis XIV side chair to pace his grandmother's front parlor.

In evening clothes he looked the part of the Bester-Skimmerhorn heir. It was only his eyes, as he stared down at the flickering fire, that reflected the other paths he'd chosen, and the internal struggle to find his true place.

He wouldn't have minded a visit. Of all of his relatives, Honoria was the only one he'd had generous feelings for during his youth. As fate would have it, she was the only relative he had left. But the command performance grated.

He'd refused to take Honoria to the Winter Ball, twice—directly and concisely. She had simply ignored his refusal and, using a combination of guile, guilt, and tenacity had wheedled him into dragging out his tux.

"Well, Jedidiah, you're still prompt."

Honoria stood in the parlor doorway. She had sharp New England cheekbones and brilliant blue eyes that missed little. Her snowy hair was softly coiffed around her narrow face. Her lips, still full and oddly sensuous, were curved. Smugly. Honoria knew when she'd won a match, whether it be a rousing game of bridge or a battle of wills.

"Grandmother." Because it was expected, and because he enjoyed it, Jed crossed over to take her hand and lift it to his lips. "You look beautiful."

It was quite true, and she knew it. Her Adolpho gown of royal blue set off both her eyes and her stately figure. Diamonds glittered at her throat, at her ears, at her wrists. She enjoyed the gems because she had earned them, and because she was vain enough to know they would turn heads.

"Pour me a drink," she ordered, in a voice that still carried a hint of Boston from her youth. "That will give you time to tell me what you're doing with your life."

"We won't need much time for that." But he walked obediently to the liquor cabinet.

He remembered when she had caught him filching from that same cabinet nearly twenty years before. How she had insisted that he drink from the decanter of whiskey—and keep drinking while she watched, steely-eyed. And after, when he'd been miserably sick, she had held his head for him.

"When you're old enough to drink like a man, Jedidiah, you and I will share a civilized cocktail. Until then, don't take what you can't handle."

"Sherry, Grandmother?" he asked, and grinned.

"Now, why would I want an old woman's drink when there's good whiskey around?" Silks rustling, she sat near the fire. "When am I going to see this hovel you've moved yourself into?"

"Anytime you like, and it's not a hovel."

She snorted and sipped at the whiskey in a heavy crystal tumbler. "A drafty apartment above some seamy little shop."

"I haven't noticed any drafts."

"You had a perfectly adequate home."

"I had a twenty-room mausoleum that I hated." He'd known this was coming. After all, it was from her he'd inherited the tenacity that had made him a good cop. Rather than face the chair again, he leaned against the mantel. "I've always hated it."

"It's wood and brick," she said dismissively. "It's a foolish waste of energy to hate the inanimate. In any case, you would have been welcome here. As you always were."

"I know." They'd been through it all before. But because he wanted to erase the concern from her eyes, he grinned. "But I didn't want to interfere with your sex life."

She didn't miss a beat. "You'd hardly have done so from the east wing. However, I have always respected your independence." And because she sensed some subtle lightening in him since the last time she'd made the offer, she let that part of the argument rest. "When do you intend to go back to your badge, and your work?"

His hesitation was brief. "I have no intention of going back."

"You disappoint me, Jedidiah. And, I think, you disappoint yourself." She rose, regally. "Fetch my wrap. It's time we left."

DORA loved a party. One of her favorite ways to reward herself for a hard day was to primp, dress up and spend an evening in a crowd. It didn't matter if she knew a single soul, as long as there were plenty of people, chilled champagne, music and interesting food.

As it happened, she knew a great many people attending the Winter Ball. Some were friends, some were customers, some were patrons of her family's theater. She was able to entertain herself by mingling, moving from group to group to exchange pecks on the cheek and fresh gossip. Though she'd taken a chance wearing the strapless white gown, the press of bodies heated the room and kept her comfortable.

"Dora, darling, you look fabulous." Ashley Draper, a social climber of the first order who had recently shed her second husband, swooped down on Dora in a cloud of Opium.

Because Ashley fell slightly below the borders of friendship, Dora was amused by the quick air kiss. "You look radiant, Ashley."

"You're a dear to say so, even though I know I'm a bit washed out. Right after the first of the year, I'm going to spend a week at the Green Door. The holidays are so fatiguing, aren't they?"

"God knows how we get through them." Dora popped a stuffed olive into her mouth. "I thought you'd be in Aspen."

"Next week." Ashley waved a fuchsia-tipped hand toward another couple. "What a ghastly dress," she murmured through her smiling lips. "It makes her look like a stuffed eggplant."

Because it was a killingly accurate statement, Dora laughed and remembered why she tolerated Ashley. "Are you here stag?"

"Lord no." Ashley scanned the crowd. "My escort's that amazing hunk of beefcake with the Samson locks."

Once again Ashley's description was on the money. Dora picked him out quickly. "My, my."

"An artist," Ashley purred. "I've decided to be a patron. Speaking of the men in our lives, I heard that Andrew broke off your business association."

"Did you?" It only amused Dora that Andrew, or more likely his mother, had twisted the facts. "Let's just say I'm looking for someone a bit more substantial to stand between me and the IRS."

"And how is your little shop doing?"

"Oh, we manage to sell a trinket now and again."

"Mmm, yes." Finances didn't interest Ashley, as long as the alimony check came on time. "We missed you the other night at the Bergermans'. Christmas Eve?"

"I was . . . unexpectedly detained."

"I hope he was worth it," Ashley purred, then grabbed Dora's hand in a crushing grip. "Look, here." She lowered her voice to confidential tones. "It's the grand dame herself. She rarely puts in an appearance here."

"Who?" Curiosity piqued, Dora craned her neck. She lost the rest of Ashley's hissed explanation the minute she saw Jed. "Surprise, surprise," she murmured. "Excuse me, Ashley, I have to go see a man about a tux."

And he did look fabulous in it, she mused as she circled the ballroom to come up behind him. She waited until he'd procured two glasses of champagne.

"I know," she said at his shoulder. "You went back on the force, and now you're undercover." She caught his soft oath as he turned. "What is it, an international jewel thief? A ring of insidious pâté burglars?"

"Conroy. Do you have to be everywhere?"

"I have an invitation." She tapped her beaded evening bag. "How about you, copper?"

"Christ. It's bad enough I have to be here at all without—"

"Jedidiah!" Honoria's authoritative voice halted any complaints. "Have you lost whatever slight degree of manners I managed to teach you? Introduce your friend to your grandmother."

"Grandmother?" On a quick laugh, Dora took Honoria's narrow-boned hand. "Really? I'm delighted to meet you, Mrs. Skimmerhorn, even though it destroys my theory that Jed was hatched from a very hard-shelled, very stale egg."

"His social graces are lacking." Honoria studied Dora with growing interest. "And it's Mrs. Rodgers, my dear. I was briefly married to Walter Skimmerhorn, but rectified the matter as soon as humanly possible."

"I'm Dora Conroy, Jed's landlord."

"Ah." There was a world of expression in the single syllable. "And how do you find my grandson as a tenant?"

"His temperament's a bit unreliable." Dora shot a look at Jed, pleased by the fire in his eye. "But he appears to be neat enough, and he's certainly not rowdy."

"I'm relieved to hear it. There were times, you know, during his youth, that I feared his landlord would be a warden."

"Then you must be pleased he chose the right side of the law."

"I'm very proud of him. He's the first and only Skimmerhorn to amount to anything."

"Grandmother." Very deliberately, Jed took her arm. "Let me get you some hors d'oeuvres."

"I'm capable of getting my own." Just as deliberately, she shook him off. "And there are several people I must speak to. Dance with the girl, Jedidiah."

"Yeah, Jedidiah," Dora said as Honoria swept off. "Dance with the girl."

"Go find somebody else to harass," he suggested, and turned toward the bar. He was going to need something stronger than champagne.

"Your grandma's watching, pal." Dora tugged on his sleeve. "Five will get you ten she'll lecture you if you don't escort me onto the dance floor and exude some charm."

Setting the champagne aside, Jed took her arm. If his fingers dug in a bit hard, she was determined not to grimace. "Don't you have a boyfriend around here?"

"I don't see boys," Dora said, grateful when Jed had to shift his grip into dance position. "If you mean do I have a date, then no. I don't usually like to bring a date to a party."

"Why?"

"Then I'd have to worry if he was having a good time, and what I prefer doing is having one myself." The orchestra was playing a silky version of "Twilight Time." "You're a nice dancer, Skimmerhorn. Better than Andrew."

"Thanks a lot."

"Of course, it would be a nice touch if you looked at me, instead of glaring at the other dancers." When his gaze lowered, she tilted her head and smiled. "What about you? Are you having a good time?"

"I hate these things." It was a shame, a damn shame, he thought, that she felt so incredibly good in his arms. "You probably love them."

"Oh, I do. You'd like them more if you accepted them for what they are."

"Which is?"

"A chance to show off." She lifted a finger from his shoulder to tease his hair. "I'm terrific at showing off."

"I'd already figured that out."

"Astonishing deductive powers. Comes from being a police captain."

He slid a hand up her back, encountered bare skin. "Do you ever go out at night in anything that doesn't glitter?"

"Not if I can help it. Don't you like the dress?"

"What there is of it." The song ended and another began, but he'd forgotten he didn't want to dance with her. Honoria glided by in the arms of a distinguished-looking man with a silver moustache. "You look okay, Conroy."

"My." She widened her eyes. "Feel my heart pound."

"If I feel your heart, I'll do it in private."

"Are you exuding charm for your grandmother's sake?"

He looked down at her again. Something in her smile encouraged one of his own. "She liked you."

"I'm a likable person."

"No, you're not. You're a pain in the ass." He stroked his hand up and down her bare back where the silk of the gown gave way to the silk of her flesh. "A very sexy pain in the ass."

"I'm getting to you, Jed." And her heart was pounding, just a little, as she trailed her fingers along his neck.

"Maybe." Testing them both, he dipped his head, brushed her mouth with his.

"Absolutely," she corrected. She felt the quickening in her stomach spread to a fluttering. She ignored the curious heads turned their way and kept her mouth an inch away from his. "We could go home tonight and tear each other's clothes off, jump into bed and relieve some of this tension."

"An interesting image, Conroy, but it sounds like there's an 'or' coming."

"Or," she said, and tried to smile, "we could get to be friends first."

"Who said I wanted to be your friend?"

"You won't be able to help yourself." She touched a hand to his cheek, as much in compassion as arousal. "I can be a pretty good friend. And I figure you need one."

She moved something in him, no matter how hard he tried to stand against it. "How do you figure that?"

"Because everyone does. Because it's hard to be alone in a room full of people, but you are."

After a violent inner struggle, he rested his brow against hers. "Goddamn it, Dora. I don't want to care about you. I don't want to care about—"

"Anything?" she finished for him. When she looked up into his eyes this time, her heart broke. "You're not dead," she murmured.

"Close enough." He pulled himself back. "I want a drink."

She went with him to the bar, ordered champagne while he chose scotch. "Tell you what." Her voice was light again. "We'll try something new. I won't give you a hard time—and vice versa. I won't make suggestive comments or clever insults."

He rattled the ice in his glass while he studied her. "What's left?"

"We'll both be agreeable and have a good time." At his lifted brow she laughed, hooked her arm through his. "Okay, I'll have a good time, and you'll make the best of the situation. Hungry?"

"I could be."

"Let's go check out the buffet. If you have a plate in your hand, none of the women who are ogling you will expect you to dance."

"Nobody's ogling me." But he went with her.

"Sure they are. I'd ogle you myself if I didn't know you." She debated between the salmon mousse and the stuffed mushrooms, settled on both. "I don't believe I've seen you at the Winter Ball before, and I've attended the last three years."

He'd always been able to use work as an excuse, Jed remembered. He plucked a cube of cheese from her plate and said nothing.

"This conversation thing is tough for you, isn't it?" She kept a smile on her face as she heaped more food on her plate, then generously held it out to share. "I'll give you a hand. I say something, then, depending on the content, you laugh, look bemused, annoyed, intrigued, and say something back. Ready?"

"You've got an awfully smart mouth, Conroy."

"Good. Good start." She sampled a thumb-sized spinach pastry. "Tell me, is your grandmother the Honoria Rodgers who purchased the Qing dynasty cloisonné enamel candleholder, in the form of an elephant, at Christie's a few months ago?"

"I don't know about elephants, but she's the only Honoria Rodgers I'm aware of."

"Gorgeous piece—at least it looked terrific in the catalogue. I couldn't get up to New York, but I put in a couple of telephone bids during that auction. Not on the Qing, though. Out of my range. I'd love to see it sometime."

"If you're wrangling for an invitation, you should talk to her."

"Just making chitchat, Skimmerhorn. Try one of these," she invited with her mouth full, and picked up another pastry. "Incredible."

Before he could accept or refuse, she had it up to his mouth and in. "Great, huh?"

"I don't like spinach." Grimacing, he washed it down with scotch.

"I used to be the same way, but my father got me hooked on it by singing 'Popeye the Sailorman.' I was twenty," she said earnestly. "And naive." When his lips quirked, she lifted her glass in toast. "There now. And you look so pretty when you smile."

"Dora, darling." With her young artist in tow, Ashley glided up to the buffet. "How do you manage to eat like that and stay so slim?"

"Just a little agreement I have with Satan."

Ashley laughed gaily and gave Jed one long sweeping glance—what Dora would definitely term an ogle. "Isadora Conroy, Heathcliff." She presented her date as though he were the prize stud at a thoroughbred farm. "I discovered him in this marvelous little gallery on South Street."

"Oh?" Dora didn't bother to remind Ashley that her shop was on South. "I've always wanted to discover something—like Christopher Columbus. Or Indiana Jones." Because Heathcliff only looked baffled, she took pity on him. After passing her plate to Jed, she offered a hand. "Ashley tells me you're an artist."

"I am. I—"

"He does the most sensual life studies." Ashley stroked Heathcliff's arm, as a woman might a favored pet. "You simply must see them sometime."

"Top of my list."

"I don't believe you've introduced us to your escort."

"I don't have one. That's an odd term, don't you think? It sounds as though you'd need someone along because you couldn't find where you were going yourself. Personally, I have an excellent sense of direction."

"Dora." Ashley gave another quick, tinkling laugh. "You're such a wit."

"Only half," Jed said under his breath.

Dora spared him even the mildest of glances. "Jed Skimmerhorn, Ashley Draper and Heathcliff."

"Oh, I recognized Captain Skimmerhorn." Ashley held out a hand, waiting until Jed had juggled the plate back to Dora. "I should say, the elusive Captain Skimmerhorn." Her fingers glided over his. "It's so rare that we're able to tempt you to one of our little affairs."

"I don't find little affairs tempting."

This time Ashley's laugh was low and throaty. "I prefer long, steamy ones myself. And how do you two know each other?"

Dora picked up the ball to save Ashley from one of Jed's nastier comments. "Jed and I share a passion," she said, and took a slow, deliberate sip of champagne. "For pincushions."

Ashley's avid eyes went blank. "For—"

"Jed has the most incredible collection. We met at a flea market, when we both reached for the Victorian blue-satin-and-lace heart-shaped—pins included." She gave a fluttery, romantic sigh.

"You collect . . . pincushions?" Ashley asked Jed.

"Since I was a child. It's an obsession."

"And he's such a tease." Dora gave him an intimate look over the rim of her glass. "He keeps dangling his horse's hoof with plated mounts under my nose. And he knows perfectly well I'd do anything—*anything*—to have it."

"Negotiations . . ." He trailed a fingertip down the line of her throat. "Are open."

"How fascinating," Ashley murmured.

"Oh, it is," Dora agreed. "Oh, there's Magda and Carl. Excuse us, won't you? I simply have to catch up."

"Pincushions?" Jed muttered against her ear as they lost themselves in the crowd.

"I thought about sardine dishes, but they seemed so pretentious."

"You could have told her the truth."

"Why?"

He thought about it. "Simplicity?"

"Too boring. Besides, if she knew you lived across the hall from me, she'd start hanging around my apartment, hoping to seduce you. We wouldn't want that, would we?"

Lips pursed in consideration, Jed glanced over his shoulder to give Ashley a thorough study. "Well . . ."

"She'd only use you and toss you aside," Dora assured him. "I see your grandmother over there. Should you join her?"

"Not if you're going to grill her about candleholders."

That hadn't been her intention—exactly. "You're just afraid she'll make you dance with me again. Tell you what, I really will go talk to Magda and Carl, and you can catch up with me later, if you like."

He took her arm, frowned down at his own hand and removed it. "Stick around."

"What a charming invitation. Why?"

"Because if I'm going to be trapped in here for a couple more hours, it might as well be with you."

"Poetry, sheer poetry. How can I resist? Let's go see if your grand-mother wants some nibbles. I promise not to bring up candleholders unless it seems appropriate."

"Jed."

A hand clamped on his shoulder. Jed braced, turned. "Commissioner," Jed said, both his face and voice neutral.

"Good to see you." Police Commissioner James Riker gave Jed a quick but thorough study. What he saw obviously pleased him as his thin, dark face creased in a smile. "You're keeping fit, I see."

"Yes, sir."

"Well, you were overdue for a vacation, God knows. How was your Christmas?"

"Fine." Because he couldn't ignore Riker's pointed look toward Dora, Jed did his duty. "Commissioner Riker, Dora Conroy."

"Hello." As both her hands were full, Dora beamed him a smile instead of a handshake. "So, you're in charge of keeping the law and order in Philadelphia."

"I'm in charge of keeping men like Jed on the job."

If Riker couldn't feel the tension shimmering off Jed, she could. The need to protect clicked in. Dora smoothly changed the course. "I suppose most of your work now is administrative."

"Yes, it is."

"Do you miss the action?" She smiled, handing Jed her empty glass. "In fiction cops always miss the action."

"As a matter of fact, I do. From time to time."

"I have to ask. I have this bloodthirsty nephew who'll want to know. Were you ever shot?"

If the question surprised him, Riker covered it well. "No. Sorry."

"That's all right. I'll lie."

"I hope you'll forgive me, Miss Conroy, but I need to steal Jed for a minute. The mayor would like a word with him."

Dora gave way graciously. "Nice to have met you, Commissioner Riker."

"My pleasure. I'll only keep Jed a moment."

Trapped, Jed handed her back her empty glass. "Excuse me."

Oh, he really hated this, she mused as she watched him walk away. It hadn't shown, not in his face, not in his eyes, but he hated it. A man faced a firing squad with more enthusiasm.

When he returned he'd be simmering with fury or tight-lipped with guilt or simply miserable. Feeling for him, Dora wondered if she could find some way to distract him, to turn whatever emotions the commissioner and the mayor managed to stir up into a different channel.

Joke him out of it? she mused as she wandered over to get a refill on her champagne. Irritate it out of him would probably be easier. It wouldn't even take much effort.

"I would think they would take more care as to who attends these affairs."

The gravelly voice was instantly recognizable. Dora turned with a bright smile on her face. "Mrs. Dawd, Andrew. How . . . interesting."

Mrs. Dawd drew air fiercely through her nostrils. "Andrew, fetch my club soda."

"Yes, Mother."

Mrs. Dawd, with her bulky frame draped in black satin, leaned forward, close enough that Dora saw the few gray hairs stabbing out of her chin that her tweezers had missed. "I knew what you were, Miss Conroy. I warned him, of course, but Andrew is as susceptible as any man to a woman's wiles."

"I had all my wiles surgically removed. I could show you the scars."

The woman ignored her. "But what would you expect, bred from a family of actors?"

Dora took a careful breath, a careful sip. She would not, absolutely not, let this idiotic old woman make her lose her temper.

"Those acting families," Dora said lightly. "The Fondas, the Redgraves, the Bridges. God knows how they can be permitted to taint society."

"You think you're clever."

"Mother, here's your drink."

Mrs. Dawd swept Andrew and the club soda back with a violent gesture. "You think you're clever," she said again, her voice lifting enough to have several onlookers murmuring. "But your little tricks didn't work."

"Mother—"

"Be still, Andrew." There was fire in her eyes now. She was the mama bear protecting her cub.

"Yes, Andrew, be still." Dora's smile was tiger sharp. "Mother Dawd was about to tell me about my little tricks. Do you mean the one when I told your slimy son to get his hand out from under my skirt?"

The woman hissed in anger. "You *lured* him into your apartment, and when your pathetic seduction failed, you attacked him. Because he recognized you for exactly what you are."

There was a laser gleam in Dora's eye now. "Which is?"

"Whore," she hissed. "Slut. Floozy."

Dora set down her glass to free her hand. She balled it into a fist and gave serious consideration to using it. She settled for upending her plate on Mrs. Dawd's heavily lacquered hair.

The resulting screech should have shattered crystal. With salmon mousse dripping into her eyes, Mrs. Dawd lunged. Dora braced for the attack, then gave out a howl of her own as she was snatched from behind.

"Jesus Christ, Conroy," Jed muttered as he dragged her toward the ballroom doors. "Can't I leave you alone for five minutes?"

"Let me go!" She might have taken a swing at him, but he locked her arms at her sides. "She had it coming."

"I don't feel like bailing you out of jail." He strode toward a sitting area with cushy chairs and potted plants. He heard the orchestra strike up "Stormy Weather."

Perfect.

"Sit." He punctuated the order with a shove that had her tumbling into a chair. "Pull yourself together."

"Look, Skimmerhorn, that was my own personal business."

"You want me to have the commissioner haul you in for disturbing the peace?" he asked mildly. "A couple hours in the tank would cool you off."

He would, too, she thought viciously. Dora huffed, tapped her foot, folded her arms. "Give me a—"

He already had a cigarette lit and was handing it to her.

"Thanks." She fell into silence.

He knew her routine. She would take three, maybe four quick shallow puffs, then stab it out.

One, he counted. Two. She shot him a furious glare. Three.

"I didn't start it." Her lips moved into a pout as she crushed out the cigarette.

Jed decided it was safe to sit. "I didn't say you did."

"You didn't threaten to have *her* arrested."

"I figured she was going to have enough problems picking pimentos out of her hair. Want a drink?"

"No." She preferred to sulk. "Look, Skimmerhorn, she was insulting me, my family, women in general. And I took it," she said righteously. "I took it even when she called me a tramp, a slut, a whore."

A great deal of his amusement faded. "She said that to you?"

"And I took it," Dora barreled on, "because I kept telling myself she was just a crazy old lunatic. I was not going to cause a scene. I was not going to lower myself to her level. Then she went too far, she went one step too far."

"What did she do?"

"She called me a—a floozy."

Jed blinked, gamely struggled to swallow the tickle at the back of his neck. "A what?"

"A floozy," she repeated, slapping her fist on the chair.

"Let's go take her down."

Dora's chin came up, her eyes narrowed. "Don't you dare laugh."

"I'm not. Who's laughing?"

"You are, damn it. You're biting your tongue right now to hold it back."

"I am not."

"You are too. You're slurring your words."

"It's the scotch."

"Like hell." She turned her head away, but he'd caught the quiver of her lips. When he brought her face back to his, they grinned foolishly at each other.

"You made it an interesting evening, Conroy."

"Well." Her temper spent, she giggled, then leaned back to rest her head on his shoulder. "I was trying to think of some way to distract you so you wouldn't be upset from the mayor and Riker."

"Why should I be upset?"

"They were pressuring you, weren't they?" Though he didn't move, she felt a part of him shift away. "Lucky for me, Mrs. Dawd came along so I didn't have to invent something."

"So you dumped food on her head to lift my spirits."

"No, it was strictly a selfish act, but it did have a nice side benefit." She turned her head. "Give me a kiss, will you?"

"Why?"

"Because I'd like one. Just a friendly one."

He put a finger under her chin to tip it up, touched his lips to hers. "Friendly enough?"

"Yeah, thanks."

She started to smile, but he shifted his hand, cupped it around her throat. With his eyes open, he lowered his mouth to hers again, teased her lips apart with his tongue and tasted the arousal on her first shaky breath.

It was like water, pure, sweet water after an agonizing thirst. He sipped easily.

She felt the rush of need, the hard, sharp-edged wave of it that left her limp. He didn't bring her closer, nor did he deepen the kiss. Instead it was slow, cool, devastatingly controlled.

When he drew back, she kept her eyes closed, absorbing the flood of sensation. Her heart was still pounding in her ears when she opened her eyes. "God," was all she managed to say.

"Problem?"

"I think so." She pressed her lips together. She could have sworn they were vibrating. "I think . . . I think I'll go." Her knees wobbled when she stood. It was very difficult, she thought, to be in charge of a situation when your knees wobbled. She pressed a hand to her stomach where the hard ball of need had hotly lodged. "God," she said again, and walked away.

11

THE new security system on Dora's building brought DiCarlo a great deal of irritation. The extra time needed to bypass it, and to get through the sturdier locks, completely wrecked his schedule. He'd hoped to get in and out of the storeroom by midnight. For surely if the Conroy woman had bought the damn painting, the damn painting was inside, regardless of what the idiot redheaded clerk had told him on Christmas Eve.

Now he'd be lucky to be inside by midnight. And worse, a nasty sleet was beginning to fall. His surgeon's gloves were hardly adequate protection against the cold.

At least there was no moon, he thought as he worked and shivered. And there were no vehicles in the graveled lot, which meant no one was home. Despite the complications, he could still be in New York by morning. He'd sleep the entire day, then catch a late flight to the coast. Once he'd handed over Finley's toys, accepted the gratitude and a generous bonus, he'd fly back to New York for a rollicking New Year's Eve.

DiCarlo shivered as the cold snuck under his collar like frigid little ants.

When the final tumbler fell, he gave a little grunt of satisfaction.

In less than fifteen minutes he was certain that the painting was not in the storeroom. Using self-control, he curbed the urge to wreck the place. If the painting was going to cause a problem, it would be best if no one knew there'd been a break-in.

He did another thorough tour of the shop, automatically picking up a few small trinkets as he went, including the jade Foo dog Terri had tried to sell him.

Resigned, DiCarlo headed upstairs. He cursed, but without much heat when he encountered the lock on the door at the top of the steps. This one was basically for looks, and he was through it quickly.

He listened, heard nothing. No radio, television, conversation. Still, he moved silently down the hall, peering out the door to be certain the parking lot was still empty.

Three minutes later he was inside Jed's apartment. That search was over almost before it had begun. There were no paintings on the wall, none tucked into the closets. He found nothing under the bed but a dog-eared paperback copy of Shirley Jackson's *The Haunting of Hill House* and a balled-up sock.

He did find the .38 in the nightstand of some interest, but after a brief examination, replaced it. Until he'd found the painting, he couldn't afford to steal anything noticeable. He gave the bench press and weights in the living room a quick glance on his way out.

He was in Dora's apartment in a matter of seconds. She hadn't bothered to lock it.

The search here was a different matter. Where Jed's apartment had held a minimum of furniture, Dora's was packed. The clutter in Jed's came from carelessness. In Dora's it was a lifestyle.

There were several paintings. A watercolor still life, two oval portraits, one of a stern-faced man in starched collar, one of an equally stern-faced woman. Other art ranged from signed lithographs, advertising posters, and pen-and-ink sketches to the finger paintings stuck to the refrigerator. But the abstract wasn't on the wall.

He moved into the bedroom to search the closet. Because he, too, had left the door unlocked, he barely had time to react when he heard it open. By the time it slammed, DiCarlo was deep in the closet hidden behind a colorful assortment of outfits that smelled erotically of woman.

"I have to be crazy," Dora told herself. "Absolutely crazy." She peeled out of her coat, laid it over the back of a chair and yawned hugely. How did she let her parents talk her into it? Why had she let them talk her into it?

Still muttering to herself, she walked straight to the bedroom. Her plans for the evening had been so simple, she thought. A nice, solitary meal of grilled chicken and wild rice; a long, fragrant bath with a glass of chardonnay as a companion. She'd intended to top it all off with a good book by the bedroom fire.

But no, she thought, and switched on the Tiffany lamp beside the bed. Oh, no, she had to fall into that old family trap of the show must go on.

Was it her fault that three stagehands had come down with the flu? Was it her fault she'd let her father badger her into joining the union?

"Absolutely not," she decided, tugging her tight-fitting black cashmere sweater over her head. "I didn't give them the damn flu. I didn't have to feel obligated to jump into the void just because I have an IATSE card."

Sighing, she bent over to unlace her black Chucks. Instead of a quiet, relaxing evening at home, she'd answered her mother's frantic call for help and had spent hours handling props and hauling scenery.

She'd even reluctantly enjoyed it. Standing backstage and listening to the voices echo, rushing out when the lights dimmed to make a scenery change, feeling a vicarious pride when the cast took their curtain calls.

After all, Dora thought with a yawn, what's bred in the bone . . .

Through the two-inch crack in the closet door, DiCarlo had an excellent view. The more he saw, the more his annoyance at being interrupted faded. The situation had possibilities, previously unexplored ones.

The woman who was bending and stretching at the foot of the bed had performed a very intriguing striptease and was now wearing only a couple of very tiny, very lacy black swatches. DiCarlo studied the smooth curve of her bottom as Dora bent to touch her toes.

She was beautifully built, in a firm, compact style. And from the way she was moving, it appeared she'd be very, very agile.

She'd changed his plans, but DiCarlo prided himself on creative thinking. He'd simply wait until the very pretty, very alone lady had gotten into bed.

Dora turned, and he took the opportunity to admire the thrust of lace-trimmed breasts.

Very nice, he thought, and smiled in the dark. Very nice indeed.

And once she was in bed, DiCarlo figured it would be a simple matter, using his considerable charms—and his .22 automatic—to convince her to tell him where the painting was.

And after business, pleasure. He might not even have to kill her afterward.

Dora shook back her hair, rolled her shoulders. It was as if she were posing, DiCarlo thought. The blood surged into his loins and throbbed impatiently. With her eyes closed and the beginnings of a smile on her face, she circled her head gently.

She lifted her hands to the front hook of the bra.

The pounding on her door had Dora jolting. In the closet, DiCarlo's breath hissed out in a combination of rage and frustration.

"Hold on!" Dora shouted, grabbing a white terrycloth robe from the foot of the bed. She struggled into it as the pounding continued. Switching on lights as she went, she hurried out to the living room. She hesitated with her hand on the knob. "Jed?"

"Open up, Conroy."

"You gave me a start," she said as she opened the door. "I was just—" The look on his face stopped her. She'd seen fury before, but never quite so intense, and never aimed so fiercely in her direction. Instinctively, she lifted a hand to her throat and stepped back. "What?"

"What the hell did you think you were doing?"

"Ah . . . going to bed," she said carefully.

"Do you think because I pay you rent you can use your fucking key and poke through my things anytime you want?"

She lowered her hand again, gripped the knob firmly. "I don't know what you're talking about."

"Cut the crap." Jed snagged her wrist and yanked her into the hall. "I know when my place has been tossed."

"You're hurting me." Her attempt at sternness failed miserably. She was afraid, really afraid he could do a lot worse.

"You took that risk when you messed with my privacy." Enraged, he shoved her up against the opposite wall. Her muffled cry of surprised pain only added to his fury. "What were you looking for?" he demanded. "What the hell did you think you'd find?"

"Let go of me." She twisted, too terrified for denials. "Take your hands off me."

"You want to go through my things?" His eyes burned into hers.

The animal was out of the cage, was all she could think.

"You figure because you've got me churned up inside you can paw through what I keep in my drawers, in my closet, and I'll let it go?" He jerked her away from the wall and, pushed by his own demons, dragged her stumbling after him. "Fine." He slammed his door open, shoved her inside. "Take a look now. Take a good one."

Even her lips had lost color. Her breath shuddered in and out through them. He was between her and the door. There was no possible hope of getting past him toward escape. As her heart drummed hard against her ribs, she saw by his face there was no chance of reason.

"You're out of your mind."

Neither of them heard DiCarlo slip down the hall and away. They stood two feet apart with Dora tugging with a shaking hand at the robe that had fallen off her shoulder.

"Did you think I wouldn't notice?" He moved too quickly for her to evade, grabbing her robe by the lapels and yanking her to her toes. Seams gave way with quick pops. "I was a cop for fourteen goddamn years. I know the signs."

"Stop it!" She shoved against him. The sound of her robe ripping at the shoulder was like a scream. Tears of terror and rage sprang to her eyes, drenching them, clouding her vision. "I haven't been in here. I haven't touched anything."

"Don't lie to me." But the first seed of doubt squeezed through his fury.

"Let me go." She tore free, falling back and ramming hard into the table. Slowly, like a woman waiting for the tiger to spring again, she backed away. "I haven't been in here. I just got home ten minutes ago. Go feel the hood of my car, for Christ's sake. It's probably still warm." Her voice hitched and sputtered in time with her heart. "I've been at the theater all night. You can call, check."

He said nothing, only watched her edge for the door. Her robe had fallen open. He could see her muscles quiver and the sheen of panic sweat. She was crying now, fast, choking sobs as she fumbled with the doorknob.

"Stay away from me," she whispered. "I want you to stay away from me." She fled, leaving his door swinging open and slamming her own.

He stood exactly where he was, waiting for his own heartbeat to slow, waiting for some grip on control, however slippery.

He hadn't been wrong. Goddamn it, he hadn't been wrong. Someone had been inside. He knew it. His books had been moved, his clothes run through, his gun examined.

But it hadn't been Dora.

Sickened, he pressed the heels of his hands to his eyes. He'd snapped. No surprise there, he thought, dropping his hands. He'd been waiting to snap for months. Wasn't that why he'd turned in his badge?

He'd come home after a miserable day of dealing with lawyers and ac-countants and bankers, and he'd snapped like a twig.

And if that wasn't bad enough, he'd terrorized a woman. Why had he picked on her? Because she'd gotten to him. She'd gotten to him and he'd found the perfect way to make her pay the price. Nice going, Skimmer-horn, he berated himself, and headed for the kitchen. And the whiskey.

He stopped himself before he poured the first glass. That was the easy way. He dragged a hand through his hair, took a long breath and walked over to Dora's to take the hard way.

At the knock, she stopped rocking on the arm of the chair. Her head jerked up. She scrambled to her feet.

"Dora, I'm sorry." On the other side of the door, Jed shut his eyes. "Damn," he whispered, and knocked again. "Let me come in a minute, will you? I want to make sure you're all right." The silence dragged on, tight-ening his chest. "Just give me a minute. I swear I won't touch you. I want to see if you're okay, that's all."

In frustration he turned the knob.

Her eyes widened as she watched it rotate. Oh God, oh God, she thought in panic, she hadn't locked it. A little sound caught in her throat. She lunged for the door just as Jed opened it.

When she froze, he saw the wild fear on her face, something he'd seen on too many faces over too many years. He hoped he remembered how to defuse fear as skillfully as he'd remembered how to incite it. Very slowly, he lifted his hands, palms out.

"I'll stay right here. I won't come any closer." She was shaking like a leaf. "I won't touch you, Dora. I want to apologize."

"Just leave me alone."

Her cheeks were still wet, but her eyes were dry now, dry and terrified. He couldn't walk away until he'd eased that fear. "Did I hurt you?" He swore at the stupidity of the question. He could already see the bruises. "Of course I hurt you." The way she'd cried out when he'd shoved her against the wall played back in his head and made his stomach clench.

"Why?"

The fact that she would ask surprised him. "Does it matter? I don't have any excuses. Even an apology's pretty lame after what I did. I'd like to—" He took a step forward, stopping when she flinched. He'd have preferred a fist to the gut. "I'd like to say it was justified, but it wasn't."

"I want to know why." Her hand clenched and unclenched on the neck of her robe. "You owe me why."

It was a hot ball in his throat. He couldn't be sure which would be more painful, holding it there or spitting it out. But she was right. He owed her why.

"Speck tossed my house a week after he killed my sister." Neither his face nor his voice gave away what it cost him to tell her. "He left a snapshot of her, and a couple of newspaper clippings about the explosion on my dresser." The nausea surged, almost as violently as it had all those months ago. He paled as he fought it back. "He just wanted me to know he could get to me, anytime. He wanted to make sure I knew who was responsible for Elaine. When I came home tonight, and I thought you'd been in, it brought it back."

She had a beautifully expressive face. He could read every emotion perfectly. The fear, and the anger that had been building to combat it, faded away. In their stead were flickers of sorrow, understanding and, like salt to his wounds, sympathy.

"Don't look at me like that." His tone was curt and, she thought, defensive. "It doesn't change what I did, or the fact that I was capable of doing worse."

She lowered her eyes. "You're right. It doesn't. When you kissed me last night, I thought something was happening with us. Really happening." She lifted her gaze again, and her eyes were cool. "But it can't be, or else this wouldn't have happened. Because you'd have trusted me. That hurts too, Jed, but that's my mistake."

He knew what it was to feel helpless, but had never expected to feel it with her. "I can move out if you want," he said stiffly. "I can leave tonight and pick up my stuff later."

"It isn't necessary, but you do what you want."

Nodding, he stepped backward into the hallway. "Are you going to be all right?"

For an answer, she walked to the door, closed it quietly and turned the lock.

She found the flowers on her desk in the morning. Daisies, a little wilted and smelling of far-off spring, were stuffed into a Minton vase. Sternly, Dora quashed the first surge of pleasure and ignored them.

He hadn't moved out. That much had been clear from the monotonous thud of weights bumping the floor when she'd passed his door earlier.

She wasn't about to let that please her either. As far as she was concerned now, Jed Skimmerhorn was a paying tenant. Nothing more. No one was going to terrify her, threaten her and break her heart, then lure her back with a straggling bunch of daisies. She would cash his monthly check, nod to him politely if they happened to pass in the hall and get on with her own life.

It was a matter of pride.

Since Terri and Lea were handling the shop, she took out her accounts payable, opened the checkbook for Dora's Parlor and prepared to work.

A few minutes later she snuck a peek at the daisies and caught herself smiling. Then the sound of boots coming down the stairs had her firming her lips and staring at her electric bill.

Jed hesitated at the base of the stairs, searching for something reasonable to say. He would have sworn the temperature had dropped ten degrees since he'd come into the storeroom. Not that he could blame her for giving him the chill, he decided. But it only made him feel more foolish for buying flowers on the way back from the gym.

"If you're going to be working in here, I can finish up those shelves later."

"I'll be doing paperwork for a couple of hours," she said. She didn't glance up.

"I've got some stuff to do downtown." He waited for a response, got nothing. "Do you need anything while I'm out?"

"No."

"Fine. Great." He started back upstairs. "Then I'll finish them up this afternoon. After I go out and buy myself a hair shirt."

Dora lifted a brow, listened to the top door slam. "Probably thought I'd throw myself in his arms because he bought me flowers. Jerk." She looked over as Terri walked through from the shop. "Men are all jerks."

Normally Terri would have grinned, agreed and added her own examples. Instead she stood in the doorway, wringing her hands.

"Dora, did you take the jade dog upstairs? The little Chinese piece? I know you like to shift things around."

"The Foo dog?" Lips pursed, Dora tapped her pen on the desk. "No. I haven't circulated any inventory since before Christmas. Why?"

Terri gave a breathless laugh, a sickly smile. "I can't find it. I just can't find it anywhere."

"It probably just got moved. Lea might have—"

"I've already asked her," Terri interrupted. Her voice sounded weak. "I showed it to a customer the other day. Now it's gone."

"Don't panic." Dora pushed away from her desk. "Let me take a look around. I might have moved it myself."

But she knew she hadn't. Dora's Parlor might have looked like a homey, cluttered space where treasure and trash were carelessly arranged side by side. But there had always been a method to the arrangement—Dora's method.

She knew her stock, and its place, down to the last silk postcard.

Lea was busy with a customer and only sent her sister a quick, concerned look, then continued to show tobacco jars.

"It was in this cabinet," Terri said quietly. "I showed it Christmas Eve, right before closing. And I'm positive I saw it here yesterday when I sold the Doulton figure. They were side by side; I would have noticed if it had been missing then."

"All right." Dora patted Terri's shoulder soothingly. "Let's look around."

Even the first glance was alarming. Dora homed in on a satinwood bonheur. She made sure to keep her voice calm and low. "Terri, have you sold anything this morning?"

"A tea set—the Meissen—and a couple of cigarette cards. Lea sold the mahogany cradle and a pair of brass candlesticks."

"You didn't sell anything else?"

"No." Terri's already pale cheeks went whiter. "What is it? Something else is gone."

"The vinaigrette, the enamel one that was there." Dora controlled a curse. "And the inkwell that was beside it."

"The pewter?" Terri turned to the bonheur, groaned. "Oh God, Dora."

Dora shook her head to ward off any more comment and did a swift tour of the entire shop.

"The Chelton paperweight," she said a few moments later. "The Baccarat perfume bottle, the Fabergé desk seal—" That one, priced at $5,200, was tough to swallow. "And the Bakelite cigarette case." Which, at roughly $3, infuriated her almost as much as the Fabergé. "All small enough to fit into a purse or a pocket."

"We haven't had more than eight or nine people in all morning," Terri began. "I don't see how—Oh, Dora, I should have watched more carefully."

"It's not your fault."

"But—"

"It's not." Though she felt sick with anger, she slipped an arm around Terri's waist. "We can't treat everyone who walks through the door like a shoplifter. We'd end up putting in those damn security mirrors and shoving all our stock behind locked glass. It's the first time we've been hit this hard."

"Dora, the Fabergé."

"I know. I'll report it to the insurance company. That's what they're for. Terri, I want you to take your lunch break now."

"I couldn't eat."

"Then go for a walk. Go buy a dress. It'll make you feel better."

Terri blew her nose. "Aren't you mad?"

"Mad? I'm furious." Her eyes narrowed and snapped. "I'm hoping they come back and try to lift something else so I can break all their sticky little fingers. Now go, clear your head."

"Okay." She blew her nose again and left Dora alone in the small side parlor.

"Bad?" Lea asked when she stuck her head in.

"Bad enough."

"Honey, I'm sorry."

"No 'I told you to lock things up'?"

Lea sighed. "I figure this should prove I was right, but after working here these past few weeks, I understand why you don't. It would spoil the atmosphere."

"Yeah." Defeated, Dora rubbed at the beginning of a headache between her eyes. "You can buy a lot of atmosphere for ten thousand."

"Ten thousand," Lea repeated. Her eyes widened. "Ten thousand *dollars?* Oh my God, Dory."

"Don't worry, I'm insured. Goddamn it. Look, put up the Closed sign for an hour. Go out and get some lunch or something. I want to go in the back and have a tantrum, and I'd like privacy."

"Are you sure?" Lea took one look at the glint in her sister's eyes. "You're sure. I'll lock up."

"Thanks."

12

JED wondered if going back to the cop shop for the first time since his resignation was just another way to punish himself. He could have set up a meeting with Brent elsewhere and avoided the wrenching reminder that he was now a civilian.

But Jed walked into his old precinct, the place where he'd spent eight of his fourteen years on the force, because he knew he had to face it. After the way he'd spun out of control the night before, he admitted there were plenty of things he was going to have to face.

Everything was the same. The air still smelled of spilled coffee, underwashed bodies and stale smoke—all with a much nastier undertone of disinfectant. The walls had been painted recently, but the color was the same institutional beige. The sounds—all familiar. Ringing phones, clattering keyboards, raised voices.

The fact that he walked in this time without the weight of his weapon strapped to his side made him feel more than awkward. This time he felt naked.

He nearly walked out again, but two uniforms turned toward the doors on their way to patrol. Recognition flickered on both of their faces. The one on the left—Snyder, Jed remembered—jerked to attention.

"Captain, sir."

They were getting younger every year, Jed mused. This one was hardly old enough to shave. The only way through it was ahead. Jed nodded to both of them as he passed. "Officers."

He stopped at the desk, waited until the bull-shouldered sergeant turned. "Ryan." The man might have had shoulders like a bull, but he had the face of a teddy bear. When he spotted Jed, that face creased into a smile so big his eyes seemed to disappear into the soft folds of ruddy Irish skin.

"Captain. Son of a bitch." He reached over the desk to grasp Jed's hand like a vise gripping steel. "Good to see you. Really good."

"IIow's it going?"

"Oh, you know. Same old same old." He leaned companionably on the counter that separated them. "Lorenzo got winged in a liquor store hit last week."

"I heard about that. How's he doing?"

"Milking it," Ryan said with a wink. "Time was, a guy took a pop, he mopped up the blood and got back on the street."

"After he chewed the bullet out with his teeth."

"That's the way." Someone shouted for Ryan, and he shouted back that they should hold on. "We miss you around here, Captain," he said, leaning on the desk again. "Goldman's okay as an acting captain. I mean he pushes paper with the best of them, but let's face it. The man's an asshole."

"You'll break him in."

"No, sir." Ryan shook his head. "Some you do, some you don't. The men knew they could talk to you, straight. Knew they'd find you on the street as often as you'd be riding the desk. With Goldman you gotta climb up the chain of command and tippytoe through regulations and procedure." His genial face wrinkled into a sneer. "You won't catch him going through the door, not unless there's a camera and three reporters on the other side."

Whatever Jed felt about Ryan's easy flow of information, he kept to himself. "Good press doesn't hurt the department. Is Lieutenant Chapman in? I need to talk to him."

"Sure, I think he's in his office. You can track him down."

Jed waited, then lifted his brow. "Give me a visitor's badge, Ryan."

Ryan turned pink with embarrassed dismay. "Shit, Captain."

"I need a visitor's badge, Sergeant."

"Makes me sick," Ryan muttered as he pulled one out. "I gotta tell you, it makes me sick."

"You told me." Jed clamped the badge onto his shirt.

To get to Brent, he had to walk through the bull pen. He would have preferred a nice slow waltz on hot coals. His stomach clenched each time his name was called, each time he was forced to stop and exchange a word. Each time he forced himself to ignore the speculation, the unasked questions.

By the time he reached Brent's door, the tension was rapping at the base of his neck like a dull spike.

He knocked once, then pushed the door open. Brent was sitting at his overburdened desk, the phone at his ear. "Tell me something I don't know." He glanced up. Instantly the irritation in his eyes cleared. "Yeah, yeah, and when you're ready to shoot straight, we'll deal. I'll get back to you." He hung up and leaned back in his chair. "I thought the noise level out there rose a few degrees. You were in the neighborhood, thought you'd drop by, right?"

"No." Jed sat down, took out a cigarette.

"I know, you needed a fix of cop coffee."

"When I get that bad, I'll have myself committed." Jed struck a match. He didn't want to ask, didn't want to get involved. But he had to. "Is Goldman being as big an asshole as Ryan claims?"

Grimacing, Brent rose to pour two cups of coffee from the pot on his hot plate. "Well, he's not exactly Mr. Popularity around here. I caught Thomas down in the locker room sticking pins in a Goldman doll. I recognized it because it had those little beady eyes and big teeth."

Jed took the coffee. "What did you do about the doll?"

"I stuck a couple pins in it myself. So far, Goldman doesn't seem to be in any particular discomfort."

Jed grinned. The first sip of coffee wiped that off his face. "You know, I could put in your name with the chief. I figure he'd listen to my recommendation."

"Not interested." Brent took off his glasses to wipe ineffectively at the smudges. "I'm lousy at delegating. Thomas might end up sticking pins in an incredibly handsome doll wearing horn-rims." He leaned against the edge of his desk. "Come back, Jed."

Jed lowered his eyes to his coffee, slowly lifted them again. "I can't. Christ, Brent, I'm a mess. Give me a badge right now and I don't know what I'd do, or who'd pay for it. Last night." He had to stop. He took a deep drag on his cigarette. "Somebody'd been in my place, in my things."

"You had another break-in over there?"

Jed shook his head. "This was slick. A couple things out of place, a drawer shut when I'd left it partway open, that kind of thing. I'd been out most of the day. Elaine's estate, the settlement on her house." Weary, he kneaded the back of his neck. "After all that, I went and had a drink, I went to a movie. I came home, took one look around and went after Dora."

He picked up his coffee again. It was no more bitter than the taste already lodged in his throat. "I mean I went after her, Brent. Saw the crime, made the collar." In disgust, he crushed out his cigarette and rose. "I pushed her around."

"Christ, Jed." Stunned, he watched Jed pace the office. "You didn't— you didn't hit her?"

"No." How could he be offended by the question? Jed wondered. "I scared the hell out of her, though. Scared myself after I pulled it in. I didn't think it through. I didn't keep it chilled. I just snapped. I'm not going to take the chance of doing something like that from behind a badge, Brent." He turned back. "That badge used to mean something to me."

"I've known you almost ten years. I never once saw you misuse it."

"And I don't intend to. Anyway, that's not why I'm here. Dora didn't go into my apartment. So who did?"

"Might have been a return from whoever broke in the other night. Looking for something to lift."

"I don't have a lot in there with me, but there was a couple hundred in cash in the drawer. My thirty-eight. A Sony Walkman. Dora's place across the hall's loaded."

"What about the security?"

"I looked it over, couldn't find anything. This guy's good, Brent. A pro. It could be a connection to Speck, somebody who wants revenge."

"Speck wasn't the kind to inspire loyalty after death." But, like Jed, Brent wasn't willing to dismiss the possibility. "I'm going to do some checking. Why don't I put a couple of eyes on the building?"

Normally Jed would have cringed at the thought of protection. Now he merely nodded. "I'd appreciate it. If somebody wants me, I wouldn't like to have Dora caught in the middle."

"Consider it done. So tell me, how are you handling things with Dora?"

"I apologized." He snorted, turned to study Brent's poster of Eastwood's Dirty Harry. "Big fucking deal. I offered to move out, but she didn't seem to care one way or the other." He muttered under his breath, but Brent's ears were keen.

"What was that? Did you say something about flowers?"

"I bought her some damn flowers," Jed snapped. "She won't even look at them. She sure as hell won't look at me. Which would be just fine and dandy, except . . ."

"Except?"

Jed whirled back, a bleak expression on his face. "Goddamn it, Brent, she's got me. I don't know how she did it, but she's got me. If I don't have her soon, I'm going to start drooling."

"Bad sign," Brent said with a slow nod. "Drooling's a very bad sign."

"You getting a kick out of this?"

"Well . . . yeah." Brent grinned and pushed up his glasses. "A big one, actually. I mean, as I recall, you've always been smooth and on top of things—no pun intended—with women. Always figured it was all that high-class breeding. Now you're standing there with this hook in your mouth. It looks good on you."

Jed just glared.

"So she's pissed," Brent continued. "She'll make you sweat for a little while, beg a little."

"I'm not begging. Screw begging." He jammed his hands in his pockets. "I'd rather she be angry than frightened." No, he realized, he didn't think he could handle having her look at him with fear in her eyes again. "I thought I might pick up some more flowers on the way back."

"Maybe you'd better think sparkles, pal. The kind you hang around your neck."

"Jewelry? I'm not going to bribe her to forgive me."

"What are the flowers for?"

"Flowers aren't a bribe." Amazed that a married man could know so little, Jed headed for the door. "Flowers are sentimental. Jewelry's mercenary."

"Yeah, and there's nobody more mercenary than an angry woman. Just ask my wife," Brent shouted when Jed kept going. "Hey, Skimmerhorn! I'll be in touch."

Chuckling to himself, Brent went back to his desk. He called up the Speck file on the computer.

JED was surprised to find Dora still at her desk when he returned. He'd been gone more than three hours, and in the short time he'd known her, he'd never seen her huddled with paperwork for more than half that time. Dora seemed to prefer the contact with customers, or perhaps it was the satisfaction of collecting money.

Probably both.

It didn't surprise him that she ignored him every bit as completely as she had that morning, but this time he thought he was prepared.

"I got you something."

Jed set the large box on the desk in front of her. When she glanced at it, he had the small satisfaction of spotting the flicker of curiosity in her eyes.

"It's, ah, just a robe. To replace the one that got torn last night."

"I see."

He moved his shoulders restlessly. He wasn't getting much of a reaction from her, and he figured he'd paid big time. Poking around a woman's lingerie department with the salesclerk beaming at him had made him feel like a pervert. At least he'd been able to settle for practical terrycloth.

"I think I got the size right, but you might want to check."

Carefully, she closed her checkbook and folded her hands on top of it. When she looked up at him, the curiosity had been replaced by glittering anger. "Let me get this straight, Skimmerhorn. Do you think that a bunch of pathetic flowers and a robe are what it's going to take to clear the path?"

"I—"

She didn't give him a chance. "You figure a handful of daisies will charm me into sighs and smiles? Is that what you think? I don't know how you've played it before, pal, but it doesn't work that way with me." She rose from the desk, slapped her palms down on the department-store box and leaned forward. If eyes were weapons, he'd have already bled to death. "Inexcusable behavior isn't reconciled by a couple of lame gifts and a hangdog expression."

She caught herself on the edge of a shout and paused to fight for control.

"You should keep going," Jed said quietly. "Get the rest of it out."

"All right, fine. You muscle your way into my apartment flinging accusations. Why? Because I was handy, and because you didn't like the way things were moving between us. You didn't even consider that you might be wrong, you just attacked. You scared the bloody hell out of me, and worse . . ." She pressed her lips together and turned away. "You humiliated me, because I just took it. I just stood there trembling and crying. I didn't even fight back." Now that she'd admitted it, she felt calmer and faced him again. "I hate that most of all."

He understood that all too well. "You'd have been crazy to take me on in the mood I was in."

"That's not the point."

"It is the point." He felt anger stirring again, viciously self-directed. "For Christ's sake, Dora, you were facing a maniac who had you by better than fifty pounds. What were you going to do, wrestle me to the ground?"

"I know self-defense," she said, lifting her chin. "I could have done something."

"You did." He remembered the way her terrified tears had defused him. "You're crazy if you let yourself be embarrassed because you were afraid."

"I don't think insulting me is going to smooth the waters, Skimmerhorn." She lifted a hand to push back her hair. It wasn't her usual casual gesture, Jed noted. It was a weary one. "Look, I've had a rough day—"

She broke off when he took her hand. Even as she stiffened, he gently straightened her arm. She'd pushed up the sleeves of her jacket to work. There was a light trail of bruises on her forearms, marks he knew would match the press of his fingers.

"I can keep saying I'm sorry." His eyes were eloquent. "That doesn't mean a hell of a lot." He released her, tucked his hands away in his pockets. "I can't tell you I've never put bruises on a woman before, because I have.

But it was always in the line of duty, never personal. I hurt you. And I don't know how to make it up to you."

He started for the steps.

"Jed." There was a sigh in her voice. "Wait a minute." Sucker, she admitted, and flipped open the top of the box. The robe was nearly identical to hers, but for the color. She smoothed a finger down the deep-green terrycloth lapel.

"They didn't have a white one." He wasn't sure if he'd ever felt more foolish in his life. "You wear a lot of bright colors, so . . ."

"It's nice. I didn't say I was forgiving you."

"Okay."

"I'd just prefer if we could put things back on some reasonable level. I'm not comfortable feuding with the neighbors."

"You've got a right to set the rules."

She smiled a little. "You must really be suffering to hand over that kind of power."

"You've never been a man buying women's lingerie. You don't know about suffering." He wanted to touch her, but knew better. "I am sorry, Dora."

"I know. Really, I do. I was nearly as mad at myself as I was at you this morning. Before I could cool off we had some trouble in the shop. So when you came back, I was ready for blood."

"What kind of trouble?"

"Shoplifting." Her eyes hardened again. "This morning, not long after you left to buy a hair shirt."

He didn't smile. "Are you sure it was all there last night when you closed up?"

That stiffened her spine. "I know my stock, Skimmerhorn."

"You said you got in a few minutes before I did last night."

"Yes, what does—"

"You were upset when I left you. You were still upset this morning. I don't suppose you'd have noticed."

"Noticed what?"

"If anything was missing from upstairs. Let's go take a look now."

"What are you talking about?"

"Somebody was in my place last night."

She caught herself before she spoke, but he saw the doubt on her face.

"I'm not saying that to excuse my behavior, but somebody was in my place," he said again, struggling to keep his voice calm. "Cops see things civilians don't. I had an idea that it might have been some of Speck's men, dropping around to hassle me, but it could have been something else. Somebody looking for some trinkets."

"What about the alarm system. Those burglary-proof locks you put in?"

"Nothing's burglary-proof."

"Oh." She closed her eyes briefly as he took her hand and pulled her up the stairs. "Well, that certainly makes me feel better. A minute ago I was happy being furious at a shoplifter. Now you've got me worried that I had some cat burglar prowling around my apartment."

"Let's just check it out. Got your keys?"

"It's not locked." His look made her bristle. "Look, ace, the outside door's locked, and I was right downstairs. Besides . . ." She shoved open the door. "Nobody's been in here."

"Mmm-hmm." He bent down to examine the lock, saw no obvious signs of tampering. "Did you leave this unlocked when you went out last night?"

"Maybe." She was beginning to sulk. "I don't remember."

"Keep any cash in the house?"

"Some." She crossed to the kneehole desk and opened a drawer. "It's right where it's supposed to be. And so is everything else."

"You haven't looked."

"I know what's in here, Jed."

He scanned the room himself, skimming, identifying knickknacks as skillfully as he would faces in a mugbook. "What happened to the painting? The one over the couch?"

"The abstract? My mother thought she liked it, so I took it over so she could live with it awhile." She gestured to the two portraits that replaced it. "I thought I'd like having those two for company. But I was wrong. They're entirely too somber and disapproving, but I haven't had the chance to—"

"Jewelry?"

"Sure, I have jewelry. Okay, okay." She rolled her eyes and headed back to the bedroom. She opened a camphorwood-and-ebony chest that sat on a lowboy. "It looks like it's all here. It's a little tougher to remember, because I lend Lea pieces, and she lends me . . ." She took out a velvet pouch and shook out a pair of emerald earrings. "If anybody was going to rifle through here, they'd go for these. They're the real thing."

"Nice," he said after a cursory glance. It didn't surprise him that she had enough jewelry to adorn a dozen women. Dora enjoyed quantity. Nor did it surprise him that her bedroom was as crowded and homey as her living room. Or as subtly feminine. "Some bed."

"I like it. It's a Louis the Fifteenth reproduction. I bought it from a hotel in San Francisco. I couldn't resist that headboard."

It was high, covered with deep blue brocade and gently curved at the top. She'd added a lushly quilted satin spread and an army of fussy pillows.

"I like to sit up late and read with a fire going." She closed the jewelry box. "One of the things that sold me on this building was the size of the rooms, and that I could have a fireplace in my bedroom. It's—as my father would say—the cat's meow." She grinned. "Sorry, Captain, it doesn't look like I have a crime to report."

He should have been relieved. But he couldn't ignore the tickle at the back of his neck. "Why don't you give me a list of the stolen goods? We—Brent can have some men check out the pawnshops."

"I've already reported it."

"Let me help." This time he went with the urge to touch her, to see if she'd back away. But when he ran a hand down her arm, she only smiled.

So he was forgiven, he thought. Just that simply.

"All right. It wouldn't be smart to turn down the services of a police captain over a simple shoplifting. Let me—" She started forward, but he didn't move with her or aside. All she accomplished was to come a step closer. Her heart stuttered in her chest with an emotion that had nothing to do with fear. Nothing at all. "The list's downstairs."

"I think you should know, you were right."

"That's always good to know. What was I right about this time?"

"I was tangled up about what was happening between us."

"Oh." It came out shaky; she couldn't help it. "What was happening between us?"

His eyes darkened. She thought of the cobalt glass on display in the shop. "I was wanting you. I was wondering what it would be like to undress you, and to touch you, and to feel you under me. I was wondering if your skin tasted like it smelled."

She stared at him while her stomach muscles danced. "Is that what was happening?"

"On my end. It was making me a little crazy."

"And it's better now?"

He shook his head. "Worse. Now I can imagine doing all those things in that bed. If you want to pay me back solid for last night, all you have to do is tell me you're not interested."

She let out the air that had backed up in her lungs. "Interested" wasn't precisely the word she would have chosen. "I think . . ." On a weak laugh, she pushed both hands through her hair. "I think I'm going to say I'm going to consider your offer carefully, and get back to you on it."

"You know where to find me."

"Yeah, I do."

He hadn't expected to fluster her, but he was enjoying it. "You want to have dinner? We could . . . discuss the terms."

The quick, wild fluttering of her heart made her feel very young, and very foolish. "I can't. I have a date—with my nephew." She picked up a silver-backed brush from her bureau, set it down again. "He's at that stage where he detests girls, so every now and again I take him out to the movies or the arcade. A kind of guys' night out."

"You're a girl."

"Not to Richie." She picked up the brush again, twisting the handle through her hands. "I don't mind sitting through ninety minutes of *Zombie Mercenaries from Hell*—that makes me one of the guys."

"If you say so." He flicked a glance down to her nervous hands and grinned. "We'll try guys' night out later, then."

"Sure. Maybe tomorrow."

"I think I can work it into my schedule." Gently, he took the brush from her restless fingers and laid it aside. "Why don't we go get that list?"

When they'd passed safely out of the bedroom, Dora let out a small, relieved breath. She was definitely going to think this over—as soon as some of the blood returned to her head.

"Got your keys downstairs?" Jed asked her when they stepped into the hall.

"What—oh, yeah."

"Good." He turned the lock before shutting the door.

DiCarlo might have enjoyed his luxurious suite at the Ritz-Carlton, with its soft, king-sized bed, a fully stocked honor bar, excellent room service and masseuse on call.

He might have enjoyed it—if he'd had the painting in his possession. Instead he fumed.

Without the man in apartment two's ill-timed arrival, DiCarlo figured he would have had the painting—or known its whereabouts.

He hesitated to call Finley. There was nothing to report for the night's work but failure, and he still had until January the second. Coming up empty for one night played hell with his schedule, but in reality it was only a delay, not a disaster.

He chewed another nut and washed it down with the Beaujolais left over from his lunch. It baffled him that the man knew his apartment had been searched. Leaning back, DiCarlo went over his moves of the night before step by step. He hadn't disturbed anything. He'd resisted taking even easily fenceable merchandise from the two apartments. What he'd taken from the store below would be attributed to simple shoplifting.

Since the man suspected the woman next door had entered his apartment, his plans didn't change.

All he had to do was go back in, DiCarlo decided. He'd do exactly what he had planned to do the night before—exactly. Only this time he would go in knowing he'd kill the woman when he'd finished.

13

THE temperature had dipped to a brisk fourteen degrees under a dazzling night sky splattered with icy stars and sliced by a thin, frosty moon. The shops along South Street were locked up tightly, and traffic was light. Occasionally someone stepped out of one of the restaurants, huddled inside a warm coat, and made a dash for a car or the subway. Then the street would be quiet again, with only the splash from the streetlamps to light the way.

DiCarlo spotted the police cruiser on his first circle of the block. His hands tightened on the wheel as he turned the corner to ride along the river. He hadn't counted on outside interference. Cops were usually too busy to stake out a building because of a possible minor break-in and a little shoplifting.

So, maybe the lady was boffing the chief of police, DiCarlo mused. Or maybe it was just bad luck. Either way, it was only one more detail. And one more reason to take the shapely Miss Conroy out when he was finished with her.

To calm himself, he tooled around aimlessly for ten minutes, switching the radio off and running through various scenarios in his head. By the time he'd circled around to South again, DiCarlo had his plan formulated. He pulled to the curb in front of the black-and-white. Taking his Philadelphia street map out of the glove box, he climbed out of the car. DiCarlo knew the cop would see only a well-dressed man in a rental car, obviously lost.

"Got a problem there, buddy?" The uniform rolled down his window. The air inside smelled of coffee and pastrami.

"I sure do." Playing his part, DiCarlo grinned sheepishly. "I was glad to see you pulled over here, Officer. I don't know where I made the wrong turn, but I feel like I've been driving around in circles."

"Thought I saw you drive by before. We'll see if we can set you straight. Where you trying to get to?"

"Fifteenth and Walnut?" DiCarlo pushed the map inside the window. "I found it on here, fine. Finding it in the car's been something else."

"No problem. You just want to go down here to Fifth and make a left. You'll run right into Walnut at Independence Square, make another left." He reached for a pen. "Let me show you."

"I appreciate it, Officer." Smiling, DiCarlo pressed his silenced pistol against the uniform's breast. Their eyes met for less than a heartbeat. There were two muffled pops. The cop's body jerked, slumped. Meticulously, DiCarlo checked the pulse, and when he found none, quietly opened the driver's door with his gloved hands, straightened the body into a sitting position. He rolled up the window, locked the door, then strolled back to his own car.

He was beginning to understand why his cousin Guido got such a kick out of murder.

Dora was disappointed that Richie hadn't taken her up on her invitation to sleep over. It seemed he'd had a better offer, so she'd dropped him off at a friend's after the movies.

She wished now that she'd swung back by Lea and John's and picked up the other kids for the night. A nice noisy pajama party would have calmed her nerves. The simple fact was, she didn't want to be alone.

No, she corrected, the complicated fact was, she didn't want to be alone and a few easy steps away from Jed Skimmerhorn. No matter how attractive and charming he'd been that afternoon, she couldn't let herself forget that he was a man capable of wild bursts of temper.

She believed—and accepted—his apology absolutely. She even understood a portion of his motivation. That didn't negate the fact that he was a crate of dynamite set with a very short fuse. She didn't want to be in harm's way when and if he exploded again.

Then again, she had a temper of her own. She might have had a longer fuse, but pound for pound she'd gauge her explosive quality equal to his.

Maybe that was just what he needed, she reflected. A woman who would stand up to him, fight back, win as often as she lost. If he had someone who understood the need to kick inanimate objects now and again, it might help him open up. It might help him squeeze out the poison in the wounds that troubled him. It might—

"Hold it, Dora," she mumbled. "You're getting this backwards. It's not what he needs, it's what *you* need." And what she didn't need was to take on a lover with more problems than a Eugene O'Neill play. She turned into the little gravel lot behind the shop. No matter how cute he was when he smiled.

The T-Bird was gone. Dora frowned a moment, then shook her head. For the best, she thought. If he wasn't around, she couldn't think about knocking on his door and inviting trouble.

Her boots crunched over the gravel, clattered up the back stairs that she usually took in a run. After entering the code into the alarm system, she unlocked the door, then secured it behind her.

She wouldn't tempt fate and listen for Jed's return, she decided, but make an early night of it. A pot of tea, a fire and that book she'd been trying to read: the perfect remedies for a troubled mind. And with any luck, they would also erase the effects of *Scream, If You Dare*—the horror movie she'd treated Richie to that evening.

She let herself into her apartment and turned on the Christmas tree. The cozy, colored lights never failed to cheer her. Once she had the stereo on low, she pried off her boots, peeled off her coat. Everything went neatly into her hall closet while she hummed along with Billie Holiday.

In her stocking feet, she padded into the kitchen to heat the kettle. Her hand on the tap jerked as a board creaked in the other room. Her heart made a beeline for her throat so that she stood frozen—water splashing into the sink—listening to the sound of her own racing heart.

"Get a grip, Conroy," she whispered. Imagine, letting a silly film give her the willies. There wasn't any seven-foot superhuman psychopath in her living room, waiting with a butcher knife. The building was settling, that was all.

Amused with herself, she put the kettle on to boil, adjusted the heat. She walked back into the living room, and stopped dead.

It was pitch dark, dark as a cave, with only the thin backwash of light from the kitchen illuminating the silhouettes of furniture. Which, of course, made the dark worse.

But she'd turned the tree on, hadn't she? Of course she had, she assured herself as her hand crept up to her throat to soothe a jittery pulse. A fuse? No, no, the stereo was still playing and they were on the same plug. She reasoned it out slowly, waiting for her heart rate to settle. The tree lights had probably shorted. Shaking her head at her overactive imagination, she started across the room to fix it.

And the kitchen light went out behind her.

Her breath sucked in on a gasp that she forced back out with a slow shudder. Slippery little fingers of fear slid over her skin. For a full minute she didn't move, listening to every sound. There was nothing but her own drumming heartbeat and shallow breathing. Lifting a hand to her head, she laughed. Of course there was nothing. A bulb blew, that was all.

Creative imagination was a killer, she mused. All she had to do was—

A hand clamped over her mouth, an arm snaked around her waist. Before she could think to struggle, she was yanked back against a hard body.

"You don't mind the dark, do you, honey?" DiCarlo kept his voice at a whisper, for practical purposes, and to add another element to her fear. "Now you stay real still and keep real quiet. You know what this is?" He loosened his grip enough to slip his gun under her sweater, run the side of it up over her breast. "It's a big, mean gun. You don't want me to have to use it, do you?"

She shook her head, squeezing her eyes tight when he stroked her flesh with steel. All capacity for thought vanished.

"Good girl. Now I'm going to take my hand away. If you scream, I'll have to kill you."

When he removed the hand from her mouth, Dora pressed her lips together to stop them from trembling. She didn't ask what he wanted. She was afraid she knew.

"I watched you the other night, in the bedroom, when you took off your clothes." His breath quickened as he slipped his free hand between her legs. "You had on black underwear. Lacy. I liked it."

She groaned, turning her head away as he rubbed through the wool of her slacks. Watched her. He'd watched her, was all she could think, repulsed.

"You're going to do that little striptease for me again, right after we take care of a little business."

"I—I have money," she managed. She kept her teeth clenched, her eyes straight ahead as she fought to distance her mind from what he was doing to her body. "A few hundred in cash. I'll give it to you."

"You're going to give me all sorts of things. Does this one fasten in the front, too?" He toyed with her bra as she whimpered. "Oh, yeah, that's just fine. What color is it?" When she didn't answer, he pressed the barrel of the gun against her heart. "You want to answer me when I ask you a question."

"R-red."

"Panties, too?"

A flush of shame rose up on her clammy skin. "Yes, yes, they're red."

"You are a hot one." He laughed, finding himself amazingly aroused by her trembling plea to stop. It was a bonus he hadn't expected.

"We're going to have a real good time, baby, and nobody'll get hurt. As long as you give me what I want. Say you understand."

"Yes."

"Yes, what?"

She bit down on the terror. "Yes, I understand."

"Good. Real good. First, I want you to tell me where it is, then we'll get down to the party."

Tears were shimmering in her eyes, burning them. She thought she'd been scared the night before with Jed. But that was nothing, nothing compared to the ice-edged horror that clawed through her now.

And she was doing nothing but whimpering, shaking and waiting to be victimized. She forced her trembling chin to firm. She wasn't helpless— wouldn't be helpless. He might rape her, but she wouldn't make it easy.

"I don't know what you're talking about." She didn't have to fake the shudders, and hoped he thought she was completely beaten when she went limp against him. "Please, please don't hurt me. I'll give you whatever you want if you don't hurt me."

"I don't want to have to." God, he felt hard as iron. Every time he slid the gun over her flesh, she quivered, and his blood sizzled. Those bleeding hearts who called rape a crime of violence were full of shit, he realized. It was about power. All about power.

"You cooperate, and we'll get on fine." He slipped the barrel of the gun under the front hook of her bra, sliding it slowly up and down the valley between her breasts. "Now, I looked all through the place and couldn't find it. You tell me where the picture is, and I'll take the gun away."

"The picture?" Her frantic mind whirled. Cooperate, he'd said, and he'd take the gun away. So she'd cooperate. But she wouldn't be powerless. "I'll give you the picture, any picture you want. Please, move the gun. I can't think when I'm so scared."

"Okay, baby." DiCarlo nipped at her earlobe and lowered the gun. "That feel better?"

"Yes."

"You didn't say thank you," he said, and teased her by bringing the gun back up her torso again.

She shut her eyes. "Yes, thank you."

Satisfied that she recognized who was in charge, he moved the gun again. "Much better. Just tell me where it is, and I won't hurt you."

"All right." She cupped her left fist with her right hand. "I'll tell you." Using the force of both arms, she rammed her elbow into his stomach. He grunted with pain as he stumbled back. Dora heard a clatter behind her as she raced for the door.

But her legs felt numb with fear. She fell into the hall, nearly lost her footing. She'd reached the rear door and was dragging at the locks when he caught her. She screamed then and, with survival her only thought, turned to claw at his face.

Swearing, DiCarlo hooked an arm around her throat. "We're not going to be able to be so nice now, are we?" Deliberately he cut off her air and began to pull her backward toward the dark apartment.

They both heard footsteps pounding up the stairs. With one desperate swipe, DiCarlo smashed the fluted hall sconce and waited in the shadows.

Jed came in low, weapon drawn.

"Toss it down," DiCarlo hissed, jerking on his arm to make Dora choke. "I've got a gun at her back. Make the wrong move and the lady won't have a spine left."

Jed couldn't see a weapon, but he could see the pale outline of Dora's face and hear her desperate struggle for air. "Ease off." With his eyes fixed on DiCarlo, he crouched, set his gun on the floor. "She won't be much of a shield if you strangle her."

"Stand up, hands behind your head. Kick the gun over here."

Jed straightened, linked his fingers behind his head. He knew Dora's eyes were on him, but he didn't look at her. "How far do you think you'll get?"

"Far enough. Kick the gun over here."

Jed nudged it halfway between himself and Dora, knowing the man who held her would have to come closer if he wanted it. Close enough, Jed figured, and they'd have a chance.

"Sorry," Jed said. "Looks like I missed the extra point."

"Back. Back against the wall, goddamn it." DiCarlo was beginning to sweat now. Things weren't going the way they were supposed to. But he had the woman. And if he had the woman, he'd get Finley's painting.

Shifting, he began to sidestep down the hall toward the open door, with Dora between him and Jed. When he reached for Jed's gun, he pulled her down with him as he crouched to retrieve it. The movement loosened his hold around her throat.

Even as Jed prepared his move, she sucked in her breath. "He doesn't have a gun," she gasped out, and threw her body back.

Her foot hit the .38, sent it skidding out the door. Jed dragged her aside and braced for DiCarlo's attack. But rather than attack, DiCarlo ran.

Jed tackled him at the door. They went through together in a violent tangle of limbs and curses. With a report like a bullet, the banister cracked in two jagged pieces under the weight. By the time they'd hit the ground, Dora was scrambling through the door and down the steps in search of the gun.

A blow glanced off Jed's kidneys. Another caught him low in the gut. He plowed his fist into the other man's face and had the satisfaction of seeing blood splatter.

"I can't find it!" Dora shouted.

"Get the hell out of here." Jed blocked the foot DiCarlo kicked toward his head and heaved his opponent backward.

Instead she let out an outraged howl when DiCarlo grabbed part of the broken banister, taking a vicious swing that missed Jed's face by inches. Teeth bared, she took three running steps and leaped on DiCarlo's back.

She bit down enthusiastically on his neck and drew blood before he flung her aside.

Pain exploded as her head hit the edge of a step. Dora reared up, managed to gain her feet again. But her vision doubled, tripled, then blacked out completely as she crumpled to the ground.

WHEN she opened her eyes again, everything swam in and out of focus. And it hurt. Dora let her eyes shut and tried to slip back into the void.

"No, you don't. Come on, baby, open up." Jed tapped Dora's cheeks with the back of his hand until the annoyance had her moaning and opening her eyes again.

"Cut it out." She shoved his hand aside and started to sit up. The room revolved like a carousel.

"Not so fast." Very much afraid her eyes were going to do that slow roll to the back of her head again, Jed eased her back down. "Try staying awake, but do it horizontal."

"My head." She touched a tentative hand to the back of her head and hissed in reaction. "What hit me?"

"It was what you hit. Just relax. How many fingers?" He held a hand in front of her face.

"Two. Are we playing doctor?"

Though he worried about a concussion, at least her vision and speech were clear. "I think you're okay." The flood of relief was instantly damned by temper. "Not that you deserve to be after that idiotic move of yours. What were you doing, Conroy? Riding piggyback?"

"I was trying to help." It all came rushing back, much too quickly, much too clearly. Her fingers gripped his, reminding him that he was still holding her hand. "Where is he?" This time, despite the flash of pain, she pushed herself up. "Did he get away?"

"Yeah, he got away. Damn it. I'd have had him if you . . ."

Her eyes narrowed, dared him. "If I what?"

"You went down like a tree. I thought you'd been wrong about the gun." The memory brought on a fast, greasy wave of nausea. "The idea that he'd shot you kind of took my mind off bashing his face in. It turned out all you'd done was crack that amazingly hard head of yours."

"Well, why didn't you go after him?" She tried to shift, noticed she was wrapped in a crocheted afghan like a moth in a cocoon.

"I guess I could have left you there, unconscious, freezing, bleeding—"

"Bleeding?" Gingerly, she checked her head again. "Am I bleeding?"

"You didn't lose much." But he began to shift into his professional mode. "You want to tell me what that was about? I don't suppose it was another of your dates gone wrong."

She stared at him, then looked away. "Should we call the cops?"

"I did. Brent's on his way."

"Oh." She glanced around the apartment. "He did have a gun, before. I don't know what happened to it."

"It was under the table. I've got it."

Her smile was weak and didn't last. "You've been busy."

"You took your sweet time coming around. Another couple of minutes and I'd have called an ambulance."

"Lucky me."

"Enough stalling." He sat beside her, took her hand again, too gently for her to refuse the contact. "Tell me what happened. Exactly what happened."

"I guess you were right about somebody breaking in here yesterday. It seems he was in here, too. I really didn't notice anything moved or taken, but he said he'd seen me undressing." She hesitated. "And since he described my style of underwear, I have to believe him."

He recognized the signs, humiliation rushing through the fear, shame jockeying with anger. "Dora, I can have Brent call in a woman officer if it would be easier for you."

"No." She took a deep breath. "He must have been hiding in here somewhere—the bedroom again maybe. I went right into the kitchen, to make tea . . . I left the water on."

"I took care of it."

"Oh, good. I'm fond of that kettle." She began to toy with the fringe of the afghan. "Anyway, when I came back in here, the tree was off. I'd just turned it on, so I figured the plug had come out of the socket or something. I started to go over and fix it, and the light in the kitchen went off. He grabbed me from behind."

Her voice had started to shake. Dora cleared her throat. "I would have fought back. I like to think I'd have fought back, but he put the gun under my sweater and started to, um, started to rub it over me." She gave a weak laugh. "I guess some guys really do look at a gun as a phallic symbol."

"Come here." He gathered her close, easing her throbbing head onto his shoulder. While his own rage ate through him he stroked her hair. "It's all right now."

"I knew he was going to rape me." She closed her eyes and burrowed in. "A bunch of us took this self-defense course last year, but I couldn't remember a thing. It was like this sheet of ice slipped over my brain and I couldn't get through it. He kept saying what a good time we were going to have, and I got so angry. He was slobbering on my neck and telling me I just had to be good, I just had to cooperate. I got so mad because he thought I wasn't going to do anything to protect myself. I guess you could say I broke through the ice, because I rammed my elbow into his stomach, and I ran. That's where you came in."

"Okay." He didn't want to think of what might have happened if he hadn't come in. "Did you know him?"

"I don't think so. I didn't recognize his voice. It was too dark in here to see, and he was behind me. I think I got a pretty good look at him outside, but he didn't seem familiar." She let out a cleansing breath. "Your brand-new banister's busted."

"I guess I'll have to fix it again. Got some aspirin?"

"Bathroom medicine chest." She smiled when she felt his lips brush against her temple. That helped, too. "Bring me a couple dozen, will you?" Calmer, she leaned back when he stood up. The crumpled towel on the coffee table caught her eye. It was her satin-edged, hand-embroidered fingertip towel. And it was dotted with blood.

"Damn, Skimmerhorn, did you have to use the good linen?" Disgusted, she leaned forward to pluck it up. "And it's wet, too! Do you know what wet cloth does when it's left on wood?"

"I wasn't thinking about the furniture." He rattled around in the medicine chest. "I can't find any aspirin."

"Let me." She'd been rather pleased to be able to stand and walk on her own, until she caught a glimpse of her reflection in the mirrored cabinet above the bathroom sink. "Oh my God."

"Dizzy?" Sharp-eyed for signs of fainting, he took her arms, prepared to sweep her up.

"No, revolted. The only makeup left on my face is what's smeared under my eyes. I look like something out of the Addams family." Reaching up, she took a small blue apothecary bottle from the top shelf. "Aspirin."

"Why isn't it in the right bottle?"

"Because plastic aspirin bottles are ugly and offend my impeccable sense of style." She shook out four, handed the bottle back to Jed.

"How do you know they aren't antihistamines?"

"Because antihistamines are in the amber bottle, aspirin is in the blue one." She ran water into a porcelain cup and downed the pills in one swallow. She winced at the sound of the knock on her door. The grandmother of all headaches was setting up residence just under her skull. "Is that the cavalry?"

"I imagine. Stay here."

She watched him, eyes widening as she saw the gun hooked in the back of his jeans. He reached for it and stood at the side of the door. "Yeah?"

"It's Brent."

"It's about damn time." He yanked open the door and a portion of his bottled-up fury descended onto his former partner. "What the hell kind of cops are you putting on these days when an armed rapist can stroll right by them and break into a locked building?"

"Trainor was a good man." Brent's mouth was tight and grim. He looked over Jed's shoulder to where Dora was standing in the bathroom doorway. "Is she all right?"

"No thanks to Philadelphia's finest. If I hadn't—" He broke off because the look in Brent's eyes had finally penetrated his temper. "Was?"

"Dead. Twice in the chest, close range. So close there are fucking powder burns on his shirt."

Dora's steps slowed as she saw the look they exchanged. "What is it? What else happened?"

"I asked Brent to put a man on the building, in case whoever broke in came back." Jed took out a cigarette. "He came back." He struck a match. "And the cop's dead."

"Dead?" The color that had come back into her cheeks washed away.

"I want you to sit down," Jed said flatly. "And run through the whole thing again, step by step."

"How was he killed?" But she already knew. "He was shot, wasn't he?"

"Let's sit down, Dora." Brent started to take her arm, but she shook him away and stepped back.

"Was he married?"

"That's not—"

"Don't tell me it's not my concern." She slapped a hand onto Jed's chest before he could finish the sentence. "A man was outside, trying to protect me. Now he's dead. I want to know if he had a family."

"He had a wife," Brent said quietly while guilt gnawed at him with small, dull teeth. "Two kids, both in high school."

Hugging her arms, she turned away.

"Dora." Jed started to reach out, to touch her, but let his hand fall back to his side again. "When a man or woman joins the force, they know what the risks are."

"Shut up, Skimmerhorn. Just shut up. I'm going to make coffee." She pushed back her tousled hair. "We'll go over it again."

Later, they sat at Dora's dining room table, going over her statement point by point.

"Funny he'd come back—we've got to figure three times." Brent checked his notes. "And taking out a cop to get inside. Not the pattern of your usual rapist."

"I wouldn't know. The more frightened I was, the better he liked it." She recited the lines as if rehearsing for a play. "I could tell he was excited, that he didn't want it to happen too quickly. Because he kept talking. He said . . ." She opened her eyes. "I forgot. He said something about a picture."

"He wanted pictures?" Brent asked.

"I—no. No, I don't think that was it. He wanted a specific picture, wanted me to tell him where it was. I wasn't really listening then, because I knew I had to do something or he was going to rape me."

"What kind of pictures do you have?"

"All sorts, I suppose. Family pictures, snapshots of vacations and birthday parties. Nothing anyone would be interested in."

"When's the last time you took any?" Jed questioned. "What did you take them of?"

"I took some at Christmas, at Lea's. I haven't even had them developed yet. Before that . . ." She pulled a hand through her hair, holding it back from her face before she let it go. "Christ, I don't know for certain. Weeks, probably months."

"I'd like to have that film developed, if you don't mind." Brent smiled. "It never hurts to check."

"I'll go get it."

"It doesn't fit," Jed said when she left the room. "A guy doesn't kill a cop, then walk across the street to rape a woman and raid her photo album."

"We have to start somewhere. He wanted a picture, we'll look at her pictures. Maybe she took a shot of something she shouldn't have."

"Maybe." But he couldn't make the piece fit into the puzzle.

"Did you get a good enough look at him for a make?"

"Six foot, a hundred seventy. Dark hair, dark eyes, slim build. He had on a cashmere coat, gray, and a navy or black suit with a red tie. Funny a guy wearing a suit and tie for a rape."

"It's a funny world."

"Here's the film." She set the container on the table. "There were a couple shots left, but I don't think I'll be using them."

"Thanks." Brent pocketed it. "I'd like you and Jed to work with the Identi-Kit. It's a little toy we have to help put together a composite."

"Sure." The show must go on, she thought miserably. "I'll get my coat."

"Not tonight." Brent adjusted his glasses and rose. "You need some rest. You'd do a better job of it tomorrow. If you think of anything else, you call, anytime."

"I will. Thanks."

When they were alone, Dora stacked the cups and saucers. It was still too difficult to look Jed in the eye. "I haven't gotten around to thanking you."

"You're welcome." He put his hands over hers. "Leave them. I should probably take you to the hospital. Let them examine that hard head of yours."

"I don't want doctors poking at me." She pressed her lips together to keep her voice from quavering. "I don't want anybody poking at me. The aspirin's taking the edge off the headache."

"It doesn't do much for a concussion."

"Neither does anything else." She turned her hands under his, linked fingers in a plea for understanding. "Don't push, okay?"

"Who's pushing?" He slipped his hands from hers to tip her head back and examine her eyes. What he saw was simple exhaustion. "Go to bed."

"I'm not tired. All this coffee will probably keep me awake for . . . I nearly brought Richie back here with me tonight." That thought churned in her stomach. "If he . . ." That was one train of thought she couldn't afford to indulge. "It should have been safe here."

"It will be." Gently he laid his hands on her shoulders and kneaded the tight muscles. "The next time I go out for cigarettes and milk, I'll take you with me."

"Is that where you were?" Because she wanted to lean back against him, a little too much, she picked up the cups and carried them into the kitchen. "I didn't see any bag."

"I left it in the car when I heard you scream."

The cups rattled when she set them down on the counter. "Good thinking. Do you always take a gun to the market?"

"They really hose you for milk in those convenience stores." He touched her hair when she managed a choked laugh.

"Don't worry, I'm not falling apart."

"I'm not worried." But he left his hand on her hair, lightly. "Do you want me to call your sister? Your father or your mother?"

"No." Dora plugged the sink, flipped on the water. "I guess I'll have to tell them something tomorrow, and that'll be bad enough."

She wasn't fooling with dishes out of a sense of neatness, he knew, but because she was postponing that moment of being alone again. At least that was something he could take care of.

"Tell you what, why don't I bunk out on the couch for tonight? I promise not to leave shaving gunk in the bathroom sink."

With one indulgent sigh, she shut off the tap and turned to bury her face against his chest. "Thanks."

He hesitated, then slipped his arms around her. "Don't thank me yet. I might snore."

"I'll risk it." She rubbed her cheek against his. "I'd tell you that you could share the bed, but—"

"Bad timing," he finished.

"Yeah. The worst." She eased away. "I'll get you a pillow."

14

SHE looked good. Really good. Jed hadn't spent much time observing sleeping women, and certainly not unless they'd shared the bed with him, but none had looked better than Dora in the morning.

She slept sprawled on her stomach, her hair, tousled from the night, was swept back from her cheek, leaving her face unframed but for the fringe of bangs. She looked enormously appealing.

He'd thought it was because of those big, dark eyes, and the way they dominated her expressive face. But the eyes were closed now, the face at rest.

And she still looked damn good.

Maybe it was her skin. Dora's skin was like silk, smooth white silk faintly blushed with rose.

He shook himself, both embarrassed and appalled by his train of thought. When a man started thinking up metaphors about a woman's skin, he was in deep.

Jed walked over, set his mug on the nightstand, then sat on the edge of the bed.

He could smell her—that carelessly sexy scent that always made his mouth go dry. Another problem, he decided, when a man fell into the obvious perfume trap.

"Isadora." He touched her shoulder over the thick quilt, shook lightly, as he had every two hours through the night to be certain she was lucid.

She made a sound that was caught somewhere between pouty and annoyed, and turned over. The movement slithered the quilt down past her shoulders. Thoughtfully, Jed studied the flannel gown she'd chosen. It looked thick as a suit of armor and was an eye-popping blue. He made out two little pink appliqués that looked like pigs' ears. Curious, he lifted the quilt. Sure enough, a fat pink pig face grinned back at him.

He imagined she'd selected it because she thought it would be warm, and completely sexless.

She'd been half right, he decided, and dropped the quilt.

"Isadora." He shook her shoulder again, then took hold of it to prevent her from turning aside. "Izzy," he whispered close to her ear. "Wake up."

"Go away, Dad."

Grinning, he leaned closer and caught the lobe of her ear between his teeth. That had her eyes springing open. It also kindled a ball of heat in the direct center of her body.

She blinked, focused, but before she could orient herself found her mouth thoroughly captured. Dazed, she lifted a hand to his shoulder, fingers digging in as the ball of heat erupted.

"You awake now?" Jed murmured, and pleased himself by nipping lightly at her lower lip.

"Oh yeah. Wide." She cleared her throat, but her voice remained sleepily husky.

"Who am I?"

"Kevin Costner." She smiled and stretched her shoulders. "Just a little harmless fantasy of mine, Skimmerhorn."

"Isn't he married?"

"Not in my fantasies."

Only a little miffed, Jed leaned back. "How many fingers?"

"Three. I thought we established I was all right last night."

"We're reestablishing it this morning." Her eyes were heavy—sexily so, he noted. But the pupils were normal. "How's the head?"

She lay still a minute, taking inventory. Besides the tingling going on, there were aches. Entirely too many of them. "It hurts. My shoulder's sore, too."

"Try these."

Dora looked down at the aspirin in his hand. "Two? Skimmerhorn, I take two when I break a nail."

"Don't be such a wimp." He knew that would do it. She scowled, took the pills, then the mug of coffee he offered.

Irritation turned to surprise at the first sip. "Pretty good coffee. Almost tastes like mine."

"It is yours—your beans, anyway. I watched you do it once."

"Quick study." Wanting to enjoy the moment, she plumped a pillow at her back and snuggled into it. "Did you sleep okay on the couch?"

"No, but I slept. I used the shower. Don't you have any soap that isn't shaped like little flowers or swans?"

"I had some sea horses, but I used them up." She leaned forward, sniffed at him as she toyed with the dark blond hair curled damply over his collar. "Mmmm. Gardenia."

He covered her face with his hand and gently shoved her back.

"Tell you what," she offered. "The next time I'm out shopping, I'll see if I can find some shaped like a little weight lifter. With that appealing masculine aroma of sweaty gym socks."

With the mug cupped in both hands, she sipped again, sighed. "I can't remember the last time anyone brought me coffee in bed." Smiling, she tilted her head and studied him. With his hair damp from her shower, his chin shadowed with stubble and his eyes nearly as annoyed as they were beautiful, he made a very appealing picture.

"You're a tough one to figure, Skimmerhorn. You had to know with minimal effort you could have been in here with me last night. You knew what buttons to push, but you didn't push them."

"You were hurt and you were tired." But he'd thought about it. Oh yeah, he'd thought about it. "I'm not an animal."

"Oh, yes you are. You're this big, restless, ill-tempered animal—and that's part of the allure." She ran her fingers along the cheek he hadn't bothered to shave. "All those hard muscles and that bad attitude. There's something irresistible about knowing you have an equal capacity for mean as you do for kindness. I'm a sucker for bad boys with soft hearts."

He took the hand she pressed to his cheek, intended to push it away. But she linked her fingers with his and sat up to kiss him. Very softly, very sweetly, so that every muscle in his body throbbed in reaction.

"You're pressing your luck, Dora."

"I don't think so."

He could have proven her wrong, would have if he hadn't been able to see the headache so clearly in her eyes. He could have pushed her back on the bed, purging that feral need she'd built inside him.

But he didn't, because there was no way to take what he wanted without hurting her.

"Listen to me." He spoke carefully, keeping his eyes on hers. "You don't know me. You don't know what I'm capable of, or what I'm not capable of. The only thing you can be sure of is that I want you, and when I'm certain you're a hundred percent, I'm going to have you. I won't ask."

"There's no need for that, since I've already answered yes."

"And I won't be kind." He looked down at their joined hands and deliberately let hers go. "It won't matter a damn to me if you're sorry after."

"When I make a choice, I don't play the hindsight game. I also know you're not warning me, you're warning yourself."

He dropped his hands and rose. "We've got other things to deal with today. What are you doing about the shop?"

"We're closed today."

"Good. We've got to get down to the station house. Get yourself together, and I'll make some breakfast."

"Can you?"

"I can pour milk on cold cereal."

"Yummy."

She tossed the quilt aside as he started out. "Oh, Conroy," he said over his shoulder, "I like your pig."

WHILE Jed and Dora were sharing a box of cornflakes, DiCarlo paced his New York apartment. He hadn't slept. He'd worked his way through half a bottle of Cutty Sark during the long night, but the effects couldn't dull his fevered mind or give him peace.

He couldn't go back to Philadelphia. The dead cop was one thing, but he'd left behind two witnesses. Two who had certainly seen his face well enough for an ID.

They'd make him, DiCarlo thought grimly, and poured another glass. And they'd tie him to the dead patrol. If there was one thing DiCarlo knew about cops, it was that they were relentless in pursuing anyone who'd killed one of their own.

So not only couldn't he return, but he'd need to go underground, at least until the weather chilled. A couple of months, he mused. Six at the most. That was no problem. He had plenty of contacts, plenty of liquid cash. He could spend a nice warm winter in Mexico, swilling margaritas. Once the cops finished chasing their tails, he would return.

The only hitch was Edmund J. Finley.

DiCarlo studied the merchandise he'd stacked against the wall beside his Christmas tree. They looked like sad, neglected presents, unwrapped and unwanted.

The bookends, the parrot, the eagle, Lady Liberty, the china dog. Counting the figurine he'd already delivered, that made six out of seven. Anyone but Finley would consider that a success.

It was only one lousy painting, he thought. Christ knew he'd given it his best shot. He had a black eye, a split lip and sore kidneys. His cashmere coat was ruined.

He'd done more than his share to correct a mistake that hadn't been his in the first place. As soon as he had time, he was going to pay back Opal Johnson for that. In spades.

In the meantime, he just had to figure out the best way to approach Finley. After all, Finley was a businessman and knew one had to take losses along with profit. So he would approach Finley just that way. Businessman to businessman. It wouldn't hurt to put Finley in a cheery mood by personally presenting him with the five newly recovered items first, then elicit sympathy and admiration by detailing the specifics.

He'd explain about the cop, too. Surely a man like Finley would understand the great personal risk taken by icing a badge.

Not enough, DiCarlo admitted, and picked up his ice pack to press it against his bruised cheekbone. He crossed to his foyer mirror to examine himself. It was just as well he was too busy to celebrate New Year's Eve. He could hardly go out in a crowd of people, since his face looked as though it had gone through a meat grinder.

He was going to have to get back to the Conroy woman, and the man across the hall as well. It would take some time. DiCarlo prodded gently beside his swollen eye, winced. He could be patient. Six months, a year. They'd have forgotten about him by then. But he wouldn't forget.

There would be no plans to kill her humanely this time. No indeed. This was one vendetta that would be executed slowly and with great pleasure.

The idea made him smile, then swear as the movement opened his split lip. DiCarlo staunched the blood with the back of his hand, turned away from the mirror. She would pay, there was no question. But his first order of business was Finley.

He knew he could run from the cops, but he wasn't certain he could escape his employer. He would use reason, practicality and flattery. And . . . DiCarlo pressed the ice bag against his mouth and smiled with his eyes only. Good faith. He would offer to put another man on the job, at his own expense.

Surely that was an offer that would appeal to Finley's business sense. And his greed.

Satisfied, DiCarlo went to the phone. The sooner he was finished in California, the sooner he could hit the beaches in Mexico.

"I want to book a flight, first class, New York to LA. First available. Not until six-fifteen?" He drummed his fingers on his desk, calculating. "Yes, yes, that will be fine. No, one way. I'll want to book another flight from LA to Cancún, on the first of January." He opened a desk drawer, took out his passport. "Yes, I'm sure the weather will be an improvement."

"I think his face was a little longer." Dora watched the computer-generated image change on the monitor to the quick rattle of the operator's fingers on the keyboard. "Yeah, that's it. And thinner, too." Unsure, Dora shook her head and looked over at Jed. "Did he have more eyebrows? I think I'm making him look like Al Pacino."

"You're doing fine. Finish going through your impressions, then we'll add mine."

"Okay." She closed her eyes and let the dark image come back, but the quiver of panic came with it, and she opened her eyes again. "I only got a quick look. He . . ." She reached for the ice water she'd requested. "I think he had more hair than that—and it might have had some curl to it."

"Okay." The operator tried on a different hairstyle. "How's that?"

"It's closer. Maybe his eyes were heavier—you know, more lid."

"Like this?"

"Yes, I think . . ." She let out a sigh. "I don't know."

Jed moved behind her chair, laid his hands on her shoulders and automatically began to knead out the tension. "Thin out the lips and nose," he ordered. "The eyes were deeper set. Yeah, that's it. She was right about the eyebrows, a little heavier. More. Square off the chin some."

"How do you do that?" Dora whispered.

"I got a better look at him than you, that's all."

No, that wasn't all, she thought. Not nearly all. He'd seen what she'd seen, but he'd absorbed and filed and retained. Now she was watching the image of her attacker taking shape on the monitor.

"Now deepen the complexion," Jed suggested, narrowing his eyes, focusing in. "Bingo."

"That's him." Shaken, Dora reached up to lay a hand over Jed's. "That *is* him. That's incredible."

Like a proud papa, Brent patted the monitor. "It's a hell of a tool. Jed had to do some fast shuffling to get it in the budget."

Dora smiled weakly and forced herself to stare into the computerized eyes. "Better than Nintendo."

"Give us a printout," Brent told the operator. "We'll see if we can come up with a match."

"I'd like a copy." Relieved to have it behind her, Dora got to her feet. "I want to make sure Lea and Terri see it, in case they notice him hanging around near the shop."

"We'll get you one." Brent nodded to the operator. "Why don't you come back to my office for a few minutes?" He took her arm, guiding her out of the conference room and down the hall. She glanced at a door, read CAPTAIN J. T. SKIMMERHORN on the glass.

It looked as though the department was keeping a light in the window.

She looked up at Jed. "T for testosterone?"

"You're a laugh a minute, Conroy."

"Oh, I forgot to mention it last night." Brent opened his office door and ushered Dora inside. "I got a call from your mother the other day."

"My mother?" Dora lifted a brow and chose a chair.

"An invitation to their New Year's Eve bash at the theater."

"Oh." Tomorrow, Dora remembered. She'd all but put it out of her mind. "I hope you can make it."

"We're looking forward to it. The Liberty Theater New Year's Eve bash has quite a rep." Brent reached in a drawer and took out an envelope. "Your pictures. We're keeping copies, but there doesn't seem to be anything unusual about them."

She slipped them out and chuckled. The first shot was of Richie's wide open mouth, taken at super-close range. Self-portrait, Dora imagined. She'd have recognized that crooked eyetooth anywhere. Obviously, the little brat had gotten hold of her camera.

"Disgusting, but not unusual." She put the envelope inside her purse. "So, where do we go from here?"

"You don't," Jed snapped. "The police do."

"Oh, are you back in command, Captain?" She only smiled at the killing look he aimed at her. "Who exactly is in charge?" she asked Brent.

He cleared his throat, pushed up his glasses. "Well, it's my case."

"Well then." Dora folded her hands in her lap and waited.

"Until we run this guy down," Brent began, watching from the corner of his eye as Jed paced, "we'll put a couple of guards on your building."

She thought of the cop, of the wife, of the children. "I don't want anyone else put at risk."

"Dora, there isn't a man in this precinct who wouldn't volunteer for the duty. Not after Trainor. This guy's a cop killer." He glanced over at Jed. "Which is why it was easy for me to put a rush on Ballistics. The bullet they took out of Trainor matched the ones we dug out of the wall in your building."

"Surprise, surprise," Jed muttered.

"I've got a case to build." Brent took off his glasses to polish them on his wrinkled shirt. "If we bring this bastard in alive, I want stacks of evidence. I'm sending out the ballistic report to other precincts throughout the city and the state. Something might match."

It was a good move. Jed only wished he didn't feel so bitter at not being able to instigate it. "Where's Goldman?"

"In Vail," Brent said under his breath. "Skiing. He took a week's vacation."

If Jed hadn't been so angry, he'd have been stupefied. "Son of a bitch. He's got a dead cop at his feet—one of his own men. He's got no business taking vacation during the holidays when his men are working double shifts."

"He had the time coming." Brent snatched up his shrilling phone. "Call back," he barked into it, and slammed it down again. "Look, I hope he breaks his candy ass. Maybe then you'll get off yours and come back where you belong. We got a dead cop, and the morale level around here's about butt high on a dwarf because we've got a commanding officer who's more worried about having his pretty teeth bonded than seeing to his men." He stabbed a finger at Jed. "What the hell are you going to do about it?"

Jed drew slowly on his cigarette, exhaled, drew again. He didn't speak, didn't dare. Instead he turned on his heel and walked out.

"Screw it." Brent looked at Dora, grimaced. "Sorry."

"Don't worry about it." Actually, she'd found the entire incident illuminating. "Do you think it did any good?"

"No." It embarrassed him to lose his temper in public. It always did. A dull flush was already working up his neck. "Once Jed's made up his mind, you couldn't change it with mortar fire." He dropped down into his chair. "Made me feel better, though."

"Well, that's something. I'd better go after him."

"I wouldn't."

She only smiled and picked up her coat. "See you tomorrow night."

Sʜᴇ caught up with him half a block away. Dora didn't bother to shout his name and ask him to wait. She was quite sure it would have been a waste of breath. Instead she trotted up beside him, matched her stride to his.

"Nice day," she said conversationally. "The temperature's up a bit, I think."

"You'd be smart to stay away from me right now."

"Yeah, I know." She tucked her hand through his arm. "I like walking in the cold. Gets the blood moving. If we turn this way, we'll end up in Chinatown. Some great little shops."

Jed deliberately turned the other way.

"Mmm, perverse," Dora commented. "You're not really mad at him, you know."

"Don't tell me what I am." He tried to shake her off, but she hung on like a silk-covered burr. "Will you get lost, Conroy?"

"Impossible. I know my way around this neighborhood too well." She studied his profile, but resisted the urge to stroke the tension out of his jaw. "You can yell at me if you think it'll make you feel better. It usually works when I'm mad at myself."

"Do I have to have you arrested for harassment?"

She batted her lashes. "Do you think it would work, a little thing like me molesting a big, tough guy like you?"

He shot her one brief, nasty look. "At least you could shut up."

"I'd rather annoy you. You know, if you keep your jaw clenched like that, you're going to break a tooth. Lea used to grind her teeth at night, and now she has to wear this plastic thing in her mouth whenever she goes to bed. It's stress. Lea's always been a worrier. Not me. When I sleep, I tune every thing out. I mean, that's the point of sleep, isn't it?"

Before they could round the next corner, Jed stopped, turned toward her. "You're not going to quit, are you?"

"Nope. I can keep this up indefinitely." Reaching down, she tugged up the zipper of his jacket, smoothed the collar. "He's frustrated because he cares about you. It's tough being cared about, because it loads all this responsibility on. You've had a potful of responsibility, I imagine. It must be a relief to toss it out for a while."

It was tough to hold on to temper with someone who understood so perfectly. But if he let go of temper, despair might creep in. "I had reasons for resigning. They still hold."

"Why don't you tell me what they were?"

"They're my reasons."

"Okay. Want to hear my reasons for leaving the stage?"

"No."

"Good, I'll tell you." She began to walk again, leading him back around the block to where he'd parked his car. "I liked acting. That's hardly surprising with all those hammy genes swimming around in my blood. I was good, too. Once I graduated from the kid parts, I took on stuff like *Our Town* and *The Glass Menagerie*. The reviews were terrific. But . . ." She glanced up under her lashes. "Piqued your interest yet?"

"No."

"But," she continued, undaunted, "it wasn't really what I wanted to do. Then, about five years ago, I got an inheritance, from my godmother. Anna Logan. Maybe you've heard of her? She made a big splash in B movies back in the thirties and forties, then went into agenting."

"I never heard of her."

"Well, she was loaded." A car zoomed by, too fast, and sent up a breeze that fluttered Dora's hair. It was still flying when she turned her head to smile up at Jed. "I was fond of her, too. But she was about a hundred years old and had had a hell of a life. Anyway, I took the money and a couple of courses in business management. Not that I needed them—the courses, I mean. Some things are innate."

"Is there a point to this, Conroy?"

"I'm getting to it. When I told my family what I was going to do, they were upset. It really hurt them that I wasn't going to use what they considered my gifts and carry on in the Conroy tradition. They loved me, but they wanted me to be something I couldn't. I wouldn't have been happy in the theater. I wanted my own shop, my own business. So even though it disappointed them, I went ahead and did what was right for me. It took a long time before I adjusted to the responsibility of being cared for, worried over and loved."

For a moment he said nothing. It surprised him that he wasn't angry any longer. Sometime during her monologue his temper had dissipated, broken up like a nasty storm and blown away on the wind of Dora's persistence.

"So the moral of your incredibly long, convoluted story is that since I don't want to be a cop, I shouldn't get pissed because a friend wants to guilt me back onto the force."

With a sigh, Dora stepped in front of him, put her hands lightly on his shoulders. "No, Skimmerhorn, you missed it entirely." Her eyes held his now, very sober and sympathetic. "I wasn't cut out to be an actor, so I made a choice that my family didn't agree with, but that I knew, inside, was right for me. You're a cop right down to the bone. You just need to wait until you're ready to admit you made the right choice in the first place."

He snagged her arm before she could walk again. "Do you know why I left?" His eyes weren't angry now, but dark and blank and, to Dora, frightening because of the emptiness of emotion. "I didn't have to kill Speck. There were other ways to bring him down, but I ignored them. I pushed the situation to the point where I knew one of us would die. It turned out to be him. I got a fucking commendation for it, even though I could have brought him in without firing a shot. If I had it to do over again, I'd do it exactly the same way."

"You made a choice," she said carefully. "I imagine most people would consider it the right one—your superiors obviously did."

Impatience vibrated from him. "It's what I consider that counts. I used my badge for personal revenge. Not for the law, not for justice. For myself."

"A human frailty," she murmured. "I bet you've had a hell of a time adjusting to the fact that you're not perfect. Now that you have, you'll probably be a better cop when you put that badge back on."

He tightened his grip on her arm, yanked her forward an inch. When her chin angled up, he eased off but kept her still. "Why are you doing this?"

For an answer, the very simplest answer, she grabbed a handful of his hair and pulled his mouth down to hers. She tasted that impatience in the kiss, but there was something else twined with it. The something else was need—deep and human.

"There's that," she said after a moment. "And I guess we'd have to say that despite what I've always considered my good common sense, I care about you, too." She watched him open his mouth, close it again. "Take responsibility for that, Skimmerhorn."

Turning away, she walked the few steps to the car, then pulled out his keys. "I'm driving."

He waited until she'd unlocked the passenger door and had scooted over to the wheel. "Conroy?"

"Yeah."

"Same goes."

Her lips curved as she gunned the engine. "That's good. What do you say, Skimmerhorn? Let's go for a ride."

15

FINLEY'S home was a museum to his ambitions, small and large. Originally built by a director of action films whose love of elaborate construction had soon outreached both his means and his skills, it was tucked high in the hills over Los Angeles.

Finley had purchased it during a flat period in the market, and had immediately set about installing a more elaborate security system, an indoor lap pool for those rare rainy days and a high stone wall that surrounded the property like a moat around a castle.

Finley was a voyeur, but he objected to being watched.

In the third-floor tower, he revamped the director's lofty screening room, adding a bank of television monitors and a high-powered telescope. Gone were the wide, reclining chairs. In their place, Finley had chosen a large, plush conversation pit in maroon velvet. He often entertained there, while home movies, starring himself, flickered on the screen.

Naturally he had hired decorators. He had gone through three companies during the six months it had taken him to furnish the house to his satisfaction.

The walls in every room were white. Some were painted, some lacquered, some papered, but all were in pure, virginal white, as were the carpet, the tiles, the bleached wood flooring. All the color came from his treasures—the figurines, the sculptures, the trinkets he had accumulated.

In room after room there were acres of glass—in windows, in mirrors, in cabinets, in breakfronts—and miles of silks in the drapes and uphol-stery, pillows, tapestries.

Every table, every shelf, every niche, held some masterpiece he had hungered for. When one began to bore him, as they always did, Finley shifted it to a less prominent position and set about acquiring more.

He was never satisfied.

In his closet, rows of suits were three deep. Wool and silk, linen and gabardine. All conservatively tailored, all in deep colors: navy, black, grays and a few more frivolous medium blues. There were no casual clothes, no sport jackets, no natty shirts with little polo players on the breast.

Fifty pairs of black leather shoes, all highly glossed, waited on glass shelves to be chosen.

There was a single pair of white Nikes to go along with his exercise clothes. It was one of his butler's responsibilities to dispose of these every two weeks and replace them with another spotless white pair.

His ties were arranged meticulously according to shade, the blacks giving way to the grays, the grays to the blues.

His formal attire was kept in a stunning rococo armoire.

In his bureau were neatly folded stacks of crisp white shirts, mono-grammed at the cuffs, black argyle socks, white silk boxer shorts and Irish-linen handkerchiefs. All were lightly scented with the lavender sachet his housekeeper replaced weekly.

The master suite included the dressing room, two walls mirrored from floor to ceiling. There was a small wet bar in case the gentleman grew thirsty while preparing for an evening out. There was a balloon-back chair and a gilded console table with a Tiffany butterfly lamp, in the event he needed to sit and contemplate his choice of attire.

To the right of the dressing room was the master bedroom. Paintings by Pissarro, Morisot and Manet graced the white silk walls, each with its own complementary lighting. The furnishings here were lushly ornate, from the Louis XVI boulle bureau to the cabriole nightstands to the gilded settee flanked by Venetian blackamoor torchères. Overhead a trio of Wa-terford chandeliers sprinkled light.

But the bed was his pride, his joy. It was a massive affair, designed in the sixteenth century by Vredeman de Vries. It had four posters complete with tester, headboard and footboard, constructed of oak and deeply carved and painted with cherubs' heads, flowers and fruit.

His vanity had tempted him to install a mirror in the tester, but the devaluation that would have caused brought him to his senses.

Instead he had a camera, discreetly hidden by the carved lintel near the ceiling, that aimed directly at the bed, operated by a remote control gun kept in the top drawer of his nightstand. He paused and flicked on the monitor.

They were preparing lunch in the kitchen, the pheasant salad he'd requested. He watched the cook and the kitchen maid work in the sunny white-and-stainless-steel room.

Finley switched the monitor to the drawing room. He watched DiCarlo sip at the club soda and lime, rattle the ice, tug at his tie.

That was good. The man was worried. Overconfidence displeased Finley. Efficiency was vital. Overconfidence bred mistakes. He supposed he should let the poor boy off the hook soon. After all, he had brought the merchandise two days ahead of deadline.

Initiative was worth something. Perhaps he wouldn't have the boy's arm broken after all.

DiCarlo tugged at his tie again. He couldn't shake the feeling that he was being watched. The sensation had him checking his hair, the line of his suit, his fly.

He took another swallow and laughed at himself. Anybody would feel as though they were being watched, he decided, if they were stuck in a room with a hundred statues and paintings. All those eyes. Painted eyes, glass eyes, marble eyes. He didn't know how Finley stood it.

He must have an army of servants to dust all this junk, DiCarlo thought. Setting his glass aside, he rose to wander the room. He knew better than to touch. Well aware of how fanatic Finley was about his acquisitions, DiCarlo kept his arms at his sides and his hands to himself.

It was a good sign, he concluded, that Finley had invited him to the house rather than demanding an office meeting. It made it friendlier, more personal. Over the phone, Finley's voice had sounded pleasant and pleased.

With enough charm, DiCarlo figured he could smooth over the missing painting, convince Finley that it was simply a matter of a little more time. All in all, DiCarlo was certain that they would part amicably and he could return to the Beverly Hills Hotel to find some willing woman to toast in the new year with him.

And tomorrow, he thought, smiling, Mexico.

"Mr. DiCarlo, I trust I haven't kept you waiting overlong."

"No, sir. I've been admiring your home."

"Ah." Finley crossed to a japanned liquor cabinet. "I'll have to give you the grand tour after lunch. Would you like some claret?" He held up a Victorian jug in the shape of a cockatoo. "I have an excellent Château Latour."

"Thank you." DiCarlo's confidence began to soar.

"Dear me." Finley lifted a brow and let his eyes scan DiCarlo's bruised face. "Did you have an accident of some sort?"

"Yes." DiCarlo touched the bandage at the back of his neck. The memory of Dora's teeth sinking in had him steaming all over again. "Nothing serious."

"I'm glad to hear it. It would be a pity if there was any scarring." He finished pouring the claret. "I hope your plans for the holiday haven't been upset by this trip. I didn't expect you for another day or two."

"I wanted to bring you the results as soon as possible."

"I like a man with a sense of responsibility. Cheers." Well satisfied, he tapped his glass against DiCarlo's. He smiled as the door chimes echoed down the hallway. "Ah, that will be Mr. Winesap. He'll be joining us to inspect the merchandise. Mr. Winesap is quite excellent with his lists, as you know. Now, I hope you'll both forgive me, but I can't stem my impatience any longer," he said as Winesap entered. "I must see my treasures. I believe they were taken into the library." He gestured toward the door. "Gentlemen?"

The hallway was tiled in white marble, and wide enough to accommodate a huge box settle and hall rack while leaving room for three to pass abreast.

The library smelled of leather and lemon and roses. The roses were arranged in two tall Dresden vases set atop the mantel. There were hundreds of books, perhaps thousands, in the split-level room, not on wall shelves but in cases and cabinets, some open, some glass-fronted. There was a charming four-tier revolving bookcase from the Regency period, as well as an Edwardian model Finley had arranged to have stolen from a castle in Devon.

He'd wanted the room to have the feel of a country squire's library, and had succeeded very well, adding deep leather chairs, a collection of antique pipes and a hunting portrait by Gainsborough.

In keeping with the cozy theme, the ubiquitous monitors were hidden behind a trompe l'oeil panel of a bookcase.

"And here we are." With a spring in his step, Finley walked to the library table and picked up a mermaid bookend.

As instructed, the butler had left a small hammer, a knife and a large wastebasket. Finley picked up the hammer and neatly decapitated a blue-eyed mermaid.

"Mustn't move too swiftly on these," he said softly, and continued to chip away, delicately, at the cheap plaster.

"This was made in Taiwan," he told his guests. "At a busy little plant I have an interest in. We ship merchandise primarily to North and South America, and make a tidy, if uninteresting, profit. These, however, are what we might call one of a kind. Some are excellent reproductions of valuable pieces, excellent enough to fool even an expert."

He took out a small square of bubbled plastic, tossing the rest of the bookend aside, then using the knife to slit the packing material open. Inside the plastic was a chamois cloth, and in that a small, very old netsuke.

He examined it, minutely, delighted. A woman crouched on hands and knees with a round-bellied man behind her, his hand clasped possessively over her breast. Her ivory head was turned slightly toward her left shoulder and up so that it appeared she was trying to see his face as he prepared to enter her from the rear.

"Excellent, excellent." After setting it aside, he carefully destroyed the second bookend.

The next piece continued the theme, with a woman kneeling at a man's feet, her head tilting back and a smile on her face as she clutched his erect penis.

"Such craftsmanship." Finley's voice shook with emotion. "Over two hundred years old, and no amount of technology can improve on it. The Japanese understood and appreciated eroticism in art while Europeans were covering their piano legs and pretending children hatched under cabbage leaves."

He took the knife and disemboweled the parrot.

"And here," he said, opening a velvet pouch. "Ah, and here." The lightest of tremors passed deliciously through him when he let the sapphire brooch drop into his waiting palm.

It was set in an intricate gold filigree encrusted with diamonds, a stone of more than eight carats, in a deep cornflower blue, square cut and majestic.

"Worn by Mary, Queen of Scots." Finley stroked the stone, the setting, turned it over to admire the back. "While she was plotting intrigue and her clandestine love affairs. It was part of the booty good Queen Bess took after she'd had her pretty cousin executed."

He could all but smell the blood and betrayal on the stones. And it pleased him.

"Oh, the trouble and expense it's taken me to acquire this bauble. It shall have a place of honor," he said, and set it gently aside.

Like a spoiled child on Christmas morning, he wanted more.

The engraved Gallé vase in the bowels of the Statue of Liberty thrilled him. Momentarily he forgot his guests as he cooed over it, stroking its long sides, admiring the lithe female forms decorating the Art Nouveau glass.

His eyes had taken on a glassy sheen that had Winesap averting his in faint embarrassment.

From within the hollowed base of the bronze eagle, Finley released a padded box. Saliva pooled in his mouth as he tore the padding aside. The box itself was a smooth rosewood, lovingly oiled and polished. But the lid was the treasure, a micro mosaic panel commissioned in Imperial Russia for Catherine the Great—perhaps by her canny lover Orlov after he'd murdered her husband and lifted Catherine onto the throne.

More blood, Finley mused. More betrayal.

Signed by the artist, it was a wonderfully delicate reproduction of the Imperial Palace fused onto glass.

"Have you ever seen anything more exquisite? The pride of czars and emperors and kings. Once this sat behind glass in a museum where un-washed tourists could come and gawk. Now it's mine. Mine alone."

"It's a beauty, all right." DiCarlo hated to interrupt, but it was nearly time to make his pitch. "You know the value of art, Mr. Finley. What's the point in having something priceless if any jerk can walk in off the street and see it?"

"Exactly, exactly. True art must be possessed, it must be hoarded. Mu-seums buy for posterity. The soulless rich for investment. Both processes are abhorrent to me." His eyes were very green now, very bright and a lit-tle mad. "To own, Mr. DiCarlo, is everything."

"I get your point there, and I'm happy to have played a part in bringing you your merchandise. Of course, there was some difficulty—"

"I'm sure." Finley waved him off before the mood was spoiled. "But we must finish here before we discuss your trails and tribulations." He used the hammer on the dog, bursting its belly open. The hound gave birth to a gold cat. "It's quite solid," Finley explained as he unwound the heavy wrapping. "A beautiful piece, of course, but all the more because of its background. It's said to have been a gift from Caesar to Cleopatra. Impos-sible to prove the validity of that, though it has been dated correctly. Still, the myth is enough," he said softly, lovingly. "Quite enough."

His hands shook with excitement as he set it down. "And now, the painting."

"I, ah . . ." It seemed a good time to stand. "There was a little trouble with the painting, Mr. Finley."

"Trouble?" Finley's smile remained fixed. He scanned the room, saw no sign of his final possession. "I don't believe you mentioned any trouble, Mr. DiCarlo."

"I wanted to get you this merchandise without any more delay. These pieces represent a great deal of time and money on your part, and I knew you'd want them in your hands at the earliest possible moment."

"We are speaking now of the painting." And now the painting was all that mattered to Finley. Cleopatra, Catherine and Mary of Scotland were all forgotten. "I don't see it here. Perhaps it's eyestrain. An optical illusion."

The sarcasm brought a dull flush to DiCarlo's cheeks. "I wasn't able to bring it on this trip, Mr. Finley. As I started to tell you, there was a problem."

"A problem?" He continued to smile pleasantly, though the acids in his stomach had begun to churn. "Of what nature?"

Encouraged, DiCarlo resumed his seat. He explained briefly about the three break-ins, reminding Finley that the first had resulted in the recovery of the china hound. He made sure he highlighted his search for the painting, at great personal risk.

"So I'm sure you'll agree, sir," he concluded, as though wrapping up a sales meeting, "that it would be dangerous for all of us for me to return to Philadelphia at this time. I do have a contact who I can put on the matter, at my own expense, of course. Since you've recovered six of the seven pieces, I'm sure you'll be patient. I see no reason why the painting can't be in your hands within, say, six weeks."

"Six weeks." Finley nodded, tapped his forefinger to his lip. "You say you shot a police officer."

"It was necessary. He was watching the building."

"Mmm. And why do you suppose he was doing that?"

"I can't be sure." Sincerity in every pore, DiCarlo leaned forward. "I left absolutely no sign of forced entry. I did overhear an argument between the Conroy woman and her tenant. He was violent. It might be that she asked for police protection."

"Interesting that she simply didn't have him evicted," Finley commented—very, very pleasantly. "You did say the tenant was the one who battered your face."

DiCarlo stiffened with wounded pride. "It was probably a lovers' quarrel. I figure the guy was getting more than a roof over his head out of her."

"Do you?" Finley let the crudeness of the remark pass. "We will have to discuss this further, Mr. DiCarlo. After lunch, perhaps."

"Sure." Relieved, DiCarlo settled back. "I'll run through all the details with you."

"That will be fine. Well, shall we dine, gentlemen?"

They enjoyed the pheasant salad along with a chilled Pouilly-Fumé in the formal dining room with its Victorian furniture and sun-swept garden view. Throughout, Finley kept the conversation away from business. It interfered with the palate, as he explained to DiCarlo. He spent an hour playing jovial host, generously refilling DiCarlo's glass himself.

When the last drop of wine and the final morsel of trifle had been consumed, Finley pushed back from the table.

"I hope you'll forgive us, Abel, but as much as I regret it, Mr. DiCarlo and I should conclude our business. Perhaps a walk around the grounds, through the garden?" he said to DiCarlo.

Pleasantly buzzed on wine, rich food and success, DiCarlo patted his stomach. "I could use a walk after that meal."

"Good, good. I'm a bit of a fanatic about exercise. I'd enjoy the company. We won't be long, Abel."

Finley led DiCarlo out into a solarium complete with potted palms and a musical fountain, through the atrium doors and into the garden.

"I want to tell you how much I admire you, Mr. Finley," DiCarlo began. "Running your business, having a home like this. You sure cut a wide path for yourself."

"I like to think so." Finley's shoes crunched lightly over the smooth white stones on the garden path. "Do you know flowers, Mr. DiCarlo?"

"Just that women are usually suckers for them."

Laughing appreciatively, Finley led him through the garden, finally stopping to admire the view. Finley stood looking out over the Los Angeles basin, drawing deeply of the fragrances around him. Flowers—early roses, jasmine. The tang of freshly watered mulch and clipped grass.

"Your plans, Mr. DiCarlo?" Finley said abruptly.

"What? Oh. It's all simple. I put my man on it. He'll take care of the Conroy woman. Believe me, after he gets through with her, she'll tell him anything." His lips thinned a moment as he grudgingly accepted he wouldn't have the pleasure of beating the painting's location out of her. "Like I said, he might have to wait a week or two, until things cool off. But he'll snatch her, put on the pressure until she leads him to the painting."

"And then."

"He'll whack her, don't worry." DiCarlo smiled a little, professional man to professional man. "He won't leave any loose ends."

"Ah, yes, loose ends. Most inconvenient. And yourself?"

"Me, I figured I'd take a few months in Mexico. Odds are they got a look at me. It was dark, sure, but I don't like to take those kind of chances. If they manage to make me, I'd rather be across the border."

"Wise, I'm sure." Finley bent over a rosebush, sniffed delicately at a pale pink bud just beginning to part its tender petals. "It occurs to me, Mr. Di-Carlo, that if they make you, they may involve me—however indirectly."

"No way. No possible way. Rest easy, Mr. Finley, they'd never tie a man like you with a couple of break-ins in a Philadelphia junk shop."

"Loose ends," Finley said with a sigh. When he straightened, he held a pearl-handled revolver in his hand. And he was smiling again, charmingly. "It's best to snip them off."

He fired, aiming just above DiCarlo's belt buckle. The sound echoed over the hills and sent terrified birds screaming skyward.

DiCarlo's eyes widened with surprise, then glazed with pain. The unbelievable fire of the pain. Dully, he looked down at his belly, pressing a hand against the spreading stain before his knees crumpled beneath him.

"You disappoint me, Mr. DiCarlo." Finley didn't raise his voice but bent low to let the words carry. "Did you take me for a fool? Did you think so much of yourself that you believed I would take your pathetic excuses and wish you bon voyage?"

He straightened and, while DiCarlo writhed in pain from the gunshot, kicked him viciously in the ribs.

"You failed!" he shouted, and kicked again, again, screaming over DiCarlo's groaning pleas for mercy. "I want my painting. I want what's mine. It's your fault, your fault I don't have it."

Spittle ran from Finley's mouth as he shot DiCarlo's left kneecap, then his right. DiCarlo's thin scream of pain faded away into animal whimpers.

"I would have killed you quickly if you hadn't insulted my intelligence. Now it may take you hours, hours of agony. And it's not enough."

He had to force himself to replace the revolver in his pocket. He took out a handkerchief and gently dabbed the perspiration from his brow.

"Not enough," he repeated. He bent down close again, pressing his face into DiCarlo's. "You had your orders. Did you forget who was in charge?"

"Please," DiCarlo moaned, too deep in shock to realize his pleas were useless, and that he was already dead. "Help me. Please."

In a fussy gesture, Finley replaced the handkerchief in his breast pocket. "I gave you plenty of time, more than enough to redeem yourself. I'd even considered giving you absolution. I can be a generous man, but you, you failed me. Failure, Mr. DiCarlo, is unforgivable."

Still shaking with rage, he straightened again. He knew he would need an hour of meditation at the very least before he would manage to compose himself for the formal affair he was attending that night.

Ineptitude, he fumed. Inefficiency in employees. He brushed dust from his sleeve as he walked back toward the solarium. Intolerable.

"Winesap!" he snapped.

"Sir." Winesap tiptoed in, folded his nervous hands. He'd heard the shots, and was very much afraid of what was coming next.

"Dispose of Mr. DiCarlo."

Winesap's shoulders slumped. "Of course, Mr. Finley. Right away."

"Not now." Finley took out a genuine tortoiseshell comb to straighten his windblown hair. "Let him bleed to death first."

Winesap glanced through the glass wall to where DiCarlo was lying on his back, babbling piteously at the sky. "Should I wait in here?"

"Of course. How else will you know when he's dead?" Finley sighed, replaced his comb. "I realize that tomorrow's a holiday, Abel, and I wouldn't dream of interfering with whatever plans you might have. So I'll ask that you focus your attention the following day on gathering all the information you can on this Isadora Conroy in Philadelphia." He sniffed his hand, wrinkled his nose at the scent of gunpowder. "I'm afraid I'm going to have to take care of this matter myself."

16

"HAPPY New Year!"

Jed was greeted at the lobby doors of the Liberty Theater by a bald beanpole of a man dressed in a red leather jumpsuit studded with silver stars. Caught by surprise, Jed found himself bear-hugged and back-patted.

His new friend smelled strongly of wine and Giorgio for Men.

"I'm Indigo."

Since the man's skin approximated the color, Jed nodded. "I can see that."

"Marvelous party." Indigo took out a slim black cigarette, tucked the end into a gold cigarette holder and posed with one hand on his narrow hip. "The band's hot, the champagne's cold and the women . . ." He jiggled his brows up and down. "Are plentiful."

"Thanks for the update."

Cautious, Jed started to ease by, but Indigo was the friendly sort and draped an arm over Jed's shoulders. "Do you need some introductions? I know everyone."

"You don't know me."

"But I'm dying to." He steered Jed through the lobby crowd toward the concession stand, where drinks were being poured by two quick-handed bartenders. "Let me guess." He stepped back half an inch, cocked his head, drew once on the European cigarette. "You're a dancer."

"No."

"No?" Indigo's mobile face creased in thought. "Well, with that body, you should be. Gene Kelly had the most marvelous athletic build, you know. Champagne here." He waved his cigarette toward a bartender. "And one for my friend."

"Scotch," Jed corrected. "Rocks."

"Scotch, rocks?" Indigo's almond-shaped eyes danced. "Of course, I should have seen it instantly. An actor—dramatic, naturally—down from New York."

Jed took his drink and dug out a buck for the tip jar. Sometimes, he decided, it was best simply to cooperate. "Yeah. I'm between parts," he said, and escaped with his drink.

The lobby of the Liberty Theater was fashioned in Gothic style, with yards of ornate plasterwork, pounds of curlicues and gremlins decorating the gilded molding. Over the doors that led into the theater itself were bronze masks of Comedy and Tragedy.

Tonight the area was packed with people who all seemed determined to be heard above the din. The space smelled of perfumes and smoke and the popcorn that erupted cheerfully in a machine beside the concession stand.

Dora would have told Jed that it quite simply smelled of theater.

Guests were milling around, and the attire ranged from white tie to torn Levi's. A group of three in somber black sat wedged on the floor in a corner and read aloud from a collection of Emily Dickinson. Through the open doors he could hear the band tear into a blistering rendition of the Stones' "Brown Sugar."

The Winter Ball, Jed mused, it wasn't.

The house lights were up. He could see people crowded in the aisles, dancing or standing, talking and eating, while onstage the band pumped out rock.

In the box seats and mezzanine and into the second balcony were still more partygoers, shooting the noise level toward sonic with the help of the Liberty Theater's excellent acoustics.

An instinct in Jed gave a fleeting thought to maximum capacities and fire codes before he set about trying to find Dora in what seemed to be the population of Pennsylvania.

Mingling had never been his forte. There had been too many enforced social occasions during his childhood, and too many humiliating public displays by his parents. He would have preferred a quiet evening at home, but since he'd dragged himself out for this, the least she could do was be available.

If she hadn't left for the party so early, with the excuse of being needed to help set up and keep her mother away from the caterers, he could have come with her, kept an eye on her.

He didn't like the idea of her being alone when her attacker was still loose. Though he could hardly call a gathering of this size being alone, he was uneasy about her nonetheless. Otherwise, he wouldn't be there.

Two parties in one week. Jed sipped scotch and worked his way toward the front of the theater. That was more than he'd chosen to attend in a year.

He squeezed between two women, was offered—and refused—a spangled party hat and gave serious consideration to squeezing his way back again and escaping.

Then he saw her. And wondered how he could have missed her. She was sitting on the edge of the stage, dead center, in what had to be an avalanche of sound, holding what appeared to be an intimate conversation with two other women.

She'd done something to her hair, Jed noted. Piled it up on her head in a tangle of dark, wild curls that looked just on the edge of control. And her eyes, he thought, watching as she gripped one of her companions' hands and laughed. She'd painted them up so that they looked bigger, deeper, sultry as a gypsy's. Her lips, which continued to curve as they moved to form words he couldn't hear, were a bold, daring red.

She'd worn a black-and-silver jumpsuit with a high neck, long sleeves and sleek legs that fit like a second skin and should have been illegal. The silver beads splattered over it caught the stage lights every time she moved, and flashed like lightning.

As she'd known they would, he mused. She might have left the stage, but she still knew how to lure the spotlight.

He wanted his hands on her. For a moment that thought and the accompanying slap of desire blocked out everything else.

Setting his glass on the armrest of an aisle seat, he pushed his way forward against the current of people.

"But he's a method actor, after all," Dora said, grinning. "Naturally if he's going to pitch the product, he'd want to catch the flu. What I want to know is what happened after he—" She broke off when hands hooked under her armpits and lifted her from the stage.

She got a quick glimpse of Jed's face before he covered her mouth with his. Fierce, hungry, urgent need rammed into her, cartwheeling from her stomach to her chest so that her heart was stuttering when he released her.

"Well, hi." Staggered, she put a hand on his arm for balance. In her spike-heeled boots she was nearly eye level with him, and the intensity of his look had every pulse point jumping in time with the band's back beat. "Glad you could make it. I—ah—this is . . ."

She turned to her two friends and went blank.

"Excuse us." Jed pulled her away until he found a corner. He couldn't call it quiet, but at least they didn't have to shout at each other. "What do you call that thing you're wearing?"

"This?" She glanced down at the spangled cat suit, then back up at his face. "Sexy. Do you like it?"

"I'll let you know as soon as I manage to roll my tongue back into my mouth."

"You have such a way with words, Skimmerhorn. Do you want a drink, some food?"

"I had a drink. I was met at the door by a seven-foot black man in red leather. He hugged me."

"Indigo." Her eyes sparkled. "He's a very sociable sort."

"He's got me pegged as an out-of-work actor from New York." Experimentally, he touched a fingertip to one of her curls, wondering what it would take to have them all tumbling down toward her shoulders.

"Indigo's a bit flamboyant, but he's an excellent director, and he has a very good eye. It's a good thing you didn't tell him you're a cop." She took Jed's hand and led him backstage, where another bar and a buffet were set up. "He doesn't like them."

"I'm not a cop." He started to order another scotch, then opted for club soda while Dora chose champagne. "Why doesn't he like them?"

"Oh, he used to work part-time at this club—as a bouncer. The cops raided this crap game in the back room and hauled him in." She angled her head, shifted her shoulders and did a dead-on imitation of Indigo. "Darling, it was a frightful experience. Do you have any idea what kind of people they put in those cells?"

"Yeah. Criminals."

"Don't say that to him. I'm the one who bailed him out, and let me tell you, the man was wrecked." In an automatic gesture, she straightened the collar of Jed's shirt. "It would be difficult for you to sympathize, I imagine, as you've only been on the outside of the bars."

"I've seen them from both sides."

"Oh, well then." With a brisk, practical movement, she brushed the windswept hair from his forehead. "You'll have to tell me about that sometime."

"Maybe I will. Have you finished grooming me?"

"Yes. You look very nice in black—a bit of the rebel, maybe. Sort of James Deanish."

"He's dead."

"Yes, of course. I meant if he'd lived to see thirty." Her smile was thoughtful and amused. "Are all cops so literal-minded, or is it just you?"

"It's a matter of fact and fantasy. I'm more comfortable with fact."

"Too bad. I spent most of my life steeped in fantasy. You could say laboring over it." She chose a radish rose from the buffet, crunched. "I prefer it to straight reality."

"When you were an actress."

Her laugh bubbled out, frothy as the wine. "Need I remind you, I'm a Conroy. I may not be on the legitimate stages these days, but I'm still an actress." Leaning closer, she nipped teasingly at his earlobe. "If you ever decided to try the stage, I might be tempted to come out of retirement."

The lance of heat arrowed straight down the center of his body. "Why don't we just stick with who we are?"

"The world will never know what they missed." She glanced down at his drink. "You don't have to play designated driver, you know. We can cab back."

"I'll stay with this." He reached out, cupped a hand under her chin. "I want a very clear head when I make love with you tonight."

"Oh." She lifted her own glass with an unsteady hand. "Well."

He grinned. "Run out of lines, Conroy?"

"I . . . Ah . . ."

"Isadora!"

Jed saw a statuesque redhead poured into a glitter of green that slicked down a regal body, then frothed out in stiff fans from the knees to the ankles. As she bore down on them, she looked exotically like a ferocious mermaid.

Blessing Trixie's timing, Dora let out a pent-up breath and turned to her mother. "Problem?"

"That caterer is a beast. God knows why I continue to hire him." She aimed a look over her shoulder that could have melted steel. "He refused, absolutely refused, to listen to a word I said about the anchovy paste."

Since it had been Will's shift to keep their mother separated from the caterer, Dora took a quick glimpse around. Her little brother was, she decided, a dead man. "Where's Will?"

"Oh, off with that pretty girl he brought with him from New York." Trixie tossed up her hands. The movement sent the colored beads that dripped from her ears dancing. A catering crisis left her no time for remembering names. "The model."

"Miss January," Dora said under her breath.

"Now, the anchovy paste," Trixie began. She drew in a deep breath, preparing to launch into an indignant speech.

"Mom, you haven't met Jed."

"Jed?" Distracted, Trixie patted her hair. Her face transformed when she took her first good look. Subtly, she angled her chin, swept her mink lashes and peered at Jed from under them. Flirting, in Trixie's opinion, was an art. "I'm thrilled to meet you."

Jed understood what was expected when he took her offered hand. He kissed her knuckles. "The pleasure's mine, Mrs. Conroy."

"Oh, Trixie, please." She nearly crooned it. "Otherwise I'll feel old and staid."

"I'm sure that would be impossible. I saw you perform *Hello Dolly* last year. You were magnificent."

Trixie's smooth cheeks pinked with pleasure. "Oh, how very kind of you to say so. I do adore Dolly Levi, such a full, richly textured character."

"You captured her perfectly."

"Yes." She sighed at the memory. "I like him, Dora. Tell me, Jed—my, you have very *large* hands, don't you?"

"Mom." Since he'd behaved so nicely, Dora took pity on him. "Jed's the tenant Dad found for me."

"The tenant—the tenant!" Instantly, maternal instincts outweighed flirtations. "Oh, my dear, dear boy!" Overcome with gratitude, Trixie threw her arms around Jed's neck. She had a grip like a linebacker. "I am so completely, so irrevocably in your debt."

Dora simply ran her tongue around her teeth when Jed shot her a helpless look.

"It was nothing," he said, awkwardly patting Trixie's back. "I just answered an ad."

"You saved my darling Isadora from that horrible burglar." Rearing back, Trixie kissed both of his cheeks. "We'll never be able to repay you for chasing him away and keeping our little girl from being robbed."

He narrowed his eyes at Dora over her mother's heaving shoulders. Dora looked aside.

"I keep an eye on her," Jed said meaningfully. "Don't worry."

"Worry is a mother's lot, dear." With a sad smile, Trixie sighed.

"There you are, passion flower." In white tie and tails, Quentin swaggered up, still steady after keeping two bartenders hopping. He gave his wife a long, lingering kiss that had Jed's brow raising. "I've come to claim my bride for a dance."

"Of course, dear." Trixie slipped her arms around him and they began to glide, tango style.

"Have you met the young man I picked out for Izzy?"

"Yes, just now." On the turn, Trixie tossed back her head and beamed at Jed. He wouldn't have been surprised if a rose had suddenly appeared between her teeth. "You have such excellent taste."

"Izzy, show Jed around the theater. There's more to our humble abode than a simple stage." Quentin winked, dipped his wife, then tangoed her away.

"Passion flower?" Jed asked after a moment.

"It works for them."

"Obviously." He couldn't remember ever seeing his parents exchange the most impersonal of embraces, much less a smoldering kiss. The only passion he had ever witnessed between them had been hurled insults and crockery.

"You never mentioned you'd been here before."

"What?"

"To the theater," she said, drawing his attention back to her. *"Hello Dolly?"*

"You didn't ask." He guided Dora away from the crowd near the bar. "You didn't tell her, did you?"

"I don't want to upset her. Don't give me that look," she snapped. "You saw how she acted when she thought about the break-in. Can you imagine what would happen if I told her some maniac held a gun on me?" When he didn't respond, she tapped her foot. "I'm going to tell her, in my own way."

"Your business," Jed said, and took out a cigarette. "But if she catches wind of it from someone else, it'll be worse."

"I don't want to think about it right now." She snatched Jed's cigarette, took one brisk puff, then handed it back. "I'll show you around. The building's mid-nineteenth-century. It used to be a popular music hall." She headed away from the stage, down one of the narrow corridors. "It started getting run-down after vaudeville died, barely escaped the wrecking ball a couple of times. After—" She pushed open the door to a dressing room. Putting her hands on her hips, she watched Will untangle himself from a torrid embrace. "Desertion," she said, "is a hanging offense."

Will grinned and slipped his arm around a curvy woman in a tiny red dress. "Lorraine was helping me run lines. I'm up for a mouthwash commercial."

"You were on duty, Will. I've had my shift and Lea doesn't come on until after midnight."

"Okay, okay." With his date in tow, Will squeezed through the door. "Catch you later."

Jed didn't bother to disguise his admiration of Lorraine's hips, which were swinging like a pendulum.

"Pop your eyes back in your head, Skimmerhorn," Dora advised. "Someone might step on them."

"In a minute." He turned back to Dora when Lorraine had swiveled out of view. "His shift for what?" Jed asked.

"For keeping Mom out of the caterer's hair. Come on, I'll take you up to the fly floor. There's a wicked view of the stage from there."

As the evening wore on, Jed stopped questioning the fact that he was enjoying himself. Although he didn't like crowds, had no use for parties and making conversation with strangers, he didn't feel any impatient urges to leave early. When he ran into the Chapmans in the first balcony, he concluded that they were also enjoying themselves.

"Hey, Jed. Happy new year." Mary Pat kissed him, then leaned on the rail again to watch the action below. "What a party. I've never seen anything like this."

Jed checked out her view. A swarm of people, streams of color, blasts of noise. "The Conroys are—unique."

"You're telling me. I met Lea's father. We jitterbugged." Her face flushed with laughter. "I didn't know I *could* jitterbug."

"She didn't have to do much more than hang on," Brent commented. "That old guy can move."

"He's probably got enough fuel in him." Jed caught a glimpse of Quentin below, with a party hat jauntily tilted on his head.

"Where's Dora?" Brent asked. "I haven't seen her since we got here."

"She moves around. Indigo wanted to dance with her."

"Indigo?" Mary Pat leaned farther over the balcony to wave back at strangers and toss confetti.

"Can't miss him. He's a giant, bald black guy in red leather."

"Oh. *Oh*," she repeated after her quick scan located him. "God, I wish I could dance like that." She propped her elbows on the rail and moved her hips gently to the beat.

"Anything turn up yet?" Jed asked Brent.

"It's early." Brent nursed a beer. "We're sending the picture around. If he's got a sheet, we'll have something after the holiday. I did some legwork myself, looking for a matchup on known sex offenders or B and E men. Nothing yet." Brent looked down in his empty glass, adjusted his horn-rims. "Let's go get a beer."

"Oh, no you don't." Mary Pat popped up from the rail and grabbed Brent's arm. "You're going to dance with me, Lieutenant. It's almost midnight."

"Couldn't we stay up here and neck?" Brent dragged his feet as his wife pulled him along. "Listen, Jed'll dance with you."

"I'm getting my own woman."

By the time the three had managed to elbow and squeeze their way down to the orchestra level, the lead singer was shouting into the mike, holding up his hands for silence.

"Come on, everybody, listen up! We got one minute until zero hour, so find your significant other—or a handy pair of lips—and get ready to pucker up for the new year."

Jed ignored the din and a couple of interesting proposals from solo women and cut through the crowd.

He saw her, stage right, laughing with her brother as they poured champagne into dozens of outstretched glasses.

She set down an empty and picked up another, turning to see that the band had full glasses to toast. And she saw him.

"Will." With her eyes on Jed's, she pushed the bottle at her brother. "You're on your own."

"There'll be a stampede!" he shouted, but she was already walking to the edge of the stage.

"Get ready, people!" The singer's voice boomed out over the theater. "Count with me now. Ten, nine . . ."

It felt as though she were moving in slow motion, through water, warm, silky water. Her heart beat hard and high in her chest.

"Eight, seven . . ."

She leaned down, put her hands on Jed's shoulders. His gripped her waist.

"Six, five . . ."

The walls shook. She stepped off into the air, into the colorful rain of confetti, felt his muscles ripple against her as she combed a hand through his hair and hooked her legs around him.

"Four, three . . ."

Inch by inch she slid down his body, her eyes locked on his, her breath already quickened.

"Two, one . . ."

Her mouth opened to his, hot and hungry. Their twin sounds of pleasure were drowned out in an explosion of cheers. On an incoherent murmur, she changed the angle of the kiss and dived deeper, both hands fisted in his hair.

He continued to lower her from the stage to the ground, certain that something in him would explode—head, heart, loins. Even when she stood, her body remained molded to his in a way that gave him painful knowledge of every curve and valley.

She tasted more dangerous than whiskey, more effervescent than champagne. He understood that a man could be drunk when he had a woman in his system.

He took his mouth from hers but kept her firmly against him. Her eyes were half closed, her lips just parted. As he watched, her tongue slipped out to skim lightly over her lips, as if she wanted to absorb the lingering taste of him.

"Give me another," she murmured.

But before he could, Quentin bounded up and swung an arm around each of them. "Happy new year, *mes enfants*." With a tilt of his head, he pitched his voice so that it flowed like wine over the din. " 'Ring out the old, ring in the new, Ring, happy bells, across the snow: The year is going, let him go; Ring out the false, ring in the true.' "

"Tennyson," Jed murmured, obscurely touched, and Quentin beamed at him.

"Quite right." He kissed Dora, then Jed, with equal enthusiasm. Before Jed could adjust to the shock, Trixie descended on them.

"I love celebrations." There were more kisses, lavishly given. "Will, come here and kiss your mother."

Will obliged, leaping dramatically off the stage and catching his mother up in a theatrical dip. He kissed his father, then he turned to Jed.

Braced, Jed held his ground. "I don't want to have to punch you."

Will only grinned. "Sorry, we're a demonstrative bunch." Despite the warning, he gave Jed a hard, tipsy hug. "Here's Lea and John."

Thinking of survival, Jed stepped back, but found himself blocked by the stage. He gave up, accepting it philosophically when he was kissed by Lea and embraced by John—whom he'd yet to meet.

Watching it all, and the various reactions that flickered over his face, Dora laughed and found a full glass of champagne.

Here's to you, Skimmerhorn. You ain't seen nothing yet.

It took DiCarlo a long, agonizing time to die. Winesap had waited patiently, while doing his best to block out the thin calls for help, the delirious prayers and the babbling sobs.

He didn't know how Finley had handled the servants. He didn't want to know. But he had wished, several times during the interminable three-hour wait, that DiCarlo would do the decent thing and simply die.

Then, when dusk began to fall and there were no more sounds from outside the solarium, Winesap wished DiCarlo had taken longer, much longer.

He didn't relish the task at hand.

Sighing, he went out of the house, past the sprawled body and across the south lawn toward a stone-sided toolshed. He had inquired, meekly, if a drop cloth or sheet of plastic might be available.

Following Finley's instructions, Winesap located a large painter's cloth, splattered with white. His back creaking from the weight, he shouldered the roll, returned to the garden and his grisly task.

It was easy to block the routine from his mind. He had only to imagine it was he who lay staring sightlessly at the deepening sky, and the entire process didn't bother him overmuch.

He spread the cloth over the white stones. They were stained liberally with blood, sticky with it. And the flies . . . Well, all in all, Winesap mused, it was a gruesome bit of business.

Crouching, breath whistling through his teeth, Winesap rolled Di-Carlo's limp body over and over until it was nicely centered on the cloth.

He took a rest then. Physical labor always made him sweat profusely. He unfolded a handkerchief and mopped his dripping face and neck. Wrinkling his nose, he tossed the handkerchief down and rolled it under the body.

He sat again, careful to avoid bloodstains, and carefully removed Di-Carlo's wallet. He held it gingerly between his thumb and forefinger and decided to burn it, money and all, at the first opportunity.

With the resignation of the overburdened, he meticulously checked the rest of DiCarlo's pockets to be certain he'd removed any and all forms of identification.

Faintly, from a second-floor window, he heard the strains of some Italian opera. Finley was preparing for his evening out, Winesap mused.

After all, tomorrow was a holiday.

17

THE night was clear as glass, the air brittle. A thin layer of frost on the T-Bird's side window sparkled like an icy spiderweb in the beam of street-lamps. Inside, the heater hummed efficiently, adding another bass note to B. B. King's "Blue Monday" from the radio.

The warmth, the blues and the slow smooth ride might have lulled Dora to sleep. If her nerves hadn't been snapping. To combat the tension, she kept up a nonstop commentary on the party, the people and the music that required little or no response from Jed.

When they pulled up behind her building, she'd nearly run dry.

"It's all right, isn't it?" she asked.

"Is what all right?"

Her fingers vised over her evening bag. "The guards Brent put on."

"Is that what's got you so wound up?"

She studied the building, the stream from the back-door light, the glow in the window from the lamp she'd left burning. "I did a pretty good job of blocking it out for most of the night."

"It's all right." Leaning over, he unsnapped her seat belt himself. "They were both there."

"Good. That's good." But her nerves didn't settle. In silence they climbed out of opposite sides of the car, started to the stairs, up.

She didn't like being jumpy, she thought as Jed unlocked the outside door. At the moment it had nothing to do with intruders and guards. It had everything to do with what was going to happen once they were inside, and alone.

Which made absolutely no sense at all, she decided. She stepped into the hallway and dug out her keys on the way to her door. She wanted him, wanted very much to finish what had started between them.

And yet . . .

Jed took the keys from her rigid fingers and unlocked the door himself.

It was a matter of control, she realized as she slipped out of her coat, laid it over a chair. Always before she'd made certain that she held the wheel in a relationship, that she steered it in the direction of her choice.

But she wasn't in the driver's seat with Jed, and they both knew it.

She heard the door close at her back, lock. Fresh nerves scrambled into her throat.

"Do you want a drink?" She didn't turn, but headed straight for the brandy.

"No."

"No?" Her fingers hovered over the decanter, fell away. "I don't either." She crossed to the stereo, switched on the CD changer without any idea what music she'd left inside. Bessie Smith picked up where B. B. had left off.

"I'll have to take the tree down in a few days." She reached out and touched a bough. "On Twelfth Night. Pack everything away, burn a few sprigs of pine in the fire. It always makes me a little sad." She jolted when Jed's hands cupped her shoulders.

"You're nervous."

"Me?" She laughed and wished she'd poured something, anything that would wash away the dry heat in her throat.

"I like it."

Feeling foolish, she turned and managed a small smile. "You would. It makes you feel superior."

"There is that." He lowered his head and kissed the corner of her mouth. "It also lets me know you'll remember this, for a long time. Come with me."

He kept her hand in his on the short walk to the bedroom.

He wanted to move slowly, discovering her inch by fascinating inch, savoring those nerves even as he was exploiting them. Until she was help-less, and his.

He switched on the bedside lamp, and looked at her.

Her breath shuddered out when he touched his lips to hers. Tenderness was the last thing she'd expected from him, and the most devastating gift he could give. Her lips parted beneath his, accepting, even as her heart jammed like a fist in her throat.

Her head fell back, a gesture of surrender that had need twisting sharp in his gut. But he continued to play her lips delicately, letting the moment spin out.

"You're shaking," he murmured, trailing his lips down her jawline, sliding his tongue over warm, smooth skin, wallowing in the flavor of flesh.

"That's you."

"You could be right." He brought his mouth back to hers, deepening the kiss until pleasure swam giddily in her head. Now there were sighs, and breathless murmurs, the hard thud of racing hearts.

"Let me turn down the bed," she whispered. But when she turned, shifted aside, he drew her back against him, nuzzling his lips at the nape of her neck.

"That can wait."

His hands were spread over her midsection where the pressure was coiled taut as a rattler. "I don't think I can."

"It's not going to be quick." He slid his hands up her sides, down again. "It's not going to be easy."

"Jed—" His name ended on a moan. His hands were over her breasts now, caressing, thumbs skimming, circling lightly over the peaks while his tongue did outrageous things to the back of her ear. Eyes closed, she relin-quished any thought of control and arched back against him.

He used his teeth now, satisfying his own primitive need for the taste of flesh while he undid the tiny buttons that ranged from her throat to the juncture of her thighs. Her breathing slowed, deepened, like a woman in a trance. The side of his thumb barely brushed her skin as he moved with tormenting laziness from button to button.

"I've had all night to wonder." He spoke softly, close to her ear, and fought to keep his hands from taking too greedily. "All night to imagine what was under here."

Slowly, he spread the material open, skimmed his fingers down her center. There was nothing but woman.

"Sweet Christ." He buried his face in her hair as desire ripped through him. Her skin was hot and soft, the muscles quivering helplessly under his hands. Each tremor rippled from her into him as they stood pressed close in the lamplight.

He hadn't known a need could be so outrageous, or the desire to give and take so brutally keen, like a blade honed and waiting for its mark. He only knew he wanted every inch of her and the satisfaction of having her crave every bit as desperately as he.

Dreamlike, she lifted an arm, hooked it around his neck. It was almost like floating, she thought. And the air was polished like silver. Then he would touch again, and that softly glowing air took on an edge, like a sword turned in the sun.

Her eyes half closed, she leaned back against him, absorbing both the pride and the wonder as his hands roamed over her skin. She turned her head so that her mouth could find his again. Her lips clung, wet and hungry, urging him to take more. She could no longer pinpoint the focus of pleasure. There were too many sensations sprinting and careening through her. His mouth, yes, there was pleasure in that, the firm pressure of lips, the scrape of teeth, the tangle of tongues.

There was more in the rock-hard press of his body against hers, the faint tremors that whispered of a violence held rigidly under control. The heat that shimmered around him that spoke of dark and desperate needs.

And there were his hands. God, his hands that stroked and molded and possessed, just a few degrees shy of rough until she was afraid she would lose all sense of self and beg for more.

Her breath came in whimpers, in low, throaty groans, and her body pressed back against his, rocking in a quickening rhythm that demanded. To please her, and himself, he ran his hand down the center of her body until he cupped her. She was already damp and heated. With fingertips only he sent her hurtling over the edge. Her body went rigid, arched back against him. She cried out as the fast, hard orgasm rammed her. When her legs buckled, he slipped deeper into her, groaning as she gasped out in stunned delight.

"More?"

Her head reeled. To keep her balance she locked her other arm around him. "Yes."

He drove her up again, arousal spurting inside him each time she moaned out his name. He understood a man could be drunk and on the edge of control without sampling a swallow of liquor. And that a woman could slip into the blood like a drug. As the greed welled inside him, he spun her around to drag the snug material over her shoulders.

There was a fierceness on his face, a violence in his eyes that should have frightened her. Though her heart gave a wild leap, it had nothing to do with fear.

"I want you." Her voice was low and thick, like honey poured over flame. The hands that tugged the shirt over his head were far from steady. But her eyes, nearly level with his, were strong and sure. She unsnapped his jeans, tossing back her head as she moved closer. "I want you inside me. Now."

In response he gripped her hips and tumbled with her onto the bed.

They rolled twice, tearing impatiently at each other's clothes until damp flesh pressed to damp flesh. But when she would have locked herself around him and taken him into her, he shifted, sliding down her body. While she writhed and moaned beneath him, he feasted on her, suckling her breasts so that the answering contractions low in her belly were all but unbearable.

Panting, she gripped his hair, her body curved in desperate invitation. "Now. For God's sake, now."

He caught her nipple between his teeth, tugging until her nails dug into his shoulders. "This time I want more."

But the more he took, the more he needed. She gave, completely, unrestrictedly, abandoning herself to the flood of sensations. Still, it wasn't enough.

As he had promised himself, he explored every inch of her, tasting, touching, possessing. Whatever he asked, she gave. Whatever she offered, he took.

He could watch her. The light sheened over her damp skin, making it gleam like one of her porcelain figurines. But she was flesh and blood, her hands as curious as his, her mouth as avid.

Beneath them the spread was as slick and smooth as water. The music drifted in, all crying sax and throbbing bass.

When he slipped inside her, her low throaty moan shuddered from her lips into his. Slowly, savoring, he slid deeper, deeper, swallowing her frantic gasps, inciting more with the play of his tongue over hers.

He braced himself over her, desperate to see her face, to watch those flickers of mindless pleasure. She came again, tightening convulsively around him so that he sucked in his breath at the storm of sensation.

Her eyes flew open, glazed and huge, to fix on his face. Her lips trembled as she tried to speak, but there was only another shuddering moan. He was all she could see, all she could feel, and all she wanted. Each slow stroke shivered through her so that her body was a mass of sparking nerves and tearing needs. He ignited them again and again until she could do nothing but wrap herself around him and let him take her where and how he chose.

She cried out again. Jed buried his face in her hair and let himself follow.

THE music had changed. Elton John was singing his ode to Marilyn. Dora lay sprawled crosswise on the bed, her numbed body barely aware of Jed's weight. She did feel his lips pressed lightly to the side of her breast, and his heartbeat, still raging. She found the strength to lift her hand, to run it over his hair and down to his shoulder.

Her touch, somehow both maternal and loverlike, caused him to stir. He felt as though he'd just tumbled down a very tall mountain without skis and had landed in a deep, warm spring. Going with the urge, he kissed the curve of her breast and watched her smile.

"You okay?" he asked her.

"No. I can't see anything."

It was his turn to smile. "Your eyes are closed."

"Oh." She opened them and sighed. "Thank God. I thought I'd been struck blind." Turning her head on the rumpled spread, she looked down at him. "I don't think I'll ask how you're doing. You look entirely too pleased with yourself."

He levered himself up to kiss her. Her hair had tumbled down, as he'd imagined it would, and was a riot of curls around her face. Her lips were swollen, her eyes sleepy.

He felt something stir—not the rekindled desire he'd expected, but something else. Something he didn't recognize as contentment. "Ask anyway."

"Okay." She brushed the hair away from his forehead. "How's it going, Skimmerhorn?"

"It's going good."

"Your gift for words stuns me."

He laughed, kissed her again, then rolled over, gathering her close to his side. "It's too bad I can't think of any Tennyson."

The idea of him quoting poetry made her smile grow misty. "How about Shelley? 'I arise from dreams of thee in the first sweet sleep of night, when the winds are breathing low, and the stars are shining bright.'"

She humbled him. "That's nice." He tipped her face up for a kiss that was both sweet and dreamy. "Really nice."

Content with that, she nuzzled closer. "As a Conroy I was raised on bards and playwrights."

"They did a good job with you." She only smiled as he continued to study her, his hand still cupped under her chin, his eyes dark and intent as they scanned her face. "I want you again."

"I was hoping you would."

"Dora, you look terrible."

"Lea, what would I do without you around to boost my ego?"

Unfazed, Lea fisted her hands on her hips as she studied her sister's pale face and shadowed eyes. "Maybe you're coming down with something. That flu's still going around, you know. I think you should close the shop for the day."

Dora walked around the counter as a customer came in. "That kind of thinking is why you're the employee and I'm the boss." She put on a sunny smile. "Good morning. May I help you?"

"Are you Dora Conroy?"

"That's right." Dora held out a hand. She knew she looked pale and wan from lack of sleep, but the woman who was currently clutching her hand looked near collapse. "Would you like some coffee? Some tea?"

"I . . ." The woman shut her eyes and pulled off her blue ski cap. "I'd love some coffee, but I'm not supposed to drink it." She laid a hand on the gentle mound of her belly. "Tea would be nice."

"Cream? Lemon?"

"No, just black."

"Why don't you sit down?" Taking charge, Dora guided the woman to a chair. "We're all starting a little slow this morning. After-holiday fatigue." When a young couple strolled in, Dora gestured for Lea to see to them. She poured two cups of tea.

"Thanks. I'm Sharon Rohman," she told Dora as she accepted her cup.

"I'm afraid I'm a little vague on details today. Oh!" It hit her all at once. Immediately she sat down and reached for Sharon's hand. "You're Mrs. Lyle's niece. I'm so sorry about what happened. The last time I called the hospital, I was told she was still in a coma."

Sharon pressed her lips together. "She came out of it last night."

"Oh, I'm so glad to hear that."

"She's still critical." Sharon lifted her cup, then rattled it back in the saucer without drinking. "The doctors can't say if or when she'll recover. She's—she's very fragile."

Dora's eyes stung in response. "It's a dreadful time for you. I don't suppose there's anything worse than waiting."

"No, there isn't." But the easy, undemanding sympathy helped her relax. "We've always been close. Really like girlfriends. The first person I told about the baby after my husband was my aunt."

"You look so tired," Dora said gently. "Why don't you come upstairs to my apartment? You can stretch out for a few minutes in private."

The kindness had Sharon's eyes welling. "I can't stay. I need to get back to the hospital."

"Sharon, this strain can't be good for you or your baby."

"I'm being as careful as I can." She brushed at a tear with the back of her hand. "Believe me, I'm doing everything the doctor tells me." She took a deep breath, then, more relaxed, Sharon said, "Miss Conroy—"

"Dora."

"Dora." Sharon took a soothing breath. "I came by this morning to thank you for the flowers you sent to the hospital. They were lovely. Aunt Alice loves flowers. Her garden is a showplace. The nurses have told me you've called several times to check on my aunt's condition."

"I'm relieved it's improving."

"Thank you. But you see, I thought I knew all of her friends. I don't know how you're connected."

"The truth is, we only met briefly. Here. She came into the shop right before Christmas."

Sharon gave a puzzled shake of her head. "She bought something from you?"

"A couple of things." Dora didn't have the heart to tell Sharon they had been gifts for her and her baby. "She mentioned she'd come in because you'd shopped here a few times."

"Yes." Baffled, Sharon smiled as Dora refilled her cup. "You always have such interesting things. I hope you're not offended, but I find it a bit strange that you'd be so concerned over a woman you'd met only once, as a customer."

"I liked her," Dora said simply. "And it bothered me a great deal that she'd been hurt so soon after she'd been here."

"She was shopping for me, wasn't she?"

"She's very fond of you."

"Yes." With an effort, Sharon drew herself in. She had to be strong, she knew, for her baby, for her aunt. "Whoever killed Muriel and hurt my aunt destroyed a lot of her things as well. It seems so senseless."

"Do the police have any leads?"

"No." Sharon blew out a helpless little sigh. "Nothing. They've been very kind, right from the beginning. I was hysterical by the time they got to her. I found her lying there on Christmas morning, and—and poor Muriel. I was really calm when I called for an ambulance and the police. And then I just went to pieces. It's helped to talk to them. The police can be so detached and analytical."

Dora thought of Jed. "I know." After a moment's hesitation, Dora made a decision. "Would you like to know what she bought for you?"

"Yes, I would, very much."

"She said that you sewed. She bought you a Victorian doorstop so you could keep the door open and hear the baby in the nursery."

"A doorstop?" A soft smile played around Sharon's mouth. "A brass elephant—like Jumbo?"

"Exactly."

"We found it in the corner of the living room." Tears threatened again, but they didn't feel so hot and desperate. "It's just the sort of thing she'd buy for me."

"She picked up a doorstop for the nursery, too. A china dog, curled up and sleeping."

"Oh, I didn't see that. It must have been broken. He shattered most of the gifts she'd wrapped, and a great deal of her things as well." She curled her fingers around Dora's. "It looked as though he'd gone crazy. I suppose he had to be crazy, didn't he, to kill one old woman and leave another for dead." But she shook the question away. "I'd like to take her something when I go to see her this morning. Could you help me pick something out?"

"I'd love to."

Twenty minutes later, Dora watched Sharon get in her car and drive away.

"What was that all about?" Lea asked. "The poor thing looked so unhappy."

"That was Mrs. Lyle's niece—the woman who was attacked on Christmas Eve."

"Society Hill? She's in a coma, isn't she?"

"She's come out of it."

Lea shook her head. "It's awful to think that someone could break into your home that way."

A quick shiver raced up Dora's spine as she remembered her own experience. "Awful," she agreed. "I hope they find him."

"In the meantime." Firmly, Lea turned Dora to face her. "Back to you. Why do you look so exhausted when you had the entire day off yesterday?"

"I haven't a clue. I spent the entire day in bed." With a smile playing around her mouth, Dora drew away to rearrange a collection of music boxes.

"Wait a minute." Eagle-eyed, Lea shifted to get another look at Dora's face. "Oh," she said, drawing the word out into three ascending syllables. "The light dawns. Jed."

Dora opened the lid on an enameled box that played the "Moonlight Sonata." "What about him?"

"Don't play that game with me, Isadora. Just whose bed did you spend the day in?"

"My own." Then she grinned and closed the box. "And it was incredible."

"Really?" Lea was all ears. "Okay, spill it."

"Well, he's . . . I can't," she realized, baffled. "This is different."

"Uh-oh," Lea said, and grinned, ear to dainty ear. "Do you remember what I did the first time John kissed me?"

"You came home, crawled into bed and cried for an hour."

"That's right. Because I was scared and thrilled and absolutely sure I'd just met the man I was going to be with for the rest of my life." The memory made her smile now, sweetly. Smugly.

"You were eighteen years old," Dora pointed out. "Overly dramatic and a virgin."

"So you're twenty-nine, overly dramatic and you've never been in love before."

A windy sigh. "Of course I have."

"No, you haven't."

Dora picked up a dust cloth. "I haven't said I'm in love with Jed."

"Are you?"

"I don't know."

"There," Lea said triumphantly. "My point exactly. If you weren't, you'd say so. Since you are, you're confused. Where is he, anyway?"

"Out." Because she felt she'd been outmaneuvered, Dora scowled. "I don't keep him on a leash."

"Testy," Lea said with a wise nod. "Another sure sign."

"Look, I'll analyze my own feelings when I have the time." She snatched up the cloth again and began to polish the already spotless countertop. "Ever since he came around, things have been upside down. The shop's broken into, the apartment's searched. I'm nearly raped and you—"

"What?" Lea was around the counter in two strides, gripping Dora's hands. "What did you say?"

"Damn." Though she tried to tug her hands away, Dora knew she'd already gone too far. "It wasn't really as bad as that. I exaggerated because you made me mad."

"Just hold on." Lea strode to the door, locked it and slapped the Closed sign up. "You're going to tell me everything, Dory, right now."

"All right." Resigned, Dora rubbed her hands over her face. "You'd better sit down."

It took some time, given that Lea interrupted frequently, but it was eventually told, beginning to end.

"I want you to promise not to tell Mom or Dad about this until I have a chance to."

"You go up and pack." Lea sprang to her feet. With her eyes glittering blue, she looked to Dora like a slim blonde angel ready to hurl her harp and halo. "You're moving in with John and me."

"I am not. Honey, I'm perfectly safe here."

"Oh, perfectly," Lea tossed back.

"I am. The police are looking for him, and they've even put guards on the building." She laughed then, adoring Lea.

"Jesus, honey, I'm sleeping with a cop."

That mollified, a little. "I don't want you left alone. Not for five minutes."

"For heaven's sake—"

"I mean it." The gleam in Lea's eyes left no room for argument. "If you don't promise, I'll get John and we'll haul you home with us. And I want to talk to Jed myself."

"Help yourself." Dora tossed up her hands in surrender. It was impossible to play big sister with a woman who was the dictatorial mother of three. "He won't tell you anything I haven't. I'm absolutely, completely safe. Guaranteed."

They both shrieked when the door rattled.

"Hey!" Terri shouted and banged. "What are we doing locked up in the middle of the day?"

"Not a word," Dora muttered, and crossed over to unlock the door. "Sorry, we were taking a break."

Terri pursed her lips as she studied the two women. The air smelled suspiciously of a family fight. "Looks like you both could use one. Busy morning?"

"You could say so. Listen, there's a new shipment in the back. Why don't you unpack it? I'll price it when you're done."

"Sure." Obliging, Terri shrugged out of her coat as she strode to the storeroom. She could always listen through the door if things got interesting.

"We're not finished, Isadora."

"We are for now, Ophelia." Dora kissed Lea's cheek. "You can grill Jed when he gets back."

"I intend to."

"And nag him, too, will you? I'd like to see how he handles it."

Lea puffed up with indignation. "I don't nag."

"World's champ," Dora muttered in her best subliminal voice.

"And if you think this is a joke, you're—"

"Hey, Dora." Terri poked her head out of the storeroom. There was a puzzled smile on her face, and the copy of the computer-generated picture of DiCarlo in her hand. "Why do you have a picture of the guy who came in Christmas Eve?"

"What?" Dora struggled to keep her voice even. "Do you know him?"

"He was our last customer Christmas Eve. I sold him the Staffordshire—the mama dog with pup?" She glanced down at the picture, wiggled her brows. "Believe me, he looks better in person than he does here. He a pal of yours?"

"Not exactly." Her heart had begun to dance in her chest. "Terri, did he pay cash?"

"For the Staffordshire? Not likely. He charged it."

Excitement rippled into Dora's heart, but she was actress enough to void it from her voice. "Would you mind digging up the receipt for me?"

"Sure." Terri's face fell. "Don't tell me the guy's a deadbeat. I got approval on the card."

"No, I'm sure it's all right. I just need the receipt."

"Okay. He had some Italian name," she added. "Delano, Demarco, something." Shrugging, she closed the door behind her.

"DiCarlo," Brent said, handing Jed a rap sheet. "Anthony DiCarlo, New York. Mostly small-time stuff: larceny, confidence games, a couple of B and Es. Did a short stretch for extortion, but he's been clean as a whistle for nearly six years."

"Not being caught doesn't make you clean," Jed murmured.

"NYPD faxed this to me this morning. There's a cooperative detective up there who's going to do some legwork for me. Shouldn't be too hard to find out if our boy has an alibi for the other night."

"If he has one, it's fantasy. This is him." Jed tossed the file photo onto Brent's desk. "Maybe I should take a trip to New York."

"Maybe you should give our friends in the Big Apple a little time."

"I'll think about it."

"You look pretty relaxed for a man who's thinking about kicking ass." Jed's lips twitched. "Do I?"

"Yep." Leaning back, Brent nodded. Lea would have commended him on his romantic radar. "That's what I thought," he murmured, and grinned. "Dora's quite a woman. Nice going, Captain."

"Shut up, Chapman," Jed said mildly on his way out. "Keep me posted, will you?"

"Sure." Brent waited until the door closed before he picked up the phone to report to Mary Pat.

18

HE did think about it. Jed knew Dora would be down in the shop, so he went straight up to his own apartment. He stripped down to gym shorts and a T-shirt before settling on the bench press. He'd think better after he'd worked up a sweat.

He had to decide how much to tell her. She had a right to know it all— but there was a matter of rights, and a matter of what was best for her. If he knew Dora, and he was beginning to think he knew her very well, she'd want to do something about it. One of a cop's biggest headaches was civilian interference.

Not that he was a cop, he reminded himself, and kept up a steady rhythm with the weights. But when a man had spent nearly half his life on the force, he couldn't be considered a civilian either.

New York could handle it. But they didn't have a vested interest. All Jed had to do was let the image of Dora's pale, unconscious face swim into his mind to remind him just how vested his interest was.

A trip to New York, some poking around wouldn't infringe overmuch on the official investigation. And if he could do something tangible, something real, he might not feel so . . .

He paused with the barbell fully extended and scowled at the ceiling. Just how did he feel? Puffing out air, he lowered the bar again, lifted, lowered.

Useless, he realized. Unsettled. Unfinished.

Nothing in his life had ever really had a closure because nothing had ever really been open to begin with. It had been easier to keep himself shut off, removed. Easier, hell, Jed thought. It had been necessary for survival.

So why had he joined the force? He supposed he had finally recognized his own need for order, for discipline and, yes, even for family. The job had given him all of that. And more. A sense of purpose, of satisfaction and of pride.

Donny Speck had cost him that; but this wasn't about Speck, he reminded himself. It wasn't about Elaine. This was about protecting the woman across the hall. The woman he'd begun to feel something for.

That was something else to think about.

He didn't stop lifting when he heard the knock, but his lips curved when she called his name.

"Come on, Skimmerhorn, I know you're in there. I need to talk to you."

"It's open."

"How come you make me lock mine?" she demanded. She walked in looking all business in a hunter-green suit, and smelling of sin. "Oh." Her eyebrows lifted as she took a long slow scan of his body stretched out on the bench, muscles oiled with sweat and rippling. Her heart did a fast somersault. "Sorry to interrupt your male ritual. Shouldn't there be drums pounding or some sort of pagan chant in the background?"

"Did you want something, Conroy?"

"I want a lot of things. Red suede shoes, a couple of weeks in Jamaica, this Böttger teapot I saw over on Antique Row." She walked over to kiss his upside down lips, tasted salt. "How soon will you be finished—I might get excited watching you sweat."

"Looks like I'm finished now." Jed rattled the bar back in the brace.

"You won't be so cranky after I tell you what I found out." She paused, dramatic timing. "Terri recognized the picture."

"What picture?" Jed slid off the bench, reached for a towel.

"*The* picture. The magic picture we put together on the computer. Jed, he was in the shop on Christmas Eve." Excitement had her pacing the room, heels clicking on bare wood, her hands gesturing. "His name is—"

"DiCarlo, Anthony," Jed interrupted, amused when Dora's jaw dropped. "Last known address East Eighty-third Street, New York."

"But how did you . . . Damn." Sulking, she shoved the receipt back in her pocket. "You could have at least pretended to be impressed with my skills as a detective."

"You're a real Nancy Drew, Conroy." He went to the kitchen, took a jug of Gatorade from the fridge and gulped it straight from the bottle. When he lowered it, she was standing in the doorway with a dangerous glint in her eye. "You did okay. The cops just work faster. Did you call it in?"

"No." Her lip poked out. "I wanted to tell you."

"Brent's in charge of the investigation," Jed reminded her. He reached out and flicked a finger over her bottom lip. "Stop pouting."

"I'm not. I never pout."

"With that mouth, baby, you're the world champ. What did Terri say about DiCarlo?"

"Brent's in charge of the case," she said, primly. "I'll go back to my own apartment and call him. He might appreciate it."

Jed caught her face in his hand, gave it a little squeeze. "Spill it, Nancy."

"Well, since you put it that way. She said he was very smooth, very polite." Moving around Jed, she opened the fridge herself, gave an involuntary and very feminine sound of disgust. "God, Skimmerhorn, what is that thing in the bowl?"

"Dinner. What else did she say?"

"You can't eat this. I'll fix dinner."

"DiCarlo," Jed said flatly, and took her by the shoulders before she could poke into his cupboards.

"He said he had this aunt he wanted to buy a special gift for. Terri said she showed him the Foo dog—which I'm now sure he helped himself to when he broke in." She scowled over that a minute. "She said he was a snappy dresser and drove a Porsche."

He wanted more than that. "Is she downstairs?"

"No, she's gone for the day. We're closed."

"I want to talk to her."

"Now?"

"Now."

"Well, sorry, I don't know where she is now. She had an early dinner date with some new guy she's seeing." Dora let out a huff when Jed walked out of the kitchen. "If it's important, you could catch her at the theater later. Curtain's at eight. We can grab her for a few minutes backstage between scenes."

"Fine."

"But I don't see what good it would do." Dora followed him toward the bedroom. "I've already talked to her, and we have the name and address."

"You don't know the questions to ask." After stripping off his T-shirt, Jed tossed it into a corner. "He might have said something. The more we know, the easier it'll be to break him down in interrogation. We've got a couple hours if you really want to cook . . ."

But she wasn't listening. When he turned back, she was standing very still, a hand pressed against her heart and a look of utter shock on her face.

"What?" Instinct had him spinning around, scanning the room through narrowed eyes.

"The bed," she managed. "Oh . . ."

His tensed muscles relaxed. The quick flutter of embarrassment annoyed the hell out of him. First she criticized his cooking, now his house-keeping. "It's the maid's year off." He frowned at the rumpled sheets and blankets. "I don't see the point in making it when I'm just going to mess it up again."

"The bed," she repeated, reverently. "French Art Nouveau, about nineteen hundred. Oh, look at the inlay." She knelt by the footboard to run her fingertips gently over the image of a slender woman in a flowing gown holding a pitcher. The sound that came from her throat was one a woman makes in the heat of passion. "It's rosewood," she said, and sighed.

Amused, Jed watched her climb onto the bed and examine the headboard on her hands and knees. "Oh, the workmanship here," she murmured. "Look at this carving." Lovingly, she caressed the curves. "The delicacy."

"I think I've got a magnifying glass around here," Jed told her when she all but pressed her nose to the wood.

"You don't even know what you have here, do you?"

"I know it was one of the few pieces in that mausoleum I grew up in that I liked. Most of the rest's in storage."

"Storage." She closed her eyes and shuddered at the thought. "You have to let me go through what you have." She sat back on her heels, all but clasped her hands in prayer. "I'll give you fair market value for whatever I can afford. Just promise me, swear that you won't go to another dealer until I can make an offer."

"Pull yourself together, Conroy."

"Please." She scrambled to the edge of the bed. "I mean it. I don't expect favors because of a personal relationship. But if there are things you don't want." She looked back at the headboard, rolled her eyes. "God, I can't stand it. Come here."

"Uh-oh." A grin tugged at his mouth. "You're going to try to seduce me so I'll lower my price."

"Seduce, hell." Her breath had already quickened when she unbuttoned her jacket, peeled it off to reveal a flimsy camisole in the same deep green. "I'm going to give you the ride of your life, buddy."

"Ah . . ." He wasn't sure which emotion was uppermost. Shock or arousal. "That's quite an offer, Conroy."

"It's not an offer, pal, it's a fact." She rose to her knees to unzip her skirt, wiggled out of it. When she'd finished, she knelt on the bed wearing the camisole, a matching garter belt, sheer black hose and spiked heels. "If I don't have you on this bed, right now, I'll die."

"I don't want to be responsible for that." God, his knees were weak. "Conroy, I'm covered with sweat."

She smiled. "I know." She made a grab, caught him by the waistband of his shorts. He didn't put up much of a fight. "You're about to get a lot sweatier."

She tugged. Jed let himself be taken down. When she rolled over on top of him, he caught at her hands. "Be gentle with me."

She laughed. "Not a chance."

She crushed her mouth to his, nipping his lips apart and plunging in a kiss that erased every rational thought from his mind. Even as he released her hands to hold her, she was pressing down on him, mercilessly rubbing heat to heat.

He pulled in air that did nothing more than clog thickly in his chest. "Dora, let me—"

"Not this time." Fisting her hands in his hair, she ravished his mouth.

She was rough, relentless, reckless, tormenting him to within an inch of sanity until he didn't know whether to curse her, or to beg. Sensation after staggering sensation whipped through him leaving his system churning and edgy and desperate for more. His hands streaked under her camisole and he tortured himself with the firm, ripe swell of her breasts.

She arched back at his touch. A low, feline sound of approval purred in her throat as she stripped the material over her head. With her head thrown back, she covered his hands with hers, riding them down over her torso, over her flat belly. Her fingers tightened on his when he drove her over the first, shuddering peak. But when he tried to roll her over, she locked her legs tight around him, laughing huskily at his oath.

She slid down, dug her teeth into his shoulder. He tasted of salt and sweat and hot-blooded male. The combination whirled in her head like a heady wind. He was strong. The muscles under her urgent hands were like rippled iron. But she could draw a breathless, vulnerable moan from him with the dance of her fingers. She could feel his heart thundering under her lips.

He clutched at the smooth flesh over the top of her stockings, too frantic now to think of bruises. Now, at last now, she let him lift her. His vision grayed when she lowered herself onto him, taking steel deep, deep into velvet. Dazed, he watched her body bow back, her eyes closed, her hands sliding up her own sweat-slicked body in an uninhibited caress as she tightened urgently around him.

Then she began to move, slowly at first, steeped in her own pleasure, absorbing shock after delirious shock. Then faster, still faster, the muscles in her thighs taut as wire, her hips rocking like pistons. Each time her body stiffened, the force of it ripped through him like a flame-tipped arrow.

He reared up, his mouth seeking her breast, her shoulder, her lips. Crazed, he dragged her head back by the hair, ravaging her throat while he made hoarse promises neither of them understood. All he understood was at that moment he would have died for her. He certainly would have killed for her.

The climax pummeled him, a violent and welcome fist that stole his breath and left him staggered. Jed banded his arms around her, pressed his face between her breasts and let it shatter him.

"Dora." He turned her head so that his lips could cruise gently over her skin. And again. "Dora." He held her close until her body had ceased to shudder. When he leaned back, his eyes narrowed. Lifting a finger to her cheek, he caught a tear on the tip. "What's this?"

She could only shake her head and gather him against her. She rested her cheek on his hair. "I thought after yesterday, it wouldn't get any better. That it couldn't."

It worried him, that tremor in her voice. "If I'd known an old bed would turn you into a maniac, I'd have brought you in here days ago."

She smiled, but her eyes were still troubled. "It's a terrific bed."

"I've got about six more in storage."

She laughed. "We'll kill ourselves."

"I'll risk it."

So would she, Dora thought. So would she. Because Lea had been absolutely right. She was in love with him.

Two hours later they arrived at the Liberty Theater in time to hear Nurse Nellie demonstrate how to wash a man out of her hair. Dora had taken Jed through the stage door and up into the wings. Her father was there, mouthing the lyrics and pantomiming the moves.

"Hey." Dora pinched his cheek. "Where's Mom?"

"In Wardrobe. A little problem with Bloody Mary's sarong. Jed, my boy." He pumped Jed's hand while keeping an eye onstage. "Glad you came by. We have an appreciative audience tonight, barely an empty seat in the house. Light cue," he muttered under his breath, then beamed at the glow of a spot. "A smooth cue is as exhilarating as a waltz."

"We just dropped by to see how things were," Dora said, and shot a warning look at Jed. "And I need a minute with Terri at intermission. Shop business."

"I don't want you pulling her out of character."

"Don't worry." She slipped an arm around his shoulders and, despite the fact that she'd seen the production countless times, was soon as absorbed in the staging as he.

Jed hung back, more intrigued by Dora and Quentin than the dialogue onstage. Their heads were tilted together as they discussed some minor bit of business that had been added to the scene. Quentin's arm came up to wrap around her waist; Dora's body angled toward his.

Jed experienced a sensation that shocked him more than a blow to the neck. It was envy.

Had he ever felt that easy affection, that simple sense of companionship with his own father? he wondered. The answer was very simple and very bleak. No. Never. He couldn't remember a single conversation that hadn't been fraught with undercurrents of tension, disillusionment, resentment. Now, even had he wanted to, it was much too late to make peace. It was certainly useless to try to understand why.

When the old bitterness threatened, he walked quietly back toward the dressing rooms. He'd have a cigarette and wait to question Terri.

Dora looked over her shoulder. Her smile faded when she saw he was no longer there.

"Dad?"

"And music," he whispered. "Good, good. Hmmm?"

"I'm in love with Jed."

"Yes, my sweet, I know."

"No, Dad. I'm really in love with him."

"I know." For no one else would he have broken his concentration. But he turned to Dora with a twinkling grin. "I picked him for you, didn't I?"

"I don't think he's going to want me to be. Sometimes I can almost see where he's bleeding inside."

"You'll fix that, given time. 'What wound did ever heal but by degrees?' "

"*Othello.*" She wrinkled her nose. "I didn't care for the ending in that one."

"You'll write your own. Conroys are excellent improvisers." A thought popped into his brain and made his eyes gleam. "Perhaps you'd like me to give him a little nudge. I could arrange a quiet man-to-man talk, with some of my special brew."

"No." She tapped a finger on his nose. "No," she repeated. "I'll handle this myself." Lowering her hand, she pressed it to her jittery stomach. "I'm scared," she confessed. "It's happened so fast."

"In the blood," Quentin said sagely. "The minute I saw your mother, I broke out in a vicious sweat. Most embarrassing. It took me nearly two weeks to get up the nerve to ask her to marry me. I kept going up on the lines."

"You never blew a line in your life." She kissed him as the applause broke out. "I love you."

"That's exactly what you should tell him." He gave her a squeeze. "Listen, Izzy, we're bringing the house down."

Responding to the applause, and the sudden chaos backstage, Jed went back to the wings just as Dora caught Terri.

"Hey, you working props tonight?"

"No." Dora got a good grip on Terri's arm. "I need to talk to you for a minute."

"Sure. How about that dance number? Those lessons I've been taking are paying off."

"You were great." With a nod to Jed, Dora steered Terri briskly through the stagehands and technicians. "We'll just need a corner of the dressing room."

Several other members of the chorus were already inside, repairing hair and makeup. Though some were stripped down to their underwear for costume changes, no one gave Jed more than a brief glance.

"Can I borrow this?" Dora asked, and commandeered a stool before anyone would refuse. "Sit down, Terri, get off your feet."

"You don't know how good that feels." She shifted toward the mirrors, choosing a makeup sponge to dab at the greasepaint moistened by sweat.

"About DiCarlo," Dora began.

"Who?" Terri stopped running lines in her head. "Oh, the guy from Christmas Eve." She smiled at Jed. "Dora's been real mysterious about him."

"What did he buy?" Jed asked.

"Oh, a Staffordshire figure. Never even winked at the price. He looked like he could afford it without any trouble though. And it was for his aunt. His favorite aunt. He said how she'd practically raised him, and she was getting really old. You know, a lot of people don't think that old people like getting nice things, but you could tell he really loved her."

Jed let her run down. "Did he show any interest in anything else?"

"Well, he looked all around, took his time. I thought he might bite on the Foo dog because he was looking for an animal."

"An animal?" Jed's eyes sharpened, but his voice remained cool and flat.

"You know, a statue of one. His aunt collects statues. Dogs," she added, relining her eyes with quick, deft movements. "See, she had this dog that died, and—"

"Was he specific?" Jed interrupted.

"Uh . . ." Terri pursed her lips and tried to think back. "Seems to me he really wanted a dog like the one his aunt had had who died—said he hadn't been able to find exactly what he'd been looking for." She freshened her lipstick, checked the results. "I remember he talked about the dog his aunt had—the dead one. I thought how we'd had that china piece that would have been perfect. It sounded like the dead dog had modeled for it. While he was alive, you know." She picked up a brush to fuss with her hair. "You know, Dora, the one you picked up at that auction. We'd already sold it, though."

Dora felt her blood drain. "To Mrs. Lyle."

"I don't know. You handled that sale, I think."

"Yes." Light-headed, Dora twisted her fingers together. "Yes, I did."

"Hey!" Alarmed, Terri turned on the stool. "Are you okay?"

"I'm fine." She forced a smile. She needed to get out. Needed air. "Thanks, Terri."

"No problem. Are you staying for the rest of the show?"

"Not tonight." Sickened, Dora fumbled for the door. "I'll see you tomorrow."

"Maybe you'd better go after her," Terri said to Jed. "She looked a little faint."

"Did you tell him about the china piece?"

"Yeah, I think so." Baffled, Terri slid off the stool and went to the door to see if Dora was in the corridor. "It seemed like such a coincidence, you know. I told him how we'd had something, but we'd sold it. I'm going to see what's wrong with Dora."

"I'll do it."

He caught up to her at the stage door, just as she was pushing through and drawing in deep breaths of air.

"Shake it off, Conroy." He held her by the shoulders at arm's length. He was afraid if he did more, she'd snap like a twig.

"I sold it to her." When she tried to jerk away, he merely tightened his hold. "For God's sake, Jed, I sold it to her. I don't know what he wanted it for, why he would have killed for it, but I sold it to her and the day after he found out—"

"I said shake it off." He all but lifted her off her feet, his face close to hers. "You sell lots of things—that's what you do. You're not responsible for what happens to the people who buy them."

"I can't be like that!" she shouted at him, and struck out. "I can't close myself off that way. That's your trick, Skimmerhorn. Make sure you don't give a damn, make sure nothing slips through and actually makes you feel. That's you. Not me."

That got through, and twisted in his gut. "You want to blame yourself, fine." Gripping her arm, he pulled her away from the door. "I'll take you home and you can spend the night beating yourself up over it."

"I don't have to apologize for having feelings. And I can get myself home."

"You wouldn't get two blocks before that bleeding heart of yours splashed on the sidewalk."

The buzzing in her ears came first. It always did when her temper snapped. Quick as a snake she rounded on him, leading with her left. He dodged that, but it was only a fake. Her sneaky right caught him in the jaw and snapped his head back.

"Son of a bitch." He saw stars. Later, he might take a moment to admire the fact that she'd all but knocked him on his ass. But now, eyes slitted with fury, he clenched his fists. She tossed her chin up in challenge.

"Try it," she invited. "Just try it."

It could have been funny—if there had been only temper in her eyes. If there hadn't been the quiver of tears beneath the dare. "Fuck this," he muttered. Ducking under her raised fists, he caught her around the waist and scooped her up over his shoulder.

She exploded with a volley of oaths, furious at the indignity of having to hammer at his back. "Put me down, you chicken-hearted bastard. You want to fight?"

"I've never coldcocked a woman in my life, Conroy, but you can be the first."

"Goddamn you, put me down and try it. They'll have to scrape you up off the pavement. When I'm finished, they'll have to pick you up with tweezers. They'll . . ." It drained out of her, as it always did, quickly, completely. She went limp, shut her eyes. "I'm sorry."

He wasn't finished being angry. "Shut up." He yanked out his keys, punched them into the door lock. In a smooth, economic move, he pulled her down, protected her head with his hand and shoved her into the car.

She kept her eyes closed, listening to him stalk around the car, open the door, slam it again. "I am sorry, Jed. I apologize for hitting you. Does it hurt?"

He wiggled his throbbing jaw. "No." He wouldn't have admitted it if it had been broken. "You hit like a girl."

"The hell I do." Insulted, she snapped up in her seat. The cool look in his eyes made her slump back again. "I wasn't angry with you," she murmured as he drove out of the lot. "I needed to vent at someone, and you were handy."

"Glad I could help."

If he was trying to chastise her with that frigid tone, she thought, he was doing a first-rate job. "You deserve to be mad." She kept her eyes lowered.

It was more difficult to take her sincerity, and her misery, than it had been to take the punch. "Just let it go. And Conroy? Don't mention to anybody that you got past my guard."

She turned back and, seeing the worst had passed, mustered up a smile. "I'll take it to my grave. If it's any consolation, I might have broken several fingers."

"It's not." But he took her hand, lifted it to touch to his lips. The stunned expression on her face had him scowling again. "What's the problem now?"

Since he'd released her hand she brought it up to her own cheek. "You threw me off a minute, that's all. The sweet routine hasn't exactly been your style with me."

Uncomfortable, he shifted in his seat. "Don't make me regret it."

"I probably shouldn't tell you, but bits of business like that—hand kissing and similar romantic gestures—make me all squishy inside."

"Define 'similar romantic gestures.'"

"Oh, like flowers, and long smoldering looks. Now that I think of it, you've done pretty well in the long-smoldering-look department. Then there's the big guns. Sweeping me up into your arms and carrying me up a curving staircase."

"You don't have a curving staircase."

"I could imagine I did." On impulse, she leaned over and kissed his cheek. "I'm glad you're not mad at me anymore."

"Who said I wasn't? I just don't want to fight when I'm driving." He lapsed into silence a moment. "About Mrs. Lyle," he began. "I'm going to need to check on her condition. If she comes out of it, she might put some pieces together for me."

"Us," Dora corrected quietly. "She's awake. Her niece came by the shop this morning." She linked her fingers again, tightly, and concentrated on keeping her voice calm and even. "She told me that Mrs. Lyle had come out of the coma, but that the doctors weren't committing themselves about her recovery."

"It's too late to try to get in to see her tonight," Jed said after a moment. "I can probably pull some strings tomorrow."

"I don't think you'd have to. I'd only have to ask Sharon—the niece." Dora kept her eyes straight ahead and tried not to resent the absence of concern in his voice. "But I won't do it unless I'm sure she's up to it. I won't let her be interrogated after what she's been through."

Tires spat out gravel when he turned into the lot. "Do I look like the gestapo, Conroy? You figure I'll shine a light in her eyes and find ways of making her talk?"

Saying nothing, she snapped down the door handle and climbed out. He reached the steps before her and blocked the way.

"Dora." Searching for patience, he took her hands. They were icy and stiff. "I know what I'm doing, and I'm not in the habit of badgering hospitalized old ladies for information." He looked down at her face. He didn't like to ask. He didn't like to need. But he found he had no choice. "Trust me."

"I do." Watching his face, she linked her fingers with his. "Completely.

This whole thing has shaken me up some, that's all. I'll get in touch with Sharon first thing in the morning."

"Good." A bit shaken himself, he lowered his head to kiss her. No, he didn't like to ask. He didn't like to need. But he did. "Stay with me tonight."

The worry cleared from her eyes. "I was hoping you'd ask."

19

DORA had never considered herself phobic about hospitals. She was young and healthy and hadn't spent a great deal of time in one, and never as a patient. When she thought of hospitals at all, she thought of babies in the nursery, bouquets of flowers and the brisk efficiency of the nursing staff striding down the corridors in crepe-soled shoes.

Yet standing outside the Critical Care Unit waiting to speak with Mrs. Lyle, she felt as if a stone were lodged in her chest. Too quiet, she thought. It was much too quiet, with death patiently lurking behind glass doors and thin curtains, waiting to choose. She could hear the muffled beats and hums from machines and monitors, like grumbling old women complaining about aches and pains. From somewhere down the corridor came the pathetic sound of low and steady weeping.

All at once she wanted a cigarette, with a razor-sharp craving.

Sharon stepped through the swinging doors. Though she looked strained, her lips curved into a smile when she saw Dora. "She's lucid. I can't tell you how good it felt to talk to her, really talk to her."

"I'm glad." Battered with both guilt and relief, Dora took Sharon's hand in both of hers. "Sharon, this is Captain Skimmerhorn and Lieutenant Chapman."

"Hello. Dora told me you want to talk to Aunt Alice."

"We've cleared it with her doctor," Brent said. "And we appreciate your cooperation."

Sharon's mouth thinned into a hard, bloodless line. "Whatever I can do to help you find the person who did this to my aunt. She's expecting you."

Jed read the concern in the way Sharon looked back toward the doors. "We won't tire her."

"I know." Her hand fluttered up, then came to rest on the child in her womb. There was family to protect. And there was family to avenge. "Dora said you'd be careful. You'll let me know, won't you, if you learn anything?"

"Of course they will." Dora steered her toward a bench. "In the meantime, you sit down. Get off your feet. Try to relax."

"We've only got fifteen minutes with her," Jed said quietly when Dora returned. "Let's make it count. You," he added with a nod toward Dora. "Do nothing, say nothing unless you get the go-ahead."

"Yes, Captain."

Ignoring her, he turned to Brent. "She shouldn't be going in at all."

"She's seen the statue, we haven't. Let's see if it means anything." He led the way through the doors, past the nurses' station and into one of the small, curtained rooms.

Dora was grateful she'd been ordered to silence. She couldn't trust her voice. The woman she remembered as elegant and enthusiastic lay on the narrow bed, her eyes closed and shadowed with dingy bruises. The formerly deeply black hair was dulled, and gray was beginning to show at the roots, and her skin was sallow against the startlingly white bandages. Her face was drawn, the cheekbones jutting up sharply against skin that looked thin enough to tear at a touch.

"Mrs. Lyle." Brent stood at the bedside, spoke quietly.

Dora could see the pale blue veins in the eyelids when they fluttered. The monitor continued its monotonous beep as Mrs. Lyle struggled to focus.

"Yes?" Her voice was weak, and rough, as if her vocal cords had been sandpapered while she slept.

"I'm Lieutenant Chapman. Do you feel able to answer a few questions?"

"Yes."

Dora watched Mrs. Lyle try to swallow. Automatically she moved forward to pick up the cup of water and slip the straw between the dry lips.

"Thank you." Her voice was a shade stronger. She focused on Dora and smiled. "Miss Conroy. How nice of you to visit."

Jed's order was easily forgotten. "I'm glad you're feeling better." She reached down to close her fingers gently over Mrs. Lyle's frail hand. "I'm sorry you were hurt."

"They told me Muriel is dead." The tired eyes filled slowly, the aftermath of a storm already spent. "She was very dear to me."

Guilt was like a wave battering against the wall of Dora's composure. She could stand against it, but she couldn't ignore it. "I'm so sorry. The police hope you'll be able to help them find the man who did this." She pulled a Kleenex out of the box beside the bed and gently dried Mrs. Lyle's cheeks.

"I want to help." Firming her lips, she looked back at Brent. "I didn't see him, Lieutenant. I didn't see anyone. I was . . . watching a movie on television, and I thought I heard Muriel—" She broke off then and her fingers shifted in Dora's for comfort. "I thought I heard her come in behind me. Then there was this horrible pain, as if something had exploded in my head."

"Mrs. Lyle," Brent began, "do you remember buying a china dog from Miss Conroy the day before you were attacked?"

"Yes, for Sharon's baby. A doorstop," she said, and turned her head toward Dora again. "I'm worried that Sharon's not getting enough rest. This stress—"

"She's fine," Dora assured her.

"Mrs. Lyle." Jed stepped forward. "Do you remember anything else about the statue?"

"No." Though she tried to concentrate, memories drifted through like clouds. "It was rather sweet. A watchdog, I thought, for the baby. Is that what he wanted?" Her hand moved restlessly again. "Is that what he wanted? The little dog? I thought—I thought I heard him shouting for the dog. But that couldn't be."

Jed leaned forward so that her eyes would focus on his. There was panic in hers, but he had to press, just a little further. "What did you think you heard him shouting, Mrs. Lyle?"

" 'Where's the dog?' And he swore. I was lying there, and I couldn't move. I thought I'd had a stroke and was dreaming. There was crashing and shouting, shouting over and over about a dog. And then there was nothing." She closed her eyes again, exhausted. "Surely he didn't murder Muriel for a little china dog."

"BUT he did, didn't he?" Dora asked when they stood together at the elevators.

"Not much doubt of it." Brent worried his glasses, stuck his hands in his pockets. "But that's not the end of it. The bullet that killed Muriel came from the same gun that killed Trainor." He looked at Jed. "Matched the ones we dug out of the plaster at the shop."

"So he came back for something else." Calculating, Jed stepped into the elevator. "The dog wasn't it—or wasn't all of it. Whatever *it* is."

"But the piece wasn't valuable or unique," Dora murmured. "It wasn't even marked. I only bid on it because it was cute."

"You bought it at an auction." Slowly, Jed turned the possibilities over in his mind. "Where?"

"In Virginia. Lea and I went on a buying trip. You remember. I got back the day you moved in."

"And the next day you sold the dog." He took her arm to pull her out of the elevator when they reached the lobby. "There was a break-in at the shop, Mrs. Lyle was attacked, then another break-in. What else did you buy, Dora?"

"At the auction. A lot of things." She dragged her hand through her hair, leaving her coat unbuttoned to the cold as she stepped outside between the two men. The brisk air helped blow away some of the sickly scent of hospital. "I have a list at the shop."

"Don't they have lots at auctions?" Brent asked. "Or groups of merchandise that come from the same place or the same seller?"

"Sure. Sometimes you buy a trunk full of junk just to get one piece. This wasn't Sotheby's; it was more of a flea market, but there were several good buys."

"What did you buy right before the dog, and right after?"

She was tired, down to the bone. The vague throb in her temple warned of a titanic headache in progress. "Christ, Skimmerhorn, how am I supposed to remember? Life hasn't been exactly uneventful since then."

"That's bull, Conroy." His voice took on an edge that had Brent's brows raising. He'd heard it before—when Jed had been interrogating an uncooperative suspect. "You know everything you buy, everything you sell, and the exact price, tax included. Now what did you buy before the dog?"

"A shaving mug, swan-shaped." She snapped the words out. "Circa nineteen hundred. Forty-six dollars and seventy-five cents. You don't pay tax when you buy for resale."

"And after the dog?"

"An abstract painting in an ebony frame. Primary colors on white canvas, signed E. Billingsly. Final bid fifty-two seventy-five—" She broke off, pressed a hand to her mouth. "Oh my God."

"Right on target," Jed muttered.

"A picture," she whispered, horrified. "Not a photograph, a painting. He wanted the painting."

"Let's go find out why."

Dora's cheeks were the color of paste as she groped for Jed's hand. "I gave it to my mother." Nausea rolled greasily in her stomach. "I gave it to my mother."

"I adore unexpected company." Trixie batted her luxuriant lashes as she hooked her arms through Jed's and Brent's. "I'm delighted you were able to find time in your busy day to drop in."

"Mom, we only have a few minutes," Dora began.

"Nonsense." Trixie was already towing the two men out of the postage-stamp foyer and into what she preferred to call the drawing room. "You must stay for lunch. I'm sure Carlotta can whip up something wonderful for us."

"That's nice of you, Mrs. Conroy, but—"

"Trixie." Her laugh was a light trill as she tapped a teasing finger against Brent's chest. "I'm only Mrs. Conroy to strangers and bill collectors."

"Trixie." A dull flush crept up Brent's neck. He didn't think he'd ever been flirted with by a woman old enough to be his mother before. "We're really a little pressed for time."

"Pressing time is what causes ulcers. No one in my family ever had stomach problems—except dear Uncle Will, who spent his whole life making money and none of it enjoying it. Then what could he do but leave it all to me? And of course, we enjoyed it very much. Please, please, sit."

She gestured toward two sturdy wing chairs in front of a crackling fire. She arranged herself on a red velvet settee, much like a queen taking the throne.

"And how is your charming wife?"

"She's fine. We enjoyed your party the other night."

"It was fun, wasn't it?" Her eyes sparkled. She draped an arm casually over the back of the settee—a mature Scarlett entertaining her beaux at Tara. "I adore parties. Isadora, dear, ring for Carlotta, won't you?"

Resigned, Dora pulled an old-fashioned needlepoint bell rope hanging on the left of the mantel. "Mom, I just dropped by to pick up the painting. There's . . . some interest in it."

"Painting?" Trixie crossed her legs. Her blue silk lounging pants whispered with the movement. "Which painting is that, darling?"

"The abstract."

"Oh, yes." She shifted her body toward Jed. "Normally, I prefer more traditional styles, but there was something so bold and high-handed about that work. I can see that you'd be interested. It would suit you."

"Thanks." He assumed it was a compliment. In any case, it seemed easier to play along. "I enjoy abstract expressionism—Pollock, for example, with his complicated linear rhythms, his way of attacking the canvas. Also the energy and verve of say, de Kooning."

"Yes, of course," Trixie enthused, bright-eyed, though she hadn't a clue.

Jed had the satisfaction of seeing sheer astonishment on Dora's face. He only smiled, smugly, and folded his hands. "And of course, there's Motherwell. Those austere colors and amorphous shapes."

"Genius," Trixie agreed. "Absolute genius." Dazzled, she glanced toward the hall at the sound of familiar stomping.

Carlotta entered, hands on the hips of the black sweatpants she wore in lieu of a uniform. She was a small, stubby woman, resembling a tree stump with arms. Her sallow face was set in permanent annoyance.

"What you want?"

"We'll have tea, Carlotta," Trixie instructed, her voice suddenly very grande dame. "Oolong, I believe."

Carlotta's beady black eyes scanned the group. "They staying for lunch?" she demanded in her harsh and somehow exotic voice.

"No," Dora said.

"Yes," her mother said simultaneously. "Set for four, if you please."

Carlotta lifted her squared-off chin. "Then they eat tuna fish. That's what I fixed; that's what they eat."

"I'm sure that will be delightful." Trixie waggled her fingers in dismissal.

"She's just plain ornery," Dora muttered as she sat on the arm of Jed's chair. It was unlikely they would escape without tea and tuna fish, but at least she could focus her mother on the matter at hand. "The painting? I thought you were going to hang it in here."

"I did, but it simply didn't work. Too frenzied," she explained to Jed, whom she now considered an expert on the subject. "One does like to let the mind rest in one's drawing room. We put it in Quentin's den. He thought it might energize him."

"I'll get it."

"An extraordinary girl, our Isadora," Trixie said when Dora was out of earshot. She smiled at Jed, but didn't quite disguise the gleam of calculation in her eyes. "So bright and ambitious. Strong-minded, of course, which only means she requires an equally strong-minded man to complement her. I believe a woman who can run her own business will run a home and family with equal success. Don't you, dear?"

Any response could spring the trap. "I imagine she could do whatever she set out to do."

"No doubt about it. Your wife is a professional woman, isn't she, Brent? And a mother of three."

"That's right." Since Jed was clearly on the hot seat, Brent grinned. "It takes a team effort to keep all the balls in the air, but we like it."

"And a single man, after a certain age . . ." Trixie aimed a telling look at

Jed, who barely resisted the urge to squirm. "He benefits from that team-work. The companionship of a woman, the solace of family. Have you ever been married, Jed?"

"No." Jed's eyes sharpened when Dora walked back in, carrying the painting.

"Mom, I'm sorry, I'm afraid you'll have to eat lunch alone. I called in to the shop to let them know I'd be delayed getting back. There's a little problem I need to see to. I'll have to leave right away."

"Oh, but darling . . ."

"We'll do lunch soon." She bent to kiss Trixie's cheek. "I think I have something Dad might like better for his den. One of you drop by and we'll see."

"Very well." With a resigned sigh, Trixie set down her cup and rose. "If you must go, you must. But I'll have Carlotta pack up lunch for you."

"You don't—"

Trixie patted Dora's cheek. "I insist. It'll just take a moment."

She hurried off, leaving Dora sighing.

"Very smooth, Conroy." Jed took the painting from her to examine it himself.

"Speaking of smooth." She turned back, smiling curiously. "Amorphous shapes?"

"I dated an artist for a while. You pick stuff up."

"It should be interesting to see what you've picked up from me."

"I don't even like tuna fish." But Dora bit into the sandwich nonetheless while Jed finished removing the frame from the canvas.

"I like the way she chopped up hardboiled eggs and pickles." Brent polished off his second sandwich with a sigh of satisfaction.

They'd chosen to work in Dora's apartment rather than the storeroom because there was both room and privacy. No one had mentioned the fact that Brent hadn't insisted on taking the painting or the information he'd gathered to his superior.

It was an unspoken fact that Brent still considered Jed his captain.

"Nothing in the frame." Still, Jed set it carefully aside. "Nothing to the frame, for that matter. We'll let the lab boys take a look."

"Can't be the painting itself." Dora washed down tuna with Diet Pepsi. "The artist is an unknown—I checked the day after I bought it in case I'd happened across some overlooked masterpiece."

Thoughtfully, Jed turned the painting over. "The canvas is stretched over plywood. Get me something to pry this off with, Conroy."

"You think there might be something inside?" She spoke from the kitchen, rummaging through drawers. "A cache of drugs—no, better. Diamonds." She brought out a screwdriver. "Rubies, maybe. They're more valuable these days."

"Try reality," Jed suggested, and went to work on the backing.

"It could be," she insisted, peering over his shoulder. "It has to be something worth killing for, and that's usually money."

"Quit breathing down my neck." Jed elbowed her away before prying at the plywood.

"It's my painting," she reminded him. "I have a bill of sale."

"Nothing," Jed muttered as he examined the backing he'd removed. "No secret compartments."

Dora glared at him. "There might have been."

"Right." Ignoring her, he tapped a hand on the back of the exposed canvas.

"That's odd. The back of that canvas has a lot of age to it." Dora pushed her way in for a closer look. "Although I suppose Billingsly could have painted over an old canvas to save money."

"Yeah. And sometimes people paint over paintings to smuggle them through customs."

"You think there's an old master behind there?" Amused, Dora shook her head. "Now who's dreaming?"

But he was paying no more attention to her than he would to a fly buzzing around the ceiling. "We need to get this paint off, see what's under it."

"Hold it, Skimmerhorn. I paid for this. I'm not going to have you screw it up over some cop's 'hinkey feeling.'"

"How much?" Impatience and disgust warred as he turned to her.

Pleased that he understood, she folded her arms over her chest. "Fifty-two dollars and seventy-five cents."

Muttering, he pulled out his wallet, counted out bills.

Dora tucked her tongue in her cheek and accepted them. Only her strong feelings for Jed kept her from recounting them. "Overhead," she said primly. "And a reasonable profit. Make it an even eighty and we'll call it square."

"For Christ's sake." He slapped more bills into her palm. "Greedy."

"Practical," she corrected, and kissed him to close the deal. "I have some stuff in the storeroom that should work. Give me a minute." Dora slipped the money into her pocket and went downstairs.

"She made you pay for it." Filled with admiration, Brent leaned back in his chair. "And made twenty-seven bucks and change on the deal. I thought she was kidding."

"I doubt Dora ever kids when it comes to money." Jed stepped back, lighted a cigarette and studied the painting as if he could see through the splashes of red and blue. "She might have a soft heart, but she's got a mind like a corporate raider."

"Hey!" Dora kicked at the door with her shoe. "Open up. My hands're full." When Jed opened the door, she came in loaded down with a drop cloth, a bottle and several rags. "You know, it might be better if we called in some expert. We could have it X-rayed or something."

"For now, we're keeping this to ourselves." He dropped the rags on the floor, then took the bottle. "What's in here?"

"A solution I use when some idiot has painted over stenciling." She knelt on the floor to roll back the rug. "We need a very careful touch. Give me a hand with this."

Brent was already beside her, grinning at the way Jed scowled when Jed noted where his eyes had focused. He crouched and spread the cloth.

"Trust me, I've done this before," she explained. "Some philistine painted over this gorgeous old credenza so it would match the dining room color scheme. It took forever to get it back in shape, but it was worth it." She sat back on her heels, blew the hair out of her eyes. "Want me to give it a try?"

"I paid for it," Jed reminded her. "It's mine now."

"Just offering to help." She handed him a rag. "I'd start on a corner if I were you. In case you mess up."

"I'm not going to mess up." But after he knelt beside her, he did indeed start on a corner. He dampened the rag and, working in slow, delicate circles, removed the end of the signature.

"Bye-bye, Billingsly," Dora murmured.

"Put a lid on it, Conroy." He dampened the rag again then gently removed the stark white paint, the primer. "Something's under here."

"You're kidding." Excitement bubbled into her voice as she leaned closer. "What is it? I can't see." She tried to crane her neck over his shoulder and got an elbow in the ribs for her trouble. "Damn, Skimmerhorn, I just want a look."

"Back off." His muscles tensed as he delicately removed more of the primer. "Pay dirt," he murmured. "Son of a bitch."

"What?" Refusing to be put off, Dora nudged him until she could crouch close to the corner. "Monet." She whispered the name, as though in church. "Claude Monet. Oh my God, I bought a Monet for fifty-two dollars and seventy-five cents."

"I bought a Monet," Jed reminded her. "For eighty."

"Children." Brent laid a hand on each of their backs. "I'm not much of an art buff, but even I know who this guy is, and I don't think anybody would have painted that abstract crap over the real thing."

"Unless it was being smuggled," Jed finished.

"Exactly. I'll run a check, see if there've been any art thefts in the last few months that included our friend here."

"It might have been in a private collection." Dora let her fingers hover over Monet's signature, but didn't touch. "Don't take off any more, Jed. You could damage it."

She was right. Jed stemmed his impatience and set the rag aside. "I know somebody who does some restoration work. She could probably handle this, and she'd keep quiet about it."

"The old girlfriend?" Dora asked.

"She isn't old." In an unconscious move he skimmed a hand over Dora's hair, resting his fingers on the nape of her neck as he looked over at Brent.

"You're going to have to take this to Goldman."

"That's the next step."

Jed looked down at the artist's signature against a deep misty green. "I shouldn't ask you, but I'm going to."

"How much time do you want?" Brent asked, anticipating him.

"Time enough to check out this auction house in Virginia and find the trail." He kept his voice even.

Brent nodded and picked up his coat. "I've got enough on my plate checking out DiCarlo. NYPD reports that he hasn't been seen at his apartment for a few days. Between that and trying to keep Philadelphia safe for women and children, I could let certain details slip my mind. You'd be doing me a favor if you could pull together what a china statue of a dog and a painting have in common. Keep in touch."

"I will."

"And watch your back. See you, Dora."

"Bye, Brent." She stayed where she was a moment. "How high a limb did he just go out on for you?"

"High enough."

"Then we'd better be sure we can pull a net under him."

"We?" He grabbed her hand as she got to her feet. "I don't remember anything about we."

"Then your memory's faulty. Why don't you call your friend the artist, then book us a flight for Virginia? I'll be packed in ten minutes."

"There's not a woman alive who can pack for a trip in ten minutes."

"Skimmerhorn." She spoke over her shoulder as she headed for the bedroom. "I was born on the road. Nobody packs faster than an actor ducking an opening-night bomb."

"I don't want you with me. It could be dangerous."

"Fine, I'll book my own flight."

"Goddamn, you're a pain in the ass."

"So I've been told. Oh, and make sure it's first-class, will you? I never travel coach."

WINESAP knocked lightly on Finley's office door. He knew his employer had just completed a forty-five-minute conference call, and wasn't sure of his mood. Gingerly, he poked his head inside. Finley was standing at the window, his hands clasped behind his back.

"Sir?"

"Abel. It's a fine day, isn't it? A fine day."

The trepidation curdling Winesap's stomach smoothed out like lake water. "Yes, sir, it is."

"I'm a fortunate man, Abel. Of course, I've made my own fortune, which makes it all the sweeter. How many of those people down there enjoy their work, do you suppose? How many go home at the end of the business day fulfilled? Yes, Abel, I am a fortunate man." He turned back, his face wreathed in smiles. "And what can I do for you?"

"I have a dossier on Isadora Conroy."

"Excellent work. Excellent." He beckoned Winesap forward. "You are of great value to me, Abel." As he reached for the file, Finley squeezed Winesap's bony shoulder with his free hand. "Of great value. I would like to demonstrate my appreciation." Opening his top desk drawer, Finley took out a velvet box.

"Thank you, sir." Humbled and touched, Winesap opened the box. "Oh, Mr. Finley," he said in a choked voice. Choked because he didn't have a clue what he was looking at.

It seemed to be a spoon of some sort with a large bowl and a short handle shaped like an eagle.

"I'm delighted you're pleased. I chose it from my own collection of caddy spoons. The pewter, I thought, suited you best. A strong, durable material often underrated."

"Thank you, sir. Thank you. I don't know what to say."

"It's nothing." Finley brushed away the gratitude. "A token only of my appreciation." He sat now, tapping his finger to his top lip. "You serve me well, Abel. I reward loyalty just as I punish betrayal. Quickly, precisely and thoroughly. Hold my calls for the next hour."

"Yes, sir. Thank you again."

But Finely had already quickly, precisely and thoroughly blocked Winesap from his reality. He opened the file and concentrated on Isadora Conroy.

20

IT was raining in thin chilly sheets when Jed drove into Front Royal. The weather had been miserable throughout the plane ride from Philadelphia International to Dulles, and promised to remain so. The defroster on the rental car worked at two speeds: blast and trickle. Each time Jed was forced to crank it up, the interior turned into a small, efficient sauna.

Dora chatted away on the drive, her easy voice and casual observations relaxing him. He wasn't required to respond, or even to listen. She had a way of making him absorb her mood even while his mind was working out the details of the next steps to be taken.

"If you ever went into the subliminal tape business," Jed commented, "you could make a fortune."

"Do you think so?" Dora flipped down the visor and used the attached mirror to freshen her lipstick. "Make the next two rights," she told him, and recapped her lipstick. "There's a parking lot in back of the building."

"Since there's a sign and an arrow, I probably could have figured that out."

"You're still ticked off because I pack faster than you do."

"I was not ticked off."

"Of course you were." With a bright smile on her face, Dora patted his arm. "It's a man thing. The way you insisted on doing the driving even though I knew the way was a man thing. I don't mind. I think it's cute."

"I did the driving because I didn't trust you not to end up in a five-car pileup because you were so busy talking about the ozone layer or ZZ Top."

"Ah." She leaned over and kissed his cheek. "You were listening."

"My ears are still ringing." Jed pulled up into a slot beside a battered Ford pickup. "Remember, Conroy, you're not here on a buying jaunt."

"I know, I know." She rolled her eyes as he climbed out of the car. "And you'll ask the questions," she continued. "I'll stand two paces behind like a good little girl and keep my mouth shut."

He waited until she'd shut her door. "That's right." He studied her while the rain dampened her hair. "It's a nice mouth—even if it runs most of the time."

"Well, that set my heart fluttering." She hooked her arm through his and started for the rear door. "It won't be warm inside," she told him as he pulled open the metal door with a screech of hinges. "But it'll be dry. Mr. Porter has a rep for extreme frugality. No frills, no shiny displays, but some pretty good bargains." She took a deep gulp of the air and her eyes kindled. "God, just look at this stuff."

He was. But what he saw was row after row of dusty furniture and smeared glass crowded with junk. There were tangles of jewelry, most of it outrageously tacky and all of it dull from disuse. An entire cabinet was stuffed with salt and pepper shakers, another with a variety of bottles that were none too clean. There was a Shriner's cap set jauntily atop a cracked gumball machine and several cardboard boxes filled with paperback books at ten cents apiece.

"I think that's a Maxfield Parrish print."

Before Dora could make a beeline, Jed snagged her arm. From the gleam in her eyes, he knew that getting her through would be similar to walking over hot coals. It would have to be done fast, and without any looking back.

"Where are the offices?"

"In the front, to the right. Jed, I only want to see—"

But he was already hauling her along while she tugged on his arm like a puppy straining at the leash. "Toughen up, Conroy. Your palms are sweating."

"This is really cruel," she muttered. But she lifted her chin. "Are you sure you don't want me to talk to Porter? Dealer to dealer?"

"I said I'd do the talking."

"Testosterone surge," Dora said under her breath.

The office was open but empty when they reached it. It looked to Jed to be the only space in the building that had seen a dust rag or scrub brush within the last decade. In contrast to the helter-skelter arrangement of the market, the desk was shining and neat, the file cabinets clean and tidily shut. The air carried the vague scent of some lemony spray wax.

"There's been some reorganizing since the last time I was here." Curious, Dora poked her head inside. The desk blotter was spotless, and on the left corner stood a good porcelain vase with fresh hothouse roses. "Last time there was a girlie calendar on the wall—from nineteen fifty-six—and the rest of it looked as though there had been a small bomb detonation. I remember thinking I didn't see how anyone could work in that kind of chaos." She caught Jed's bland stare and shrugged. "My kind of chaos is organized." She paused to look around and tried not to yearn too much toward the bargain table. "Maybe Porter's roaming through somewhere. He's easy enough to spot. He sort of looks like a ferret."

"May I help you?"

Jed put a hand on Dora's shoulder to keep her quiet and turned to the tidily dressed woman with glasses hanging from a gold chain. "We'd like to speak to Mr. Porter."

Helen Owings's eyes clouded and filled alarmingly fast with hot tears. "Oh," she said, and dug in her pocket for a tissue. And again, "Oh," as she mopped her streaming eyes.

"I'm sorry." Before Jed could react, Dora had her by the arm and was leading her into the office, into a chair. "Can I get you some water?"

"No, no." Helen sniffled, then began to tear the damp tissue into tiny pieces. "It was just such a shock, your asking for him. You couldn't have known, I suppose."

"Have known what?" Jed shut the door quietly and waited.

"Sherman—Mr. Porter's dead. Murdered." Though the word came out fruity with drama, Helen's lips trembled.

"Oh God." Dora groped for a chair herself while her brain did a slow, sickening spin.

"Right before Christmas." Helen blew her nose on what was left of her tissue. "I found him myself. There." She lifted a hand, pointed at the desk.

"How was he killed?" Jed demanded.

"Shot." Helen covered her face with her hands, then dropped them into her lap to twist them together. "Shot through the head. Poor, poor Sherman."

"Do the police have any suspects?" Jed asked.

"No." Helen sighed and began to draw on what was left of her rattled composure. "There doesn't seem to have been a motive. Nothing was taken that we can determine. There were no—signs of struggle. I'm sorry, Mr. . . . ?"

"Skimmerhorn."

"Mr. Skimmerhorn. Did you know Sherman?"

"No." He debated for a moment how much to tell her. As usual, he decided less was best. "Miss Conroy is a dealer in Philadelphia. We're here about some items that were auctioned on December twenty-first."

"Our last auction." Her voice broke. After taking a deep breath, she straightened her shoulders in an obvious effort to compose herself. "You'll excuse me for being so upset, I hope. We've just reopened today, and I'm still a little shaky. Was there a problem?"

"A question." Jed smiled with charm and sympathy. "Miss Conroy bought two pieces. We're interested in where and how you acquired them."

"May I ask why? We usually don't reveal our sources. After all, another dealer could come in and outbid us."

"We're interested in more background on the items," he said reassuringly. "We're not going to try to cut off your supply."

"Well . . ." It wasn't entirely regular, but Helen couldn't find any harm in it. "I may be able to help you. Do you remember the lot number?"

"F fifteen and F eighteen," Dora said dully. She'd remembered something else, something that made her stomach roll. But when Jed murmured her name, she shook her head.

"F fifteen and eighteen," Helen repeated, grateful for something practical to do. She rose and went to the file cabinets. "Oh yes, the F lots were from the New York shipment. A small estate sale." She smiled, taking the folder to the desk. "To be frank, Mr. Skimmerhorn, I believe most of the items were picked up at yard sales. I remember that the quality was not what I'd expected. Conroy . . . yes, you purchased both pieces. I'm afraid I can't tell you very much about them. I—"

The knock on the door interrupted her. "Miz Owings?"

"Yes, Richie?"

"We got a question out here about that Early American dry sink. People are in a hurry."

"All right, tell them I'll be right there." Helen rose, smoothed down her hair, her skirt. "Will you excuse me just a minute?"

Jed waited until she'd walked out before picking up the file himself. He scanned the lists, the inventories, the prices, then simply pocketed what he felt was relevant.

"What are you doing?" Dora demanded. "You can't do that."

"It'll save time. Come on."

"She knows my name."

"So, we'll make copies then send the originals back." He took a firm grip on her hand, but this time it wasn't necessary. She didn't try to linger or dig in her heels to study any of the dusty treasures. Once they were outside and in the car, Jed took her chin in his hand. "Okay, spill it. You went white as a sheet in there."

"I remembered Mr. Ashworth. I told you about him. He was the dealer I met at the auction that day. He bought a piece from that shipment."

"The guy who was killed during a burglary," Jed murmured. "You said his shop was around here."

"Yes, just a couple miles away."

"Then that's where we're going next." He switched on the engine. "Can you handle it?"

"Yes. But I want to stop and call the shop first."

"You've only been away a couple hours, Conroy. It should run well enough without you."

"I don't want Terri or Lea anywhere near the place." She set her jaw and stared straight ahead. "I want it closed."

"Okay." He closed his hand over hers and found it cold and rigid. "Okay."

* * *

ALTHOUGH he'd taken the precaution of packing an overnight bag, Jed had hoped to make the trip to Virginia and back in one day. There was no question of doing so after visiting Ashworth's shop.

Dora needed some downtime, and he was going to see that she got it.

She said nothing when he checked into a hotel near the airport. The fact that she'd said little throughout the rainy ride from Front Royal concerned him nearly as much as the information they'd gleaned from Tom Ashworth's grandson. In addition to Ashworth's death and the damage done during the break-in, the figurine had apparently been taken.

Jed unlocked the door of the hotel room, set the overnight bags aside, then pointed Dora toward a chair. "Sit down. You need to eat."

"I'm not hungry."

"Yes, you are." He picked up the phone and ordered two steaks, coffee and a bottle of brandy without consulting her. "Thirty minutes," he said when he hung up. "Which probably means forty. You've got time to stretch out."

"I . . ." Numb, she looked toward the bed. "I think I'll have a bath."

"Fine. Take your time."

She rose, picked up her bag. She didn't look at him. "Don't you feel anything?" she asked in a voice that cracked with fatigue. "Three people are dead—at least three. There might be more. People I care about might be in danger simply because they work for me. And you order dinner. Doesn't it make you scared? Doesn't it make you sick? Doesn't it make you anything?"

The last question lashed out like a whip as she clutched the bag to her chest and forced herself to look at his face. Jed met her eyes levelly. "Yeah, it makes me something. It makes me pissed off. Go take your bath, Dora. Tune it out for a while."

Wearily, she turned away. "It doesn't work like that." She closed the door quietly behind her. In a moment, he heard the water running in the tub.

He lighted a cigarette, swearing under his breath as he fought with the matches. She was disappointed in him—that's what had been in her eyes when she'd finally looked at him. And it mattered, maybe too much, what she thought of him, what she felt for him, how she looked at him.

She mattered too much.

He crossed to the bathroom door, lifted his hand to knock. Then dropped it again. There was nothing to be said, he thought. Actions were necessary. He went back to the phone and called Brent.

"Lieutenant Chapman."

"It's Jed."

"What have you got?"

"A couple of dead guys." Jed blew out smoke and automatically kept his voice low. "Sherman Porter, owned the auction house where Dora picked up the painting and the dog. Shot in his office right before Christmas. You might want to call the locals here for details."

"I've got it."

"Ashworth, Thomas, local antique dealer, killed during a burglary about the same time Porter bought it. He'd been at the auction with Dora, bought a porcelain figurine." Jed consulted his list. "A man and a woman, about two feet high, in period dress. Antebellum. He didn't keep it long."

"Value?"

"Negligible. I've got a rundown here of what else was in the shipment, and who bought what."

"You've been busy, Captain. Read it off, but take it slow. My short-hand's rusty."

When he'd finished the list, Jed crushed out his cigarette. "I'd appreciate it if you'd put a rush on running these people down."

"You don't have to ask."

"The shipment came down from New York, supposed to be from some estate sale, but the woman in charge seemed to think the stuff was yard-sale junk—not exactly what she'd been expecting. I've got the name of the guy who sent it down. I'm going to check him out tomorrow, in person."

"Let me have the name. We'll run a make on him just in case."

"Franklin Flowers, Brooklyn address. Any more on Mrs. Lyle?"

"Her condition seems to be stabilizing. She doesn't remember any more than what she told us."

"The painting?"

"Your old girlfriend's still working on it. Nice thought to have her working in your grandmother's place." A hint of amusement lightened

Brent's voice. "Your grandmother told me, in no uncertain terms, that the process wouldn't be rushed."

"You've got a man on her?"

"Twenty-four hours. I've had to blow a little smoke in Goldman's direction, call in a few favors. Reports are the duty includes petits fours and café au lait. I wouldn't mind pulling it myself. Give me your number in case I come up with anything tonight."

Jed read it off the phone. "Are you taking any heat on this?"

"Nothing I can't handle. Goldman decided to take an interest in Trainor's shooter. Did a standup in front of the courthouse. You know: 'When one of my men is killed, I won't rest until the perpetrator is brought to justice.' Film at eleven."

"We'll dump DiCarlo right in his lap."

The disgust in Jed's voice gave Brent hope. "If we can find him. Our boy seems to have gone underground."

"Then we'll dig him up. I'll call you from New York."

He hung up, leaned back against the headboard and smoked another cigarette. The water had stopped running. He hoped she was lying back in the tub, her eyes closed and her mind blank.

Dora was lying back. She did have her eyes closed while the hot water and bath salts slowly relaxed her body. It was more difficult to relax her mind. She kept seeing the way Helen Owings's eyes had filled and overflowed. She kept hearing the way Thomas Ashworth III's voice had thickened when he'd spoken of his grandfather. She kept remembering how pale and fragile Mrs. Lyle had looked lying in a hospital bed surrounded by machines.

Even in the warmth of the bath she could feel the memory of the cool barrel of a gun pressed against her breast.

Worse, she could still hear Jed's flat, dispassionate voice questioning the victims, and see his eyes, so gorgeously blue, blank out all emotion. No heat, no ice, no sympathy.

Wasn't that its own kind of death? she wondered. Not to feel—no, she corrected, not to *allow* yourself to feel. And that was so much worse. To have the capacity to permit yourself to stand to the side and observe and dissect without any of the grief touching you.

Perhaps she'd been wrong about him all along. Perhaps nothing really touched him, nothing got through all those carefully constructed layers of disinterest and frigid objectivity.

He was simply doing a job, putting together a puzzle, yet none of the pieces meant any more than a step taken toward a solution.

She stayed in the water until it began to cool. Postponing the moment when she would have to face him again, Dora dried off carefully, soothed herself by slowly creaming her skin. She let the towel drop, then reached for her robe.

Her hand hesitated, then brushed over the vivid green terrycloth. She'd let herself forget that side of him, she realized. The gentle side, the perhaps reluctantly-kind-but-kind-nonetheless side.

Sighing a little, she slipped into the robe. It was her own fault, she decided. She always seemed to look for more, and was always disappointed if more wasn't available. But it was so hard to settle, she thought, and secured the belt. So goddamn hard to settle.

She opened the door, letting out a flow of steam and scent. He was standing at the window, looking out at the rain. The room-service cart was beside him, set for two. He'd already poured himself a cup of coffee from the pot and was lifting the cup to his lips as he turned to her.

It was like a fist in the solar plexus, watching her come into the room. The bath had brought color back to her cheeks, yet her skin had that soft, fragile glow brought on by exhaustion. The hair she'd pinned carelessly up was damp from the steam. And quite suddenly, the air smelled only of her.

He'd dimmed the lights, not for romance but because he'd thought the softer light would comfort her. In it she looked fragile and lovely, like a flower under glass.

He forced himself to bring the cup the rest of the way to his lips and drank deeply. "Dinner's here," he said as he set the cup aside. "You'd better eat while it's hot."

His eyes weren't blank now, she noted. Nor were they disinterested. It was more than desire she saw in them, more basic, more needy than lust. It was hunger for woman. For her.

"You're trying to make things easier for me." Why hadn't she realized that before? she wondered.

"I got you some fuel, that's all." He started to pull out a chair, but she was crossing to him. Her arms went around him, her body pressed close, she buried her face against his neck. She made it impossible for him not to offer whatever he had in comfort. He held her like that, his hands stroking her back, and watched the rain stream down the window.

"I was scared," she murmured.

"You don't need to be." His grip on her tightened fractionally, then relaxed again. "Nothing's going to happen to you."

"I was scared of more than that. I was scared that you wouldn't be here to hold me like this when I needed you to. Or that if you were, it would be because it was a part of the job you couldn't graciously avoid."

"You're being stupid. I don't worry about doing anything graciously."

She laughed a little, surprised that she could. "I know. I know that. But you see, I got in your way." She tilted her head back so that she could watch his face, so that she could see what she needed to see there. "Pushing you to feel things you can't afford to feel if you're going to do what you have to do. Wanting you to have feelings for me you don't want to have."

"I don't know what I feel for you."

"I know that, too." She lifted a hand to his cheek, smoothing away the tension. "Right now you want me, so we'll make that enough." She touched her lips to his, gently, gently deepening the kiss. "Make love with me."

Need coiled in his gut. "That isn't what you need now."

"Yes, it is." She drew him toward the bed. "Yes, it is."

LATER, she curled against him, steeped and sleepy. He'd been so gentle, she thought. He'd been so patient. And, she knew, he'd been absorbed. It hadn't been only she who had forgotten, for that one stretch of time, why they were there. He'd given everything she'd asked for, and had taken everything she'd needed to offer. Now she listened to the rain and let her consciousness hang suspended just above sleep.

"The food might be cold," Jed said. "But you still need to eat. You looked ready to keel over when we walked in here."

"I'm feeling better." She smiled when he linked his hand with hers. He was doing things like that more often, she thought. She wondered if he realized it. "Tell me what we do next."

"We go to New York in the morning."

"You said 'we.'" She cuddled closer. "You're making progress, Skimmerhorn."

"Just saving myself an argument."

"Uh-uh. You like having me around. You might as well admit it."

"I like having you in bed. Most other times you're a pain in the neck."

"That may be, but you still like it." Dora pushed herself up, ran a hand through her tangled hair. "You did make me feel better."

He skimmed a fingertip over her nipple. "My pleasure."

She laughed and shook back her hair. "Not just that—though it was exceptional." Smiling gently, she rubbed her knuckles over his chin. "I like having you around, too."

He caught her wrist, held it. "Maybe you shouldn't. Maybe you should be running hard in the other direction."

"I don't think so."

"You don't know me, Dora. You don't have any idea where I come from, and you wouldn't understand it if you did."

"Try me."

He shook his head, started to get up.

"Try me," she said again, and made it a dare.

"I want dinner." He tugged his jeans on again and turned his back on her to uncover their cold steaks.

"Fine. We can talk while we eat." It wasn't an opportunity she was going to let slip by. Pulling on her robe, she took a seat at the room-service cart. He'd gotten only one cup for coffee. Obviously, she mused, he'd figured it would keep her awake when he wanted her to sleep. She poured some into the brandy snifter and drank it black and cool. "Where do you come from, Skimmerhorn?"

He was already regretting his words and the position they put him in. "Philadelphia," he said simply, and cut into his steak.

"Moneyed Philadelphia," she corrected. "I know that." So, she would prime the pump. "I also know that the money came from both sides, and that your parents' marriage had the scope of a high-powered merger." She shook salt onto her steak. "And that they indulged in a number of public spats."

"They hated each other, for as long as I can remember." He shrugged, but the movement was stiff. "You got the merger right. Neither of them was willing to let go of any of the joint assets, so they lived together in mutual disgust and animosity for twenty-seven years. And ironically—or maybe suitably—died together when their driver lost control of the limo and crashed."

"It was hard for you, losing them both that way."

"No." He lifted his eyes, met hers. "It wasn't. I didn't feel anything for them when they were alive but a kind of mild contempt. I told you, you wouldn't understand."

She waited a moment, eating because the food was there and filled a hole. "You're wrong. I think I do. You didn't respect them, and somewhere along the line you'd given up loving them."

"I never loved them."

"Of course you did. A child always loves until the love is abused badly enough—and often long after. But if you stopped, it was because you needed to. So when they died, if you felt anything, it would have been guilt because you couldn't feel more." She paused again, measuring him. "Close enough?"

It was a bull's-eye, but he wasn't ready to say so. "They had two children they didn't particularly want," he continued. "Elaine, and then me, because it was important to carry on the name. I was reminded of that over and over while I was growing up."

You're a Skimmerhorn. You're the heir. The least you can do is—not be so stupid. Show some gratitude. Be less of a nuisance.

"My responsibilities," Jed continued tightly, fighting back the ghosts of resentment. "And their expectations. Your parents wanted you to go into the theater; mine wanted me to make more money from the family fortune."

"And in our own ways, we let them down."

"It's not the same, Dora. Your parents' ambitions for you came out of pride. Mine came out of greed. There was no affection in my house."

He hated saying it, hated remembering it, but she'd spun the wheel and he couldn't stop it until it had completed the circle.

"Your sister—"

"Meant no more to me than I meant to her." He said it flatly, without passion, because it was pathetically true. "An accident of fate made us both prisoners in the same cell, but inmates don't always develop a fondness for each other. The four of us spent most of our time avoiding one another." He smiled a little at that, humorlessly. "Even in a house that size it wasn't always easy."

Though she knew he hadn't intended it, her sympathy was stirred. "Wasn't there anyone you could talk to?"

"About what?" He gave a short laugh. "It wasn't any secret that my parents hated each other. The fights they had in public were only the preliminaries. They'd always finish them up at home. If they weren't at each other's throats, they were at mine or at Elaine's. I turned to petty larceny, malicious mischief and short cons. She turned to men. She'd had two abortions before she was twenty. They managed to keep them quiet, just as they managed to keep my trouble with the law quiet. Shipping us off to boarding school didn't help. I got kicked out of mine, and Elaine had an affair with one of her teachers.

"In the end, they threw up their hands—it was one of the few things they agreed on. They made a deal with Elaine, settled a tidy sum of money on her if she married a handpicked candidate. I went to live with my grandmother. Elaine's first marriage lasted just shy of two years. I went into the police academy about the same time she was divorced. That really pissed them off." He picked up the brandy and poured generously. "They threatened to cut both of us out of the will, but they didn't want to let all those holdings fall out of the family. So Elaine went through another husband, I got my badge. And they died."

She felt too much—much more, she knew, than he would want her to offer. The pity for the child, the outrage on his behalf, the sorrow for a family that had had nothing to bind them together.

"Maybe you're right," she said slowly. "I can't understand how people could stay together when there was no love. Or how they could be incapable of giving it to their children. That doesn't mean I don't understand you."

"What you need to understand is that I may not be able to give you what you want."

"Then that's my problem, isn't it?" She took the brandy and poured. "It occurs to me, Skimmerhorn, that you're more worried I might be able to give you exactly what you want."

21

DORA had always loved New York. Years before, she had imagined herself living there. A loft in the Village, a favorite ethnic restaurant, a circle of Bohemian friends who always dressed in black and quoted from the latest esoteric literature. And a wacky neighbor, of course, who was always falling in and out of love with the wrong man.

But she'd been fourteen at the time, and her vision had changed.

Yet she still loved New York, for its unrelenting pace, its energy, its arrogance. She loved the people hurrying down the sidewalks careful not to make eye contact with anyone else, the shoppers burdened with bags from Saks and Macy's and Bendel's, the electronics shops that were perpetually having going-out-of-business sales, the sidewalk vendors with their roasted chestnuts and bad attitudes, and the blatant rudeness of the cabdrivers.

"Son of a bitch," Jed muttered as a cab cut him off with little more than a coat of paint to spare.

Dora beamed. "Great, isn't it?"

"Yeah. Right. I doubt a cop's written a moving violation in this hellhole since the turn of the century."

"It wouldn't be very productive. After all—oh, look!" Dora rolled down her window, craned her neck.

"You breathe out there, you're going to die."

"Did you see that outfit?" Dora narrowed her eyes, not against exhaust fumes, but to try to make out the name and address of the shop. "It was fabulous. It would just take me five minutes if you could find a place to park."

He snorted. "Get real, Conroy."

She huffed and plopped back in her seat. "Maybe after we're done, we could come back by. All you'd have to do is circle the block."

"Forget it. Aren't there enough shops in Philadelphia?"

"Of course there are. That's not the point. Shoes," she said with a long sigh and studied another storefront while Jed fought Madison Avenue traffic uptown. "They're having their after-Christmas sale."

"I should have known better. Goddamn it, get out of my lane!" he shouted, and took the aggressive route by gunning it past another cab. "I should have known better," he repeated, "than to have driven you through Manhattan. It's like offering a steak to a starving dog."

"You should have let me drive," she corrected. "I'd be more good-natured about it, and I wouldn't have been able to look at the shops. Besides, you're the one who wanted to check out DiCarlo's apartment."

"And we may get there alive yet."

"Or we could have taken a cab from the airport."

"I stress the word *alive*."

Dora was feeling very much alive. "You know, we could stay over tonight, book into some hideously expensive midtown hotel. Catch Will's play." She looked longingly at a boutique. "Shop."

"This isn't a sight-seeing trip, Conroy."

"I'm just trying to make the best of the situation."

Ignoring her, Jed made the turn onto Eighty-third. After a quick scan for a spot big enough to slip the rental car into, he did the sensible thing and double-parked. "I'm going to have to trust you."

"All right." She prepared to be trustworthy. "About what?"

"I want you to sit behind the wheel while I go in and check out Di-Carlo—run down the super, maybe a couple of neighbors."

Her mouth moved dangerously close to a pout. "How come I can't come in?"

"Because I want the car to be here when I get back. If you have to move it, you drive around the block, making no stops whatsoever for outfits or shoes, and park it right back here. Got it?"

"I'm not an idiot," she began, but he kissed her and got out.

"Lock your doors, Conroy."

When five minutes passed into ten, and ten into twenty, Dora began to consider leaving Jed a note telling him to pick her up at the boutique, then hailing a cab to get her there. She was just reaching into her purse for a notepad when Jed jogged back to the car.

He switched on the engine and waited for a chance to jump back into traffic. "Now, how the hell do we get to Brooklyn?"

"Is that all you have to say? You leave me sitting here for nearly half an hour, now you want a map to Brooklyn?"

"The super let me into DiCarlo's apartment."

"That's hardly an excuse." She fumed a moment in silence, but curiosity prevailed. "So? What did you find?"

"A couple dozen Italian shoes. Several Armani suits. A few bottles of Dom Perignon and silk underwear in a rainbow of colors."

"So, DiCarlo likes the finer things."

"I also found a checkbook with a balance of a little over seven thousand, a porcelain Madonna and several dozen framed family photos."

"He saves his money, hasn't forgotten his religious roots and appreciates his family. So far he doesn't sound like a cold-blooded murderer."

"And Ted Bundy had a pretty face and a nice smile." He turned on Lexington and headed downtown. "I also found some letterhead from E. F., Incorporated, based in LA with a branch here in Manhattan, a lot of paperwork from the same and about a dozen messages on his phone machine from Mama, cousin Alphonso, Aunt Sophia and some bimbo named Bambi."

"Why, because a woman is named Bambi, do you assume she's a bimbo?"

"My mistake." He snuck through an amber light. "Just because she called DiCarlo Tony-kins, giggled and left a message in squealing baby talk is no reason for me to assume she's a bimbo."

"That's better."

"What I didn't find was an address book, a passport or any cash. Given that, and the fact that his messages were unanswered, no one in the building has seen him for more than a week and his mail hasn't been picked up, leads me to believe he hasn't been around in a while."

"That's a reasonable deduction. Do you think he's still in Philadelphia?"

She said it lightly, but he caught the undertone of worry. "It's a possibility. No one's going to bother your family, Dora. There's no reason to."

"I think you're right. If he's there, he's waiting for me to come back." She grimaced. "Cheerful thought."

"He won't get near you. That's a promise."

Jed fought his way from Manhattan to Brooklyn Heights, fueled on cigarettes and the not entirely unpleasant sensation of jousting in traffic. By the time he found Franklin Flowers's address, he had fit together the pieces he had so far, jumbled them and let them reassemble. He slipped smoothly into a parking spot.

"Looks like you're in on this one, Conroy." He leaned toward her, ducking his head to get a better look at the storefront through her window.

F. FLOWERS

WE BUY AND SELL

"Who doesn't?" he wondered. "Don't forget, Conroy—"

"I know. You'll do the talking."

They entered the shop. It was hardly bigger than the average living room and crammed with merchandise ranging from ratty teddy bears to pole lamps. Though it was deserted, Jed heard a voice coming from the back room behind a beaded curtain. As the sign on the counter instructed, he rang a brass bell that had once graced the front desk of a small-time bawdy house in the Bronx.

"One moment, please." The voice was male, the words delivered like a song.

Flowers was as good as his word. Before Dora could finish her survey of a group of Avon bottles, he came through the curtain with a rattle of beads and a puff of fragrant smoke.

He was a big man, perhaps six-four, gone soft in the middle. Like his teddy bears, he had a round, homely face that radiated sweetness. His hair was parted nearly at his ear to allow him to comb strands of thin blond hair over a wide bald spot. Between two thick fingers he held a slim brown cigarette.

"Good morning!" Again he sang, like a kindergarten teacher reciting the ABCs. "No, no." Clucking his tongue, he glanced toward a row of ticking clocks. "It's afternoon already. Where does the time go? I never seem to be able to keep up. The world seems to move too quickly for me. And what may I do for you?"

Since Dora was busy admiring the jovial giant, she had no trouble letting Jed take the lead.

"Mr. Flowers?"

"Yes, I'm Frank Flowers, and this is my own little place." He drew delicately on his cigarette, exhaled through lips pursed as if for a kiss. "As you can see, we buy and sell almost anything. What can I interest you in today?"

"Do you know Sherman Porter?"

Flowers's jolly expression disintegrated. "Poor Sherman. I received word just two days ago. Tragic. The world we live in so often appalls me. Shot down like a dog at his own desk." He shuddered. "Hideous. Simply hideous."

"You sent a shipment to him," Jed continued when Flowers took time to sigh and smoke. "It arrived in Virginia on the twenty-first of December."

"Oh yes." Flowers smiled sadly. "Who would have guessed it would be the last time Sherman and I would do business together? Fate is such a cruel and capricious mistress. Nearly six years. We were associates and, I like to think, friends."

Jed pulled out the papers he'd taken from Helen's file. "There seems to be a question about the shipment."

"Really?" Flowers shuffled grief aside and frowned over the idea. "I find that odd. Helen never mentioned it—of course, it's understandable under the tragic circumstances, I suppose. But she certainly could have phoned me with any problem rather than sending you to New York."

"We had other business here," Jed said smoothly. "You purchased the merchandise from an estate sale?"

"A small one, yes, in the Catskills. Such air, such scenery. I picked up several minor gems. Several of the larger pieces I sold to other clients. It was impractical to ship heavy furniture to Virginia when I have outlets much closer to home."

He blew two neat smoke rings. "You see, I most often act as an agent for dealers. This little place"—he gazed fondly around his shop, a doting parent at a slow-witted child—"it's very dear to me, you see, but can hardly keep the wolf from the door. As I recall, I chose some very nice pieces for Sherman." Flowers put out his cigarette in a marble ashtray. "I can't imagine what problem there might be."

"The painting," Jed began.

"Painting?" Flowers frowned, set a fist on his hip. "I didn't send a painting."

"The abstract, signed E. Billingsly."

"Abstract?" Tilting his head, Flowers giggled like a girl. "Oh, my dear, no. I would *never* touch an abstract. Too bizarre for my tastes. And they're so hard to sell. No, I'm afraid there's been some mistake."

"Do you have a list of the inventory you shipped?"

"Naturally. I'm a bear for organization. An abstract painting, you say? No wonder Helen has a problem. I'll be back in a jiff."

He disappeared behind the curtains.

"Maybe he has a partner," Dora whispered. "And his partner put the painting in the shipment. Or maybe—" She broke off when Flowers stepped back in, carrying two files, one in sunny yellow, the other in bright red.

"I color-code, you see." Smiling, he set the files on the counter. "The yellow will be exactly what I purchased at the sale. He flipped open the folder. Inside were meticulously typed sheets listing merchandise, with descriptions. "Now that would have been . . . December twelve, I believe." He flipped briskly through. "And here we are, in January already. The time passes too quickly. Here now." Carefully placing the top pages facedown, he tapped a finger on the file. "Woodlow Estate, Catskills, December twelve. You can see this is the entire list, with the receipt attached. There's no painting."

Nor was there a china dog, Jed observed. Or a figurine matching the description of the one Tom Ashworth had died for.

"And this is one of my shipping files, specifically dealing with Sherman—God rest him. As you can see," he said as he opened it, "the top shipment was the last shipment—packing slip attached. Not a painting in sight." He grinned cheerfully. "It must have gotten mixed up with my things after uncrating. Sherman, bless him, was a teensy bit careless."

"Yes," Jed said. "I'm sure you're right."

*   *   *

"He's wrong," Dora stated as she pulled open the car door. "I saw the stockboy setting up that entire lot. It had just arrived."

"Yeah." Jed took out his keys, but he didn't start the car. His eyes were opaque as he jiggled them restlessly in his hand.

"There was a painting. I bought the damn thing."

"There was a painting," Jed agreed. "There was a china dog and a lot of other things. None of which are listed on Flowers's file. Not one item matches."

"Maybe he was lying." She looked back across the street and shook her head. "But I don't think he was lying."

"No, he wasn't lying." Shifting in his seat, Jed turned to her. "Tell me this, Conroy. If you were smuggling a Monet and several other illegal valuables, for your own use or for someone else's, and you'd taken the time to conceal them, to make them look ordinary—"

"I wouldn't have them shipped to auction," she interrupted, her eyes darkening with inspiration. "I wouldn't let them be purchased by people scattered all over the east coast."

"Because then you'd have to go to the trouble, and take the risk, of getting them back again—when you'd had them in the first place."

"So somebody messed up. DiCarlo?"

"Might be."

"What else?" she demanded. "There's a 'what else' in your eyes."

"The packing slips. The one in Flowers's file, and the one I lifted from Porter's. They were both from Premium Shipping." He started the car. "I've got some calls to make."

Dora drank endless cups of coffee and toyed with a club sandwich, using her time in the small Brooklyn restaurant while Jed made his calls from the pay phone to think the puzzle through. Taking out her pad, she began to make notes and diagrams.

"Looks like the Monet's genuine." Jed sat down and pulled Dora's plate to his side of the booth. "They'll need to run tests to be a hundred percent, but my grandmother and her pal gave it thumbs up."

"Who's her pal?"

"A guy she knows. Used to be a curator at the Met." He wolfed down a triangle of sandwich and signaled for coffee. "It also turns out that every name on the list, everybody who bought from the shipment, was hit during the period between the twenty-second of December and New Year's."

"Hit?" The blood drained out of her face. "You mean, they're dead?"

"No." Jed took her hand and gave it a solid squeeze. "Robbed. In each case, the piece they'd bought at the auction was taken. Sloppy jobs. From what Brent tells me they look like deliberately sloppy jobs. And there's still no sign of DiCarlo. He's some sort of vice president of the New York branch of E. F., Incorporated. He hasn't shown for work since before Christmas. He did call in a few times, but not since the end of the year. His secretary and his staff claim not to know his whereabouts. His mother filed a missing-person's report with the NYPD this morning."

"So, he's on the run." Dora picked up her coffee and missed the flicker in Jed's eyes. "Good. I hope he keeps running until he falls off a cliff. What do we do now?"

Jed moved his shoulders and chose another section of the sandwich. "If we can put enough evidence together to tie him to the murders in Philly and in Virginia, we can call in the Feds."

"You don't have to tell me you don't want to do that. I'm beginning to read you, Captain."

"I like to finish what I start." Idly, he turned her notebook around so he could read it. A smile tugged at his mouth. "Playing Nancy Drew again?"

"You're not wearing a badge, Skimmerhorn. I guess that makes you Joe Hardy."

He let that pass. Her diagrams interested him. At the top she had Premium Shipping, with lines leading off right and left. At the end of one she'd written Porter. The tail of the other ended in a question mark. Below it was a list of the inventory Flowers claimed to have shipped. Shooting down from Porter were all the names of buyers from the auction and their purchases. Another line connected her name with Mrs. Lyle's.

"What are you getting at here, Nancy?"

"It's a theory." Her spine stiffened at his tone. "I have two, actually. The first is that DiCarlo was double-crossed. Whoever he had handling the valuables pulled a fast one and shipped them to Virginia."

"Motive?"

"I don't know." She huffed and snatched up her coffee. "Some disgruntled underling he hadn't promoted, a woman scorned—or maybe just some hapless clerk who screwed up."

"That might work if the disgruntled underling or the scorned woman had kept some of the loot. And even a hapless clerk would be hard-pressed to screw up by sending a shipment of merchandise to some dinky auction house in Virginia where it's unlikely DiCarlo had any ties."

"For all you know, DiCarlo might have been using Porter's as a clearinghouse for smuggled merchandise for years." She tossed her hair back and scowled at him. "I suppose you have a better theory?"

"Yeah, I got one. But let's look behind door number two." He was grinning now, enjoying himself. He tapped her diagram. "What have you got here?"

"I don't have to take your superior amusement, Skimmerhorn."

"Indulge me." He lifted her hand, nipped at her knuckles. "Just for a minute."

"Well, it's obvious to me there were two shipments. The one from the estate sale, and the one with the smuggled goods. Since we agree that it would have been impossibly stupid for DiCarlo to have purposely shipped off his loot to Virginia where it would be offered for sale to the highest bidder, the logical conclusion is that the two shipments were mixed up."

"Keep going," he encouraged. "You're about to earn a merit badge."

"And since both packing slips originated from Premium, one could deduce that the mix-up happened there."

"Nice going, Nancy." Pleased with her, he pulled out his wallet and tossed bills on the table. "Let's go check out Queens."

"Wait a minute." She caught up with him at the door. "Are you saying you think I'm right?"

"I'm saying we should check it out."

"Nope, not good enough." She shifted her body to block the door. "Look me in the eye, Skimmerhorn, and say you think I'm right."

"I think you're right."

She let out a whoop of triumph and yanked open the door herself. "Then what are we waiting for?"

*   *   *

"You know," Dora said after they'd cooled their heels in Bill Tarkington's office for fifteen minutes, "most of police work is really boring."

"Thinking about giving it up, Conroy?"

She braced her elbow on the arm of her chair, cupped her chin in her hand. "Is this the sort of thing you did every day for all those years?"

He kept his back to her, watching the belts and the shipping clerks. "I couldn't calculate the number of hours I spent waiting."

She yawned, hugely. "I suppose it teaches you patience."

"No. Not necessarily. You juggle enough hours of tedium with enough moments of terror, and it teaches you not to relax your guard."

She could see his profile from where she sat. Only a part of him was in the room with her, she realized. Another part was somewhere he wouldn't let her follow. "How do you handle the terror?"

"By recognizing it, by accepting it."

"I can't imagine you being afraid," she murmured.

"I told you that you didn't know me. I think this is our man now."

Tarkington bounced up to the door, beaming his cheery smile. "Mr. Skimmerhorn?" He pumped Jed's hand enthusiastically. "And Miss Conroy. I apologize for making you wait. How about some coffee? A doughnut. Maybe a nice Danish."

Before Jed could decline, Dora was beaming at Tarkington. "I'd love some coffee."

"Just let me pour you a cup." Happy to serve, Tarkington turned to fill three cups. Dora sent Jed a smug look.

"We know you're busy, Mr. Tarkington. I hope we won't keep you long."

"Don't you worry about it. Always got time for a customer, yes sir. Cream? Sugar?"

"Black," Jed told him, and watched, slightly appalled, when Tarkington dropped a flood of sugar into one of the cups.

"Now then." He passed out the coffee, took a sip from his own heavily sweetened cup. "You had some question about a shipment, didn't you?"

"That's right." Jed reached in his pocket to read off the numbers of the shipping invoice he'd copied from Flowers. "A package shipped out of this building on December seventeenth from a Franklin Flowers, destination Sherman Porter, Front Royal, Virginia. Number ASB-54467."

"That's fine." Tarkington settled himself behind his desk. "We'll just call that right on up. What was the problem, exactly?"

"The merchandise shipped was not the merchandise received."

Tarkington's fingers dropped away from the keys of his computer. His face took on a pained look, as though he were suffering from intestinal gas. "Oh Lordy, Lordy, not again."

"You had this happen before?" Jed demanded.

Recovering, Tarkington punched keys. "I assure you, Mr. Skimmerhorn, Premium has a top-notch reputation. I can only say that the Christmas rush this year was unusually bad. December seventeenth, you said." His little eyes brightened. "That could be it!"

"What?"

"There was another complaint about a shipment that went out that very same day. The client was very upset, let me tell you. Not nearly as patient as you and Miss Conroy."

"DiCarlo," Dora said involuntarily.

Before Jed could snarl at her, Tarkington was beaming again. "Righto. Do you know him?"

"We've met." Dora kept an easy smile on her face.

"Isn't that a coincidence?" Shaking his head at the way of the world, Tarkington happily tapped keys. "This takes a weight off these old shoulders, let me tell you. I've done everything possible to locate Mr. DiCarlo's merchandise, and now it seems likely that the two shipments were mismarked and misdirected. I can't come up with a ready answer as to how that could have happened, but the solution seems simple as apple pie. I'll contact Mr. DiCarlo immediately."

"We'll take care of that." Jed scanned the computer screen over Tarkington's shoulder and noted the shipping clerk's name.

"That would save me an embarrassing moment." He slurped at his coffee and winked, showing Jed and Dora that they were, indeed, happy campers. "We will, of course, reimburse both you and Mr. DiCarlo for all shipping charges."

"Fine."

"I was right," Dora said under her breath as they walked away.

"Pat yourself on the back later." Jed walked up to the nearest clerk. "Where's Johnson?"

"Opal?" The clerk jerked his head toward another conveyor belt. "Over there. Line six."

"What are we doing now?" Dora asked.

"Checking tedious details."

Dora didn't find it tedious at all. Not when they'd sat with Opal in the employee lunchroom and listened to her story. Because she was obviously fascinated and sympathetic, Jed sat back, lighted a cigarette and let Dora play good cop.

He wasn't about to tell her, but he'd have said she'd been born for it.

"Can you believe it?" The excitement was drumming again as they made their way across the parking lot. "She drops a handful of invoices, and we end up with a smuggled Monet." She grinned as Jed unlocked the car door. "Maybe I like police work after all."

"Stick with selling knickknacks," Jed advised.

"At least you could say I did a good job."

"You did a good job. Don't get cocky."

"I'm not cocky." She slipped out of her shoes. "But now we know how, we know why and we know who. All we have to do now is find DiCarlo."

"Leave that one to the big boys, baby."

"You're going to turn it over?" Astonishment shimmered out of every pore. "You're going to turn it over now?"

"I didn't say that. I said it's time for you to step back."

"You're not making one move without me, Skimmerhorn. If I hadn't bought smuggled goods and ended up in the middle of this mess, you'd still be sulking and lifting weights."

"You want me to thank you for that?"

"You will. When you come to your senses." Relaxed, she sighed and smiled. "Sure you don't want to take me up on that expensive hotel?"

"I've seen enough of New York, thanks."

And he had something else to check out now. Bill Tarkington's computer screen had been a fount of information, including the intended recipient of DiCarlo's illicit shipment. Abel Winesap of E. F., Incorporated, Los Angeles.

22

THE chill in the air didn't prevent Finley from his morning ritual. Every day, regardless of the weather, he swam fifty laps in his hourglass-shaped pool while Vivaldi poured out of the speakers hidden in the jasmine plants. It was, to him, a matter of discipline. Of course, the water was heated to a pleasant eighty-three degrees—exactly.

As he cut through the warm water with strong, sure strokes, thin fingers of steam curled up into the cool winter air. He counted the laps himself, gaining arrogance and satisfaction with each turn.

The pool was his, and his alone. Finley allowed no servant, no companion, no guest, to sully his waters.

Once, when he had been entertaining, a tipsy acquaintance had tumbled in. The following day Finley had had the pool drained, scrubbed out and refilled. Needless to say, his hapless guest had never been invited back.

Now, he rose in the water, enjoying the sensation of having the water slice off his skin. Gooseflesh popped out over his body as he strode up the wide, curving steps, onto the terra-cotta skirt and into the snowy-white robe his butler held for him.

"Time?" he said, rubbing down briskly.

"Twelve minutes, eighteen seconds, sir."

The butler always stopped the clock at precisely that time. Once, he made the mistake of timing Finley at a bit over thirteen minutes. An ugly scene had followed, during which the man had nearly lost his well-paying job. Finley never went over twelve-eighteen again.

"Excellent." Smugly satisfied, Finley accepted his vitamin drink, a concoction created especially for him by his personal trainer. Even served in a Waterford tumbler, the thick, nasty-looking mixture of herbs, vegetables and Chinese roots tasted foul. Finley drank it quickly, as though it were the fresh, clear water of the Fountain of Youth. He'd convinced himself it was exactly that.

Finley dismissed the butler by handing him back both the damp towel and the empty glass.

Now that the first part of his morning ritual was behind him, Finley allowed himself to consider the problem of Isadora Conroy. It was not an altogether unpleasant problem, he mused. One couldn't become overly disgruntled at the prospect of dealing with a young, beautiful woman. He strode in through the French doors of the parlor as he reflected on the possibilities.

Secure in his power, Finley showered and groomed and dressed. He enjoyed a pleasant breakfast of fresh fruit, whole-wheat toast and herbal tea on the patio a few feet from where he had gut-shot DiCarlo. All the while he considered Isadora. When the solution came to him, he smiled, even chuckled softly, and blotted his lips.

It would work, he decided. And if it didn't—well then, he would simply kill her.

DORA was trying not to be annoyed. It was too predictable a reaction, she told herself, much too typical. Any woman would be annoyed if she awakened alone in bed without a clue as to where her lover had gone, or when he might be returning.

She wasn't *any* woman, Dora reminded herself. And she wasn't going to be annoyed—she wasn't even going to be mildly miffed. They were each free to come and go as they pleased. She wouldn't even ask him where the hell he'd been.

But when she heard the knock on the door, she tugged down the hem of her oversized sweatshirt, lifted her chin and marched into the living room.

"Okay, Skimmerhorn, you pig," she muttered. "This better be good."

She yanked open the door, searing words ready to leap off her tongue.

She had to swallow them back when she stood face-to-face with Honoria Skimmerhorn Rodgers.

"Oh." Dora pushed at the hair she'd bundled untidily on top of her head. "Mrs. Rodgers. Hello."

"Good morning, Dora." Not by the flicker of an eyelash did Honoria reveal her amusement in watching the changes in Dora's expressive face. The fury, the shock, the embarrassment. "Have I caught you at an awkward time?"

"No. No. I was just . . ." Dora swallowed a nervous giggle and smiled. "If you're looking for Jed, he doesn't seem to be around."

"Actually, I was hoping for a word with you. May I come in?"

"Of course." Dora stepped back, miserably regretting that she hadn't opened the shop that day and therefore hadn't dressed for work. She felt like a used dust rag in her Steelers sweatshirt and bare feet while Honoria swept in smelling of Paris and wrapped in a luxurious fur jacket.

"How charming!" The sincerity in Honoria's voice did a great deal to put Dora back on keel. "How utterly charming." Her appreciative gaze roamed the room while she tugged off her gloves. "I must confess, I often wondered about these apartments over shops on South Street. It's quite large, isn't it?"

"I need a lot of room. May I take your coat?"

"Yes, thank you."

As Dora hung up the mink, Honoria continued to wander the room. "I peeked in your shop window downstairs. I was disappointed to find it closed. But this"—she ran a fingertip along the sinuous, female lines of a Deco lamp—"is every bit as delightful."

"One of the best things about selling is that I can live with my stock as long as I like. Would you like some coffee, tea?"

"I'd love some coffee, if it's not too much trouble."

"Not at all. Please, sit down, make yourself at home."

"Thank you. I believe I'll do just that."

Honoria didn't consider herself nosy—simply interested. She was interested enough to study and approve Dora's view of bustling and artsy South Street from the tall living room windows. She also enjoyed and approved the decor of the apartment—warm and cozy, she decided, while remaining eclectic and a tad theatrical. Yes, she liked the room very much—a perfect mirror of Dora's personality.

The girl would do, she thought, and lifted up a tortoiseshell tea caddy to admire it. The girl would do very, very well.

"Here we are." Dora carried out a tray laden with a Fiesta ware pot and cups. She wished she could find some tactful way to dash into the bathroom and put on her lipstick. "Shall we take it in here?"

"That would be fine. Let me make room on the table for you. What a marvelous aroma. Scones?" Her eyes brightened. "How delightful."

"I always keep some around." Honoria's simple pleasure had Dora relaxing again. "There's something so civilized about scones."

With a laugh, Honoria settled herself. "You're very polite not to ask me what I'm doing knocking on your door at nine in the morning." Honoria sipped her coffee, paused, sipped again. "This is quite exceptional."

"I'm glad you like it." Dora waited as Honoria added a dab of blackberry jelly to a scone. "Actually, it's harder for me not to ask you about the painting."

"Good." Honoria let the scone lay on her tongue, sighing a little as she swallowed. "My dear, my mother would have been delighted with you. I haven't tasted better since she died."

"I'd be happy to give you the recipe for your cook."

"I'd appreciate it. Now." She sat back, balancing her cup and saucer with the uncanny skill only women of a certain class seem to acquire. "I believe you and I can trade information."

"Oh? I don't think I understand."

"My grandson asks me to keep a certain painting in my home, and to allow an old friend to work on this painting. I'm to do this in the strictest confidence, and with police protection." She smiled, inclined her head. "There is no explanation accompanying the request, of course."

"Of course." Returning the smile, Dora leaned forward. "Tell me, Mrs. Rodgers, why do we go along with him?"

"Call me Ria—my husband always did. We go along with him, dear child, because we care too much not to." A delicate pause. "Am I right?"

"Yes. Yes, you are. That doesn't make *him* right." Dora's earlier irritation returned in full force. "I'll tell you everything I know, Ria, then you can tell me the results."

"Precisely what I had in mind."

Dora started at the beginning. Jed would have several logical reasons, she assumed, why his grandmother should be spared the knowledge and the concern that accompanied it. Yet she rationalized that he had already involved Honoria, completely voluntarily. She was only providing the background as a matter of courtesy.

Honoria listened without interruption. She sipped her coffee, her reaction showing only in the darkening of her eyes, a thinning of her mouth, the occasional lift of a well-shaped eyebrow. There was temper, but there was also breeding.

And here, Dora thought, was where Jed had inherited his control.

"This has been terrible for you," Honoria said at length.

"Mrs. Lyle's the worst. No matter what Jed says, I feel responsible."

"Of course you do." This was said staunchly, and made Dora feel more comforted than a dozen polite denials. "You wouldn't be the woman you are if you didn't. This DiCarlo . . ." The name came through Honoria's lips ripe with cultured distaste. "Do the authorities have any idea where he might be hiding?"

"I don't think so." In a frustrated gesture, Dora lifted her hands, let them fall. "If they do, they haven't found it necessary to mention it to me."

"So like men. Do you know, I believe it goes back to when they had to crawl out of the cave and hunt for meat with rocks and clubs. The hunter." She smiled when she said it, with a kind of cool indulgence Dora admired. "Women, of course, were left in the cave to give birth in the dirt and the dark, to cook the meat on a dung fire and tan the hides. But men still thought they knew best."

"Jed hasn't even told me what's going to be done with the painting."

"There, you see?" Her point proven, Honoria refilled her coffee cup, then Dora's. "I wish I could tell you what his plans are, but he hasn't deemed it necessary to share them with me either. I can, however, tell you about the painting itself. It's brilliant."

Her face shone with emotion. "Though there are tests to be run, there's no doubt as to its authenticity. Not to me. It's one of his water lily studies, no doubt painted at Giverny." Her eyes went misty with dreams. Her voice softened like a woman speaking of a lover. "Ah, the light—ethereal and lyrical. That soft, seductive power that pulls you into the painting, makes you believe you can smell the damp flowers and still water." Her eyes cleared again. "He painted more than seventeen in that series."

"I know. Coincidentally, he's my favorite impressionist painter. I never thought I'd own one, even indirectly."

"I have one—a gift from my husband on our tenth anniversary. One of Monet's garden studies. Side by side, those paintings are breathtaking. Before the police took it away, I stood in my bedroom, looking at them, and weeping. I wish I could believe this DiCarlo had stolen it because of its beauty and not for its monetary value. That would make it almost understandable."

"You'd think they'd have let me see it," Dora complained. "I did buy it. But no, I wake up this morning and the bed's empty. Jed's gone off somewhere—and does he let me know where, or what he's up to? No. Not even a note under a refrigerator magnet. It seems to me—" She broke off, appalled. This was Jed's grandmother. His *grandmother*. "I beg your pardon," she managed.

"Not at all." To prove it, Honoria tossed back her head and laughed. "Oh no, not at all. I'm delighted. I do hope, my dear, that you'll give him hell when he returns. He's always needed it from someone who loved him. God knows he took enough of it from those who didn't. It's not at all the same thing, you know."

"No, I suppose not." Most of her embarrassment faded, but the flush remained. "Mrs. Rodgers—Ria, I wouldn't want you to think that I usually . . . develop intimate relationships with my tenants."

"You still expect me to be shocked." Thoroughly enjoying Dora's reaction, Honoria smiled and helped herself to a second scone. "I'll tell you why I married Jed's grandfather, shall I? He was an incredibly handsome man—very strong and blond and physically exciting. In other words, I was hot for him."

She nibbled delicately at the scone, her eyes alive with amusement. "Fortunately, Jed has inherited many of his grandfather's physical traits and none of his emotional ones. Walter Skimmerhorn was a cold, often cruel and incessantly boring man. All of which are unforgivable flaws in a husband. It took me less than a year of marriage to realize my mistake. To my regret, it required a considerably longer amount of time to correct it."

And the bitter dregs of that resentment still festered.

"You, on the other hand," Honoria continued, "have already discovered there is much, much more to my grandson than an excellent physique. If I were to give any advice to the young people of today in such matters, it would be that they live together—as you and Jed are essentially doing now—before marriage."

"We're not—" Dora's heart gave a quick and, to her embarrassment, decisively female flutter. "I hope I haven't given you the impression that we're thinking of marriage."

"Not at all," Honoria said lightly. Giving in to sentiment, she imagined the beautiful great-grandchildren Jed and Dora would make for her. "Now, Jed tells me your parents are Liberty Theater. I've enjoyed many productions there. I hope I'll be able to meet them."

"Ah . . ." Before Dora could answer, they were interrupted by another knock on the door. "Excuse me a minute."

More than a little frazzled by the mention of marriage, and the neat segue into her family, Dora opened the door. Jed stood on the other side of the threshold. He took one long look, running his gaze from her bare feet to the top of her tousled hair. She looked rumpled and sexy and deliciously flushed.

"Conroy." He snatched her to him and before she could speak had engaged her mouth in a hot, steamy kiss. "You got anything on under there?"

"Skimmerhorn." If she'd been flushed before, she was now painfully pink. "Your—"

"I'll find out for myself." He scooped her up and, covering her mouth again, stepped inside with her.

Desperately embarrassed, she shoved against his chest. "Skimmerhorn." After tearing her mouth from his, she sucked in a deep breath. "I think you'd better put me down and say hello to your grandmother."

"What?"

"Good morning, Jedidiah." Honoria brushed her fingers over her linen napkin. "Dora and I were just having some coffee. Perhaps you'd like to join us."

"Grandmother." To his credit, he said it easily, even if he did set Dora on the floor rather abruptly. "Were you waiting to see me?"

"Not at all, I paid a friendly call." She glanced over as Dora walked in with an extra cup and saucer. "Dora and I were exchanging views on Monet. It happens he's a favorite with both of us."

"It's police business now."

"Then where's your shield, Skimmerhorn?" Dora asked sweetly, and poured him a cup of coffee.

"Shut up, Conroy."

"His manners are my failing," Honoria explained. "I hope you'll forgive me."

"Think nothing of it," Dora told her. "I don't. Jedidiah," she said, delighted when he bared his teeth at her, "your grandmother and I would like to know what's being done with the Monet."

It seemed easier to give them something than to fight them both. "We—Brent," he corrected, "took the whole business to Commissioner Riker this morning. It's being kept under wraps for the time being."

"So," Honoria mused. "He went over that detestable Goldman's head. Wise. The man is a horse's ass and has no business being in command."

"Is that your *professional* opinion, Grandmother?" Jed asked, and earned the mild stare that had caused him to flush in his youth.

"You know, Dora," Honoria continued, "I made the mistake of never completely approving of Jedidiah's decision to become a police officer, until he resigned. I'm afraid I didn't tell him I was proud of him soon enough."

"It's always soon enough," Dora said.

"You have a very fluid sense of compassion." Well pleased with her morning's work, Honoria rose. "He'll need that. Thank you so much for the coffee. I hope I'll be welcome back."

"Anytime." Dora took Honoria's hand and did what Jed had yet to do. She kissed the woman's cheek. "I'll get your coat."

"I have an appointment shortly." Honoria tugged on her gloves. "So I don't have time to see your apartment."

"There's nothing to see," Jed told her flatly. But he took the coat from

Dora and helped his grandmother into it. "I appreciate your help in this." He bent down and kissed her, despite the discomfort of having Dora looking on. "I'd appreciate it more if you'd forget it now."

She only smiled. "I'd like you to bring Dora for dinner soon. Call me and we'll arrange it. Thank you again, dear," she said to Dora. "I'll come back when the shop's open. There was a piece in the window—the bronze huntress."

"Yes, I know the one."

"I'm very interested." With a quick wink at Dora, she sailed out.

"What a terrific lady."

"What did she want?"

"The basic courtesy of information." Dora started to lift the tray, then set it down with a rattle when Jed took her shoulder.

"If I'd wanted her to have information," he began with barely controlled fury, "I'd have given it to her."

"You opened Ria up when you took the painting to her. I'm sorry, Jed, if you're angry, but when she asked me directly, I answered."

"Damn it." Her calm sincerity was the pin that burst the balloon of his temper. "Do you know the tap dancing we're doing to keep this quiet?"

"I have some idea." She lifted a brow. "Do you think your granny's going to take out a full-page ad?"

His mouth twitched at the idea of the elegant Honoria being called his granny. "The fewer people who have the details, the better."

"Including me." Now she did lift the tray and walked stiffly into the kitchen with it. "That's why I woke up alone in bed this morning, without any explanation from you as to where you were going, what you were doing."

"Hold it. What the hell are you talking about?"

"Nothing." Her voice low and furious, she began to load the coffee things into the sink for rinsing. "Nothing at all. Go kill a bear with your bare hands, why don't you?"

"Conroy." Caught between amusement and exasperation, he leaned against the doorjamb. "You're ticked because I went out this morning?"

"Why should I be?" She rounded on him with hurt anger in her eyes. "I'm used to waking up in bed alone."

"Damn." Baffled, he scrubbed his hands over his face. "Look, I got up early. I didn't want to wake you. . . ." He remembered exactly the way she'd looked, curled in the bed, her hair spread on the pillow. Yes, he'd wanted to wake her up, he thought. But it hadn't been to tell her he was going out. "I went to the gym for an hour, caught breakfast with Brent. We had some things to go over."

"Did I ask you for an explanation?" Her voice was cold, but her temper was not as she shoved by him.

"Yeah." Cautious, he followed her back into the living room. "You did."

"Oh, forget it!" Disgusted with herself, she pinched the bridge of her nose between her thumb and forefinger.

"I really need to satisfy my curiosity. What does a woman wear under baggy football sweats?" He scooped her up again, nuzzled her neck on the way to the bedroom.

"Nothing important. In fact . . ." She laughed as they tumbled like wrestling children onto the bed. "Nothing at all."

"There's a hole in the shoulder."

"I know. I was mortified when your grandmother caught me in it."

"And a stain." He ran his finger between her breasts. "Right here."

"A nice full-bodied burgundy. It splashed on me when I was making lasagna." She sighed and slid her fingers into his hair. "I've been meaning to cut it up for rags, but—" She gasped, stunned when he ripped the shirt down the center.

"That ought to take care of it." Before she could decide whether to laugh or swear at him, he took her breast into his mouth and sent a quick and urgent greed swimming in her blood. "I've wanted to rip your clothes off since the first time I saw you."

"You—" Staggered, and aroused, she gulped in air as his hands stroked possessively down to her waist. "You shut the door in my face the first time you saw me."

"It seemed a more rational reaction at the time." He tore the sweatpants with one powerful twist of his hands. "I could have been wrong."

He leaned back, his hands over hers on the spread. The sun was bright through the open curtain, spilling generously over her face, her skin, her hair. The ruined clothes lay in tatters beneath her. It made him feel, however fancifully, like a warrior about to reap the spoils of war.

Her body, aware, aroused, alluring, quivered as though it were his hands rather than his eyes that skimmed over it. Her breasts were small, firm, milk-white, the nipples temptingly erect.

Lowering his head, he circled each rose-colored peak with his tongue until her breath was short and shallow and her body taut as a bowstring. The pulse at her wrists pounded like gunshots under his fingers.

"I want to watch you." His voice was thick as he took a hand from hers to slide between her thighs. From silk to velvet to damp satin.

The orgasm curled inside her like a snake, striking quickly, violently, so that her body reared up in shock when she cried out.

"It never seems to be enough," he whispered. He was surprised he could breathe. Watching Dora in pleasure was unspeakably erotic, uncannily seductive. She greedily consumed it, and she generously released it. Her capacity for giving and for taking passion was unstintingly honest and impossible to resist.

So he watched as she absorbed the aftershocks of sensation as he pulled off his clothes.

He needed to see her, to see every flicker and flash of emotion on her face. Kneeling, he lifted her hips, slid her slowly toward him, slipped slowly into her.

The sound she made at the mating was feline and throaty. He never took his eyes from her face, even when his vision dimmed and his control shattered.

"I owe you a sweatshirt." In a friendly gesture, Jed tugged his own over her head.

Dora examined it. "This is even rattier than the one you tore up." And she wouldn't have parted with it for diamonds. "Besides, you owe me sweatpants, too."

"Mine wouldn't fit you." He pulled them on, then stood looking at her as she sat on the edge of the bed. Reaching down, he twined a lock of her hair around his finger. "We could start a fire, and spend the rest of the morning in bed watching game shows."

She tilted her head. "That sounds incredibly tempting, Skimmerhorn. Why do you suppose I have this odd feeling that you're trying to keep me out of the way?"

"Out of whose way?"

"Yours."

"How can you be out of my way when I'm planning on spending as much time as possible on top of you?"

"You and Brent are working on something and you don't want me to know what it is." It was disappointing, and enormously frustrating, that he showed no reaction at all to her accusation. "That's all right." She shrugged it off and smoothed a hand over the rumpled spread. "I'll find out anyway."

"How?"

She smiled. "When I'm on top of *you*, I'll vamp it out of you."

"Vamp?" But he fought back a laugh as he worked a flattened cigarette out of his pack. "You can't expect me to concentrate on Bob Barker or Vanna White after a statement like that."

"Bob Barker?" She laughed, so thoroughly delighted with him she gave in to the need to leap up and into his arms. "Bob Barker? God, Skimmerhorn, I love you."

She started to lean back and kiss him senseless when she felt him stiffen. Very slowly, very quietly, her heart sank to her knees.

"Whoops." She fought for a light tone as she untangled herself from him. "Wasn't supposed to let that one out, was I? Sorry." Because the hurt was still swelling, she turned away, avoiding his eyes. "Chalk it up to the heat of the moment, or whatever works for you."

He wasn't sure he could get his tongue around a word, but finally managed her name. "Dora—"

"No, really." Oh God, oh God, she thought, panicked. She was going to cry if she didn't do something quickly. "It was just a slip of the tongue, nothing to get worried about."

Forcing a smile, she turned back. It was as bad as she'd feared. His face was set, his eyes absolutely blank.

"Listen, Skimmerhorn, the 'L' word comes real easy to me. My family boots it around like a football—you know us theatrical types."

She lifted her hand again, running it through her hair in that restless and lovely feminine gesture he'd grown so fond of.

"So look." Her voice was bright again, excessively cheerful. "Why don't you start that fire? I'll make us something appropriate to snack on while watching game shows."

She took a step forward, stopped. He hadn't moved, but had blocked her retreat through simple will.

"You meant it, didn't you?" He said it quietly, and the eyes that had fastened on her face made it impossible for her to hedge.

"Yes, I meant it." The defense came automatically. He watched as her shoulders straightened, her chin firmed. "They're my feelings, Jed, and I know how to deal with them. I'm not asking you to match them, or even to accept them if that's difficult for you." The first licks of temper glinted in her eyes. "And since it obviously bothers you so much to hear them, I'll be careful not to mention them again. Ever. All right?"

No, it was far from all right. He couldn't pinpoint the moment when things had changed between them any more than he could pinpoint his own feelings. But he could do something to stabilize what was becoming a dangerous situation.

"Get dressed," he told her. "I've got something I want to show you."

23

THE weather, at least, was promising. The sun beat hard against the T-Bird's windshield, giving Dora an excuse to slip on tinted glasses. However thin the defense, she felt better shielded.

As Jed drove north on Germantown Avenue under a vividly blue sky, she passed the time watching the pedestrian traffic. The temperature had risen to nearly fifty, allowing people to walk with a more cheerful step. They drove through the center of the city, far from the rivers with their frisky breezes, toward Chestnut Hill.

Not such a long way from South Street mile for mile, just vast distances of ambience and income.

He hadn't spoken since they'd started the drive. She didn't ask where they were going. She was almost sure she knew. His reasons for making the trip would soon become apparent—just as the consequences of her rash and impulsive declaration of love.

Rather than dwell on what was to come, Dora sat back and tried to enjoy the scenery, the beautifully restored homes and storefronts, the glitter of crystal and gold in the shops, the charm of the cobblestones beneath the T-Bird's monster tires.

Far up the hill the trees were old and stately, the homes trim and elegant. It was a neighborhood of minks and diamonds, of heirlooms and fat portfolios, of country club memberships and well-behaved lapdogs. She wondered fleetingly how it had appeared to a small boy growing up.

Jed pulled up in a narrow driveway beside a lovely old colonial. The brick had mellowed to a soft dusky rose and the trim was an elegant and unfaded Wedgwood blue. Tall windows glinted and winked in the strong sunlight, tossing back reflections while preventing the curious from seeing the secrets within.

It was a fine house, Dora mused. Beautifully maintained, perfect in its setting and somehow strongly feminine, with its neat lines and dignity. If she had picked it herself, she realized, for herself, it couldn't have been more perfect. The age, the tradition, the setting all clicked quietly into place with her image of the ideal family home.

She imagined it in the summer when the roses planted beneath those tall windows would be sumptuously blooming, carrying bold color and womanly scent. And in the fall when the big, leafy trees would burst into golds and scarlets. The picture was completed with lace at the windows and a dog in the yard.

And because she imagined so well, her heart broke a little. She doubted very much that Jed saw the house as she did.

Saying nothing, she alighted from the car to stand and study. Only a discreet portion of the city noise traveled up here, on the hill. There would be no camera-snapping tourists here searching for monuments, no bold flash of a blade skater careering down the sidewalk, no tempting scents of pizza and hoagies from a corner deli.

And wasn't that what she wanted? she asked herself. The noise, the smells and the freedom of being in the center of it?

"This is where you grew up?" she asked.

"That's right." He led the way to the door flanked with lovely beveled glass inserts. When he'd unlocked it, he stepped back and waited for Dora to go in ahead.

The foyer was two stories, tipped with a many-tiered chandelier that would graciously light the way up the grand oak staircase. The floor was tiled with large black-and-white squares of marble. Her soft suede half boots barely made a sound as she crossed it.

There is something richly fascinating about empty houses. There is the thin, echoing air and the sense of vastness. There is the curious wonder of

who had lived there, and what they had lived with, and the automatic pro-
jection of self into the rooms. There I would put my favorite lamp, and
here my little table.

Dora felt that fascination now, but it was tinged with a deeper curiosity
for where Jed had fit into the architecture and design.

She couldn't feel him here. Though she knew he stood beside her, it was
as though the part of him that mattered most had stepped back at the
threshold, and left her to enter alone.

The wallpaper with its tiny tea roses had faintly lighter rectangular
sections where paintings had hung. The bare foyer cried out for flowers,
she thought. Tall urns with freesia spilling out, bold stalks of lilies lancing
up and some pretty, welcoming rug over that cold marble to soften the
rigid formality of the entrance.

She ran her hand over the gleaming newel post at the base of the banister—a banister, she thought, fashioned for a child's bottom or a woman's
trailing fingers.

"You're planning to sell it."

He was watching her, carefully, as she wandered from the foyer into
the front parlor. Already, by simply entering, his muscles had tensed. Dora
was right, Jed wasn't seeing pretty flowers or welcoming rugs.

"It's on the market. Elaine and I inherited it fifty-fifty, and she wasn't
happy with any of the offers we received. I didn't really give a damn one
way or the other." Because they wanted to fist, he tucked his hands into the
pockets of his jacket. "So since she had a house of her own, I lived here
awhile." He stayed where he was when Dora walked over to study the
scrubbed and empty hearth. "It's mine now, and the Realtor's starting
over."

"I see." There should be family photos framed on the mantel, she
thought. Crowds of them jockeying for position, celebrating the births and
passage of generations. There should be an old Seth Thomas deep in their
center, gently ticking off the time.

Where were the heavy candlesticks with their tapers burned low? she
wondered, almost desperately. Where were the deep-cushioned chairs with
petit point footstools tilted toward the fire?

A fire would take away the chill, she thought, rubbing her arms absently as she wandered out again and down the hall. It was much colder than it needed to be.

She found a library, stripped of books; another parlor with a view of a cobbled patio that begged for flower boxes; the dining room, vast and empty but for another chandelier, and finally the kitchen, with its charming hearth and brick oven.

Here's where the warmth should center, she thought, with the sun streaming through the window over the sink and bread baking fragrantly. But she found no warmth there, only the cold, echoing silence of a house untenanted and unwanted.

"It's a pretty view from here," she said for no other reason than to fill the void. There should be a sandbox in the yard, she thought, linking her tensed fingers together. A swing hanging from the thick bough of the big maple.

"We weren't allowed in here."

"Excuse me?" She turned back from the window, certain she'd misunderstood.

"We weren't allowed in here," he repeated, and his eyes were on her as if the pecan cupboards and rosy countertops didn't exist. "Only the servants. Their wing was through there." He gestured but didn't look toward a side door. "Along with the laundry and utility rooms. The kitchen was off limits."

She wanted to laugh and accuse him of making it up. But she could see quite clearly that he was telling the truth. "What if you had a desperate craving for some cookies?"

"One didn't eat between meals. The cook, after all, was paid to produce them, and we were expected to do them justice—at eight A.M., one P.M. and seven in the evening. I used to come in here at night, just for the principle of it." Now he did look around, his eyes flat and blank. "I still feel like a trespasser in here."

"Jed—"

"You should see the rest of it." He turned and walked out.

Yes, he wanted her to see it, he thought grimly. Every stone, every curve of molding, every inch of paint. And once she had, once he had walked through with her, he hoped never to walk through the door again.

She caught up with him at the base of the stairs, where he was waiting for her. "Jed, this isn't necessary."

"Let's go upstairs." He took her arm, ignoring her hesitation.

He remembered how it had smelled here—the air heavy with beeswax and funereal flowers, the expensive clashes of his mother's and sister's perfumes, the sting of cigar smoke from one of his father's Havanas.

He remembered, too, when it hadn't been silent. When there were voices raised forever in anger and accusation, or lowered in disgust. How the servants had kept their eyes downcast, their ears closed and their hands busy.

He remembered being sixteen, and being innocently attracted to one of the new maids. When his mother had come across them harmlessly flirting in the upstairs hall—right here, he thought—she had dismissed the girl on the spot.

"My mother's room." Jed inclined his head toward a doorway. "My father's was down the hall. As you can see, there were several rooms between."

She wanted to sigh and tell him she'd had enough, but knew it wasn't enough for him. "Where was yours?"

"There."

Dora moved down the hall and peeked into the room. It was large and airy, bright with afternoon light. The windows overlooked the rear lawn and the tidy privet hedge that marched along the verge of the property. Dora sat on the narrow window seat and looked out.

She knew there were always ghosts in old houses. A building couldn't stand for two hundred years and not carry some memories of those who had walked in it. These ghosts were Jed's, and he was violently possessive about them. What good would it do, she wondered, to tell him how easy it would be to exorcise them?

It only needed people. Someone to run laughing down the steps or to curl up dreaming by a fire. It only needed children slamming doors and racing in the halls.

"There used to be a chestnut tree out there. I'd go out that way at night, hitch a ride and go down to Market Street to raise hell. One night, one of the servants spotted me and reported it to my father. He had the tree cut down the next day. Then he came up here, locked the door and beat the hell out of me. I was fourteen." He said it without emotion, took out a cigarette, lighted it. "That's when I started lifting weights." His eyes flashed through the smoke. "He wasn't going to beat me again. If he tried, I was damn well going to be strong enough to take him. A couple of years later, I did. And that's how I earned boarding school."

Something sour rose up in her throat. She forced herself to swallow it. "You expect that to be hard for me to understand," she said quietly. "Because my father never raised a hand to us. Not even when we deserved it."

Jed considered the tip of his cigarette before tapping the ash on the floor. "My father had big hands. He didn't use them often, but when he did, it was without control."

"And your mother?"

"She preferred throwing things, expensive things. She knocked me unconscious once with a Meissen vase, and then took the two thousand in damages out of my college fund."

Dora nodded, continued to stare out the window while she struggled not to be sick. "Your sister?"

"They vacillated between treating her like a Dresden doll and an inmate. Tea parties one day, locked doors the next." He shrugged. "They wanted her to be the perfect lady, the virginal debutante who would follow the Skimmerhorn rules and marry well. Whenever she didn't conform, they put her in solitary."

"Excuse me?"

"Locked her in her room, a couple of days, maybe a week. Then they'd bribe her with shopping sprees or parties until she did what they wanted." To combat the bitterness in his mouth, he took another drag. "You'd have thought sharing the misery would have made us close, but somehow it never did. We didn't give a damn about each other."

Slowly, she turned her head, looked at him over her shoulder. "You don't need to apologize to me for your feelings."

"I'm not apologizing." He snapped the words out. "I'm explaining them." And he refused to let her unquestioning compassion soothe him.

"I got the call to go see Elaine—supposedly from one of her staff, but it was one of Speck's men. They wanted me on the scene when it happened.

They knew she went out every Wednesday at eleven to have her hair done. I didn't." His gaze lifted again, latched onto Dora's. "I knew nothing about her, wanted to know nothing about her. I was minutes away from her house, and royally pissed at being summoned, when the dispatch came through with the bomb threat. You could say Speck had a good sense of timing."

He paused a moment, walked over to the small hearth and crushed out the cigarette on the stone. "I was first on the scene, just as Speck planned. I could see her in the car when I was running. The roses were blooming," he said softly, seeing it all perfectly again, not like a film, not like a dream, but stark reality. "She looked toward me. I could see the surprise on her face— and the irritation. Elaine didn't like to have her routine interrupted, and I imagine she was ticked off at the idea of the neighbors seeing me run across the lawn with my weapon out. Then she turned the key, and the car went up. The blast knocked me back into the roses."

"You tried to save her, Jed."

"I didn't save her," he said flatly. "That's for me to live with, and the guilt of it because she meant no more to me than a stranger. Less, because she wasn't a stranger. We lived in this house together for nearly eighteen years, and we shared nothing."

She turned back then, and sat quietly. Jed felt a quick jolt of surprise at how lovely, how perfect she looked there with the sun pouring liquidly around her, her eyes calm and watchful, her mouth solemn. Odd, he thought, there had never been anything in this house he'd considered beautiful. Until now.

"I understand why you brought me here," she began. "Why you felt you had to—but you didn't have to. I'm glad you did, but it wasn't neces- sary." She sighed then and let her hands rest in her lap. "You wanted me to see a cold, empty house where very little is left but the unhappiness that used to live here. And you wanted me to understand that, like the house, you have nothing to offer."

He had a need, an almost desperate one, to step forward and rest his head in her lap. "I don't have anything to offer."

"You don't want to," she corrected. "And considering the role models in your life, it's certainly logical. The problem is, Skimmerhorn, emotions just aren't logical. Mine aren't." She tilted her head and the sun creamed over her skin, warming it, as her voice was warm, as the room was warm with her in it. "I told you I love you, and you'd probably have preferred a slap in the face, but there it is. I didn't mean to say it—or maybe I did."

In a vulnerable and weary gesture, she brushed a hand through her hair. "Maybe I did," she repeated softly. "Because even though I understood how you might react, I'm just not used to bottling my feelings inside. But they are my feelings, Jed. They don't ask you for anything."

"When a woman tells a man she loves him, she's asking for everything."

"Is that how you see it?" She smiled a little, but her eyes were dulled with sadness. "Let me tell you how I see it. Love's a gift, and can certainly be refused. Refusing doesn't destroy the gift, it simply puts it aside. You're free to do that. I'm not asking for a gift in return. It's not that I don't want it, but I don't expect it."

She rose then and, crossing the room, took his face gently in her hands. Her eyes were still sad, but there was a bottomless compassion in them that humbled him. "Take what's offered, Jed, especially when it's offered generously and without expectations. I won't keep throwing it in your face. That would only embarrass us both."

"You're leaving yourself open, Dora."

"I know. It feels right to me." She kissed him, one cheek, the other, then his mouth. "Relax and enjoy, Skimmerhorn. I intend to."

"I'm not what you need." But he gathered her close and held on. Because she was what he needed. She was so exactly what he needed.

"You're wrong." She closed her eyes and willed the threatening tears away. "You're wrong about the house, too. You're both just waiting."

HE kept losing his train of thought. Jed knew the details he and Brent discussed were vital, but he kept seeing Dora sitting on the window seat of his old, hated room, with sunlight pooling around her.

And he kept remembering the way her hands had felt against his face when she'd smiled and asked him to accept love.

"Jed, you're making me feel like a boring history teacher."

Jed blinked, focused. "What?"

"Exactly." Blowing out a breath, Brent leaned back in his desk chair. "You want to tell me what's on your mind?"

"It's nothing." He washed the mood away with some of the station house's atomic coffee. "What you've picked up on Winesap makes it look like he's another underling. I still think the best way to handle this is to approach the top man, Finley. Not directly. The longer we can keep the smuggled painting under wraps, the better."

"What I can gather on the guy wouldn't fill a teacup," Brent complained. "He's rich—rich enough to make you look like a piker, pal—successful, single, obsessively private."

"And as the head of a large import-export firm, would be the perfect warehouse for smuggled goods."

"If wishing only made it so," Brent murmured. "We've got no hard evidence on Finley. Sure, the shipment was addressed to his assistant, and DiCarlo works for him."

"DiCarlo's small-time, a hustler. You've only got to look at his rap sheet."

"And Finley has no rap sheet. He's the American ideal, a modest self-made man and a solid citizen."

"Then a little digging shouldn't hurt him," Jed pointed out. "I want to take a trip to LA."

"I thought that was where this was leading." Uncomfortable, Brent shifted. "Listen, Jed, I know you've got a personal investment in this. The department wouldn't have diddly without you."

"But," Jed interrupted, "I'm not with the department."

Feeling miserable, Brent pushed at his glasses, fiddled with papers on his desk. "Goldman's asking questions."

"Maybe it's time you answered them."

"The commissioner thinks so."

"I'm a civilian, Brent. There's nothing to stop me from taking a trip to the coast—at my own expense, on my own time."

"Why don't you cut the crap?" Brent blurted out. "I know you've got a meeting with the commissioner in an hour, and we both know what he's going to say. You can't keep straddling this. Make my life easier and tell me you're coming back on the job."

"I can't tell you that. I *can* tell you I'm thinking about it."

The oath dried up on Brent's tongue. "Seriously?"

"More seriously than I ever thought I would." Jed rose and paced to the frosted glass door, to the scarred file cabinets, to the coffeepot thick with dregs. "Goddamn, I miss this place." Nearly amused at himself, Jed turned back. "Isn't that some shit? I miss it—every minute of the tedium, the fucking reports, the candy-assed rookies. Nine mornings out of ten I reach for my shoulder harness before I remember it's not there. I even thought about buying one of those frigging police scanners so I'd know what the hell's going on."

"Hallelujah." Brent folded his hands, prayerlike. "Let me tell Goldman. Please, let me be the one."

"I didn't say I was coming back."

"Yeah, you did." On impulse Brent leaped up, grabbed Jed by the shoulders and kissed him.

"Christ, Chapman. Get a grip."

"The men are going to welcome you back like a god. What does Dora think about it?"

Jed's foolish grin faded. "She doesn't think anything. We haven't talked about it. It doesn't concern her."

"Oh." Brent tucked his tongue in his cheek. "Uh-huh. Mary Pat and I have a bet. She says I'll be renting a tux as best man by the end of the school year. I say Easter vacation. We tend to mark time by the school calendar."

The quick flutter of panic in Jed's stomach staggered him. "You're off base."

"Come on, Captain, you're crazy about her. Ten minutes ago you were staring into space daydreaming. And if she wasn't the star of the show, I'll kiss Goldman on the mouth."

"You're awful free with your affections these days. Drop it, will you?"

He knew that tone of voice—the verbal equivalent of a brick wall. "Okay, but I've got dinner for two at the Chart House riding on you." Brent leaned back on the edge of his desk. "I'd appreciate a rundown of what you and the commissioner come up with. Whether you go to LA officially or not, I can arrange some backup."

"We'll touch base tomorrow."

"And, Captain," Brent added before Jed made it to the door. "Do me a favor and let them bribe you back, okay? I can make you a list of the things we could use around here."

Brent grinned and settled down to fantasize about breaking the news to Goldman.

It was nearly midnight when Dora gave up the attempt to sleep and bundled into her robe. An ordinary case of insomnia. It wasn't because Jed hadn't come home, or called.

And things were really bad, she admitted, when she started lying to herself.

She switched on the stereo, but Bonnie Raitt's sultry blues seemed entirely too appropriate, so she turned it off again. Wandering into the kitchen, she put the kettle on to boil.

How could she have blown it like this? she wondered as she debated without interest between Lemon Lift and chamomile. Hadn't she known that a man would head for the hills when he heard those three fateful words? Nope. She tossed a tea bag into a cup. She hadn't known because she'd never said them before. And now that she was in the real show, she'd rushed her cue.

Well, it couldn't be taken back, she decided. And she was sorry she and Jed hadn't read the same script.

He hadn't echoed the words back, or swept her up in delight. He had systematically and subtly withdrawn, inch by inch, since that fateful moment some thirty-six hours earlier. And she was very much afraid he would continue to withdraw until he had faded completely away.

Couldn't be helped. She poured the hot water into the cup and let the tea steep while she rummaged for cookies. She couldn't force him to let her show him what it could be like to give and take love. She could only keep her promise and not throw it in his face again. However much that hurt.

And she had some pride left—Bonnie Raitt was wrong about that, she thought. Love *did* have pride. She was going to pull herself together and get on with her life—with him, she hoped. Without him, if necessary. She figured she could start now by going downstairs and putting her wide-awake brain to work.

Carrying her tea, she headed out, remembering at the last minute to slip her keys into her robe pocket and lock the door behind her. She hated that, that sensation of not being completely safe in her own home. Because of it, she felt compelled to switch on lights as she went.

Once settled in the storeroom, she picked up the tedious task of continuing the reorganization of the files DiCarlo had upended.

As always, the steady work and the quiet relaxed and absorbed her. She enjoyed putting the proper thing in the proper place, and pausing occasionally to study a receipt and remember the thrill of the sale.

A paperweight commemorating the New York World's Fair, at $40. A marquetry toilet mirror, at $3,000. Three advertising signs, Brasso, Olympic ale and Players cigarettes, at $190, $27 and $185, respectively.

Jed stood midway down the stairs watching her. She'd set all the lights burning, like a child left home alone at night. She was wearing the green robe and an enormous pair of purple socks. Each time she leaned down to read a piece of paper, her hair fell softly over her cheek and curtained her face. Then she would push it back, the movement fluid and unstudied, before she filed the paper away and reached for another.

His heart rate, which had spiked when he'd seen the hallway door open, settled comfortably. Even with the desire that seemed to nag him whenever she was close, he was always comfortable looking at her.

He'd already settled his weapon back under his jacket when she turned.

She caught a glimpse of a figure and stumbled back. Papers went flying as she choked on a scream.

"What are you doing?" she said furiously. "Trying to scare me to death?"

"No." He came down to the base of the steps. "What the hell are you doing, Conroy? It's after midnight."

"What does it look like I'm doing? I'm practicing the minuet." Humiliated by her reaction, she crouched down to pick up scattered papers.

"You were very graceful." He bent down, placed a hand over hers. "I'm sorry I scared you. I guess you were too involved to hear me."

"Never mind."

"You should be in bed." He tilted her face up toward the light. "You look tired."

"Thanks so much."

"And you're bitchy, too."

"I am not bitchy." She sucked in an insulted breath. "I resent that term both as a feminist and as a dog lover."

Patiently, he tucked her hair behind her ear. She'd managed to cover it remarkably quickly, he mused. But her eyes had been worried and wary after the first fright had faded. He'd hurt her already, and was very likely to do so again.

"Come on upstairs, baby."

"I haven't finished yet."

He lifted a brow. There was the faintest edge of resentment in her tone. It made him feel small and incredibly stupid.

"You're pissed at me."

"I'm not." She straightened, drew a deep breath and, with an effort of will, made the statement the truth. "I am not," she repeated, calm again. "If I'm out of sorts it's because I feel useless having to keep the shop closed, and deceitful because I'm lying to my family."

"You don't have to do either of those things. There's no reason not to open tomorrow, and you'd feel better if you came clean with your family."

She considered it. "I will open," she decided, "but I'm not telling my family. Not yet. It's for me to deal with."

He started to argue and found he couldn't. Wasn't that the same rationale he was using to ease his conscience? He wasn't going to tell her about his meeting with the commissioner or his decision to pick up his badge. Not yet.

"Come upstairs," he repeated. "I'll give you a back rub."

"Why?"

"Because you're tense," he said between his teeth. "Damn, Conroy, why do you care why? All you have to do is lie there and enjoy it."

Eyes narrowed, she stepped back. "You're being nice to me. Why? You're setting me up for something, Skimmerhorn. You're planning on doing something you know I won't like." She raced up the steps after him.

"Don't keep things from me." She laid a hand on his arm as he unlocked his door. "Please. It's something about DiCarlo, isn't it? About the painting, the whole mess."

It was more than that. And less. He wondered if it was the coward's way out to give her that one part.

"I'm going to LA to have a talk with DiCarlo's boss."

"Winesap?" Her brow creased as she concentrated. "That's who the shipment was supposed to go to, wasn't it?"

"The top man's name is Finley, Edmund G.," Jed told her. "I'll start with him."

"And you think he—Finley—was expecting the shipment, that he arranged for the smuggling?"

"Yeah." He poured whiskey, for both of them. "That's what I think."

"What do you know about him?"

"Enough to buy a ticket for LA." He handed her the glass, then offered a brief rundown.

"Import-export," she mused when he'd finished. "Then he's probably a collector. They almost always are. It's possible that he was unaware of DiCarlo's sideline—after all, you said it was a big company. But if he isn't . . ."

He caught the gleam in her eye and bit back a sigh. "Don't think, Conroy. You can be dangerous when you think."

"But I am thinking." She lifted the whiskey, tossed it back in one burning swallow. "And what I think is, you aren't the one who should talk to Finley." She held out the glass for a refill. "I am."

24

"You're out of your mind."

"That is a perfectly sane, rational statement." Since Jed made no move to share, Dora took the bottle and refilled her glass herself. "And if you'd put that male ego on hold a minute, you'd see why."

"It has nothing to do with ego." Although it did, however slightly, and that fact burned the hell out of him. "It has to do with simple common sense. You're in no position to tackle something like this."

"On the contrary." She was warming up to the idea now, and began moving around the room, swirling her whiskey, relishing the part to be played. "I'm in the perfect position. I, after all, was the victim of his employee. I, the baffled innocent, will appeal to Finley's sympathies if he, in turn, is innocent and, since I too am a collector, to his imagination if he's guilty. In short, Skimmerhorn—" She circled back and tapped her glass to his. "This part is tailor-made for me."

"It's not a damn audition, Conroy."

"But it is, essentially. Lord, when are you going to get some furniture in here?" In lieu of a decent chair, she scooted up to sit on the table. "What was your plan, Captain, to barge into his offices, gun blasting?"

"Don't be any more ridiculous than necessary."

"I thought not. You would, if I may interpret the scene, request a meeting to discuss the ugly situation informally, possibly soliciting his help to locate DiCarlo?"

She lifted a brow, waiting for his denial or assent, and got neither. Undaunted, she plowed ahead. "Meanwhile, you'd be looking for a chink in his armor, if indeed he has any armor or chinks. While doing so, you'd get a firsthand view of his operation, his style, and develop an informed opinion as to his culpability."

"You sound like a freaking lawyer," he muttered. "I hate lawyers."

"That's the cop talking. I have some very good friends who are lawyers—and my father was an excellent Clarence Darrow in a production of *Inherit the Wind*. Now, let's see." She crossed her legs; the robe shifted open over long smooth thighs. "How would I play this?"

"You're not, Conroy." Because he felt something essential slipping neatly out of his fingers, he spoke with a snap and caught her chin in his hand. "You are not going."

"Yes, I am," she said, unperturbed. "Because we both know it's the perfect solution." Smiling, she took his hand off her chin then kissed it. "You can come with me. Keep me away from Rodeo Drive."

There was only one way to deal with her, Jed thought, and that was calmly. "Dora, I don't have a handle on this guy. We can't get any hard data. He might be some nice, grandfatherly type who collects stamps in his spare time, and has nothing to do with smuggling. Or DiCarlo might just have been the trigger on his gun. Walking onto his turf is risky, and I'm not taking risks with you."

"Why?" She said it softly. "One would almost think you care."

He jammed his frustrated hands in his pockets. "Damn it, you know I care."

"I know you want, but caring is entirely different. Still, it's nice to hear."

"Don't circle around me on this." She wasn't going to lure him into a dangerous discussion of feelings again. "The point is Finley. If he's involved, he's going to take one look at you and see through that pretty face of yours like plate glass."

"My, my, you tell me you care and that I'm pretty in one night. My heart swells."

"I ought to smack you," he said through clenched teeth.

"But you won't." She smiled and held out a hand. "Lots of bark and little bite, that's you, Skimmerhorn. Let's get some sleep. We can hash this out in the morning."

"There's nothing to hash. I'm going. You're not."

She let her hand fall away. "You don't trust me. That's it, isn't it?" She clamped her teeth over her bottom lip to still the trembling, but her voice thickened and shook even as her eyes filled.

"It's not a matter of trust." He dragged a hand out of his pocket, through his hair. "Don't take it so personally."

"How else can I take it?" The first tear spilled over, ran a lonely trail down her cheek. Her eyes were glistening with more, combined with fragile hurt. "Don't you understand that I need to do something? That I can't just sit in the background after me and my home have been violated this way? I can't bear it, Jed. I can't bear having you think of me as some helpless victim who only gets in your way."

"Stop it." Her tears weakened him, unmanned him. "Come on, baby, don't." He awkwardly lifted a hand to her hair. "I can't stand that." Gently he kissed her quivering lips. "I don't think of you as helpless."

"Useless, then," she said on a hitching sob.

"No." He brushed her tears away with his thumbs and was nearly ready to beg. "You're not trained to do this. If he suspects anything, the whole sting could fall apart before it gets started."

She sniffled, pressed her face to his throat. "Do you suspect—?"

"What?"

"Do you suspect?" she demanded in a perfectly controlled voice. Leaning back, she grinned at him without a trace of remorse. "Fell for it, didn't you?" Laughing, she patted his cheek while he stared at her through slitted and infuriated eyes. "Don't feel too stupid, Skimmerhorn. I told you once I was good." She lifted her glass again to toast herself. "And I am very, very good. And that was just an impromptu performance."

"Maybe I will smack you. You ever turn on tears again like that, I swear I will."

"Made you feel like a heel, didn't I?" She sighed, lustily. "Sometimes I do miss the stage." Then she shrugged. "But not very often. Be assured, Captain, that our Mr. Finley will see exactly what I want him to see. I'll play him like an accordion."

She could do it. He hated the fact that he was certain she could do it perfectly. "And if I lose my mind enough to consider agreeing to this hare-brained idea, you'd do exactly as you were told?"

"No—but I'd try to do exactly as I was told. It's just a fishing expedition, Jed."

He'd thought so, but he preferred to know his water, and bait his own hook. "I don't want you hurt."

She softened all over, eyes, mouth, heart. "That's one of the nicest things you've ever said to me."

"If he hurts you, I'd kill him."

Her easy smile vanished. "Don't put that weight on my shoulders. Okay? It scares me."

He lifted her off the table, set her on her feet. "Conroy, I said I didn't think you were helpless, and that I didn't think you were useless, but I never told you what I think you are."

"No, you didn't." She grimaced, braced.

"Important," he said simply, and melted her heart. "Very important."

By noon the next day, Dora felt at least one part of her life was shifting back into normal gear. The shop was open for business. The first sale warmed her soul so that she gave her customer an impulsive ten percent off. When Lea walked in to help with the afternoon flow, Dora greeted her with a fierce hug.

Laughing, Lea untangled herself. "What's all this? Did you win the lottery?"

"Better. We're open."

Lea peeled off her coat and fluffed her hair. "You never explained why we were closed."

"Too complicated," Dora said breezily. "I needed a day or two of downtime."

"That break-in bothered you more than you let on." Lea's nod was self-satisfied. "I knew it."

"I guess it did. Anyway, we've got a couple of browsers, and I just bought those tea cookies from the bakery again—the ones with the chocolate filling."

Lea took a deep breath. "How am I supposed to lose the four pounds I gained during the holidays?"

"Willpower."

"Right. Oh, Mom said to ask you about the painting."

The cookie box nearly slipped out of Dora's fingers. "Painting?"

"Something about you lent her a painting and had to take it back." Lea gave up on willpower and chose a frosted cookie. "She's thinking about buying it for Dad for Valentine's Day. Seems he really took a shine to it."

"Oh . . . I, ah, sold it." At least that was true, she reminded herself. She still had Jed's $80 tucked in her jewelry box like love letters.

"Are you okay?" Lea's keen eyes scanned Dora's face. "You look a little flustered."

"Hmm? No, I'm fine. Just getting back in the swing. Actually, I'm a little scattered. I may have to go to LA for a couple of days."

"What for?"

"There's an import business out there that I may want to cultivate. I don't want to close the shop again." No reason to, she assured herself. Since Brent was still pulling strings to ensure police protection.

"Don't worry about it. Terri and I can keep things going." The phone on the counter rang twice. Lea raised a brow. "Want me to get that?"

"No." Dora shook off the guilt and lifted the receiver that was an inch away from her hand. "Good afternoon, Dora's Parlor."

"I'd like to speak to Miss Isadora Conroy, please."

"Speaking."

"Miss Conroy." From his desk in Los Angeles, Winesap turned to his meticulously rehearsed notes. "This is, ah, Francis Petroy."

"Yes, Mr. Petroy," Dora said as Lea turned to greet a customer.

"I hope I'm not disturbing you, but I was given your name and number by a Mrs. Helen Owings of Front Royal, Virginia."

"Yes." Dora's fingers tightened on the receiver. "What can I do for you?"

"I hope it's what we can do for each other." Winesap read the words "genial chuckle" in his notes and did his best imitation of one. "It concerns a painting you bought at auction in December. A Billingsly."

All moisture evaporated in her mouth. "Yes, I know the piece. An abstract."

"Exactly. As it happens, I'm a collector of abstract work. I specialize in unknown and emerging artists—in a regretfully small way, you understand."

"Of course."

"I was unable to attend that particular auction—a family emergency. It gave me some hope when Mrs. Owings informed me that the painting had been sold to a dealer, rather than an art collector."

"Actually," Dora said, playing for time. "I'm a little of both."

"Oh dear." He shuffled through his papers. Nothing in his copious notes addressed that particular response. "Oh dear."

"But I'm always interested in a legitimate offer, Mr. Petroy. Perhaps you'd like to come in and see the painting. It would have to be sometime late next week, I'm afraid." She paused and mimed flipping through an appointment book. "My schedule's rather hectic until then."

"That would be excellent. Really excellent." Relieved, Winesap mopped his sweaty neck with a handkerchief. "What day would be good for you, Miss Conroy?"

"I could fit you in on Thursday, say at two?"

"Perfect." Hurried, Winesap scribbled down the date. "I hope you'll hold the painting until then. I'd hate to miss the opportunity."

"Oh, I'd hate you to miss it, too." She smiled grimly at the wall. "I promise, it won't go anywhere until we have the chance to discuss terms. Do you have a number where I can reach you in case something comes up?"

"Certainly." As his notes instructed, Winesap recited the number for one of Finley's fronts in New Jersey. "During business hours," he said. "I'm afraid I keep my private number unlisted."

"I understand perfectly. Next Thursday then, Mr. Petroy."

She hung up, almost too furious to enjoy the sense of elation. He thought she was an idiot, Dora fumed. Well, DiCarlo or Finley or Petroy or whoever the hell you are, you're in for a rude surprise.

"Lea! I have to go out for an hour. If Jed comes in, tell him I have to talk to him."

"Okay, but where—" Lea broke off, fisting her hands on her hips as she stared at the closing door.

SHE should have called ahead. Dora turned back into the parking lot after a fruitless trip to the police station. Lieutenant Chapman was in the field. Sounded as though he were out hunting pheasant, she thought grumpily.

How was she supposed to tell anyone she'd made contact if there wasn't anyone around to tell? Then she spotted Jed's car and allowed herself a smug smile. He was about to learn that he wasn't the only one who could think on his feet.

She found him in the storeroom, calmly painting shelves.

"There you are. I hate to use a cliché, but where's a cop when you need one?"

He continued to paint. "If you'd needed a cop, you should have called nine-one-one."

"I went to the source instead." Wanting to prolong the excitement, she peeled off her coat. "But Brent was out. How come they call it a field? I don't recall passing through any fields in Philadelphia."

"Just our little way of impressing civilians. Why did you need Brent?"

"Because." She paused for drama. "I made contact."

"With what?"

"With whom, Skimmerhorn. Don't be dense. I got a call from Mr. Petroy—only I don't think it was Mr. Petroy. It could have been DiCarlo, but the voice didn't really jibe. Maybe he disguised it, but I'm pretty good with voices. He could have had someone else make the call," she said, considering. "Or it could have been Finley, but—"

"Sit down, Conroy." Jed laid the brush across the top of the paint can. "Try a Jack Webb."

"A Jack Webb? Oh." Her eyes brightened. "Just the facts. I get it."

"You're a real whip. Sit."

"Okay." She settled and imagined herself filing a report. As a result, she related the entire phone conversation precisely, thoroughly and without embellishments. "How's that?" she asked when she was done.

"What the hell were you thinking of, making an appointment to meet him without checking with me?"

She'd expected him to be impressed, not irritated. "I had to do something, didn't I? Wouldn't he have been suspicious if a dealer had seemed reluctant to meet with him?" Her back stiffened defensively. "But it's definitely fishy. An art collector inquiring about a painting from an artist who probably doesn't even exist. I checked on Billingsly. There isn't any Billingsly, so why should anyone go to the trouble to track down a Billingsly painting? Because," she said, and lifted a finger for emphasis, "he wants a Monet."

"That's brilliant, Conroy. Just goddamn brilliant. And it's not the point."

"Of course it is." She blew out a breath, stirring her bangs. "He thought I was stupid. He thought I was some money-grubbing junk dealer who doesn't know her butt from a delft vase, but he's going to find out differently."

"That's also beside the point. You should have put him off until I got back."

"I did very well on my own, thank you. I'm not an idiot."

"Do you have star sixty-nine on your phone system?"

Her face went blank. "Excuse me?"

"Return call. You press a couple of buttons and your phone rings back whoever called you last."

"Oh." As the wind leaked out of her sails, she examined her nails. "Yeah. I guess I do."

He studied her bowed head. "I don't suppose you thought to try it?"

"I can't think of everything," she mumbled. Hopefully, she looked up. "We can try it now."

"The phone's rung three times since I got back."

"Oh." She pushed up from the chair. "Go ahead, tell me I blew it."

"I don't have to, you just did." He gave her hair a tug. "Don't take it too hard, Nancy Drew, even amateur sleuths screw up now and again."

She knocked his hand away. "Take a leap, Skimmerhorn."

"Brent and I will work out how to handle Petroy on Thursday. We'll be back by then."

"Back? Are you and Brent going somewhere?"

"No, you and I are." He tucked his thumbs in his pockets. He still wasn't happy about it, but she'd made an odd sort of sense. "We're leaving for LA tomorrow."

"I'm going to do it?" She pressed a hand to her heart, then tossed her arms wide and vaulted into his. "I'm actually going to do it." Thrilled with the prospect, she raced kisses over his face. "I knew you'd see it my way."

"I didn't. I was outvoted." He wasn't going to admit he'd seen the simple beauty of her idea and had recommended it to Brent.

"Whatever." She kissed him again, hard. "Tomorrow?" she said, rearing back. "God, that's so quick. I have to decide what I'm going to wear."

"That's the least of your worries."

"No, no, no, the proper presentation is essential to character. My navy pinstripe," she considered. "It's very polite and businesslike. Or maybe the red double-breasted—more power and sex. I could distract him with my legs."

"Go for the businesslike."

Because she enjoyed the faint trace of annoyance in the tone, she smiled. "Definitely the red."

"For all you know, he won't even see you."

"Of course he'll see me." She stopped, frowned. "How are we going to make him want to see me?"

"Because you're going to call him, and you're going to say exactly what I tell you to say."

"I see." She tilted her head, lifted a brow. "Have you written me a script, Skimmerhorn? I'm a quick study. I can be off book in no time."

"Just do what you're told."

In Los Angeles, Winesap entered Finley's office with a worried frown creasing his face. "Mr. Finley, sir. Miss Conroy, she's on line two. She's waiting to speak with you."

"Is that so?" Finley closed the file he'd been studying, folded his hands on top of it. "An interesting development."

Winesap's hands twisted together like nervous cats. "Mr. Finley, when I spoke with her earlier today, she was quite cooperative. And I certainly never mentioned my connection with you. I don't know what this might mean."

"Then we'll find out, won't we? Sit, Abel." He lifted the receiver and, smiling, leaned back in his chair. "Miss Conroy? Edmund Finley here."

He listened, his smile growing wider and more feral. "I'm afraid I don't follow you, Miss Conroy. You're inquiring about one of my employees— Anthony DiCarlo? I see. I see." He picked up a letter opener from his desk and tested the honed point with the pad of his thumb. "Of course, I understand if you feel a personal meeting is important. I don't know if I'll be able to help. We've told the police all we know about Mr. DiCarlo's unexplained disappearance, which is, unfortunately, nothing. Very well," he added after a moment. "If you feel you can't discuss it over the telephone, I'd be happy to see you. Tomorrow?" His brows raised. Gently he scraped the point of the letter opener over the Conroy file. "That is rather short notice. Life and death?" He barely suppressed a chuckle. "I'll see if it can be arranged. Will you hold? I'll give you to my assistant. He'll check my calendar. I'll look forward to meeting you."

With a flourish of wrist, Finley punched the Hold button. "Give her four o'clock."

"You have a meeting at three-thirty, sir."

"Give her four o'clock," Finley repeated, and held out the phone.

"Yes, sir." Winesap took the receiver in his damp hand, engaged the line. "Miss Conroy? This is Abel Winesap, Mr. Finley's assistant. You'd like an appointment for tomorrow? I'm afraid the only time Mr. Finley has open is at four. Yes? You have the address? Excellent. We'll be expecting you."

"Delightful." Finley nodded approval when Winesap replaced the receiver. "Simply delightful. 'Fools walk in,' Abel." He opened Dora's file again and smiled genially at her dossier. "I'm certainly looking forward to this. Clear my calendar for tomorrow afternoon. I want no distractions when I see Miss Isadora Conroy. She will have all my attention."

"TOMORROW, four o'clock," Dora said, and turned to Jed. "He sounded puzzled but cooperative, pleasant but reserved."

"And you sounded on the verge of hysteria but controlled." Impressed despite himself, he tipped her face up with his finger and kissed her. "Not bad, Conroy. Not bad at all."

"There's something else." Though she wanted to, she didn't take his hand. If she had, he'd have seen that hers was chilled. "I think I just spoke with Mr. Petroy."

"Finley?"

"No." She forced a thin smile. "His assistant, Winesap."

25

DORA was pleased, and impressed, when the cab pulled up in front of the pink stucco villa that was the Beverly Hills Hotel. "Well, well, Skimmerhorn, you surprise me. This makes up for not springing for a night at the Plaza in New York."

"The room's booked in your name." Jed watched Dora gracefully offer her hand to the doorman. The gesture was one of a woman who'd been sliding out of limos all her life. "You have to put it on your credit card."

She cast a withering look at him over her shoulder. "Thanks a bunch, big spender."

"You want to advertise the fact that you're traveling out here with a companion?" he asked when she sailed through the doors and into the lobby. "A cop?"

"You left out the 'ex.' "

"So I did," he murmured, and waited while Dora checked in. The tony lobby of the BHH didn't seem exactly the right setting to tell her that the "ex" wouldn't apply much longer.

Dora covertly scanned the lobby for passing movie stars when she handed the desk clerk her card for imprint. "I'm going to bill you for this, Skimmerhorn."

"It was your idea to come."

True enough. "Then I'll only bill you for half." She accepted her card, and two keys, passed one to the waiting bellman. "Some of us are not independently wealthy."

"Some of us," he said as he slipped an arm around her waist, "paid for the airfare."

She was touched by the easy way he'd linked them together as they trailed the luggage to the elevator and up to the room.

Dora quickly slipped out of her shoes and padded over to the window to check out the view. There was nothing quite so Californian, she mused, as lush lawns, regal palms and cozy stucco cottages.

"I haven't been in LA since I was fifteen. We stayed in an incredibly bad hotel in Burbank while my father did a part in a small, forgettable film with Jon Voight. It did not distinguish either of their careers."

She stretched her back, rolled her shoulders. "I guess I'm a snob. An east coast snob, because LA doesn't do it for me. It makes me think of unnecessary eye tucks and designer yogurt. Or maybe it's designer eye tucks and unnecessary yogurt. After all, who really needs yogurt in their lives?"

She turned back, her smile becoming puzzled when he only continued to stare at her. "What is it?"

"I just like looking at you sometimes, that's all."

"Oh."

When he saw that the statement had both pleased and flustered her, he smiled back. "You're okay, Conroy. Even with the pointy chin."

"It's not pointy." She rubbed it defensively. "It's delicately sculptured. You know, maybe we should have booked a suite. This room's hardly bigger than a closet. Or maybe we can just go out for a while, get something to eat, soak up some smog."

"You're nervous."

"Of course I'm not nervous." She tossed her bag onto the bed and undid the straps.

"You're nervous," Jed repeated. "You talk too much when you're nervous. Actually, you talk too much all the time but there's a different quality to the babble when you're nervous. And you can't keep your hands still." He laid his gently over hers.

"Obviously I've already become too predictable. The first death knell in any relationship."

He simply turned her around, keeping her hands in his. "You've got a right to be nervous. I'd be more worried about you if you weren't."

"I don't want you to worry." Because she didn't, she willed her hands to relax in his. "I'm going to be fine. Classic opening-night jitters, that's all it is."

"You don't have to do this. I can keep the appointment for you."

"I never give the understudy a chance to steal my thunder." She inhaled and exhaled twice, deeply. "I'm okay. Wait till you read the reviews."

Since she so obviously needed him to, he played along. "What did you used to do before opening night?"

Thinking back, she sat on the edge of the bed. "Well, you'd pace a lot. Pacing's good. And you'd keep running lines in your head and going over the blocking. I'd get out of my street clothes and into a robe—sort of like a snake shedding. And vocalize. I used to do a lot of tongue twisters."

"Such as?"

"Moses supposes his toeses are roses, that kind of thing." Grinning, she waggled her tongue between her teeth. "You've got to limber the tongue."

"Yours has always seemed pretty limber to me."

"Thanks." She laughed and looked back at him. "Good job, Skimmerhorn. I feel better."

"Good." He gave her hair a brotherly tousle, then turned to the phone. "I'll order up some room service, then we'll go over the routine again."

Dora groaned and flopped back on the bed. "I hate heavy-handed directors."

BUT he didn't let up. Two hours later they had eaten, argued, discussed every possible contingency, and he was still unsatisfied. He listened to her reciting tongue twisters in the bathroom and frowned at the door. He'd have felt better if she'd been wearing a wire. Foolish, he supposed, as she'd be walking into a fully staffed office building in broad daylight, but it would have eased his mind. If he hadn't been concerned that Finley's security might have picked up on it, he'd have insisted.

It was a simple job, he reminded himself. One with little to no risk. And he'd already taken the precaution of seeing that the minimal degree of risk was all but eliminated.

It was the *all but* that nagged at him.

The door opened, and Dora stepped out wearing the red suit that showed off every glorious curve in that sexy body, highlighting her legs in a way that would make any man this side of the grave salivate.

"What do you think?" She was holding two different pairs of earrings up to each lobe. "The drops or the knots?"

"How the hell should I know?"

"The knots," she decided. "More discreet." She fastened them on. "I'd forgotten how much better you feel once you're in costume. There's just those little ripples of nerves that keep the adrenaline up." She reached for her bottle of perfume.

He frowned as she spritzed on scent—the throat, the back of the neck, the wrists, the backs of her knees. Something about the female ritual made his stomach jitter. When she picked up her antique silver brush and pulled it slowly through her hair, he knew what that something was. It made him feel like a voyeur.

"You look fine." He had to clear his throat. "You can stop primping now."

"Brushing your hair isn't primping. It's basic grooming." While she gave it another sweep, she caught his gaze in the mirror. "I'd swear you're more nervous than I am."

"Just stick to the plan and try to remember everything you see. Don't bring up the painting. You haven't got a clue about the painting. Try to go through Winesap. We're running him down, but I want your impressions—not your speculations, your impressions."

"I know." Patiently she set the brush aside. "Jed, I know exactly what to do and how to do it. It's simple. Simpler because I might have done just this if I hadn't known about the painting. It's a very logical step."

"Just watch your ass."

"Darling, I'm counting on you to do that for me."

DORA was impressed with the decor of Finley's outer office, trying to pick up helpful clues. As she'd suspected, he was a collector, and their mutual interest would give them a firm foundation. Her hands were chilled. That was good, too. The honest nerves she projected were just what she needed to set the tone for her visit.

It was difficult to hang on to those nerves, and character, when she really wanted to walk over and examine some of Finley's treasures firsthand. She felt favorably toward anyone who put malachite vases and Chiparus figures in his waiting area. And the settee she was using was no reproduction. Early Chippendale, Dora thought reverently, high-style rococo.

She sincerely hoped Finley would prove himself to be in the clear. She'd love to develop a business relationship.

But if he wasn't . . .

The thought of that had the nerves creeping back. She fiddled with the calla lily pin at her lapel, brushed at her skirt, looked at her watch.

Damn, it was four-ten, she thought. How long was he going to keep her waiting?

"EXCELLENT. Excellent," Finley murmured to Dora's video image. She was every bit as lovely as he'd expected from the faded newspaper photos Winesap had unearthed from old Show and Style sections. Her wardrobe showed a flair for color and line as well as an affection for the feminine. He respected a woman who knew how to present herself to her best advantage.

He enjoyed the way her hands moved restlessly through her hair, over her body. Nerves, he thought, pleased. A spider gained more thrill from a panicky fly than a resigned one. And despite the nerves, he noted, her eyes were drawn again and again to pieces in his collection. That flattered him.

They would do very well together, he decided. Very well indeed.

He buzzed his receptionist. It was time to begin.

"Mr. Finley will see you now."

"Thank you." Dora rose, tucked her envelope bag under her arm and followed the woman to the double doors.

When she entered, Finley smiled and stood. "Miss Conroy, I'm so sorry to have kept you waiting."

"I'm just happy you could see me at all." She crossed the rug, that pool of white, and took his extended hand. Her first impression was one of vitality and health and of well-channeled power.

"It seemed important to you. What can we offer you? Some coffee, tea or perhaps some wine."

"Wine would be lovely." And would give her the prop of a glass to twist in her hands as she told her story.

"The Pouilly-Fumé, Barbara. Please sit, Miss Conroy. Be comfortable." In a move calculated to disarm her, he rounded the desk and took the chair beside her. "And how was your flight?"

"Long." Dora's smile was fleeting. "But I shouldn't complain. The weather was turning nasty at home. But of course, I'll go back tomorrow."

"So soon?" His bright eyes glinted with just the right touch of curiosity. "I'm flattered to have such a pretty young woman travel all this way just to see me."

His receptionist had uncorked the bottle. Obviously, Dora mused, her duties included those of a wine steward. She passed Finley the cork and tipped an inch of wine in his glass for approval.

"Yes," he said after rolling the wine on his tongue and swallowing. "That will do nicely." When the wine was poured in both glasses, the secretary slipped soundlessly out of the room. Finley raised his glass. "To your health, Miss Conroy, and a safe journey home."

"Thank you." It was beautiful wine, silk on the tongue, with just a hint of smoke. "I know it might sound foolish, coming all this way just to see you, Mr. Finley. But I honestly felt compelled." As if overcome, she looked down into the pale gold wine in her glass, let her fingers tighten on the stem. "Now that I'm here, I don't know where to start."

"I can see you're upset," Finley said kindly. "Take your time. You told me on the phone this had to do with Anthony DiCarlo. Are you . . ." He paused delicately. "A friend?"

"Oh no." There was horror in her voice, in her eyes as she dragged them back to Finley's. She imagined DiCarlo's voice whispering in her ear to bring the rusty edge of revulsion into her voice. "No. He—Mr. Finley, I need to ask how much you know about him."

"Personally?" Thinking, he pursed his lips. "I'm afraid I don't know many of my branch employees as well as I might. The company is very large now, and unfortunately that depersonalizes matters. We had a meeting here just before Christmas. I noticed nothing out of the ordinary. He seemed as competent as always."

"Then he's worked for you for some time?"

"Six years, I believe. More or less." He sipped more wine. "I have studied his file since this odd disappearance, to refresh my memory. He has an excellent record with the company. Mr. DiCarlo worked his way up the corporate ladder rather quickly. He showed initiative and ambition. Both of which I believe in rewarding. He came from a poor background, you know."

When she only shook her head, he smiled and continued. "As I did myself. The desire to better oneself—this is something I respect in an employee, and also tend to reward. As one of my top executives on the east coast, he's proven himself to be reliable and cunning." He smiled again. "In my business, one must be cunning. I'm very much afraid of foul play. As Mr. DiCarlo's work record would indicate, he isn't a man to neglect his responsibilities this way."

"I think—I think I might know where he is."

"Really?" There was a flash in Finley's eyes.

"I think he's in Philadelphia." As if to bolster her courage, Dora took another quick sip, and her hand shook lightly. "I think he's . . . watching me."

"My dear." Finley reached for her hand. "Watching you? What do you mean?"

"I'm sorry. It's not making sense. Let me try to start at the beginning."

She told the story well, with several pauses for composure, and one significant break in which she described the attack.

"And I don't understand," she finished, with her eyes wet and shimmering. "I don't understand why."

"My dear, how horrible for you." Finley was all baffled sympathy while his mind performed rapid calculations. It appeared DiCarlo had left out a few significant details, he mused. There had been no mention in his report of an attempted rape, nor of a knightly neighbor coming to the rescue. It explained the bruises on his face during his last, and final, visit, however.

"You're telling me," Finley began, his tone lightly shocked, "that the man who broke into your shop, the man who attacked you, was Anthony DiCarlo."

"I saw his face." As if overcome, Dora covered her own with her hand. "I'll never forget it. And I identified him to the police. He's killed a police officer, Mr. Finley, and a woman. He left another woman for dead, one of my customers." The thought of Mrs. Lyle urged the first tear down her cheek. "I'm sorry. I've been so upset, so frightened. Thank you," she managed when Finley gallantly offered his handkerchief. "None of it makes any sense, you see. He only stole a few trinkets, and as for Mrs. Lyle, my customer, he took nothing of any real value. Just a china dog, a statue she'd bought from me the day before. I think he must be crazy," she murmured, lowering her hand again. "I think he must be mad."

"I hope you understand this is difficult for me to take in. Mr. DiCarlo has worked for me for years. The idea of one of my own staff attacking women, murdering police officers. Miss Conroy—Isadora." He took her hand again, gently, a father comforting a child after a bad dream. "Are you absolutely certain it was Anthony DiCarlo?"

"I saw his face," she said again. "The police said he had a record. Nothing like—like this, and nothing for several years, but—"

"I knew he'd had some trouble." With a sigh, Finley sat back. "Just as I felt I understood the need to overcome the past mistakes. But I would never have believed . . . It seems I misjudged him, badly. What can I do to help you?"

"I don't know." Dora twisted the handkerchief in her hands. "I guess I'd hoped you'd have some idea what to do, where the police might look. If he contacted you—"

"My dear, I assure you, if he contacts me, I will do everything in my power to lead the authorities to him. Perhaps his family knows something?"

She dried her tears and, calmer, shook her head. "The police have questioned them, I believe. I actually thought of going to see his mother myself, but I couldn't. I couldn't face that."

"I'll make some calls. Do whatever I can to help you."

"Thank you." She let out a shaky sigh followed by a shaky smile. "I feel better doing something. The worst is the waiting, the not knowing where he is or what he's planning. I'm afraid to go to sleep at night. If he came back—" She shuddered, sincerely. "I don't know what I'd do."

"You have no reason to think he will. Are you sure he gave you no idea why he chose your shop?"

"None. That's what's so terrifying. To be picked at random that way. Then Mrs. Lyle. He shot her housekeeper and left Mrs. Lyle for dead, all for some little statue." Her eyes, still wet, were guileless and trusting. "A man doesn't kill for that, does he?"

"I wish I knew." Finley heaved a heartfelt sigh. "Perhaps, as you say, he's gone mad. But I have every confidence in the authorities. I'll say, with full confidence, that you won't be bothered by Mr. DiCarlo again."

"I'm trying to hold on to that. You've been very kind, Mr. Finley."

"Edmund."

"Edmund." She smiled again, courageously. "Just talking it out has helped. I'd like to ask, if you find anything, anything at all, that you'd call me. The police aren't very free with information."

"I understand. And, of course, I'll keep in touch with you. We have an excellent security team on retainer. I'm going to put them on this. If there's a trace of DiCarlo, they'll find it."

"Yes." She closed her eyes, let her shoulders relax. "I knew I was right to come here. Thank you." When she rose, he took both her hands in his. "Thank you so much for listening to me."

"I only regret I can't do more. I'd consider it a favor if you'd agree to have dinner with me tonight."

"Dinner?" Her mind went sheet blank.

"I don't like to think of you alone, and upset. I feel responsible. DiCarlo is, after all, my man. Or was," he corrected, with a small smile.

"That's very kind of you."

"Then indulge me. Ease my conscience a bit. And, I admit, I would find it very pleasant to spend the evening with a lovely young woman who shares some of my interests."

"Your interests?"

"Collecting." Finley gestured toward a curio cabinet. "If you run an antique and collectibles shop, I think you'd be interested in some of my treasures."

"Yes, I am. I'm sure you're much more knowledgeable than I, but I've already admired several of your pieces. The horse's head?" She nodded toward a stone figure. "Han dynasty?"

"Precisely." He beamed, a professor to a prize student. "You have a good eye."

"I love things," she confessed. "Owning things."

"Ah, yes. I understand." He reached up to brush a fingertip lightly over her lapel pin. "A plique-à-jour—early nineteen hundreds."

She beamed back at him. "You, too, have a good eye."

"I have a brooch I'd like you to see." He thought of the sapphire, and the pleasure it would give him to taunt her with it. "I only recently acquired it, and I know you'd appreciate it. So it is decided. I'll have a car pick you up at your hotel. Say, seven-thirty."

"I . . ."

"Please, don't misunderstand. My home is fully staffed, so you'll be well chaperoned. But I don't often have the opportunity to show off my treasures to someone who recognizes their intrinsic worth. I'd love your opinion on my pomander collection."

"Pomanders?" Dora said, and sighed. If she hadn't been on a mission, she'd have agreed in any case. How could she resist a collection of pomanders? "I'd love to."

DORA strolled back into the hotel room filled with the warmth of success. She found Jed pacing, the air blue with smoke and rattled by an old war movie on television he wasn't watching.

"What the hell took you so long?"

"It was only an hour." She slipped out of her shoes as she walked to him. "I was brilliant," she said, and wrapped her arms around his neck.

"I'll tell you if you were brilliant." He put a hand on top of her head and pushed her into a chair. Snatching the remote, he ended the war with a fizzle. "You tell me about Finley. Everything, from the top."

"Is there any coffee left?" She picked up a room-service pot, sniffed the contents. "Let me savor the moment, will you?" She poured coffee and sipped it black and tepid. "I want some cheesecake," she decided. "Order us up some cheesecake, okay?"

"Don't push it, Conroy."

"You know how to take the fun out of things. All right." She took a last sip, sat back and told him.

"He really was nice," she concluded. "Very understanding, and properly shocked by my story. I, of course, played the part of the high-strung, spooked-at-every-shadow heroine to perfection. The police simply aren't doing enough to ease my mind, so he very gallantly offered to do whatever he could, down to hiring a private firm to track down DiCarlo."

"What about Winesap?"

"He wasn't there. I asked for him at first, but the receptionist told me he was out of the office today."

"If he's the one who's going to keep the appointment next Thursday, he couldn't afford having you see him."

"I thought of that. So I stopped to talk to the security guard in the lower lobby on the way out. I told him I'd seen Abel Winesap's name on the board, and that my father had worked with an Abel Winesap once, years ago, and had lost touch. So I asked if this guy was tall and heavyset with red hair. It turns out this Winesap is short and skinny, round-shouldered and balding."

"Good girl, Nancy."

"Thanks, Ned. Do you think Nancy and Ned ever made love? You know, in the back of her coupe after a particularly satisfying case."

"I like to think so. Get back on track, Conroy."

"Okay." Now came the hard part, Dora mused. She would have to work up to it carefully. "Finley's office is incredible—oh, I forgot to mention the monitors. He has a whole wall of them. Kind of creepy, you know? All these television shows running silently side by side with different parts of the building. I guess he has security cameras everywhere. But that's not why it's incredible. He had a Gallé lamp in his office that made me want to sit up and beg. And a Han horse. That barely touches on it. Anyway, I'll see his personal collection at dinner tonight."

Jed snatched her wrist before she could bound up. "Play that back, Conroy, slow speed."

"I'm having dinner with him."

"What makes you think so?"

"Because he asked me, and I accepted. And before you start listing all the reasons why I shouldn't, I'll tell you why I should." She'd worked it out point by point in the cab on the way back. "He was kind to me in the office—very concerned and avuncular. He believes I'm in town alone, and that I'm upset. He knows I have a rabid interest in collectibles and antiques. If I'd said no, it would have set the entirely wrong tone."

"If he's involved, the last place you should be is alone with him, at his house."

"If he's involved," she countered, "the last place he'd want anything to happen would be his own house. Especially when I tell him I called my parents to check in and told them I'd be having dinner with him."

"It's a stupid idea."

"It isn't. It will give me more time to cultivate him. He likes me," she added, and walked over to the closet. She'd brought a little black dress along, and had paired it with a glittery bolero jacket in red and gold stripes. Holding them in front of her, she turned to the mirror. "He doesn't like the idea of me spending the evening alone in LA while I'm upset."

Jed watched the sequins glimmer through narrowed eyes. "Did he come on to you?"

Dora paused in the act of unbuttoning her suit jacket. "Are you jealous, Skimmerhorn?" The laugh bubbled out, quick and delighted. "Isn't that cute?"

"I am not jealous." He'd never been jealous of a woman in his life. Never. He wasn't about to admit it now. "I asked you a simple question, and I'd like an answer."

She took off the jacket, revealing the creamy lace and silk of the camisole beneath. "You're going to put yourself in the awkward position of making me tell you I love you again. We wouldn't want that, would we?"

When his stomach clenched, he swore under his breath, grabbed another cigarette. "Maybe I'm fed up with watching you deck yourself out for another man."

"That's what I'm here for, isn't it? To meet him, gain his sympathy and confidence and to find out everything I can." With her head tilted to the side, she studied Jed's set face. "Would you feel better if I told you I didn't have any intention of sleeping with him?"

"Yeah, I'll rest easy now." He blew out a frustrated stream of smoke. "I don't like you going in there alone. I don't have enough on him, and I don't like it."

"You'll have more when I get back, won't you?" She walked over to hang up the jacket. He crossed the room so quietly she jumped when his hands touched her shoulders.

"I'm not used to being the one who waits."

She arranged the jacket meticulously on the hanger. "I guess I can understand that."

"I never had anyone to worry about before. I don't like it."

"I can understand that, too." She unzipped her skirt and clipped it neatly on another hanger. "I'll be fine."

"Sure you will." He lowered his cheek to the back of her head. "Dora . . ." What could he say? he wondered. Nothing that was churning inside him seemed right. "I'll miss you tonight. I guess I've gotten used to having you around."

Wonderfully touched, she smiled and lifted a hand to cover one of his. "You're such a sentimental slob, Skimmerhorn. It's always hearts and flowers with you."

"Is that what you want?" He turned her to face him. "Is that what you're looking for?"

Her smile didn't quite reach her eyes as she brushed her knuckles over his cheek. "I've got a heart, thanks, and I can buy flowers anytime I like." To comfort him, she nuzzled her lips to his. "I've also got an hour before I have to get ready. Why don't you take me to bed?"

It would have been a pleasure, and a relief, but both pleasure and relief would have to wait. "We've got work to do, Conroy. Put on your robe, and we'll go over the ground rules for your dinner."

Huffing, she stepped back. "I'm standing here in little more than a lace garter belt and you're telling me to put on a robe?"

"That's right."

"You have gotten used to me," she muttered.

26

DORA stepped off the curb and into a white Mercedes limo at precisely seven-thirty. There was a single white rosebud laid across the seat, and a Beethoven sonata playing softly on the stereo. A bottle of champagne was iced beside a crystal bowl of beluga.

Brushing the rose petals across her cheek, she looked up toward the window where she knew Jed would be watching.

Too bad, she mused as the car pulled smoothly away. It appeared that she did need hearts and flowers, and was unlikely to receive them from the man who mattered most.

Because she was looking back she noticed a man in a gray suit slip into a dark sedan and cruise out into traffic behind them.

Dora closed her eyes, slipped out of her shoes to run her bare feet luxuriously over the plush carpet and put all thoughts of Jed behind her.

For the next few hours, she was alone.

Armed with a glass of champagne and a toast point of caviar, she enjoyed the ride up into the hills. Though under other circumstances she might have struck up a conversation with the driver, she hugged the silence to her and prepared for Act Two.

After her impressions of his office, she'd expected Finley's house to be lavish. She wasn't disappointed. The sweeping drive up, the quick, teasing peeks of the building through screening trees. Then the full impact of stone and brick and glass simmering in the last fiery lights of the dying sun.

A well-set stage.

She took the rose with her.

There was only a moment to appreciate the Adam door knocker in the shape of a dolphin before the door was opened by a uniformed maid.

"Miss Conroy. Mr. Finley would like you to wait in the drawing room."

Dora didn't bother to disguise her open-mouthed admiration for the magnificence of the entrance hall. In the parlor she gave the maid a murmured assent at the offer of wine, and was grateful when she had the glass in hand and was alone to worship.

She felt as though she had entered some personal museum, one structured for her alone. Everything she saw was spectacular, and every piece her eyes feasted on seemed more glorious. So glorious it was impossible not to gorge.

She saw herself reflected in the George III mirror, ran her fingers delicately over a mahogany armchair of the same period, crooned over a Japanese Kakiemon tiger.

When Finley joined her she was mentally devouring a collection of netsukes.

"I see you're enjoying my toys."

"Oh yes." Eyes dark and brilliant with appreciation, she turned from the curios. "I feel like Alice, and I've just stumbled into the best corner of Wonderland."

He laughed and poured himself a glass of wine. He'd known he would enjoy her. "I was certain I'd find it pleasant to share my things with you. I'm afraid I spend too much time alone with them."

"You've made my trip very worthwhile, Mr. Finley."

"Then I'm content." He walked over, placed a light hand at the small of her back. It wasn't a suggestive move. She had no explanation as to why her skin crawled under the friendly pressure. "You were looking at the netsukes." He opened the curio and deliberately chose one of the pieces of erotica that had been smuggled in the mermaid bookends. "Not everyone can appreciate the humor and the sexuality, as well as the artistry of these pieces."

Chuckling, she took the figure of the man and woman into her palm. "But they look so pleased with themselves, trapped forever in that moment of anticipation. It's hard to imagine some stoic samurai with something like this dangling from his obi."

Finley merely smiled. "And yet that's precisely how I like to imagine it. Worn by a warlord, into bed and into battle. One of the Tokugawa family, perhaps. I enjoy giving a history to each of my possessions." He replaced the figure. "Shall I give you the tour before dinner?"

"Yes, please." Agreeably, she slipped a hand through his arm.

He was knowledgeable, erudite and entertaining, Dora thought. Why, before an hour was up, she was violently uncomfortable she couldn't have said.

He took a greedy delight in all that he'd acquired, yet she understood greed. He was unfailingly correct in his manner toward her, yet she felt increasingly as though she were being subtly violated. It took all of her skill and control to play out her prescribed role as they moved from room to room. By the time they were nearly finished, she'd begun to understand that one could have too much of even the beautiful and precious.

"This is the pin I mentioned earlier." Excited by the fact that he was showing her each and every one of the smuggled items, Finley offered her the sapphire brooch. "The stone is, of course, magnificent, but the workmanship of the setting, and again, the history, add intrigue."

"It's beautiful." It was, the gleaming blue eye winking up at her from its bed of delicate gold filigree and fiery diamonds, both beautiful and tragic. Tragic, she realized, because it would be forever behind glass, never again to grace a woman's silks or make her smile when she adorned herself with it.

Perhaps that was the difference between them. She passed her treasures on, gave them a new life. Finley locked his away.

"It was said to belong to a queen," Finley told her, waiting, watching her face for a sign of recognition. "Mary, Queen of Scots. I often wonder if she wore it when she was arrested for treason."

"I'd rather think of her wearing it when she was riding across the moors."

"And this." He chose the etui. "This belonged to another queen with a sad fate. Napoleon gave it to Josephine. Before he divorced her for being barren."

"You give your treasures a sad history, Edmund."

"I find poignancy increases their meaning for me. The trinkets of the rich and the royal, now a part of the collection of a commoner. Shall we dine?"

There was lobster bisque and Peking duck so delicate it all but melted on the tongue. The meal was served on Limoges and eaten with Georgian silver. Dom Perignon was poured into antique Waterford that glittered like crystal tears.

"Tell me about your shop," Finley invited. "It must be exciting for you to buy and sell every day, to handle lovely things time and again."

"I do love it." Dora fought to relax and enjoy the meal. "I'm afraid most of what I have falls far below your collections. What I stock is a mixture of antiques and estate items, along with . . ." Junk—she all but heard Jed's sneering and comforting voice. "Novelty items," she said a bit primly. "I love the foolish as well as the beautiful."

"And, like myself, you appreciate the having, the control. There's something innately satisfying about making your own business out of something you love. Not everyone has the opportunity, or the courage, to make it a success. I believe, Isadora, that you have a great deal of courage."

Her stomach fluttered, but she managed to swallow the bite of duck. "My family considers it stubbornness. I hate to confess, but I frighten very easily."

"You underestimate yourself. After all, you came here, to me." He smiled, watching her over the rim of his glass with eyes as sharp as carved jade. "For all you knew, DiCarlo might have been acting on my orders. After all, he is—was—an employee."

When she went pale and set down her fork with a rattle, he laughed, patted her hand. "Now I have frightened you. I apologize. It was merely said to illustrate my point. What sense would it make for me to have DiCarlo break into your shop and steal a few trinkets when I could so easily acquire them myself?"

"I doubt I'd have very much you'd find interesting."

"Oh, I disagree." He smiled and signaled for dessert. "I believe I'd find a great deal of what you have to offer of interest. Tell me," he said, "do you ever come across any Grueby?"

"I once had a statue of a boy—badly chipped, I'm afraid." She fisted and unfisted her hands in her lap as the creamy chocolate soufflé was served. "I noticed your vase in the library. It's lovely."

She relaxed into the discussion of pottery, and began to believe that she'd imagined he'd been baiting her.

Later, they had coffee and brandy before a sedate fire in the drawing room. The conversation was easy again, like that of old friends. All the while Dora's nerves drummed. She'd never wanted to escape so badly in her life.

"I'm sorry you can't extend your visit." Finley passed a small porcelain nude from hand to hand.

"Running a business doesn't give one as much flexible time as some people think. I'm sure you'd understand."

"Yes, indeed. There are times when I feel a prisoner of my own success. Do you?" He skimmed a fingertip over the nude's glossy breast. "Feel trapped?"

"No." But she couldn't shake the sensation that the walls of the room were shrinking in on her. "You must have marvelous contacts." Again she scanned the room. She couldn't watch the way he was fondling the nude. "Do you do much of the traveling and acquiring?"

"Not as much as I'd like. Over the years I've had to delegate that pleasure. But I take the occasional trip to the Orient, or Europe. I even get to the east coast from time to time."

"I hope you'll let me return your hospitality if you're ever in Philadelphia."

"I wouldn't think of taking the trip without paying you a call."

"Then I hope you find the time to come east soon. It was a wonderful meal, Edmund, a delightful evening." She rose to play her final scene, the contented guest taking a reluctant leave.

"Believe me, it was my pleasure." He stood, took her hand and kissed it gallantly at the knuckles. "I'd be happy to arrange for my car to take you to the airport tomorrow."

"That's so nice." It made her feel ashamed of the urge she had to rub her hand clean on her jacket. "But I've already arranged transportation. Please, call me if you—if there's any news about DiCarlo."

"I will. I have a feeling it will all be sorted out very soon."

*   *   *

WHEN she returned to the Beverly Hills Hotel, Dora waited until the limo had driven away, then simply stood on the sidewalk breathing slowly and waiting to calm. She didn't want to face Jed until she had herself under control.

She felt idiotic to be shaken. Though she knew she would have to tell him how the evening had affected her, she wanted to be cool and precise when she did so.

Then she saw the dark sedan pull up across the street. And the man with the gray suit.

On a skidder of panic she bolted into the lobby.

Jumping at shadows, Conroy, she berated herself while her heartbeat roared in her ears. Chin up, she punched the button for the elevator. It was just jet lag. It helped a great deal to believe it. She was overtired and over-stressed. Once she'd gotten through relaying everything to Jed, she'd get a good night's sleep and be fine again.

By the time she'd ridden up to her floor and slipped the key into the lock, she had herself back in line. She was even able to smile when she walked in and saw Jed scowling out of the window.

"Ah, you waited up for me."

"You're always good for a laugh, Conroy. You really ought to—" He broke off after he'd turned and gotten a look at her. He hadn't known any-one could appear so exhausted and still stand on both feet.

"What?" Such were her nerves that she groped at her throat and stepped back. "What is it?"

"Nothing. My mind was wandering. Have a seat."

"I'd just as soon get out of this dress first." Habit had her going to the closet for a hanger.

"Let me give you a hand." He tugged down the zipper for her. Casually, he gave her shoulders a quick massage and found them, as he'd suspected, knotted with tension. "You want a nightgown or something?"

"Or something." She sat tiredly on the edge of the bed to remove her hose. "You had something for dinner, didn't you?"

"I'm a big boy now, Conroy." He unhooked the black strapless bra, tossed it aside, then slipped the thin nightshirt over her head.

"We had duck."

"Beats the hell out of my cheeseburger."

"It was excellent. The house—really, you should see it. It's immense, with all these lofty rooms leading into other lofty rooms. I've never seen so many museum-quality pieces in one place."

When her eyes began to droop, she shook her head. "I need to wash my face. You should see if you can get some kind of financial report on E. F., Incorporated." In the bathroom she ran the water cold, scooping it up with both hands to splash on her face. "The butler served coffee out of a Meissen worth ten, twelve thousand." She yawned and splashed more water. "And a paperweight in the library—an Alméric Walter. I watched one go at Christie's a couple of years ago for fifteen big ones. Plus this—"

"I don't want an inventory."

"Sorry." After choosing a tube from the bathroom counter, she began creaming off her makeup. "I've never seen a collection to compare with it. Never heard of one to compare with it. You can't even call it a collection, really. It's more of a private little empire." Dutifully, she dabbed on moisturizer. "And there was something odd about the way he showed it to me."

"In what way?"

"Like he was waiting for me to do something, say something." She shook her head. "I don't know. I can't explain exactly, but the atmosphere was different than it had been in his office." Her eyes met his in the mirror. There were faint bruises of fatigue under hers and a fragility to her skin now that it was without the shield of cosmetics. "He spooked me, Jed. He was a perfect gentleman, a perfect host. And being alone with him terrified me."

"Tell me." He combed a hand through her hair. "It doesn't have to make sense."

Relieved, she nodded and walked back in to sit on the side of the bed. "He took me all through the house," she began. "And like I said, there was something off about the way he showed off his pieces. A handful of them in particular. I could feel him watching me when I looked at them, and it was . . . it was like watching someone masturbate. I kept telling myself I was imagining it because he was being so charming. We had dinner, this elegant dinner in this elegant room on elegant china. And we discussed art and music, and so forth. He never touched me in a way that wasn't perfectly correct, but . . ."

She laughed a little. "I'd really appreciate it if you wouldn't say I was being an overimaginative female when I tell you this, because that's exactly how I feel. But I felt as though he was seeing me naked. We're spooning up this incredibly delicate soufflé with Georgian silver and I felt as though he could see right through my dress. I have no explanation for it, just that unshakable and very creepy feeling."

"Maybe he was thinking of you that way. Men do, even elegant ones."

She could only shake her head. "No, it wasn't like that—not really sexual on either side. It was more like being defenseless."

"You were alone."

"Not really—or not often. He has an army of servants. I wasn't really afraid that he'd hurt me. I was afraid he wanted to. And there was that business in the bathroom."

"He took you into the bathroom?"

"No. I went into the powder room after dinner. I was freshening my makeup, and I kept feeling like he was right there, watching over my shoulder."

She blew out a breath, grateful that Jed didn't snort and tell her she was being a fool. "I honestly didn't think he had anything to do with this whole business after I'd left his office this afternoon. And now, I don't know what to think. I do know that I wouldn't want to go back into that house even if he offered me my pick of his pomanders. Which, I might add, were wonderful."

"You don't have to go back. We'll see if the IRS wants to poke a few fingers into Finley's pie."

"Good." There was a throbbing over her left eye she couldn't quite rub away. "You might see what you can find out about a sapphire brooch— possibly sixteenth-century. The stone looked to be about eight carats in a horizontal setting of gold filigree with some small, round-cut diamonds. He made a real issue of showing it to me."

"Fine. You did good."

"Yeah." She gave him a sleepy smile. "Do I get a detective's gold star?"

"That's gold shield, Nancy. And no. You're retiring."

"Good."

"You want something for that headache?"

She stopped rubbing her temple long enough to grimace. "Morphine, but I didn't bring any along. I do have something less effective in my makeup bag."

"I'll get it. Stretch out."

She took him up on it without bothering to crawl under the sheets. "I forgot. I saw this guy in a dark sedan—God, that sounds like a Charlie Chan movie. Anyway, I saw him pull out after the limo when we left. Then he drove up a few minutes after I got back. I don't know why Finley would have me followed to and from his house though."

"He didn't. I did. Where the hell do you keep pills? You've got all these little bottles."

"The pills aren't in a bottle, they're in a box. What we call a pillbox in the trade."

"Smartass."

"The little one with the enameled violets. What do you mean you had me followed?"

"I've had you tailed all day. Local PI."

She was smiling when he walked out with the pills. "Almost as good as flowers," she murmured. "You hired a bodyguard for me."

"I hired him for me," he said lightly.

After pillowing her head on her folded arms, she shut her eyes.

Straddling her, he began to rub her neck and shoulders. "Relax, Conroy, you don't get rid of a stress headache by tensing up."

But his fingers were already working their magic. "Jed?" Her voice was a thick murmur, hardly audible.

"Yeah."

"Mirrors. I forgot. He has dozens of them. You couldn't walk into a room without seeing yourself coming and going."

"So he's vain."

"I've got a cheval glass I could probably sell him."

"Shut up, Conroy. You're off the clock."

"Okay, but I don't think he just likes to watch himself. I think he likes to watch."

"Okay. He's a vain pervert." He ran the heels of his hands down the sides of her spine.

"I know. That doesn't make him a smuggler. I wish . . ."

"Wish what?"

But whatever she wished, it would remain unsaid. She was asleep.

Quietly, he turned down the covers and, lifting her, slipped her between the sheets. She never stirred. Jed studied her a moment before he turned off the lights, got in bed beside her. After a little while, he gathered her close to hold her while he joined her in sleep.

BECAUSE his arms were around her, her first shudders awakened him. Instinctively he tightened his grip, his hand soothing at her neck.

"Hey. Hey, Dora, come on. Pull out of it." He heard her gasping gulp of air, and her body trembled hard as she broke through the surface of the dream. "Bad one, huh?" he murmured.

She responded by pressing her face to his chest. "Can you reach the light? I need the light."

"Sure." Keeping an arm firm around her, he shifted to grope for the switch. The light flashed, cutting through the unrelieved dark. "Better?"

"Yeah." But she continued to shiver.

"Want some water?"

"No." The instant panic in the word had her biting down on her lip. "Just stay right here, okay?"

"Okay."

"And don't let go."

"I won't."

And because he didn't, her fluttering heart began to settle again. "That was the first nightmare I've had since I reread Stephen King's *The Shining*."

"Scary book." Though his eyes were far from calm, the kiss he brushed over her hair was light and easy. "Too bad about the movie."

"Yeah." Her laugh was shaky, but it was a laugh. "I didn't know you went in for horror stuff, Skimmerhorn."

"It relieves tension. It's tough to worry about life's little problems when you're reading about kiddie vampires or the walking dead."

"I've always been a sucker for the walking dead." Because he didn't ask, didn't press, she found herself able to tell him. "I was in that house, Finley's house all those rooms and mirrors. All those things, those beautiful things. Did you ever read *Something Wicked?*"

"Bradbury. Sure."

"In the carnival, that house of mirrors? Remember, if you bought a ticket, they promised you you'd find what you wanted inside. But it was a very nasty trick. That's what it was like. I wanted to see all those beautiful things. Then I couldn't get out. DiCarlo was in there, too, and Finley. Every time I turned, one of them was there, reflected all around me. I kept running into walls of glass." Taking comfort in the heat of Jed's body, the press of muscle, she cuddled closer. "I feel like a jerk."

"You shouldn't. I've had some beauts."

"You have?" Intrigued, she tilted her head to study his face. "Really?"

"My rookie year I responded to a 'shots fired.' I was lucky enough to be first on the scene of a murder-suicide." He didn't add that what was left of a human head after a shotgun blast was not a pretty sight. "My subconscious pulled that little scene out on me in the middle of the night for weeks after. And after Elaine . . ." He hesitated, then continued. "I kept reliving that. Running across the lawn, through the roses. Watching her turn her head to look at me. The sound of the blast when she turned the key. I'll take the kiddie vampires any day."

"Yeah. Me too." They lay for a moment in silence. "Jed?"

"Hmmm?"

"You want to see if there's an old horror movie on TV?"

"Conroy, it's nearly six in the morning."

"It's too dark to be nearly six in the morning."

"The drapes are closed."

"Oh."

"Tell you what." He shifted, rolling on top of her and catching her chin between his teeth. "Why don't I show you something really scary?"

She chuckled, and slipped her arms around his neck just as the phone shrilled beside them. Her heart shot to her throat and pushed out a shriek.

"Hold that thought," he murmured, then lifted the receiver. "Skimmerhorn."

"Jed. Sorry to wake you." But the edge of excitement in Brent's voice had nothing to do with apology. "I've got something you might want to check out."

"Yeah?" Automatically Jed rolled over and picked up the pen from the nightstand.

"I just picked up a fax from the sheriff's department out there. A couple of hikers stumbled over a body a few days ago wedged in a shallow ravine in the hills. There was enough left for a couple of prints. We can stop looking for DiCarlo. He's real dead."

"How long?"

"They're having a tough time pinpointing it, given the exposure and the wildlife. Sometime around the first of the year. Since you're out there, I figured you might want to talk to the coroner, the investigating officers."

"Give me the names." Jed wrote down the information.

"I'm going to fax them back as soon as I hang up with you," Brent continued. "Tell them that you were on a related investigation out there. They'll be ready for you."

"Thanks. I'll be in touch."

Dora was sitting up in bed, her chin resting on her drawn-up knees, studying Jed when he hung up the phone. "You've got cop all over your face. It's an interesting metamorphosis to witness."

"Why don't you order up some breakfast?" He was already out of bed and on his way to the shower. "We're going to have to take a later flight."

"All right." She heard the water start. Her jaw clenched. Tossing back the covers, she marched into the bathroom, yanked back the shower curtain. "It's not enough to give orders, Captain. Some of us recruits require minimal information."

"I've got something to check on." He scooped up the soap. "In or out, Conroy, you're getting water all over the floor."

"What do you have to check on?"

He decided the issue himself by reaching out and tugging the nightshirt over her head. She didn't object when he lifted her up and into the tub with him. Saying nothing, she adjusted the hot water so that it wouldn't blister the skin. She dragged the wet hair out of her eyes. "What do you have to check on?" she repeated.

"DiCarlo," he said flatly. "They've found him."

27

SHERIFF Curtis Dearborne harbored an innate distrust of outsiders. Since he considered any member of the LAPD an outsider, an East Coast cop was an entity to be watched with extra care.

He was a towering, well-muscled man who wore his uniform proudly starched, kept his sandy moustache well trimmed and lightly waxed, and spit-polished his boots. Beneath his military sense of polish and style lurked a well of country-boy charm that he used cleverly and with great success.

He rose from his desk when Jed and Dora entered. His square, handsome face was set in serious lines, his handshake was dry and firm.

"Captain Skimmerhorn. Pretty handy you being out our way when we identify the John Doe."

Jed summed up his man instantly. Dearborne was going to be territorial. Jed's first move was to acknowledge Dearborne's authority.

"I appreciate your passing on the information, Sheriff. I'm sure Lieutenant Chapman filled you in on the mess we've got back home. This quick work on your part will be some comfort to Officer Trainor's widow."

It was exactly the right button. Dearborne's eyes frosted, his mouth thinned. "Your lieutenant told me the corpse was a cop killer. I'm only sorry the coyotes didn't take more of an interest in him. Sit down, Captain, Miss Conroy."

"Thanks." Stemming impatience, Jed took a seat. If he rushed Dearborne, it would probably cost him hours of time in diplomacy. "I was told there was no identification on the body."

"Not a lick." Dearborne's chair creaked comfortably as he sat back. "But we ruled out robbery right off. The wallet was gone, but the guy had a diamond on his pinkie and one of those gold chains around his neck." Dearborne sneered just enough to let Jed know he considered such trappings suspiciously unmasculine. "The body wasn't in such good shape, but I didn't need the coroner to tell me how he bought it. He'd been gut-shot. Not much blood on the tarp he'd been wrapped in though. Stands to reason the body had been moved after he bled to death. Probably took a good long nasty time. Begging your pardon, ma'am," he said for Dora's benefit. "Coroner confirmed it."

"I'd like a look at the coroner's report, if that's all right," Jed began. "And any physical evidence you've gathered. The more I go back with, the better."

Dearborne drummed his fingers on the desk as he considered. East Coast wasn't pushy, he decided. "I think we can accommodate you there. We've got the tarp and what's left of his clothes downstairs. I'll have the rest of the paperwork brought in after you've finished. If you want a look at the body, we'll take a run down to the coroner's."

"I'd appreciate that. If Miss Conroy could wait here?" he said as Dora started to rise.

"That's fine." Dearborne admired a woman who knew her place. "You just make yourself comfortable."

"Thank you, Sheriff. I wouldn't want to get in the way." The sarcasm was thinly veiled, but Dearborne wasn't a man for subtleties. "May I use my credit card to make a call?"

"Help yourself." Dearborne gestured toward the phone on his desk. "Use line one."

"Thank you." There was no use being annoyed with Jed, she mused. In any case, while he was off doing cop things, she could let her family know she was being delayed a few hours. After Jed and Dearborne trooped off, she settled behind Dearborne's desk. And she smiled. She wondered if Jed realized that Dearborne had called him "Captain"—and that Jed hadn't even winced at the title.

He'll have his badge back by spring, she predicted, and wondered what Jed Skimmerhorn would be like when he was completely happy.

"Good afternoon, Dora's Parlor."

"You've got a great voice, honey. Ever think about phone sex?"

Lea answered with a rich chuckle. "All the time. Hey, where are you? At thirty thousand feet?"

"No." Dora pushed back her hair and sent a smile to the officer who carried in a mug of coffee and a file folder. "Thank you, Sergeant," she said, deliberately mistaking his rank.

"Oh, it's just deputy, ma'am." But he flushed and grinned. "And you're welcome."

"Sergeant?" Lea demanded. "What, are you in jail or something? Do I have to post bond?"

"Not yet." She picked up the mug, tapping a finger idly against the file the deputy had set on the desk. "Just taking care of a little business Jed wanted to handle while we were here." No need to mention dead guys and gut shots, she mused. No need at all. "So we'll be taking a later plane. Everything there okay?"

"Everything's fine. We sold the Sherbourne desk this morning."

"Oh." As always with a particularly loved piece, Dora felt the twin tugs of pleasure and regret.

"No haggling either." The smug pride came through. "Oh, how did your meeting go?"

"Meeting?"

"With the import-export guy."

"Oh." Hedging, Dora thumbed at the file tab. "It went. I don't think we'll be doing business after all. He's out of my league."

"Well, I don't suppose you'd consider the trip a waste. See any movie stars?"

"Not a one, sorry."

"Oh well. You had Jed along to help you soak up the LA sunshine."

"There was that." She didn't add that she calculated she'd spent more time with Jed on the plane than she had since they'd landed.

"Call me when you get in so I'll know you're safe and sound."

"All right, Mommy. I don't imagine we'll make it much before ten your time, so don't start worrying until after eleven."

"I'll try to restrain myself. Oh, I should warn you, Mom's planning on having an informal gathering—so she can check Jed out on a more personal level. I thought you should know."

"Thanks a lot." Sighing, Dora idly flipped open the folder. "I'll try to prepare Jed for—" Her mouth went dust dry as she stared down at the photo. Through the buzzing in her head, she heard her sister's voice.

"Dora? Dory? Are you still there? Shoot. Did we get cut off?"

"No." With a herculean effort, Dora leveled her voice. Even when she lifted her gaze to stare at the wall, the photo's grim image remained imprinted on her mind. "Sorry, I have to go. I'll call you later."

"Okay. See you tomorrow, honey. Safe trip."

"Thanks. Bye." Very gently, very deliberately, Dora replaced the receiver. Her hands had gone icy cold beneath a sheer layer of sweat. Breathing shallowly, she looked back down.

It was DiCarlo. There was enough of his face left for her to be sure of that. She was also sure that he hadn't died well, that he hadn't died easy. With numb fingers she shifted the first police photo aside and stared at the second.

She knew now just how viciously cruel death could be to human flesh. No amount of Hollywood horror fantasies had prepared her for this ghastly reality. She could see where the bullet had ripped, where the animals had feasted. The desert sun had been every bit as merciless as the bullet and the carrion. The color photo was both lurid and dispassionate.

She couldn't stop looking, couldn't take her eyes away even when the buzzing in her head became a roar. She couldn't stop looking even when her vision blurred and grayed until the bloated body seemed to float off the surface of the photo toward her horrified eyes.

Jed let out one concise oath when he walked in and saw her white face and the open file. Even as he strode toward her he watched her eyes roll back. He had her chair pushed away from the desk and her head between her knees in two brisk moves.

"Just breathe slow." His voice was drum tight, but the hand on the back of her head was gentle as he reached up and slapped the file closed.

"I was calling Lea." Dora swallowed desperately as her stomach heaved. Bile tickled gleefully in the back of her throat. "I was just calling Lea."

"Keep your head down," he ordered. "And breathe."

"Try a little of this." Dearborne held out a glass of water to Jed. There was sympathy in his voice. He remembered his first murder victim. Most good cops did. "There's a cot in the back room if she wants to stretch out."

"She'll be all right." Jed kept the pressure light on Dora's head as he accepted the water. "Would you give us a minute, Sheriff?"

"Sure. Take your time," Dearborne added before he closed the door behind him.

"I want you to come up real slow," Jed told her. "If you feel faint again, put your head back down."

"I'm okay." But the trembling was worse than the nausea, and much more difficult to control. She let her head fall back against the chair and kept her eyes closed. "I guess I've made a lasting impression on the sheriff."

"Try some of this." He brought the cup to her lips, urging her to swallow. "I want you to feel better before I yell at you."

"You might have to wait awhile." She opened her eyes as she sipped. Yes, his were angry, she realized. Really angry. But she couldn't worry about that just yet. "How can you face that?" she said softly. "How can you possibly face that on a regular basis?"

He dipped his fingers in the cool water and rubbed them on the back of her neck. "Do you want to lie down?"

"No, I don't want to lie down." She looked away from him. "And if you have to yell, get it over with. But before you do, you should know I wasn't prying or playing detective. Believe me, I didn't want to see that. I didn't need to see that."

"Now you can start working on forgetting it."

"Is that what you do?" She made herself look at him again. "Do you just file this sort of thing away and forget it?"

"We're not talking about me. You have no business being this close, Dora."

"I have no business?" She moistened her dry lips and set the cup aside before she forced herself to stand. "The man inside that file tried to rape me. He would certainly have killed me. That brings me pretty goddamn close. Even knowing that, knowing what he did and what he tried to do, I can't justify what I saw in those pictures. I just can't. I guess I want to know if you can."

He'd seen enough to know just what kind of afterimage she'd be carrying with her. He'd seen enough to know it was worse than most. "I don't justify, Dora. If you want to know if I can live with it, then yeah, I can. I can look at it. I can go down to the coroner's right now and take a good long look at the real thing. And I can live with it."

She nodded, then walked shakily to the door. "I'm going to wait in the car."

Jed waited until she was gone before he picked up the file and studied the photos. He swore, not at what he saw, but at what Dora had seen.

"She okay?" Dearborne asked as he came back in.

"She'll do." He handed the file over. "I'd like to take you up on your offer of talking to the coroner."

"Guess you want to see the stiff, too."

"I'd appreciate it."

"No problem." Dearborne picked up his hat, settled it on his head. "You can read the autopsy report on the way. It's interesting. Our pal had a hell of a last meal."

DORA refused the snack the flight attendant offered and stuck with icy ginger ale. Her system balked at even the thought of food. She did her best to ignore the scents of deli meat and mayo as the other passengers dug in.

She'd had a lot of time to think, stretched out on the front seat of the rental car while Jed had been with Dearborne. Time enough to realize that she'd taken her shock and revulsion out on him. And he hadn't taken his anger out on her.

"You haven't yelled at me yet."

Jed continued to work his crossword puzzle. He'd have preferred to read through Dearborne's reports again, but they would wait until he was alone. "It didn't seem worth it."

"I'd rather you did, so you'd stop being mad at me."

"I'm not mad at you."

"Could've fooled me." She wasn't certain what she was feeling herself, only knew it had to be put behind them. "You've hardly spoken since we left LA. And if I hadn't been making a fool of myself in the sheriff's office, you'd have torn into me." His eyes flicked up from his paper to meet her strained smile. "You wanted to."

"Yeah, I wanted to. But I wasn't mad at you. I was mad because you'd seen those pictures. Because I knew you'd walked through a door you wouldn't close easily, and never completely. There was nothing I could do about it."

She put a hand over his. "I can't go as far as saying I'm glad I opened that file. But you were right, it brings me closer. I think I'd handle it all better if you told me what you found out from Sheriff Dearborne and at the coroner's. Speculation can be even worse than reality."

"There isn't that much to tell." But he let the paper fall into his lap. "We know DiCarlo flew out to the coast on New Year's Eve, rented a car, booked a hotel room. He didn't sleep in the room that night, he didn't return the car. That hasn't turned up yet, either. Apparently he'd also booked a flight for Cancún, but he didn't use the ticket."

"So he didn't plan on coming back east anytime soon." She left her hand over his as she tried to think it through. "Do you think he came out to see Finley?"

"If he did, he didn't sign in. There's no record of him going to the offices on that date. If we go by the theory that he was working for himself, DiCarlo might have run into some bad luck on his way out of the country. Or he could have had a partner, a business disagreement."

"Makes me glad I'm in business for myself," Dora murmured.

"Or, choice number three, and my personal favorite, he worked for Finley, came out to report, and Finley killed him or had him killed."

"But why? DiCarlo hadn't finished the job, had he? I still had the painting."

"That might be the reason." Jed shrugged. "But there's no physical evidence to link Finley to any of it at this point. We know DiCarlo came to LA, and he died there. He was murdered sometime between December thirty-first and January second—as far as the coroner can pinpoint at this time. He died from a single gunshot wound to the abdomen, then, from the lack of blood on the tarp, was moved several hours later. Someone had the presence of mind to take his wallet to slow up the identification if and when his body was found. The bruises on the face were several days old. I put them there myself. Other traumas occurred after death."

He couldn't bring himself to tell her that DiCarlo had also been kneecapped.

"I see." To keep her voice clear and steady, she continued to sip the ginger ale like medicine. "That's like no signs of struggle, right?"

"That's right, Miss Drew." He gave her hand an approving squeeze. She was toughing it out, he thought, and admired her for it. "The condemned man had enjoyed a hearty last meal that had included pheasant, a considerable amount of wine and raspberries with white chocolate."

Nope, Dora thought as her stomach curdled, she definitely wouldn't be eating anytime soon. "Then one would assume," she began, pressing her free hand surreptitiously to her roiling stomach, "that the deceased was relaxed before he died."

"Kind of tough to put away a meal like that if you're tense. Dearborne's going to have his hands full checking restaurant menus. There were also some white stones and mulch found rolled up in the tarp. The kind you find in flower beds and around ornamental shrubs."

"I wonder how many flower beds there are in the LA area."

"I told you police work was tedious. Did Finley have gardens?"

"Extensive ones." She let out a shaky breath. "He's very proud of them, and was disappointed that there was a cloud cover so he couldn't show them to me properly in natural starlight. I admired part of them from his solarium." Her color had drained again when she turned to look at Jed, but her voice was level. "They were very neat and tidy, well mulched with narrow pathways of white stone."

"You've got good eyes, Conroy." He leaned over and kissed her. "Now close them for a while."

"I think I'd be better off watching the movie." She reached unsteadily for the headphone. "What did they say it was?"

"It's the new Costner flick." Jed plugged the cord in for her. "I think he plays a cop."

"Perfect." Dora sighed, slipped on the headphones and escaped.

*   *   *

IN LA Winesap entered Finley's office. Timid men, like small dogs, often sense the mood of their master by the scent of the air. Winesap was wringing his hands.

"You wanted to see me, Mr. Finley?"

Without looking up from his paperwork, Finley gestured Winesap in. With a stroke of his pen he initialed changes in a contract that would eliminate nearly two hundred jobs. His eyes were blank when he sat back.

"How long have you worked for me, Abel?"

"Sir?" Winesap moistened his lips. "Eight years now."

"Eight years." Nodding slowly, Finley steepled his index fingers and tapped his top lip. "A fair amount of time. Are you happy in your work, Abel? You feel you're well treated, well compensated?"

"Oh, yes, sir. Absolutely, sir. You're very generous, Mr. Finley."

"I like to think so. And just, Abel. Do you find me a just man, as well?"

"Always." Unbidden, the image of DiCarlo's bloody body flashed into his brain. "Without exception, sir."

"I've been thinking of you this morning, Abel, all through the morning and into the afternoon. And as I did so, it occurred to me that over these—eight years, did you say?"

"Yes, eight." Winesap began to feel like a spider stunned by a hornet. "Eight years."

"That over these eight years," Finley continued, "I've had very little cause to criticize your work. You are prompt, you are efficient, you are—in most cases—thorough."

"Thank you, sir." But Winesap only heard the words "most cases." He felt fear. "I do my best."

"I believe you do. Which is why I find myself so disappointed today. I believe you did your best, and it wasn't quite enough."

"Sir?" Winesap's voice was a squeak.

"You perhaps haven't found the time in your busy schedule to read the morning paper?"

"I glanced at the headlines," Winesap said apologetically. "Things have been a bit hectic."

"One should always make time for current events." With his eyes glittering on Winesap's face, Finley stabbed a finger at the newspaper on his desk. "Such as this. Read it now, Abel, if you will."

"Yes, sir." All but shaking in terror, Winesap approached the desk and took the paper. The article Finley referred to was circled over and over again in bloodred ink. " 'Body discovered by hikers,' " Winesap began, and felt his bowels loosen. " 'An-an unidentified body was discovered several days ago in a r-ravine—' "

Finley snatched the paper away with a snap. "Your reading voice is weak, Abel. Let me do it for you." In flowing, melodious tones, Finley read the sketchy report, ending with the standard line about the police investigating. "Of course," he added, smoothing the paper out on his desk, "we would be able to identify the body, wouldn't we, Abel?"

"Mr. Finley. Sir. It was found miles from here. No one would possibly . . ." He cringed, lowering his eyes.

"I expected better from you, Abel. That was my mistake. You were not thorough," he said, spacing each word carefully. "They will, of course, identify the body sooner or later. And I will be forced to answer more questions. Naturally, I'm confident that I can handle the police, but the inconvenience, Abel. I really believe you should have spared me this inconvenience."

"Yes, sir. I'm terribly sorry." Winesap thought of the miserable drive into the mountains, the hideous trek with the body dragging behind him. His shoulders sagged. "I can't apologize enough."

"No, no, I don't believe you can. However, since I have considered your work record carefully and found no unsightly blemishes, I will try to overlook this one. You'll be leaving for the east in a day or two, Abel. I trust you'll handle Miss Conroy with more finesse than you handled Mr. DiCarlo."

"Yes, sir. Thank you. I'll be . . . thorough."

"I'm sure you will." Finley offered a glittering smile that made Winesap think of sharks feeding. "We'll put this unfortunate mistake out of our minds. I don't believe we need to discuss it again."

"That's very understanding of you, Mr. Finley." Cautious, Winesap backed out of the room. "Thank you."

"Oh, and Abel." Finley enjoyed watching the man stop on a dime and cringe. "I really think, under the circumstances, you should return the caddy spoon."

"Oh." Winesap's face fell. "Of course."

In much better spirits, Finley leaned back as the door closed respectfully. He'd been in a state of mental turmoil since reading the article, and now calmed himself by doing his deep-breathing exercises. There was nothing quite like yoga for soothing the soul.

He would have to keep a closer eye on Abel, he thought sadly. A much closer eye. If things got too sticky over DiCarlo, he would simply throw dear, devoted Abel to the wolves like so much dead meat.

But he sincerely hoped it wouldn't be necessary.

He wasn't worried for himself. When a man was rich enough, and powerful enough, Finley mused, he was above the common reach of the law.

The police couldn't touch him. No one could. And if, by some minor miracle, they came too close, there would always be small prey—like Abel—to throw off their scent.

But he was a forgiving man. Smiling, Finley took the etui he'd brought back to his office with him from his desk and fondled it. A very forgiving man—sometimes to a fault.

As long as Abel followed instructions carefully and managed Miss Conroy, there would be no need to kill him. No need at all.

28

IT was good to be home in the simple routines of each day. Dora comforted herself with that and tried not to think of the meeting with Mr. Petroy she still had to face.

She hadn't realized she was ordinary enough, mundane enough, to wish for a lack of adventure. But the bald truth was, she wanted her simple life back. More, she wanted the chance to be bored.

At least Jed hadn't noticed her lack of appetite. Dora was certain he'd have made a few choice remarks if she hadn't covered it so well. The same held true for the female art of cosmetics. Her eyes might have been shadowed, her skin pale and drawn, but with facials and creams and powders, she presented a very competent mask.

She hoped it didn't slip until after Thursday.

She was rubbing at the throbbing between her eyes that the doses of aspirin seemed unable to ease when the shop door opened. Nothing could have made her happier than her father's smiling and slightly tipsy face.

"Izzy, my sweet."

"Dad, my own true love." She stepped away from the counter to kiss him, then found herself pressing her face against his shoulder and hugging him fiercely.

He returned the embrace. Though concern clouded his eyes, they were smiling again when he drew back. "All alone, little girl?"

"Not anymore. It's been a slow morning. Want some coffee?"

"Half a cup." He speculated, watching her move to the coffee service and pour. He knew his children—their faces, the tones of their voices, the subtleties of their body language. Isadora was hiding something, he mused. He would find out what easily enough.

"Your mother sends me as ambassador." He accepted the cup, then pulled out his flask to add a generous dollop of whiskey. "To extend an invitation to cocktails and conversation to you and your young man."

"If you're referring to Jed, I think he might object to the description, but accept the invitation. When?"

"Thursday night." His brow lifted as he saw something flicker over her face. "Pretheater, of course."

"Of course. I'll be happy to check with him."

"I'll extend the invitation myself. Is he upstairs?"

"No, I think he's out." She sipped her coffee, grateful when a couple of window-shoppers passed on without coming in. "You can check with him later, if you like."

Quentin watched her toy with the sugar bowl. "Have you had a lovers' tiff?"

"We don't tiff." She managed a smile. "We do fight now and then, but tiffing isn't part of our ritual." She picked up a cookie, put it down again. "You know, I'm feeling a little restless today. Do you want to take a walk?"

"With a beautiful woman? Always."

"Let me get my coat."

Quentin's eyes narrowed in speculation, wondering if his handpicked partner was making his little girl so unsettled. But he was all smiles again when she returned, buttoning her coat. "I seem to recall someone who enjoys busman's holidays. Perhaps we should take a little ride over to New-Market and check out some shop windows."

"My hero." Dora flipped the Closed sign over, then hooked her arm through her father's.

HE bought her jelly beans, and she didn't have the heart not to eat them. They stayed outside, enjoying the cold and the cobblestones, the cosmopolitan air of the window displays. Dora knew she was feeling better when she was tempted by both a Limoges box and a cashmere sweater.

The wind whistled through the bare trees as they sat on a bench to enjoy more coffee. Quentin's was again stiffly laced.

"Shall I buy you a present?" he asked. "It always made you smile when you talked me into some little trinket."

"I've always been mercenary, haven't I?" Amused at herself, she leaned her head companionably on his shoulder.

"You've always loved pretty things—and appreciated them, as well. That's a gift, Izzy, not a flaw."

She felt foolish tears prick at her eyes. "I guess I'm having a mood. I always thought Will had the moods."

"All of my children had wonderful moods," Quentin said staunchly. "It's the theater in your blood. Artists are never easy, you know. We aren't meant to be."

"What about cops?"

He paused a moment to drink, to enjoy. "I see law enforcement as an art as well. Some would say science, of course. But the timing, the choreography, the drama. Yes, it's quite an art." He draped a comforting arm around her. "Tell me what you're feeling, Izzy."

And she could. She had always been able to tell him what she felt without fear of criticism or disapproval. "I'm so in love with him. I want to be happy about it. I nearly am, most of the time, but he doesn't trust those kind of emotions. He doesn't have any experience with them. His parents didn't give him anything of what you and Mom gave us."

She sighed and watched a young mother wheel a stroller over the stones. The toddler inside was rosy-cheeked and laughing. The yearning tug came quickly, with equal parts surprise and discomfort. I want to do that, she realized. I want to spend an hour pushing my child in the sunlight and smiling.

"I'm afraid we can't give each other what we need," she said carefully.

"First you have to discover what those needs are."

Wistfully, she watched mother and child roll away. "I think I have a pretty good handle on mine. How can you expect a man whose childhood was a study in misery to take the first step toward creating a family of his own? It isn't fair for me to push him toward that step, and it isn't fair for me to deny myself taking it."

"Do you think only people from happy families make happy families of their own?"

"I don't know."

"Jed's grandmother seems to think he's already taken that first step, and is cautiously debating over the second."

"I don't—" She stopped, straightened to frown at her father. "His grandmother? You've spoken to her?"

"Ria, your mother and I had a very nice visit while you were in California. A lovely woman," he added. "She's quite taken with you."

Dora's eyes slitted. "It appears I have to remind you that I'm a competent adult, and so is Jed. I don't think it's right that you would sit around discussing us as though we were slow-witted children."

"But you are our children." He smiled benignly and patted her flushed cheek. "When you have children of your own, you'll understand that the love never stops, and neither does the concern, the pride or the interference." He beamed at her. "I love you, Izzy, and I have great faith in you." He pinched her chin. "Now, tell me what else is worrying you?"

"I can't." And she was sorry for it. "But I can tell you it should be resolved in a few days."

"I won't pry," he said. At least not when she was so obviously on her guard. "But if you don't look happier soon, I'll sic your mother on you."

"I'm smiling." She bared her teeth. "See, couldn't be happier."

Satisfied for the moment, he rose. After tossing his empty cup in a wastebasket, he held out a hand. "Let's go shopping."

"She's a ball of nerves." Jed met Brent in the gym so that he could release some tension by pummeling the heavy bag. "She won't admit it, but she's tied up inside." More than a little tied up himself, Jed gave the bag a rapid series of sharp punches. As he'd been delegated to hold the bag steady, Brent grunted as the power sang up his arms. "I'm not helping."

"We're moving on it as fast as we can." Brent felt sweat trickle down his shirt and wished he'd talked Jed into meeting at some nice coffee shop. "After Thursday's meet, we should be able to keep her out of it."

"It's not just that." Jed moved from the heavy bag to the light, relieving

Brent immeasurably. Eyes narrowed, Jed sent the bag flying into a blur. "She's in love with me."

Brent took off his glasses to clean the lenses of fog. "Is that supposed to be news?"

"She needs more than I can give her. She should have more."

"Maybe. Is she complaining?"

"No." Jed blinked sweat out of his eyes and kept his fists flying.

"Then relax and enjoy the ride."

Jed whirled on him so swiftly, so violently, that Brent braced for the blow. "It's not a fucking ride. It's not like that with Dora. It's—" He broke off, furious at the smug smile creasing Brent's face. "Don't play me," he said very softly.

"Just testing the waters, Captain." When Jed turned over his gloves, Brent obligingly unlaced them. "Speaking of which, the unofficial word is that you'll be back in command the first of the month. Goldman's sulking."

"He'll feel better when I sign his transfer papers."

"Oh, let me worship at your feet."

A grin tugged at Jed's mouth as he flexed his fist. "We'll make an official announcement on Monday. And if you try to kiss me in here, pal, I'll have to deck you." He picked up a towel to dry his face. "For now, Goldman's in charge. Is everything set for Thursday?"

"We'll have two men in the shop. Another pair outside, and a surveillance van a half block away. As long as Dora follows instructions, we'll pick up every word."

"She'll follow them."

SPENDING an hour with her father had given Dora a need for family. She indulged it by closing the shop an hour early and spending the evening at Lea's. The din from the family room soothed her soul.

"I think Richie's definitely improving on the trumpet," Dora commented.

Head cocked, Lea listened to the wet musical blats with a mixture of pride and resignation. "There's a band concert at school in three weeks. I'm saving you a front-row seat."

"God bless you." There was a series of muffled thumps from the next room, what was—if you had enough imagination—a stirring cavalry charge and an excellent rebel yell. "I needed this." Content, Dora slipped onto a stool by the counter.

"I'd be happy to leave you in charge for a couple hours." Lea added another touch of burgundy to the stew she had simmering.

"I don't need it that much." Dora drank a hurried sip of wine. "No. I spent some time with Dad this afternoon, and it made me think what it would be like if he wasn't so handy. That's all."

"Something's going on." Frowning, Lea tapped the spoon on the side of the pot, set it on a spoon rest shaped like a duck. "You've got that line between your eyebrows. And you're pale. You always get pale when you're worried about something."

"You'd be worried too if you had to find a new accountant right before end-of-January inventory."

"Not good enough." Lea leaned closer, probing. "You're edgy, Dory, and it has nothing to do with business. If you won't tell me, I'll have to turn Mom loose on you."

"Why does everyone threaten me with Mom?" she demanded. "I'm unsettled, okay? My life's taken a couple of odd turns. I'd like my family to respect my privacy enough to allow me to work out my own problems."

"Okay. I'm sorry. Really."

Passing a hand over her face, Dora took a cleansing breath. "No, I'm sorry. I shouldn't have snapped at you. I guess I'm still a little jet-lagged. I think I'll go home, take a hot bath and sleep for twelve hours."

"If you don't feel better tomorrow, I can come in early."

"Thanks. I'll let you know." She started to slide off the stool as the knock sounded on the back door.

"Hi." Mary Pat stuck in her head. "I came to pick up my share of the monsters." She listened a moment to the shouting and the blare of the trumpet. "Ah, the patter of little feet. Wonderful, isn't it?"

"Have a seat," Lea invited. "Unless you're in a hurry."

"I'd love a seat." She sighed as she took the one beside Dora. "I've been on my feet for eight straight hours. We had two codes back to back." She took a deep breath of air. "God, how do you manage to raise kids, hold down a job and cook like that?"

"I have an understanding boss." Smiling, Lea poured Mary Pat a glass of wine. "She gave me the day off."

"Speaking of work, terrific news about Jed, isn't it?"

"What news?"

"About him coming back on the job." With her eyes closed, she circled her neck and missed Dora's blank look. "Brent's really flying. He detested Goldman, of course. Who didn't? But it's more than that. The department needs Jed and Jed needs the department. Now that he's made the decision to come back, it's pretty clear he's got his head on straight again. I don't think he's going to wait until the first of the month to take command, either. Otherwise . . ." One look at Dora's face made Mary Pat stumble to a halt. "Oh, damn. Did I jump the gun? When Brent told me it would be official on Monday, I just assumed you knew."

"No, Jed didn't mention it." She fought to work a smile onto her lips, but couldn't make it reach her eyes. "It's good news, though. No, great news. I'm sure it's just what he needs. How long have you known?"

"A couple of days." Idiot, Mary Pat thought, but wasn't sure if she was referring to herself or to Jed. "I'm sure he planned to tell you himself. Once he, ah . . ." But she couldn't think of any handy excuses. "I'm sorry."

"Don't be. I really am glad to hear it." After sliding off the stool, Dora reached mechanically for her coat. "I've got to get going."

"Stay for dinner," Lea said quickly. "There's plenty."

"No, I have some things to do. Say hi to Brent," she told Mary Pat.

"Sure." When the door closed, Mary Pat lowered her forehead onto her fisted hands. "I feel like I ran over a puppy. Why the hell didn't he tell her?"

"Because he's a jerk." Lea's voice was low with fury. "All men are jerks."

"That's a given," Mary Pat agreed. "But this was major. And this was cold. Lea, I've known Jed a long time, and he's not cold. Careful, but not cold."

"Maybe he forgot the difference."

*   *   *

Odd things happen to the mind at two o'clock in the morning. Particularly to a man who's waiting for a woman. He begins to speculate, to project, to worry and to sweat. Jed paced his living room, strode through the door he'd propped open and paced the corridor.

As he had numerous times over the last four hours, he strode to the back door and stared out at the gravel lot. His car was as alone out there as he was alone inside. There was no sign of Dora.

Where the hell was she? He strode back to his apartment to look at the clock, to check its time with his watch. Two-oh-one. If she wasn't home in ten minutes, he promised himself, he would call in all his markers and put out an APB.

He stared at the phone. It wasn't until he'd picked up the receiver that he realized his hand was sweating. Swearing, he slammed the phone back on the cradle. No, he wasn't going to call the hospitals. He wasn't even going to let himself think that way.

But where the hell was she? What the hell could she have to do at two in the morning?

He started to reach for the phone again and stopped as a fresh idea sharpened in his brain. Unless she was paying him back. It was a safe, even a comforting thought, so he played with it. Was this how she'd felt when he'd come in late without leaving any word? Was she doing this to show him how it was to agonize over silence when the person who mattered was out of reach?

She wasn't going to get away with it, he decided. She damn well was going to pay for it. But he was reaching for the phone again when he heard her key in the outside lock.

He was out in the hall and at the door before she'd opened it.

"Where the hell have you been?" The demand burst out of him, ripe with worried fury. "Do you have any idea what time it is?"

"Yes." Very deliberately she closed the door and locked it. "Sorry. I didn't realize I had a curfew."

She walked past him only because he was too stunned to stop her. But he recovered quickly. He caught up with her at the door of her apartment and spun her around.

"Just a goddamn minute, Conroy. We'll forget the personal stuff for now. The fact is you're a prime target, and it was incredibly irresponsible of you to be out of contact for half the night."

"I'm responsible to and for myself." She jammed the key in the lock and shoved the door open. "And as you can see, I'm perfectly fine."

He slapped a hand against the door before she could close it. "You had no right—"

"Don't tell me about rights," she interrupted, very cool, very calm. "I spent the evening as I chose to spend it."

Anger and resentment bubbled inside him. "And how was that?"

"Alone." She took off her coat and hung it in the closet.

"You did this to get under my skin, didn't you?"

"No." She walked past him toward the kitchen to pour a glass of water. "I did it because I wanted to. I'm sorry if you were worried. It didn't occur to me that you would be."

"It didn't occur to you." Incensed, he grabbed the glass out of her hand and tossed it into the sink. It shattered effectively. "Fuck that, Conroy. You knew damn well I'd be half crazy. I was about to call out a goddamn APB."

"Interesting, isn't it, the way those police terms slide right off your tongue? It's a good thing you're going back on, Skimmerhorn. You make a lousy civilian." Her eyes were as dull as her voice. "Are congratulations in order, Captain, or just best wishes?" When he didn't respond, she nodded. "Well, you can have both."

"It's not official until next week." He spoke carefully, studying her. He'd never seen her eyes that cold, or that detached. "How did you find out?"

"Does it matter? It's more to the point that I didn't find out from you. Excuse me." She brushed past him and into the living room.

He closed his eyes a moment and cursed himself for a fool. "So you're pissed. Okay. But that—"

"No," she interrupted. "It's not okay. And I'm not pissed." Because she was tired, unbearably so, she gave in and sat on the arm of a chair. "You could say I've been illuminated. You could even say that I'm devastated, but no, Jed, I'm not angry."

The quiet resignation in her voice reached him. "Dora, I didn't do it to hurt you."

"I know that. That's why I'm illuminated. You didn't tell me because you didn't think it was any of my concern. You didn't want it to be any of my concern is probably more accurate. It was a major decision in your life. Your life," she repeated with stinging emphasis. "Not mine. So why should you bother to tell me?"

She was slipping away from him. He was standing two feet away from her and watching the distance grow by leaps and bounds. It terrified him. "You make it sound as though I was keeping it from you. I needed to work it out, that's all. I didn't think you'd understand."

"You didn't give me the chance, Jed," she said quietly. "Did you think I could have felt the way I did about you and not understand how important your work was to you?"

Her use of the past tense had a quick skidder of panic sprinting up his spine. "It had nothing to do with you." As soon as the words were out of his mouth he knew they were ill chosen. Her eyes remained dry, but hurt filled them. "I didn't mean it that way."

"I think you did. I wish I didn't blame you for it, but I do. I know you had it rough, but you've been making your own choices for a long time. You chose not to accept my feelings for you, and you chose not to let yourself feel anything back. And I do blame you for that, Jed."

Her voice didn't waver, her eyes remained steady, but the hands in her lap were clenched tight. "I blame you very much for that, and for hurting me. I told you I don't handle pain very well, and I don't pretend it's not there when it is. Since you're the first man who's ever broken my heart, I think you should know it."

"For Christ's sake, Dora." He started toward her, but the way she jumped up and stepped back unmanned him.

"I don't want you to touch me now." She spoke very quietly, clinging to the slippery edge of control. "I really don't. It's humiliating for me to finally understand that's all we had."

"That's not true." He fisted his hands at his sides, but already knew he couldn't beat his way through the wall he'd thrown up between them. "You're blowing this out of proportion, Dora. It's just a job."

"I wish it were. But we both know it's not. It's the most important part of your life. You gave it up to punish yourself, and you're taking it back because you can't be happy without it—and maybe not even whole without it. I'm glad for you, Jed. I truly am."

"I don't need the analysis. I need you to stop this and be reasonable."

"I am being reasonable, believe me. So reasonable I'm going to make it easy for both of us. The day after tomorrow you should be able to tie up the loose ends about the painting. Or most of them. You shouldn't need me after that."

"Goddamn it, you know I need you."

Her eyes filled then, and she fought back tears like bitter enemies. "You can't imagine what I would have given to hear you say that before. Just once, for you to have been able to look at me and say that you needed me. But I'm not a courageous woman, Jed, and I have to protect myself."

No, he couldn't break through the wall she'd put between them, but her hurt could. It snuck through the cracks and battered at him. "What do you want, Dora?"

"When we're finished on Thursday, I intend to close the shop for a couple of weeks, take a trip someplace warm. That should give you plenty of time to find other accommodations and move out."

"That's no way to handle this."

"It's my way. And I figure I'm in the position of calling the shots. I'm sorry, but I don't want you here when I get back."

"Just like that?"

"Yes."

"Fine." He had his pride. He'd been rejected before. If it burned a hole in him this time, he'd find something to fill it with. But he wouldn't beg. He'd be damned if he'd beg. "I'll go as soon as things are wrapped up." Because it hurt, it hurt unbelievably, he covered the wounds with a professional shield. "There'll be a team in tomorrow after closing. They'll set up the wires. We'll go over procedure when they're done."

"All right. I'm very tired. I'd like you to go now." She walked to the door, held it open. "Please."

It wasn't until he'd reached her that he realized his hands were unsteady. When he heard the door close behind him he had the sick and certain feeling that he'd just been shut out of the best part of his life.

29

"WHAT'S with you two?" Brent asked as Jed climbed into the surveillance van.

Ignoring the question, Jed pulled out a cigarette. "How's the sound?"

"Loud and clear." Though Brent offered the headphones, he was far from finished. "Loud enough and clear enough to hear the two of you talking in there like polite strangers. Don't you think she could have used a little morale boost instead of a lecture on procedure?"

"Drop it." Jed slipped on the headphones and checked the rear window of the van to be sure he had a clear view of the shop. "Everybody in place?"

"We're set," Brent assured him. "Look, maybe you'd feel better if you were on the inside."

"She'll be more comfortable if I'm not. Look, I'll handle my end." Jed drew deeply on the cigarette. "You handle yours."

"You're not running the show yet, Captain." The edge of anger in Brent's voice sent off an answering ripple in Jed's blood. Before he could respond, the radio crackled.

"Base, this is Unit One. A man answering subject's description just got out of a cab on the corner of South and Front streets. He's walking west."

"Looks like it's show time," Brent murmured, but Jed was already reaching for the portable phone. Dora answered on the first ring.

"Good afternoon, Dora's Parlor."

"He's half a block away," Jed said flatly. "I've got him in view."

"All right. Everything's ready here."

"Keep loose, Conroy."

"Sure."

"Dora—" But she'd already broken the connection. "Fuck." He said it softly, finally, helplessly.

"She can handle it, Jed."

"Yeah. But I don't know if I can." He watched Winesap mince hurriedly down the sidewalk, shoulders hunched against the wind. "I just figured out I'm in love with her." Ignoring the throbbing at the back of his neck, he slipped on the headphones in time to hear the bells jingle as Winesap opened the shop door.

"Good afternoon." Dora stepped away from the counter and offered her best new-customer smile. "May I help you?"

"Miss Conroy? I'm Francis Petroy."

She let the smile broaden. "Yes, Mr. Petroy. I was expecting you." She walked to the door to flip the Closed sign around. Her eyes slashed to the van, then away. "I'm so glad you could make it. Can I get you some coffee? Tea?"

"I wouldn't want to trouble you."

"Not at all. I always keep both on hand for customers. It makes business so much more pleasant."

"I'd love some tea, then." It might soothe his stomach more than the Alka-Seltzer he'd downed an hour before. "Your shop is very impressive."

"Thank you." She saw, with satisfaction, that her hand was rock steady on the teapot. "I like to surround myself with beautiful things. But you'd understand that."

"Excuse me?"

"Being an art collector." She offered him a cup of tea and a smile. "Cream? Lemon?"

"No, no, nothing, thank you."

"You said you specialize in abstract, but you might find some of my nostalgia prints interesting." She gestured to a car manufacturer's sign for a Bugatti, which hung beside a Vargas girl.

"Yes, ah, very nice. Very nice indeed."

"I also have several good *Vanity Fair* caricatures in the other room." Watching him, she sipped her own tea. "But as an abstract buff, you'd be more interested in say, a Bothby or a Klippingdale," she said, making up names.

"Yes, of course. Exceptional talents." The tea soured like vinegar in Winesap's stomach. He'd tried, really tried to be thorough by studying book after book on the subject of abstract art. But all the names and pictures swam through his head. "My collection isn't extensive, you see. Which is why I concentrate on the emerging artist."

"Such as Billingsly."

"Exactly," he said on a sigh of relief. "I'm very anxious to see the work, Miss Conroy."

"Then, by all means." She led the way into the side room. Jed's artist friend had worked overtime to reproduce the painting. Now it stood, like a gaudy stripper among prim Victorian ladies, in the pretty sitting room.

"Ah." The sense of satisfaction was so great Winesap nearly wept with it. It was horrid, of course, he thought. Absolutely horrid, but it matched the description.

"Such a bold, arrogant style," Dora commented. "I was really taken with it."

"Yes, of course. It's everything I'd hoped for." He made a show of examining the brush strokes. "I'd very much like to add this to my collection."

"I'm sure you would." She let a touch of amusement color her voice. "Did you have an offer in mind, Mr. Petroy?"

"In mind, naturally," he said, trying to be coy. "I'd prefer if you'd set a price, for negotiation."

"I'd be happy to." Dora sat in a tufted-back chair and crossed her legs. "Why don't we start at two hundred and fifty thousand?"

Winesap's prim mouth fell open. He made a choked sound in the back of his throat before he managed to find his voice. "Miss Conroy, Miss Conroy, you can't be serious."

"Oh, but I am. You look as though you need to sit down, Mr. Petroy." She gestured to a petit-point stool. "Now, let's be frank," she began when he'd sunk onto the seat. "You don't know diddly about art, do you?"

"Well, really." He tugged at his strangling tie. "As I told you, I have a small collection."

"But you lied, Mr. Petroy," she said gently. "You haven't a clue about abstract. Wouldn't it be simpler, and more friendly, if we admitted that we're both more interested, at the moment, in Impressionism rather than Expressionism?"

For a moment he didn't follow her. Then his pasty face blanched. "You know about the painting."

"I bought it, didn't I?"

"Yes, but, that was a mistake." His frantic eyes widened. "No? You knew—knew all along about the Monet? You were working with DiCarlo? You—you cheated," he accused, miserably.

Dora merely chuckled and leaned forward. "You needn't sound so offended. After all, you sent DiCarlo here, didn't you?"

"It's been his fault." Disgusted, Winesap threw up his hands. "All this confusion is his fault. I can't imagine why I was sorry he died so badly."

The image in the police photo flashed obscenely in her mind. "So you killed him," she murmured. "For this."

But Winesap wasn't listening. "Now I have to clean up the entire mess, again. I'm not happy about the two hundred and fifty thousand, Miss Conroy. Not happy at all."

He rose. So did Dora. Even as he reached under his coat, two officers were bursting through the rear door.

"Freeze."

Winesap took one look at the guns pointing at him and fainted dead away. His checkbook slipped out of his hand and flapped onto the floor.

"He was going to pay me for it," Dora said dully. She watched, light-headed, as two officers escorted a babbling and cuffed Winesap out of the shop. She hadn't needed to lower her head between her knees, but she remained sitting. It was an even bet as to whether or not her legs would support her. "He was going to write me a check." A laugh bubbled out, lightly tinted with hysteria. "Jesus Christ, I wonder if I'd have asked him for two forms of ID."

"Here." Jed shoved a cup into her hands.

"What is it?"

"That tea you drink—with a little brandy."

"Good idea." She knocked it back like water and felt it warm her jittery stomach. "I guess you guys got all you needed."

"We got plenty." He wanted to touch his fingertips to her hair, but he was afraid she'd cringe away. "You did good, Nancy."

"Yeah, I did." She lifted her eyes then, made herself meet his. "I guess on some level we didn't make such a bad team."

He stared down at her for a long time. "It's been hard on you."

"I come from pretty tough stock, Skimmerhorn. Conroys don't fold easily."

"You were brilliant." Brent swept in to lift Dora out of the chair by her elbows. He kissed her, hard. "A stand-up job, Dora. You want a job on the force, you've got my recommendation."

"Thanks. But I'm putting my magnifying glass and coupe in mothballs."

"Come again?"

"Nancy Drew," Jed muttered, and felt his heart sag. "I'm going down to Interrogation with Brent. Are you going to be all right?"

"I'm going to be fine. Terrific, in fact." Her smile was blinding, but she lowered herself carefully to the arm of the chair. "It's still tough for me to believe that pathetic little man engineered all this, and killed DiCarlo."

Brent opened his mouth, then shut it again at a swift, warning look from Jed. "We have enough on the tape to pry the rest out of him." Because they felt useless, Jed jammed his hands in his pockets. "Are you sure you'll be all right?"

"I said I would. Go be a cop." She softened the words with a smile. "It looks good on you." She pushed a hand through her hair. Jed watched as the strands fell beautifully back into place. "I'd appreciate it if you'd give me a call, let me know what the result of the interrogation is."

"You'll get a full report," Brent promised her.

"In the morning." Steadier, she rose again. "I'm going upstairs and sleep around the clock. If you're finished in here, I'll lock up behind you."

She followed them to the door. When he reached it Jed turned, closed his hand over hers on the knob. He couldn't help it. "I'd like to talk to you tomorrow, when you're feeling up to it."

She nearly gave in. Very nearly. There was as much hurt in his eyes as she was holding inside her. But a fast break was a clean one. "My schedule's a little tight, Jed. I've booked an early-morning flight to Aruba. I've got to pack."

There was nothing in her voice, nothing in her face that offered the slightest opening. "You move fast."

"It seemed best all around. I'll send you a postcard." Because she hated the bitter aftertaste of the statement, she turned her hand under his and gave it a quick squeeze. "Give 'em hell, Captain."

She closed the door quickly and turned the lock.

"WHY didn't you tell her we've asked LAPD to move on Finley?" Brent demanded when Jed stood on the sidewalk.

He hurt, all over, as if someone had pounded him ruthlessly and methodically with foam-covered fists. "Do you think that would have made her sleep any better?"

"No," Brent murmured to Jed's retreating back. "Guess not."

AND she was telling herself that sleep was exactly what she needed. She hadn't had a decent night of it in more than a week. Dora pulled the shade on the front door, then drummed up the energy to lift the coffee-and-tea tray.

Once she got to Aruba, she promised herself, she'd do nothing but sleep. She'd sleep in bed, on the beach, in the ocean. She'd bake this aching depression out of her body and mind with the Caribbean sunshine, beat those midwinter blues and come back tanned and revitalized.

She set the tray on her desk to carefully lock the storeroom door and engage the security alarm before heading up to her apartment.

It was habit more than desire that had her taking the tray into the kitchen to wash. When she turned from the sink, she was standing face-to-face with Finley.

He smiled and took her nerveless hand in his. "I've taken you up on your offer of hospitality, Isadora. And may I say you have a charming home."

"I really don't think I should make any sort of statement without a lawyer." Winesap chewed on his ragged nails and glanced fitfully at Brent and Jed. "I really don't."

"Suit yourself," Brent shrugged and straddled a chair. "We've got plenty of time. Do you want to call one, or do you want a PD?"

"A public defender?" That pricked the pride enough to have his sagging shoulders lift. "Oh no, I can afford counsel. I have a very good position." But his lawyer was in Los Angeles, he thought. "Perhaps if you could explain again why I'm here, we could dispense with the formality of an attorney."

"You're here on suspicion of theft, smuggling, conspiracy to murder a police officer and murder, among other things," Brent added.

"That's really absurd." Pride deflated again, Winesap hunched down in his seat. "I don't know where you could have gotten such a ridiculous idea."

"Maybe you'd like to listen to the tape of your conversation with Miss Conroy." Jed made the suggestion as he crossed to the recorder.

"That was a simple transaction—and a private one." Winesap tried to lever some indignation through the fear in his voice. But when Jed switched on the recorder, he said nothing at all. It was painfully clear after only a few moments that he hadn't been thorough at all—and that he'd been remarkably stupid.

While his mind worked, he began to suck on his knuckles. He didn't think he would care for prison. No indeed. Winesap thought of Finley and knew he would like his employer's brand of punishment a good deal less.

"Perhaps we can make an arrangement. Might I have a cup of water, please?"

"Sure." Agreeably, Brent went to the watercooler and pumped out a paper cupful.

"Thank you." Winesap sipped it slowly while he considered his options. "I think I would like immunity, and a place in the witness-protection program. I think that would suit me very well."

"I think it would suit me very well to see you rot in a cell for the next fifty years," Jed said pleasantly.

"Captain." Brent fell into the classic interrogation rhythm. "Let's give the guy a chance. Maybe he's got something to trade."

"I promise you, I do. If I have assurance that my cooperation will be rewarded, I'll give you everything you need to make a very big arrest." Loyalty, a chain around his neck for eight long years, slipped easily off. "A very big one," he repeated.

Jed gave an imperceptible nod as Brent's eyes met his. "I'll call the DA."

* * *

"Why don't we sit down?" Finley kept his hand firm on Dora's arm as he pulled her into the living room. "And have a nice chat."

"How did you get in?"

"There was such a lot of confusion this evening, wasn't there?" He smiled as he pushed her into a chair. "I wasn't at all sure that Abel—Mr. Winesap—could handle this matter efficiently on his own. I came to supervise. A very good thing, too."

Finley took the chair beside her and folded his hands comfortably. He saw Dora's eyes cut toward the door and shook his head. "Please don't attempt to run, Isadora. I'm very strong and very fit. I'd hate to resort to physical violence."

She would hate it, too. Especially since she was certain she wouldn't get two feet. Her best bet was to play for time and wait for help. "It was you who sent DiCarlo."

"It's a long, sad tale. But I find you such good company." He settled back comfortably and began to talk. He told her of the carefully planned robberies in several different countries. The network of men and finances it required to operate a successful business—legally and illegally. When he reached DiCarlo's part in it, he paused, sighed.

"But I don't have to go into that with you, do I, dear? You're an excellent actress. One wonders why you decided to give it up. I realized quite soon after your visit to my office that you and DiCarlo had been in league together."

For a moment she was too stunned to speak. "You think I was his partner?"

"I'm sure you found him an adequate lover." Truly disappointed in her, Finley plucked at his cuffs. "And I can certainly see how you could have lured him into betraying me. A pity, too," Finley added softly. "He had potential."

"What I told you in your office was exactly the truth. He broke in here and attacked me."

"I'm quite sure you had some sort of falling out. Greed and sex working against one another, I would assume." His eyes narrowed, glinting dully. "Did you find another, more inventive man, Isadora, one you could maneuver and pit against poor Mr. DiCarlo so that he came to me with some feeble excuse for not returning my property?"

"The painting was not your property. You stole it. And I was never involved with DiCarlo."

"And when he didn't return," Finley continued as if she hadn't spoken, "you became concerned and decided to test the waters with me yourself. Oh, you were very clever. So charming, so distressed. I very nearly believed you. There was just one niggling doubt in my mind, which proved sadly true once I witnessed the events of this afternoon. I'm disappointed that you turned to the police, Isadora. Settling for a finder's fee." He wagged a finger at her scoldingly. "I thought more of you than that. You've cost me two very good men, and a painting I wanted very much. Now how are we to reconcile?"

Too terrified to sit, she sprang to her feet. "They have your Mr. Winesap down at police headquarters. He'll be telling them all about you by now."

"Do you think he would have the nerve?" Finley considered it a moment, then moved his shoulders in elegant dismissal. "Perhaps. But don't be concerned. Mr. Winesap will very soon suffer a tragic and fatal accident. I would much rather talk about my painting, and how you think I can retrieve it."

"You can't."

"But surely, since you've been such a help, the police have told you where they've secured it."

She said nothing, only because it surprised her so much that she hadn't thought to ask.

"I thought so." Finley smiled broadly as he rose. "Just tell me where it is, Isadora, and leave the rest to me."

"I don't know where."

"Don't lie, please." He slipped his hand into the inside pocket of his Savile Row suit and pulled out a highly polished Luger. "Gorgeous, isn't it?" he asked when Dora's eyes fastened on the barrel. "A German make, used in World War II. I like to think that a Nazi officer killed quite efficiently with it. Now, Isadora, where is my painting?"

She looked helplessly into his eyes. "I don't know."

The force of the bullet slammed her back against the wall. Even as the fire erupted in her shoulder, she didn't believe he'd shot her. Couldn't believe it. Dazed, she touched a finger to the worst of the heat and stared blindly at her blood-smeared fingers. She was still staring at them when she slid limply down the wall.

"I really think you'd better tell me." All reason, Finley stepped up to where Dora lay in a boneless heap. "You're losing a great deal of blood." He crouched down, mindful not to stain his suit. "I don't want to cause you unnecessary distress. It took DiCarlo hours to die after I shot him. But there's no need for you to suffer like that." He sighed when she only whimpered. "We'll give you a little time to compose yourself, shall we?"

Leaving her bleeding, he began to methodically examine her treasures, one by one.

"The little bastard sure did sing." Brent felt like singing himself as he cut through traffic toward South Street.

"I don't like cutting deals with weasels," Jed muttered.

"Even for a big fat weasel like Finley?"

"Even for that." He checked his watch. "I'll feel better when I know that LAPD's picked him up."

"The warrant's in the works, pal. He won't be sleeping in his own bed tonight."

There was some comfort in that. Some small comfort. Jed would have been happier if he could have taken the man down himself. "You didn't have to come this far out of your way. I could have caught a cab."

"Nothing's too good for the captain. Not tonight. And if I were you, I wouldn't wait until morning to give a certain gorgeous brunette the good news."

"She needs to sleep."

"She needs some peace of mind."

"She ought to get plenty of it in Aruba."

"Come again?"

"Nothing." Jed turned to scowl at the light sleet that began to fall as they turned onto South.

*   *   *

"Now then." Finley sat down again, pleased when Dora found the strength to push herself to a sitting position against the wall. The blood seeping out of the wound on her shoulder had slowed to a sluggish ooze. "About the painting."

Her teeth were chattering. She'd never been so cold, so cold that even her bones felt like frigid sticks. While her arm and shoulder spurted fire, the rest of her seemed cased in ice. She tried to speak, but the words hitched one moment and slurred drunkenly the next. "The police . . . The police took it."

"I know that." The first sizzle of anger crept into his words. "I'm not a fool, Isadora, as you obviously believe. The police have the painting, and I intend to get it back. I paid for it."

"They took it away." Her head lolled on her shoulder, then rolled weakly against the wall. The room was losing its color, going gray. "To grandmother's house," she said, edging toward delirium. "Then away. I don't know."

"I can see you need incentive." He set the gun aside and loosened his tie. Dully, Dora watched him slip out of his jacket. When he reached for the gold buckle of his belt, slippery fingers of horror crept through the shock.

"Don't touch me." She tried to crawl away but the room revolved sickeningly so that she could only curl in a ball in a congealing puddle of her own blood. "Please, don't."

"No, no. Unlike DiCarlo, I have no plans to force myself on you. But a good whipping with this belt may loosen your tongue. It may be hard for you to believe, but I actually enjoy inflicting pain." He wrapped the end of the belt around his hand, the buckle loose to add bite to the beating. "Now, Isadora, where is the painting?"

She saw him pick up the gun and raise the belt at the same time. All she could do to try to block both weapons was close her eyes.

"You can drop me out front," Jed told Brent.

"Nope. Door-to-door service." He whipped into the parking lot, spitting gravel. "If you had any heart, you'd ask me up for a beer."

"I haven't got any heart." Jed pushed the door open and glanced back at

Brent's engaging grin. "Sure, come ahead." If nothing else, it would put off the time he'd have to spend alone, waiting for morning.

"You got any of that imported stuff?" Brent slung a friendly arm over Jed's shoulders as they trooped toward the steps. "Mexican, maybe? I really feel like—"

When they heard the thin cry, they each slapped a weapon into their hands. They charged through the door in a dead run. Years of partnership clicked seamlessly into place. When Jed kicked open Dora's door, he went in high, Brent low.

The faintest flicker of irritation crossed Finley's face as he whirled. Two police issues fired simultaneously. Two 9mm bullets caught Finley high in the chest.

"God. Oh God." With terror singing in his head, Jed rushed to Dora. He said her name over and over like a prayer as he ripped off her blouse and used it to staunch the oozing blood. "Hang on, baby. You hang on."

There was so much blood, he thought frantically. Too much. And because it had begun to clot, he knew too much time had passed. When he looked at her still, white face he had one moment of unspeakable horror when he thought she was dead. But she was shaking. He could feel the racking trembles of shock even as he peeled off his jacket to cover her.

"You're going to be okay. Dora, baby, can you hear me?"

Her eyes were wide and dilated and remained unfocused. The second bullet had gone through the fleshy part of her upper arm. She hadn't even felt it.

"Use this." Brent pushed a towel into Jed's shaking hands and folded another to place under Dora's head. "Ambulance is on the way." He spared a glance at the body sprawled on the rug. "He's dead."

"Dora, listen to me. You listen to me, damn it." Jed worked quickly as he spoke to her, using the towel to pad the upper wound and what was left of her blouse to fashion a pressure bandage. "I want you to hold on. Just hold on." Then he could think of nothing else but to gather her close and rock her. "Please. Stay with me. I need you to stay with me."

He felt the light brush of her hand on his cheek. When he looked down at her face, her lips trembled open. "Don't—don't tell my parents," she whispered. "I don't want them to worry."

30

HE would have wept if it would have helped. He'd tried everything else. Swearing, pacing, praying. Now he could only sit, his head in his hands, and wait.

The Conroys were there. Jed wondered if Dora would be surprised at how tough they were. He doubted it. There had been tears, and there had been terror, but they had all drawn together, a solid wall, in the hospital waiting room to count the minutes while Dora was in surgery.

He'd waited for recriminations. They had given him none. He'd wanted blame. But it hadn't come from them. Not even when he had stood, smeared with Dora's blood, and told them that he'd left her alone, left her defenseless, had they blamed him.

He wished to Christ they had.

Instead, John had gotten them all coffee, Lea had gone down to wait for Will to arrive from New York and Quentin and Trixie had sat side by side on the sofa, holding hands.

After the second hour had crawled by, Trixie murmured to her husband. When she received his nod of agreement, she rose and went to sit beside Jed.

"She was always a tough little girl," Trixie began. "She used to pick fights in school—well, not pick them, precisely, but she never would walk away from one without dignity. It used to amaze me that she would scream like a banshee if she fell and banged her knee. But if she came home with a split lip or a swollen eye, you never heard a peep. A matter of pride, I suppose."

"This wasn't her fight." Jed kept the heels of his hands pressed hard against his eyes. "It shouldn't have been."

"That's for her to decide. She'll want lots of pampering, you know. She was never sick often, but when she was—" Trixie's voice broke, betraying her. She mopped quickly at her eyes and steadied it. "When she was, she expected everyone's devoted attention. Dora's never been one to suffer in silence."

Gently she touched the back of his hand. When he lowered it enough, she gripped it firmly. "It's so much harder to wait alone."

"Mrs. Conroy . . ." But he didn't have the words. He simply leaned against her and let himself be held.

They all rose to their feet at the quick slap of crepe-soled shoes on tile. Still in her scrubs, Mary Pat stepped through the doorway. "She's out of surgery," she said quickly. "It looks good. The doctor will be out soon."

It was then Trixie began to cry, with hard, racking sobs and hot tears that burned through Jed's shirt. His arms went around her automatically as he met Mary Pat's eyes.

"When can they see her?"

"The doctor will let you know. She's a tough one, I can tell you that."

"Didn't I say so?" Trixie managed. She stumbled blindly into Quentin's arms so they could weep out their relief together.

It wasn't until he was alone again that Jed started to shake. He'd gone outside, had fully intended on going home. It was a time for family, he'd told himself. Now that he knew she was going to pull through it, there was no need to hang around.

But he couldn't make it across the street to hail a cab, so he sat down on the steps and waited for the tremors to subside. The sleet had turned to snow that fell quick and light and damp. There was something otherworldly about the way it danced in the streetlights, something hypnotic. He stared at one beam of light as he smoked one cigarette, then another. Then he walked back in and rode the elevator to the floor where Dora lay sleeping.

"Figured you'd be back." Mary Pat smiled at him out of eyes red-rimmed with fatigue. "Damn it, Jed, you're soaked. Am I going to have to dig up a bed for you?"

"I just want to see her. I know she's sedated, I know she won't know I'm there. I just want to see her."

"Let me get you a towel."

"MP."

"You're going to dry off first," she told him. "Then I'll take you in."

She was as good as her word. When she was satisfied he was dry enough, she led him into Dora's room.

Dora lay, still and white as death. Jed's heart careered into his throat. "Are you sure she's going to be all right?"

"She's stabilized, and there were no complications. Dr. Forsythe's good. Believe me." She didn't want to think about the amount of blood they'd had to pump into Dora, or how long it had taken to get that feeble pulse to steady. "The bullet's out—and there's some tissue damage, but it'll heal. She's going to be weak as a baby for a while, and she's going to hurt."

"I don't want her to hurt." His control slipped a dangerous notch. "You make sure she gets whatever she needs so she isn't in pain."

"Why don't you just sit with her for a while?" Mary Pat ran a soothing hand up and down his back. "It'll make you feel better."

"Thanks."

"I go off duty in an hour. I'll check back."

But when she did, one look had her stepping back and leaving them alone.

He was still there in the morning.

She awakened slowly, as if swimming toward the surface of still, dark water. The air seemed too thick to breathe, and there was a whooshing sound in her head like waves lapping gently on the shore.

He watched her break through, every flicker of the eyelid. Her hand flexed once in his, then lay still again.

"Come on, Dora, don't go back yet." He brushed his fingers over her hair, over her cheek. She was still too pale, he thought, much too pale. But her lashes fluttered again, then her eyes opened. He waited for them to focus.

"Jed?" Her voice sounded hollow, lifeless, and the sound of it almost broke him.

"Yeah, baby. Right here."

"I had a nightmare." He pressed a kiss to her hand, fighting the need to simply lay his head on the bed and let go.

"It's all right now."

"It seemed awfully real. I—Oh God!" She shifted, sending an arrow of pain radiating through her arm.

"You've got to lie still."

Like the pain, memory burst back. "He shot me. Jesus." She started to move her hand to the fire blooming in her shoulder, but he clamped his fingers on hers. "It was Finley."

"It's all over now. You're going to be fine."

"I'm in the hospital." The panic came quickly, surging along with the pain. "How—how bad?"

"They fixed you all up. You just need to rest now." None of his fourteen years on the force had prepared him to deal with the terrified pain clouding her eyes. "I'm going to get a nurse."

"I remember." Her fingers trembled as she groped to hang onto his. "He was in the apartment, waiting for me. He wanted the painting back. I told him I didn't know where it was, and he shot me."

"He won't ever hurt you again. I swear it." He pressed his brow against their joined hands and felt himself crack. "I'm sorry, baby. I'm so sorry."

But she was swimming down through the dark water again, away from the pain. "Don't leave me alone here."

"I won't."

THE next time he saw her conscious, she was surrounded by flowers, banks and bouquets of them from sweet little nosegays to towering exotic blooms. Rather than the drab hospital gown, she was wearing something frilly and pink. Her hair was washed and she was wearing makeup.

But to Jed she looked horribly frail.

"How you doing, Conroy?"

"Hi." She smiled and held out a hand. "How'd you break in? They're vicious about proper visiting hours around here."

"I pulled rank." He hesitated. The hand in his felt as fragile as bird wings. "If you're too tired, I can stop back by later."

"No, if you stay you can chase them away when they come in with their needles."

"Sure, my pleasure." Miserably awkward, he turned away to study the forest of flowers. "Looks like you ought to go into a different business."

"Great, isn't it? I love being fawned over." She shifted, winced and was grateful his back was to her. "You ratted on me, Skimmerhorn."

"What?"

"You told my family."

"I figured it was better than having them read it in the papers."

"You're probably right. So what's happening in your world? Mary Pat tells me you kicked Goldman out early and went back to work."

"Yeah." He'd had to have something filling his days, or go quietly mad.

"Can I see your badge?"

"What?"

"Really." She smiled again. "Can I see it?"

"Sure." He pulled out his shield as he crossed to the bed. She took it, studied it, opened and closed it a couple of times.

"Pretty cool. How does it feel?"

"Right," he told her as he slipped it back into his pocket. There was no possible way he could stand there and make small talk when he kept seeing the stark white bandage peeking out beneath that frilly pink nightgown. "Listen, I just stopped by to see how you were doing. I've got to go."

"Before you give me my present?" When he said nothing, she drummed up another smile, though it was becoming harder as her medication wore off. "That box you're holding? Isn't it for me?"

"Yeah, it's for you." He set it on her lap. "I've been by a couple of times when you were zonked out. After I saw the flower shop in here, I figured you wouldn't need any more posies."

"You can never have too many." She reached for the fussy bow, then sat back again. "Give me a hand, will you? I have a little trouble using my arm."

He didn't move, but his eyes were eloquent. "They told me there wouldn't be any permanent damage."

"Right." Her mouth moved into a pout. "Like a scar isn't permanent damage. I'm never going to look the same in a bikini."

He couldn't handle it, simply couldn't. Turning abruptly, he strode to the window and stared blindly out with the heavy scent of roses tormenting him.

"I should have been there," he managed after a moment. "You shouldn't have been alone."

His voice was so angry, his shoulders so stiff, that Dora waited for the storm. When it didn't come, she plucked at the bow with her good hand. "From what Brent tells me, Finley slipped right through LAPD. Nobody had a clue he'd left California. I don't see how anyone could have imagined he'd waltz right into my apartment and shoot me."

"It's my job to know."

"So, it's going to your head already. What do they call that super-cop thing—the John Wayne syndrome, right?" She'd managed to pull and tug the ribbon off and was lifting the top off the box when he turned. "Well, pilgrim," she said in a very poor Wayne imitation. "You just can't be everywhere at once." Though her arm was beginning to throb, she dug happily into the tissue paper. "I love presents, and I'm not ashamed to say so. I don't particularly care to get shot to . . . Oh, Jed, it's beautiful."

Stunned, really completely stunned, she lifted out the old wooden-and-gesso box, delicately painted and gilded with figures from mythology. When she opened the lid, it played "Greensleeves" softly.

"It was hanging around in storage." He dipped his hands into his pockets and felt like a fool. "I figured you'd get a kick out of it."

"It's beautiful," she said again, and the look she sent him was so sincerely baffled he felt even more foolish. "Thank you."

"It's no big deal. I figured you could put junk in it while you're stuck in here. I've really got to take off. You, ah, need anything?"

She continued to run her fingers over the box as she looked at him. "I could use a favor."

"Name it."

"Can you pull some strings, get me out of here?" It shamed her to feel tears pricking at her eyes. "I want to go home."

IT took him several hours, and a great deal of negotiation, but Dora finally laid her head down on her own pillow, in her own bed.

"Thank you, God." Dora closed her eyes, sighed deeply, then opened them again to smile at Mary Pat. "Nothing against your workplace, MP, but personally, I hated it."

"You weren't exactly the ideal patient either, kiddo. Open up." She stuck a thermometer in Dora's mouth.

"I was a jewel," Dora muttered.

"A diamond in the rough, maybe. Very rough. But I'm not going to complain; a few days of private duty suits me just fine." Efficiently, she wrapped a blood-pressure cuff around Dora's uninjured arm. "Right on the money," she announced when she took the thermometer out to read. But Dora caught the quick frown over blood pressure.

"What's wrong?"

"Nothing that quiet and rest won't fix."

"I've been quiet. I never thought I'd hear myself say this, but I'm tired of being in bed."

"Live with it." Sitting on the edge of the bed, Mary Pat took her hand—and her pulse. "I'm going to be straight with you, Dora. You're going to be just fine with the proper rest and care. But this wasn't any skinned knee. If Jed hadn't gotten you in when he did, you wouldn't be here to complain. As it was, it was close."

"I know. I remember it all a bit too clearly for comfort."

"You're entitled to moan and bitch. I won't mind a bit. But you're also going to follow orders, to the letter, or I'll report you to the captain."

Dora smiled a little. "You nurses have ranks?"

"I'm talking about Jed, dimwit. He's financing this operation."

"What do you mean?"

"I mean you've got round-the-clock home care for as long as you need it, courtesy of Captain J. T. Skimmerhorn."

"But—I thought insurance was arranging it."

"Get real." Chuckling at the thought, Mary Pat plumped the pillows, smoothed the sheets. "Now, get some rest. I'm going to go fix you something to eat."

"He shouldn't feel guilty," Dora murmured when Mary Pat started out of the room.

Mary Pat stopped, looked back. "He feels a lot more than guilt where you're concerned. Did you know he didn't leave the hospital for the first forty-eight hours?"

"No." Dora looked down at her hands. "I didn't."

"Or that he checked on you every night."

Dora only shook her head.

"A lot of women wait their whole lives for someone to feel that guilty."

Alone, Dora reached for the music box. She opened the lid, closed her eyes and wondered what to do.

AT the end of her shift, Mary Pat passed her patient's progress on to her replacement. But she didn't consider herself off duty yet. Marching across the hall, she rapped sharply on Jed's door. When Jed opened it, she jabbed a finger into his chest.

"Couldn't you find the energy to walk across the goddamn hall and—" She broke off, scowling. "What are you doing?"

"I'm packing."

Darts of righteous fury shot out of her eyes. "The hell you are." Incensed, she stomped over and upended a box of books onto the floor. "You're not walking out on her when she's flat on her back and defenseless."

"I'm not walking out." He struggled for calm. He'd convinced himself, very logically, that what he was doing, he was doing for Dora. "She *asked* me to leave. It's only going to upset her if she finds out I haven't moved yet."

Mary Pat fisted her hands on her hips. "You're an idiot. I can almost accept that. But I never thought you were a coward."

"Back off, MP."

"Not a chance. Can you stand there and tell me you're not in love with her?"

He reached for a cigarette. Mary Pat snatched it out of his hand and broke it in two. He glared. She glared right back.

"No, I can't. But that's not the point. The doctor was real clear about keeping her free from stress. She doesn't need me hanging around upsetting her."

"Sit down. Sit down, damn it." She gave him a quick shove. "I'm going to tell you exactly what she needs."

"Fine." He slumped into a chair. "I'm sitting."

"Have you ever told her you loved her?"

"I don't see that that's any of your business."

"I didn't think so." Impatient, she took a quick turn around the room, barely preventing herself from kicking his weight bench. "Have you ever picked her wildflowers?"

"It's fucking February."

"You know exactly what I'm talking about." She turned on him, slapped both hands on the arm of his chair to cage him in. "I'll lay odds you never lit candles for her, or took her for a walk by the river, or brought her some silly present."

"I gave her a damn music box."

"Not enough. She needs to be wooed."

Incredibly, he felt a flush creeping up on his neck. "Give me a break."

"I'd like to break your butt, but I'm sworn to heal. You almost lost her."

His eyes whipped up, sharp as a sword. "Don't you think I know that? I wake up in a sweat every night remembering how close it was."

"Then do something positive. Show her what she means to you."

"I don't want to push myself on her when she's vulnerable."

Mary Pat rolled her eyes. "Then you are stupid." Feeling sorry for him, she kissed him. "Find some wildflowers, Jed. My money's on you."

THE box arrived the following afternoon.

"More presents," Lea announced, struggling to shove the huge box across the living room to where Dora sat on the couch. "I'm thinking of getting shot myself—as long as it's a flesh wound."

"Believe me, it's not worth it. Get the scissors, will you? Let's get the baby open." She leaned down to study. "No return address."

"Ah, a secret admirer." Tongue caught in her teeth, Lea attacked the packing tape. "Oh," she said, deflating when she opened the lid. "It's just books."

"God. Oh my God. Carolyn Keene." She was down on her knees, rummaging. "Nancy Drew—it looks like the complete set. And first editions. Look, look. It's *The Clue of the Leaning Chimney, The Hidden Staircase*." All at once she clutched the books to her breasts and began to weep.

"Honey, oh, honey, did you hurt yourself? Let me help you to bed."

"No." She pressed *Password to Larkspur Lane* against her cheek. "They're from Jed."

"I see," Lea said carefully, and sat back on her heels.

"He went to all this trouble just to be sweet. Why is he being so sweet? Look, a few days ago he sent me this bracelet." She held out her arm and continued babbling even when Lea oohed and aahed over it. "And that silly cow, and the watercolor. Why is he doing this? What's wrong with him?"

"Love sickness would be my guess."

Dora sniffled and rubbed tears away with the sleeve of her robe. "That's ridiculous."

"Honey, don't you know when you're being romanced?" Lea picked up a book, turned it over, shook her head. "I myself might prefer a slightly different style, but this certainly seems to have punched your buttons."

"He's just feeling sorry for me. And guilty." She hitched back tears, blinked them away. "Isn't he?"

"Honey, the man I saw haunting that hospital wasn't there out of guilt." She reached over to tuck her sister's hair behind her ear. "Are you going to give him a break?"

She laid a book on her lap, running her hands gently over the cover. "Before I was shot, I broke things off with him. I told him to move out. He hurt me, Lea. I don't want him to hurt me again."

"I can't tell you what to do, but it seems awfully unfair to make him keep suffering." She kissed Dora's forehead, then rose to answer the knock on the door. "Hi, Jed." Lea smiled and kissed him as well. "Your surprise hit the mark. She's in there right now crying over the books."

He stepped back automatically, but Lea took his hand and pulled him inside. "Look who's here."

"Hi." Dora brushed at tears and managed a shaky smile. "These are great." Her eyes overflowed again. "Really great."

"Their value's going to plummet if they're water-damaged," he warned her.

"You're right. But I always get sentimental over first editions."

"I was just on my way out." Lea grabbed her coat, but neither of them paid any attention to her departure.

"I don't know what to say." She continued to press *The Hidden Staircase* like a beloved child to her breast.

"Say thanks," he suggested.

"Thanks. But, Jed—"

"Listen, I've got the go-ahead to spring you for a while. You up for a drive?"

"Are you kidding?" She scrambled to her feet. "Outside? All the way outside and not to the hospital?"

"Get your coat, Conroy."

"I can't believe it," she said a few minutes later as she slid luxuriously down in the seat of Jed's car. "No nurses. No looming thermometers or blood-pressure cuffs."

"How's the shoulder doing?"

"It's sore." She opened the window just to feel the rush of air on her face and missed the way his fingers tightened on the wheel. "They make me do this physical therapy, which is—to put it mildly—unpleasant. But it's effective." She jockeyed her elbow to a right angle to prove it. "Not bad, huh?"

"That's great." There was such restrained violence in the statement she lifted a brow.

"Everything all right at work?"

"It's fine. You were right all along. I shouldn't have left."

"You just needed some time." She touched his arm, letting her hand fall away when he jerked. It was time, she thought, to clear the air. "Jed, I know that we were in a difficult position before—well, before I was hurt. I know I was unkind."

"Don't." He didn't think he could bear it. "You were right. Everything you said was right. I didn't want you to get too close, and I made certain you couldn't. You were one of the main reasons I went back on the job, but I didn't share it with you because I would have had to admit that it mattered. That what you thought of me mattered. It was deliberate."

She rolled up the window again, shutting out the wind. "There's no point in raking it up again."

"I guess it would sound pretty convenient if I told you that I was going to ask you to forgive me, that I'd have been willing to beg for another chance, before you got hurt." He shot her a look, caught her wide-eyed stare then scowled back through the windshield in disgust. "Yeah, that's what I thought you'd say."

"I'm not sure," she said cautiously, "what another chance might entail."

He was going to try to show her. He pulled up in the driveway, set the brake, then rounded the hood to help her out. Because she was staring at his house, she moved wrong and bumped her arm against the car door.

"Damn." Her gasp of helpless pain broke him.

"I can't stand to see you hurt." Shielding her arm, he gathered her close. "I just can't stand it. It rips at me, Dora, every time I think of it. Every time I remember what it was like to see you on the floor, to have your blood on my hands." He began to tremble, all those honed muscles quivering like plucked strings. "I thought you were dead. I looked at you and I thought you were dead."

"Don't." She soothed automatically. "I'm all right now."

"I didn't prevent it," he said fiercely. "I was too late."

"But you weren't. You saved my life. He'd have killed me. He wanted to, as much as he wanted the painting. You stopped him."

"It isn't enough." Fighting for control, he gentled his grip on her and stepped back.

"It suits me pretty well, Jed." She lifted a hand to his cheek. He grasped at it, pressed it hard to his lips.

"Just give me a minute." He stood there a moment, with the air cool and crisp, whispering through denuded trees and sleeping winter grass. "You shouldn't be standing out in the cold."

"It feels great."

"I want you to come inside. I want to finish this inside."

"All right." Though she no longer felt weak, she let him support her as they went up the walk. She thought he needed to.

But it was he who was unsteady as he unlocked the door, opened it, led her inside. His nerves jumped as she let out a quiet gasp of pleasure.

She stepped onto the welcoming Bokhara rug. "You've put things back."

"Some." He watched the way she ran her fingertips over the rosewood table, the curved back of a chair, the way she smiled at the fussy gilded mirror. "My landlord kicked me out, so I took a few things out of storage."

"The right things." She walked on into the front parlor. He'd put back a curvy pin-striped settee, a lovely Tiffany lamp on a satinwood table. There was a fire burning low in the hearth. She felt both a surge of pleasure and grief. "You're moving back in."

"That depends." He slipped her coat carefully off her shoulders, laid it on the arm of the settee. "I came back here last week. It wasn't the same. I could see you walking up the stairs, sitting on my window seat, looking out the kitchen window. You changed the house," he said as she turned slowly to face him. "You changed me. I want to move back in, and make it work. If you'll come with me."

Dora didn't think the sudden dizziness had anything to do with her healing injuries. "I think I want to sit down." She lowered herself to the striped cushions and took two careful breaths. "You're going to move back here? You *want* to move back here?"

"Yeah, that's right."

"And you want me to live with you?"

"If that's the best I can get." He took a small box out of his pocket and pushed it into her hands. "I'd like it better if you'd marry me."

"Can I—" Her voice came out in a squeak. "Can I have some water?"

Frustrated, he dragged a hand through his hair. "Damn it, Conroy— sure." He bit back on temper and a terrible fit of nerves. "Sure, I'll get it."

She waited until he was out of the room before she worked up the courage to open the box. She was glad she had because her mouth fell open. She was still staring dumbfounded at the ring when he came back in carrying a Baccarat tumbler filled with lukewarm tap water.

"Thanks." She took the glass, drank deeply. "It's a whopper."

Disgusted with himself, he fumbled out a cigarette. "I guess it's over-stated."

"Oh no. There isn't a diamond in the world that's overstated." She laid the box in her lap, but kept a hand possessively around it. "Jed, I think these past few weeks have been as hard on you as they have on me. I might not have appreciated that, but—"

"I love you, Dora."

That stopped her cold. Before she could gather her wits, he was beside her on the settee, crunching several bones in her hand. "Goddamn it, don't ask me for another glass of water. If you don't want to answer yet, I'll wait. I just want a chance to make you love me again."

"Is that what all this has been about? The presents and the phone calls? You were trying to undermine my defenses when I was down."

He looked down at their joined hands. "That about sizes it up."

She nodded, then rose to walk to the window. She'd want tulips out there in the spring, she thought. And lots of sunny daffodils.

"Good job," she said quietly. "Damn good job, Skimmerhorn. It was the books that really did it, though. How could I possibly hold out against a complete set of first-edition Nancy Drew?" She looked down at the bold square-cut diamond still in her hand. "You exploited my weaknesses for nostalgia, romance and material gain."

"I'm not such a bad deal." Nerves screaming, he came up behind her to touch a hand to her hair. "I've got some flaws, sure, but I'm loaded."

Her lips curved. "That approach might have worked once, but I'm pretty well set myself, since I'll be awarded a fat finder's fee on the Monet. I might be greedy, Skimmerhorn, but I have my standards."

"I'm crazy about you."

"That's better."

"You're the only woman I've ever wanted to spend my life with." He brushed a light kiss at the curve of her shoulder and throat and made her sigh. "The only woman I've ever loved, or want to love."

"That's excellent."

"I don't think I can live without you, Dora."

Tears burned her throat, thickening her voice. "Direct hit."

"So does that mean you're going to fall in love with me again?"

"What makes you think I ever stopped?"

The hand he had in her hair fisted and made her wince. "And the marriage thing? You'll give it a shot?"

She grinned into the sunlight. It might not have been the world's most romantic proposal, but it suited her. It suited her just fine.

"We'll need lace at the curtains, Jed. And I have a Chippendale bench that's waiting to sit in front of that fire."

He turned her around, brushing her hair back so that his hands could frame her face. He only had to see her eyes for the nerves to vanish. "Kids?"

"Three."

"Good number." Overwhelmed, he rested his brow against hers. "There's a bed upstairs, in the master suite. I think it's a George the Third."

"Four-poster?"

"Tester. Stay here with me tonight."

She laughed her way into the kiss. "I thought you'd never ask."